CORINNA

LAUREN ROYAL
DEVON ROYAL

June 2021 Edition

SWEET CHASE BRIDES: THE REGENCY

CORINNA by Lauren Royal & Devon Royal

Published by Novelty Books, a division of Novelty Publishers, LLC, 205 Avenida Del Mar #275, San Clemente, CA 92674

May 2021 Edition

Cover by Kimberly Killion

Learn more about the authors and their books at www.LaurenandDevonRoyal.com.

ISBN: 978-1-63469-174-1

MORE SWEET CHASE BRIDES BOOKS

~

SWEET CHASE BRIDES

The Earl's Unsuitable Bride

The Marquess's Scottish Bride

The Laird's Fairytale Bride

The Duke's Reluctant Bride

The Viscount's Wallflower Bride

The Baron's Inconvenient Bride

The Gentleman's Scandalous Bride

The Cavalier's Christmas Bride

A Chase Brides Christmas

SWEET CHASE BRIDES: THE REGENCY

Alexandra

Juliana

Corinna

SWEET CHASE BRIDES: THE RENAISSANCE

Alice Betrothed (coming soon)

For Uncle Bert

We will miss you forever and ever!

PROLOGUE

IRISH WHISKEY CAKE

Take butter with sugar and put in this eggs and flour and a bit 'o coffee to make a nice flavour.

Put in your pan and bake in your oven. Make a syrup of coffee with much sugar and a wee

dram 'o whiskey and pour this into your cake. Bring to table with sweet whiskey cream and a

sprinkle of nuts.

My mother used to caution, "Who gossips with you will gossip of you." Nonetheless, she surely
did love to gossip. She used to serve this cake when the womenfolk came for tea. She claimed it
loosened ladies' tongues.

—Deirdre Delaney Raleigh, 1819

Kilburton, Ireland
November 1809

ON A DAMP Tuesday shortly after he turned sixteen, life as Sean Delaney had known it ceased to exist.

First he received a letter, an event in itself. Everyone Sean knew lived in the village of Kilburton—nobody had reason to write him a letter. A very official letter it looked, too. As Sean watched the lad who'd delivered it retreat down the lane, his mother came in from the sitting room where she'd been serving tea to some womenfolk from the parish.

"Was it not Mary McBride, then?" Ma asked. "She's late."

"It wasn't Mrs. McBride." Sean shut the door and turned to her, the single folded sheet clutched in a hand. "It's a letter. For me."

"For you?" Her pleasant, guileless face looked as surprised as he felt. "Well, open it, then, won't you?"

He nodded and broke the seal.

"Who is it from?" she asked impatiently.

"A solicitor." Below the imposing engraved letterhead, he scanned down the page. "'On behalf of Mr. Patrick Delaney—'"

"Never heard of him."

He shrugged. "One of Da's relations, perhaps."

"Your father has no living relations." She frowned. "What is he wanting, then?"

"He's wanting..." He read further and gasped. "Begorrah!" His head shot up. "He's not wanting anything. He's dead. And he left ten thousand pounds. To me."

"Ten *thousand* pounds?"

To a vicar's wife like Ma, the number was incomprehensible —enough to support a villager and his family and even a servant or two for fifty years. Staring at Sean, she slowly lowered herself to a plain oak chair. Muffled feminine voices could be heard from the sitting room—her guests were having a gossip, no doubt. Uncharacteristically, she ignored them.

"Ten thousand pounds, Sean. Whatever will you do with so much money?"

"I don't know," he said.

But he did know. He'd known instantly. He just didn't want to tell her.

He didn't want to disappoint her, not yet.

"I'm after going for a walk." He grabbed a heavy wool cloak

from the peg by the door. "I shan't be gone long," he promised before slipping outside.

It was raining, as usual this time of year. As usual all year, come to that. Tucking the letter inside the cloak where it would stay dry, he hurried down the lane.

Such a vast amount of money, more than Ma had seen in her entire lifetime. She would want him to do good with it. Charitable works or some such. She was a vicar's wife, after all, and a kindly one at that.

But Sean had something else in mind. Oh, he'd pay the expected tithe, of course. He *was* a vicar's son, after all. The amount would be an unprecedented windfall for the parish, one Sean would be pleased to give. He'd been raised by this congregation—spent his entire life surrounded by them, cocooned in their comforting familiarity—and it seemed right that they should share a tenth of his good fortune.

But after that, he was going to leave Ireland.

He was going to London.

He was going to make a life for himself, something better than he'd ever imagined growing up in wee Kilburton.

He was still quite young. People in London might not take him seriously at first. And it wouldn't be easy to leave kinfolk and friends, to strike out on his own. He knew that. His heart seemed both heavy and light as he turned away from the village, crossed the harvested fields, wandered the age-old riverbank. Touching the precious letter beneath his cloak, he alternately laughed, pondering his immense luck, and trembled, wondering what lay ahead.

Hours passed—tense, exhilarating hours—before he took a deep breath and started home. It had stopped raining. When he reentered the village, the sun was setting low on the horizon, its last rays fighting through the cloud cover as he trod the lane toward the vicarage. Just before he reached the squat house, two figures came out of it, dark shadows against the silvery glow.

"You have no choice." The Honorable Mr. William Hamilton's voice came low and angry through the gloom. An imposing man if not a tall one, he was the same height as the son he pulled toward their fancy carriage. "Not this time."

Wondering what was going on but not wanting to be seen, Sean hid himself behind a tree.

"You paid off the last one," young John Hamilton whined. "And the maid—"

"Two. Two maids, there were." His father pushed him up the carriage's steps. "This one's not some servant's get, you idiot," he muttered, following his son inside. "I'd lose face should you not—"

The door shut, and Sean heard nothing else. As the carriage rumbled off, he stepped from behind the tree and hurried into the house.

It was warm, welcoming, filled with the soft light of oil lamps and the scent of the whiskey cake his mother had baked earlier for her guests. A good home, simple but clean and cared for. Sean had a fine family, a sister two years older and parents who had always been there for both of them, giving of their hearts although they'd never had much to give materially.

He felt sad, knowing he'd soon be leaving all of this, and also excited about his new life. But mostly, he was mighty curious to learn what had made the Hamiltons leave their huge manor house to pay a call at the modest vicarage.

Hearing voices from the sitting room, he headed there. And stopped short when his sister turned to him with a grin. "I'm marrying John Hamilton."

Sean gaped at eighteen-year-old Deirdre. He couldn't have heard her right. "What did you just say?"

Her golden hair gleamed in the firelight as she bounced to her feet. "Mr. Hamilton told John he'd have to marry me."

"But why?" His gaze shot from his father's bloodless face to his mother's eyes, swollen from weeping. There could be only one reason they looked like that, one reason John Hamilton might be forced to wed Deirdre. "Don't tell me you're…" As he looked back to his sister, the rest of the sentence stuck in his throat.

Her grin widened as she folded her hands over her deceivingly flat middle. "Aye, little brother, I'm with child. And I'll be the wife of John Hamilton, the handsomest, richest young man in all of Kilburton."

In all of the county, more like. The Hamiltons' lofty new manor house sat in the shadow of their ancestral home, centuries-old Kilburton Castle. John Hamilton's father was the younger brother of the Earl of Lincolnshire, sent years ago to oversee Kilburton, one of the earl's many lesser estates.

Growing up, Sean and Deirdre had been educated in a chilly one-room schoolhouse, while John had a parade of private English tutors. The boy had always been temperamental, and Sean had thought him haughty, unfeeling, and selfish. But since there were no other lads near their age in Kilburton, Sean's mother had told him to play with John anyway. After all, as she'd often say, it was the Christian thing to do.

Being a dutiful sort of son, Sean did as he was told. But John had always made them stay inside fiddling with paste and paint, instead of engaging in the outdoor pursuits Sean preferred, like fishing and building forts. He'd never really liked John Hamilton.

Deirdre, on the other hand, a rather wild girl and the bane of her parents' existence, obviously liked John Hamilton just fine.

Fine enough to let John…

Sean couldn't finish the thought.

Still and all, he loved his sister. She was lovely and fun, the best of companions, always ready with a smile and a plan for mischief. Looking at her now, her eyes dancing, he sadly shook his head. She had no idea what she was in for. John might seem nice when he wanted something from you, but once he'd got what he wanted...

Sean clenched his fists.

He no longer disliked John Hamilton. He hated him.

For life.

ONE

Eight years later
The British Museum, London
April 1817

"WE WANT TO see the Rosetta Stone," two impatient voices chorused.

For the third time.

"Just a few more minutes," Lady Corinna Chase promised her sisters, her gaze focused on her sketchbook.

"A few is three," Alexandra, the oldest, pointed out.

"Or maybe five," added Juliana, the middle sister.

"But certainly not thirty," Alexandra went on. "You said 'a few more minutes' half an hour ago."

"And half an hour before that," Juliana put in.

Corinna was used to ignoring her sisters' chatter, but the squeak of wheels threatened her concentration. Alexandra was rolling a perambulator back and forth in hopes of soothing Harold, her infant son. Though ladies generally didn't make a habit of carting their babies around town—most aristocratic mothers happily left their children in the care of wet nurses and nannies—Alexandra had insisted on buying one of the newfangled contraptions, because she rarely let little Harry out of her sight.

Squeak. Squeak. Squeak. "How can you gaze at statues for so long?"

"I'm not gazing. I'm sketching." Corinna drew another line, following the curve of the marble figure's muscled thigh. "And as you see, this is not a statue, it's a panel. Part of a frieze from the famous Parthenon in Greece, to be exact. And more importantly, the figures carved on it are anatomically correct."

Which was the reason she'd come, of course. The reason she'd been willing to drag herself out of bed at a preposterous hour to come see the Elgin Marbles. Corinna wanted nothing more than to study human anatomy so she could improve her skills in portraiture. Unfortunately, the anatomy classes at the Royal Academy of Arts were entirely forbidden to girls.

Entirely.

Forbidden.

It was infuriating. Corinna's fondest wish was to be elected to the Royal Academy, an honor no woman had attained since 1768. Though she harbored no illusions of accomplishing this goal at the tender age of seventeen—for one thing, Academicians were required to be at least twenty-four years old—earning a nomination was a long, involved process, and she hoped to take her first step within a matter of weeks, by getting one of her paintings accepted for the Royal Academy's Summer Exhibition.

That was something girls *did* accomplish on a regular basis, although not usually with portraits. Proper ladies painted only landscapes and still lifes—painting people was considered unseemly. But Corinna's heart lay in portraiture. As she'd grown older, she'd found herself more and more drawn to the human figure, fascinated by the challenge of capturing a personality on canvas.

But how was she supposed to paint people accurately if she wasn't allowed to attend anatomy classes?

"We cannot stay much longer," Juliana said. "I need to make sure everything's in place for Cornelia's wedding." Cornelia, Juliana's mother-in-law, was marrying Lord Cavanaugh at her home later that evening. "And I want to see the Rosetta Stone," she added for the fourth time.

"So go see it."

"And I want to see the gems and minerals," Alexandra said. "And the jeweled—"

"Go see it all. Go see every rock in the museum." Corinna flipped a page, refocusing on the nude form of the gorgeous Greek god before her. "I'll be right here."

"That would take an hour or more." *Squeak. Squeak.* "We cannot leave you here in the Elgin Gallery alone."

"I'm not alone. There are people everywhere." Too many people, constantly jostling her and blocking her view.

"The Rosetta Stone is in the main building."

"It's perfectly proper for two married ladies to cross the museum grounds together." Unlike Corinna, who was a bit of a free spirit, her sisters seemed always concerned with being proper. "I knew I should have brought Aunt Frances along instead. She's more patient than either of you."

"She's also nine months gone with child," Alexandra retorted. She sighed. "We'll be back in an hour."

"Make that two or three," Corinna muttered as they left. Hearing the pram *squeak-squeak* away, she smiled. She and the Greek god were alone at last.

Holy Hannah, he was magnificent.

～

*M*AJOR CHANGES in Sean Delaney's life always seemed to be heralded by a letter.

The first had been the letter informing him of his unexpected inheritance, of course, but more letters had followed. A year later, a letter had relayed the devastating news that he was now an orphan, his parents having succumbed to smallpox. In the years that followed, he'd received numerous letters each time he'd established a new enterprise, each time he'd bought an ongoing concern, each time he'd purchased a piece of property. And six months ago, a letter had arrived from his older sister, Deirdre, confessing her unhappiness in her marriage (surprise, surprise) and announcing her intention to leave John Hamilton and come live with her brother instead.

But when Sean's butler brought him a letter this fine spring morning in Hampstead, he broke the seal without a second thought. Opened it. Scanned the scrawled message quickly.

Then crumpled it into a ball and hurled it into his library's fancy white marble fireplace.

"Who was it from?" Deirdre asked from the plush blue velvet chair where she'd draped herself with a book.

She was still a beauty, though you wouldn't have known it when she'd first arrived. After eight long, bitter years of fighting with her weasel of a husband, Deirdre had looked haggard when she'd shown up on Sean's doorstep. She'd looked run-down and wretched and much older than twenty-six.

As Sean feared, John Hamilton had treated her like dirt. Or less than dirt, considering one usually noticed dirt and did something about it. In contrast, Hamilton preferred to ignore his Deirdre completely, while amusing himself with an endless parade of other women. None of whom he bothered to try to conceal from his wife.

The worst of it was that she'd miscarried three months into their marriage, losing not only a child, but the only bright spot in her gloomy new life. Poor, heartbroken Deirdre remained child-less and lonely, while Hamilton, who'd gained a reputation as a talented young artist as well as a notorious scoundrel, had illegitimate offspring all over Great Britain.

Sean sipped his tea, glaring at at the paper ball in the empty fireplace, wishing it weren't such a warm, sunny day. Had there been a proper fire on the hearth, the letter would have been ashes by now. "It was from your husband." The final word left a bad taste in his mouth.

"From John? What did he say?" She shook her head. "Never mind. I don't want to know. I'm done with him."

Sean *wished* she were done with him. The reason Deirdre looked so much better lately was that she'd met Daniel Raleigh, a prosperous merchant Sean sometimes worked with. The two had fallen head-over-heels in love and wanted to marry. But despite her desperate pleas, Hamilton refused to grant her a divorce.

Maddeningly, women weren't given the same rights as men when it came to ending a marriage. Only the husband could sue for divorce, and it seemed Hamilton preferred to stay wed. Apparently he found Deirdre a convenient prop for deflecting any woman who might dare ask for commitment after finding herself carrying Hamilton's child. Such conversations could grow tiresome, you see.

And what could Deirdre's screaming anguish possibly matter, next to Hamilton's slight discomfort?

The weasel.

"He wants me to meet with him at noon," Sean told his sister. "At the British Museum. He claims he has 'something important' to discuss."

Hope leapt into her eyes. "My divorce?"

He shook his head. "It sounded more like a favor. What makes him think I'd do him a favor? Me, of all people?"

She sighed and returned to her book. "It doesn't signify.

Divorce or no, Daniel wants me to come live with him, and I've decided I will."

Sean nearly spat out a mouthful of tea.

Raleigh had a fine house and could provide well for Deirdre. He was a steady man of good character. Sean liked him, and he treated Deirdre like a princess.

But all of that was beside the point.

"Begorrah,Deirdre! You'll live with him as his *mistress*?"

"I made a mistake, Sean. I'll be the first to admit that. But haven't I suffered for it long enough? John's already stolen nearly a decade of my life." She set her book aside. "I'd *much* prefer to marry Daniel, but that isn't an option. He's willing to have me anyway, and it's time I lived again."

"What would Ma say? And Da?" For the first time ever, Sean was almost glad they were gone. They'd both have been mortified. Though their daughter had always been a wild one, this went beyond inappropriate. It was unthinkable.

Sean pushed his chair back from the table and rose. "Deirdre, you're not thinking this through. You've a chance for a fresh start here in London. If you want to be accepted by society, you need to abide by its rules."

"I'm not part of *society*."

He'd begun to pace. "I'm not meaning in the sense of the aristocracy, and you know it. The public in general, Deirdre, the respectable people. Someday you'll have children. Do you want them to be outcasts?"

"No, I *won't* have children, not if I stay with my husband!" she snapped. "Better to be an outcast than never to be born, don't you think?"

He strode to the fireplace, snatched out the crumpled paper, and smoothed it on his rosewood desk. "I'll meet with Hamilton. We'll work this out. There's just enough time to get to the British Museum by noon—"

"Don't." She leapt from her chair to seize his arm. "This is my mess, little brother. And you've got your own work to attend to."

"I've no work that matters as much as this."

"I won't have you begging on my behalf. It's humiliating."

"And your living in sin won't be? I'm going. You cannot stop me."

He shook her off and went to summon his curricle. On the ride into town, he prayed fervently that, instead of a favor, "something important" would turn out to be the divorce that would save Deirdre from being ruined (again).

TWO

"*I* HAVE A problem," Hamilton drawled when Sean met him in the museum lobby. "I require your help." He beckoned. "I wish to view the new Elgin Marbles exhibition."

"That hardly presents a problem," Sean said dryly, waving toward the back of Montagu House. "You need only walk through here and outside."

Never one for humor, Hamilton slanted a look at him as they fell into step. "My uncle, the Earl of Lincolnshire, is dying."

"My condolences," Sean said automatically, though Hamilton looked cheerful enough (for him). As always, he was flamboyantly dressed. His waistcoat appeared brown to Sean, which likely meant it was actually a bright red or green. "Though I'm not sure how I can help with *that*."

"*That* is not the problem. I'm Lincolnshire's heir, you see," he said smugly. "But the old man wishes to acquaint himself with me before he dies. He hasn't seen me for many years—not since I was an infant, in fact."

"So he wants to meet the fellow who's inheriting his title and fortune. I don't find that surprising," Sean said as they stepped outdoors. "Or particularly problematic."

Hamilton's estrangement from his uncle was no surprise, either. Deirdre's dear husband was an infamous recluse. He claimed that keeping to himself—with the exception of female companionship, of course—helped maintain his artistic vision. But Sean had known the weasel long enough to realize what he really meant to maintain was his pretentious, "mysterious" persona. And maybe his distance from those he disliked.

Which was nearly everyone.

"Go see your uncle if that's what he wants." Sean stopped before the Elgin Gallery building, which his experienced eye told him was nothing but a large, prefabricated shed.

"He doesn't want to just *see* me. He's demanded I come live with him through his final days."

"Sounds fair enough to me. How long is he expected to live?"

"A week or two," Hamilton spat. "And he swears that if I ignore his request, I'll only inherit what is required by law—the title and the entailed estates. He'll leave the rest of his fortune to charity."

And how the angels would weep.

Sean shook his head in disgust. "So go stay with him, man. For pity's sake, it won't kill you." He turned to leave, thinking he'd obviously get no human decency out of the weasel today.

"I cannot." Hamilton moved to block Sean's way. "I've an invitation to paint the waterfall on the Llewelyn estate in the Tanat Valley. Lady Llewelyn's message came in the same mail as Lincolnshire's. I'll be leaving before nightfall."

It was common knowledge that Lady Llewelyn was Hamilton's latest conquest. How he could think of abandoning his sick and dying uncle for the sake of a tryst—while his own lovely wife languished in isolation, no less!—was far beyond Sean.

It was the second most unthinkable suggestion he'd heard today.

"I suppose Lord Llewelyn will be conveniently absent," Sean said tightly.

"Abroad," Hamilton confirmed.

"And I suppose you'll be quite busy *painting*."

"Naturally. The falls have never been opened to a landscape artist before. And it's spring, the season when their volume is greatest. This very month of April, in fact, is said to be when the monk and the lady are most likely to appear. If I can capture them in paint, it will be a work for the ages."

"The monk and the lady?"

"A monk in his long robes, the Guardian of the Falls, said to materialize in the pattern of rushing water. And the Lady of the Waterfall. She peeks out from behind the towering gush, wearing flowing skirts, her face hidden by her long hair—"

"You believe this blarney?" Sean interrupted. "This utter fairy tale nonsense?"

"You don't? You're Irish, for heaven's sake. You have to believe in the fairies."

Sean snorted. Hamilton didn't want to see fairies. He wanted to see his fair Lady Llewelyn. "Your uncle needs you, Hamilton. Paint the falls another time."

"There won't *be* another time. Llewelyn never grants access, and he hasn't left the country in years."

Why on earth was the weasel coming to *him* with this problem? "Well, I suppose if that's the way you feel, you'll have to forgo Lincolnshire's unentailed holdings."

"Lincolnshire's unentailed holdings make up the majority of his fortune!"

"And what on earth do you expect *me* to do about that?" Sean was done with this conversation. "Cancel your trip, Hamilton. You'd best stay and pray that your uncle goes quickly and without pain," he added contemptuously.

Once again, his exit was blocked. "There *is* something you can do about it." Hamilton had a firm grip on his shoulder. "I want you to go to the old man, tell him you are John Hamilton, and live with him until his death."

Sean could do nothing but gape. He couldn't imagine he'd heard correctly.

After a long pause, he finally recalled which muscles to use for the purpose of talking. "I'd be sure you were jesting," he said slowly, "except I know you haven't any sense of humor to speak of." Looming over his shorter brother-in-law, Sean gripped Hamilton's wrist and squeezed until the weasel let go of his shoulder. "Why would I, of all people, do this favor—or any favor—for the person who ruined my sister's life?"

"Why?" Hamilton's lazy-lidded eyes sharpened. "Because if you help me, I'll grant your sister her precious divorce." He cocked his head. "And because if you refuse, I won't. Ever."

The words knocked the wind out of Sean.

He was being offered an impossible choice: condemn Deirdre to the shameful, miserable life of a social pariah...or defraud a sick, dying old man out of his final wish.

He couldn't wrap his mind around either option.

Unfortunately, neither could he commit murder (however justified) in the middle of a crowded museum. So Sean chose another tack. "You'll soon be an earl," he pointed out. "You're going to need an heir—a *legitimate* one—to carry on the line. With or without my cooperation, you'd best divorce Deirdre and remarry."

"That doesn't signify." Hamilton waved a smooth, pale hand. "I shall simply force her to return to my house until she bears me a male child."

Monstrous as that declaration was, Sean couldn't argue. He knew Deirdre would have to comply. The law was clear on this matter: A husband had the right to compel his wife to live wherever he pleased. Just thinking about the possibility made him feel sick.

"It has to be you, Delaney," Hamilton pressed. "You're the one person who's not only similar in age and appearance, but also knew my father, my mother, our estate in Ireland...everything my uncle would expect you to know."

All of this was true. Though Sean was taller, they both had similar dark hair and green eyes. And Lincolnshire hadn't seen his nephew since infancy. No doubt Sean *could* pull it off.

Except...

"I'm color-blind."

"What of it?"

"What if your uncle notices? He'll never believe I'm a color-blind *painter*."

Hamilton scoffed. "People will believe whatever you tell them. In fact..." With a mean-spirited glint in his eye, he opened the flimsy door to the Elgin Gallery and dragged Sean inside. Hamilton scanned the crowd..."There!" He pointed out a girl seated before a magnificent marble frieze, busily sketching. "I'll bet I can fool that girl—an artist—into believing *you're* an artist."

Sean rolled his eyes. "I'm not going along with—"

"Hush. You haven't heard the terms of the bet. If I manage to convince the girl, you'll agree to do as I've asked, thereby securing my inheritance and your sister's liberation. If I fail, I swear I'll march out of this building and straight to the clerk to start the divorce proceedings. Either way, Deirdre wins." A slow, devious smile stretched across his face. "Take it or leave it, Delaney."

Before Sean could protest any further, Hamilton pushed him toward the girl.

THREE

*I*F ONLY SHE could find a young man who looked like *this*, Corinna mused as she sketched another Greek god, she'd have nothing left to wish for.

Not that she had the slightest intention of wedding anytime soon, much to her brother's displeasure. Griffin wanted nothing more than to marry her off, to have her—his last unwed sister—out of his house and off of his hands. To make her someone else's responsibility.

To that end, he'd been dragging Corinna to balls and to Almack's and to every other social event on the calendar, for the express purpose of hurling her at every eligible gentleman he could find. The season had been underway only a few weeks, yet already she was grumbling more than Juliana had all last year.

Griffin really *did* take all the fun out of it.

True, she was fond of dancing, and she also liked gentlemen, of course. Especially the ones who'd managed to get her alone, behind a potted palm in a ballroom or in a dark corner on a terrace, for a stolen kiss. But those had been few and far between this year—her brother was a much more vigilant chaperone than dear, oblivious Aunt Frances.

Artists were supposed to be creatures of passion, were they not? Well, Corinna's life seemed to be sorely lacking in passion. After the shattering consecutive deaths of her father, mother, and eldest brother had kept her hidden away in mourning through much of her adolescence, she'd emerged a fresh-faced sixteen-year-old eagerly anticipating her first season. Anticipating glamour, gaiety, novelty, intrigue, and most of all, passion. And when she'd finally made it to London, finally come out in society, finally experienced her first kiss, it had all been...

Rather pleasant.

But that was all.

So excuse her if she was in no great hurry to put aside her grand, exhilarating, ambitious artistic dreams in favor of the *rather pleasant* pastime of finding love.

Especially since, now that she was seventeen and the last unmarried sister, Griffin was making it *rather annoying*.

Catching her lower lip between her teeth, she was using her pencil to shade the fascinating muscles on the god's toned bare chest when something caught her eye. Glancing up, she spotted two young gentlemen heading in her direction. Not an unusual sight—the gallery was crowded with people—but something about these gentlemen held her interest. Actually, it was just one of the gentlemen. The taller one.

The one who bore a striking resemblance to the Greek god she'd been sketching.

Flipping to a new page, she started sketching him instead. Quickly, before he disappeared from view.

His angular, sculpted face was framed by crisp black hair that grew long at the back of his neck. His eyes were the greenest she'd ever seen. Sadly, he was somewhat more clothed than the marble gods, but having sketched quite a few of them, she fancied she could imagine what he looked like beneath his smart but conservative trousers, waistcoat, and tailcoat. Her pencil outlined broad shoulders—

She froze midsketch as the two gentlemen walked right up to her.

"Good afternoon," the shorter one said.

Like his taller companion, he was dark-haired and green-eyed and good-looking. And he was much more fashionably dressed. But all in all, she decided, not nearly of the same godly caliber.

Still, she felt flustered. She wasn't accustomed to handsome young men introducing themselves. Good manners dictated they ask permission of a young lady's chaperone, who would then provide the introduction.

Of course, Corinna's chaperones were currently off who knows where, looking at rocks.

"Good afternoon," she returned guardedly. "Mr....?"

"Delaney," he drawled. "Sean Delaney, at your service. And this," he added, indicating the taller man, "is my good friend Mr. John Hamilton. Having noticed you sketching, he wished to greet a fellow artist. You've heard of him, I presume?"

Had she heard of him? Corinna's sketchbook and pencil fell to the floor. *Everyone* had heard of John Hamilton, the young renowned and reclusive painter of landscapes.

She turned to him, positively stunned. Her Greek god was John Hamilton—John Hamilton!—and he wanted to meet her. *Her*, Corinna Chase, possibly the most *un*renowned artist in all of London.

"Mr. Hamilton," she gushed, "I cannot tell you how I much I admire—"

"Please stop," he interrupted, bending to scoop up her fallen supplies. He straightened and, with a roll of his gorgeous green eyes toward Mr. Delaney, handed the items to her. "I'm sorry, but I'm not John Hamilton." His lilting voice was distracting. The melodic Irish accent didn't quite mesh with the Greek physique. "I'm Sean Delaney. And I'm afraid my brother-in-law here—the *real* John Hamilton—has a horrible sense of humor."

"Now, Hamilton." The other fellow dolefully shook his head. "There's no need to hide your identity from this charming young lady."

"It's *your* identity, and you feel the need to hide it from everyone." The Irishman drew a line in the air that traced his companion from head to toe. "You'll note he's the one dressed with artistic flair," he pointed out to Corinna before brushing at his own plain black clothes. "I'm merely a common man of business."

"Please forgive Mr. Hamilton." Mr. Delaney—or perhaps he was Mr. Hamilton—raised a brow toward Corinna. "He's much too self-effacing."

"Blarney!" the Greek god shot back. "You're a dunce, Hamilton."

Corinna felt like a tennis ball bouncing back and forth between two players. She didn't know which one to believe. But since she didn't expect to see either of them ever again, she figured it didn't signify.

While they'd volleyed, she'd regained her senses enough to recall Mr. Hamilton was a member of the committee that chose artwork for the Summer Exhibition. *That* was what truly mattered.

She clutched her art supplies to her chest. "I'm an oil painter myself," she told both of them, praying one really was John Hamilton. "I'm here sketching the marbles to learn anatomy so I can improve my technique for portraits. It's my fondest hope that one of my canvases will be selected for this year's Summer Exhibition."

"I'm certain Mr. Hamilton will vote for it," the shorter one assured her gravely.

"I will not." The Greek god's fists were clenched, and his Irish lilt came through gritted teeth. "I mean, he won't. Or perhaps he will, but I'm *not* Hamilton."

"Pshaw." His friend waved a smooth, graceful hand.

"He's—"

"Corinna!" She looked away to see her sisters and the pram squeaking their way toward her. "I'm sorry we took so long," Alexandra said. "Are you finished yet?"

Corinna beckoned them eagerly, certain Juliana would discern which fellow was John Hamilton. An inveterate meddler, Juliana could ferret out any secret. "I'd be pleased for you to meet Mr. Hamilton," she said, turning back to the gentlemen.

They were gone.

Lifting sweet little Harry from the pram, Alexandra frowned. "Mr. Hamilton?"

"The landscapist, John Hamilton. He was just here." Corinna scanned the crowded gallery, to no avail. "He's gorgeous. Or perhaps it's his friend who's gorgeous, or his brother-in-law—"

"Whatever are you on about? Everyone knows John Hamilton never appears in public." Looking sympathetic, Juliana touched her arm. "I think we should go. I must get home well before my mother-in-law's wedding, and in any case, you've clearly been sketching too long."

~

SEAN HAULED Hamilton back toward Montagu House, one hand clenched on the weasel's upper arm.

"It's a shame girls cannot study anatomy," Hamilton drawled as though they were on a leisurely stroll, "because sketching statues isn't going to help her learn anything."

"Is that so?" Sean gritted out.

"I've yet to see a portrait painted by a female that was any good, and I never expect to, so I seriously doubt I'll vote for that girl's painting."

Sean had no wish to continue this conversation. In fact, he'd gladly pay a thousand pounds to avoid speaking with Hamilton ever again. But he felt sorry for the girl in question. "What if her picture *is* good? Will you still refuse to vote for it simply because it was painted by a lady?"

"Of course I wouldn't. As it happens, I wouldn't be aware a lady painted it, since I don't look at signatures before I vote. Most of the Summer Exhibition judges take an artist's status into consideration, but I believe each work should stand on its own. Regardless of what the other Academicians think, I believe a painter's identity should never influence a judge's opinion."

It was the most decent thing Sean had ever heard Hamilton utter. Surprisingly decent. Until the weasel added, "But I'm certain her paintings won't be any good. Especially since she's never studied anatomy."

"She might surprise you," Sean shot back. "You shouldn't be so judgmental. You might vote for her painting and later on have to eat humble pie."

"I doubt it," Hamilton said blandly. "We failed to learn her name, so in the unlikely event I ever did vote for one of her works, I'd never know it, would I?"

"Corinna."

"Pardon?"

"Her name is Corinna. Another girl called her Corinna as I was dragging you off."

She'd had wide blue eyes and gleaming dark hair. Sean remembered the way she'd bitten her plump lower lip. For some reason, that had made him imagine kissing her.

"You had no right to drag me off." Wrenching his arm from Sean's hand, Hamilton pulled open the door to Montagu House. "I won the bet," he added smugly.

"You did not. She didn't believe I was you."

"She didn't know what to believe. Which means I won. I succeeded in convincing her you may be an artist."

"Blarney."

Hamilton shrugged. "Whether you agree or not doesn't

signify. You'll still pretend to be me for Lincolnshire's sake if you want to see your sister divorced."

"I believe you'll want to rethink that demand. When society discovers you deceived your uncle for your own gain, your reputation will be torn to threads. Your impressive art career will end in shame."

"Blarney," Hamilton mimicked in disdain. "No one will ever find out. Lincolnshire is incapacitated and housebound. And the man lived to make others miserable—especially my family—so who would give a care if he's duped? The mean old brute deserves it."

Maybe Hamilton had a point there. Who would complain if a man like Lincolnshire got tricked? Sean had heard tell of his infamous deeds throughout his childhood. William Hamilton—Lincolnshire's younger brother—had dreamed of a fulfilling career in the church, but Lincolnshire couldn't be bothered to help him secure a position. He'd been willing to instead commit his service to the military, but Lincolnshire had refused to buy him a commission. Being a younger son, William had no means to support himself, his wife, and his young child, so he hadn't a choice when his brother banished him to Kilburton to oversee his foreign interests. Left to rot among village rabble in the dreary backwoods of Ireland, far from all their friends and relations, the family had languished in bitterness and despair, their desperate pleas to return home falling on deaf ears.

Perhaps those years of bitterness were the reason Hamilton could act so callously toward poor Deirdre. Like uncle, like nephew?

Sean stood in the museum's busy lobby, fighting his better judgment. Though he'd normally abhor lying to a man on his deathbed (or anywhere else, for that matter), maybe the mean old earl had it coming. But more than that, Sean loved his sister. He didn't want to see her forced to bear Hamilton's child or living in sin with Daniel Raleigh. And he knew that if he didn't agree to the deception, the weasel would never free Deirdre.

"This won't interrupt your routine," Hamilton went on. "You'll have to move to Lincolnshire's Berkeley Square town house for a couple of weeks, but you need only sleep there at night. You can tell the old man you must paint during the day and go off to do your usual work. It shan't affect Delaney and Company at all."

"What if he wants to see your paintings?"

"You mean *your* paintings," Hamilton returned with a smirk. He frowned a moment, then nodded. "I'll leave you some money to lease studio space near the square—"

"I don't want your money," Sean growled. "And I don't need to lease anything. I own half of Piccadilly Street." He normally hated advertising his wealth, but, even more, he hated being bullied. And Hamilton was a bully. Sean couldn't resist firing back with whatever he could use to intimidate the weasel.

Hamilton raised an eyebrow. "Do you, now? Well, that's excellent. If you've a vacant garret nearby, that would be ideal. Something very private with north-facing windows. I've a few canvases in the apartments I've been renting. I shall fetch them posthaste and put them in there for you to show him." He nodded again, more enthusiastically. "Perhaps I'll lease the space from you permanently. Once I inherit the title, I'll be forced to spend some time at Lincolnshire House, so I'll need it when I return from Wales."

An awkward silence stretched between them while people walked in and out, asking the porter directions to find the Rosetta Stone or the Egyptian mummies.

"You'll do it, won't you?" Hamilton pressed. "Otherwise—"

"I'll do it," Sean snapped. He knew what *otherwise* entailed: doom for Deirdre.

To avoid that, he'd sell his very soul if he had to.

Which he very probably just had.

FOUR

ORANGE BRANDY

Take a quart of Brandy, the peels of eight Oranges thin pared, keep them in the Brandy forty-
eight hours in a closed pitcher, then take three pints of Water, put into it three quarters of a
pounde of loaf Sugar, boil it till half be consumed, and let it stand till cold, then mix it with the
Brandy.

*This was served at my grandparents' wedding breakfast, and their marriage was blessed with
love and health. We have had it at family weddings ever since.*
—Eleanor, Marchioness of Cainewood, 1730

*L*ADY STAFFORD and Lord Cavanaugh's wedding was
a modest affair, just family and a few friends in the
gorgeous Painted Room at Stafford House. The chamber
was a bit tight even for the small number of guests; the equally
impressive Palm Room downstairs would have been more
comfortable. But the Painted Room was perfect for the occasion,
because its theme was marriage.

A famous Roman fresco was re-created on the chimneypiece,
and other wedding scenes were painted directly on the plaster
walls. Panels depicted music, drinking, and dancing. Cupid and

Venus cavorted overhead, nymphs danced on the ceiling, lovers courted on gilt-framed canvas, and a frieze of rose wreaths and garlands of flowers went all around the cornice.

The house wasn't actually Lady Stafford's anymore. Cornelia had been the Dowager Lady Stafford for several years now, which meant Stafford House belonged to her son, James Trevor, who was the current Earl of Stafford and, of course, Juliana's husband.

While the minister droned on, Juliana leaned close to Corinna and whispered, "Your turn will come next."

"I'm not concerned about having a turn," Corinna hissed back.

Juliana rolled her eyes.

On Corinna's other side sat Aunt Frances, hugely pregnant and watching the ceremony with a sappy, romantic smile on her face. Love and marriage had come late to Aunt Frances, but she looked happier now than her niece had ever seen her. And love had transformed Corinna's sisters as well. Juliana and James had wed last August—right after Aunt Frances and Lord Malmsey—and the two of them still had trouble keeping their hands to themselves in public. Alexandra and Tristan had been married nearly two years and seemed to live in awe of each other and their infant son.

Although Corinna sometimes worried she'd never find that sort of love for herself, she also worried she'd never fulfill her artistic potential. Of the two, she felt the art was more under her control. It was the thing that defined her, the thing she had that others didn't.

She was happy for Aunt Frances and her sisters. It was brilliant that they'd all found love, but to Corinna's mind, the three had little else. They'd *needed* love to complete them, but she had her art.

She had her landscapes and her still lifes, and most of all, her portraits. If only she could get one of her works accepted into the

Summer Exhibition, her future would look bright whether or not there was a gentleman in the picture.

No sooner had the minister announced that the Dowager Lady Stafford was now Lady Cavanaugh than Juliana began distributing glasses of orange brandy, a concoction some ancient Chase ancestor had claimed would guarantee a lifetime of marital bliss. How her sisters believed such nonsense, Corinna would never fathom. But she had to admit that Lord and Lady Cavanaugh looked very happy for now. Perched together on an amazing green silk sofa with gilt arms carved to look like winged lions, they both beamed as they accepted congratulations. Apparently Cornelia had found *her* Greek god, even if he was somewhat aged and silver-haired.

Her husband in tow, Juliana returned. She handed Corinna the last glass with a satisfied sigh. "Don't the two of them look perfect together? I knew they'd end up married."

Juliana always knew what was best for everyone, and she never hesitated to say so. Last season she'd suggested Lord Cavanaugh and James's mother share a dance, and now here they were, man and wife.

"Her new title even begins with C," Juliana added proudly.

Corinna sipped the sweet spirits. "Why should that signify?"

James laughed, slipping an arm around Juliana's waist. "My aunts," he reminded Corinna, "are Aurelia, Lady Avonleigh, and Bedelia, Lady Balmforth. But until today my mother—their sister —was Cornelia, Lady Stafford."

"Now she's Cornelia, Lady Cavanaugh, and the three sisters are Ladies A, B, and C," Juliana concluded.

"Holy Hannah," Corinna said, shaking her head.

She'd never understand how Juliana's mind worked.

James dropped a kiss on Juliana's head and moved off, just as Lady A herself made her way over. "Wasn't the ceremony beautiful? My baby sister, married again." With a teary but joyful little sniff, she tore her gaze from the new Lady C and focused on Corinna. "How are you these days, my dear?"

"Very well, thank you."

"And your art?"

"I've been painting madly. I think I'm close to finishing my submissions for the Summer Exhibition."

"Don't forget, I promised to help."

"Thank you," Corinna said, although she had no idea how Lady A *could* help. But the woman seemed quite determined. Years ago, her youngest daughter had tragically ended her own life by jumping off the London Bridge, taking her unborn baby with her. The poor girl had been artistic and ambitious, and dreamed of entering the Royal Academy just like Corinna, so Lady Avonleigh dearly wished to see Corinna succeed in her daughter's stead.

Unfortunately, wishing didn't accomplish much. The kindly woman's heart was in the right place, Corinna knew, but she had no connections or influence in the art world. "I appreciate your good intentions," Corinna told her sincerely.

"I have a plan," Lady A announced.

"You do?"

"Yes, indeed. I've made a rather large donation to the Royal Academy, earmarked to provide yearly grants for deserving students to study abroad. A noble cause, don't you think?"

"Very much so," Corinna said. The Royal Academy had sponsored student travel years ago, but such grants had been suspended since the wars had begun, making journeys to the Continent impossible. Following Napoleon's recent defeat at Waterloo, travel had once again resumed, and artists were now clamoring to go.

But Lady A's grants would all go to males, of course, since females were barred from the Royal Academy schools.

Corinna sighed. "I would love to go study in Italy."

"I'm sure you would, dear. My daughter always wanted to

go, too." Lady A rested a sympathetic hand on her arm. "I've made a stipulation that the yearly awards be titled the Lady Georgiana Cartwright Scholarships, in her honor. I do hope that seeing a lady's name on the grant will encourage the Academy to consider admitting girls in future. And in the meantime"—she smiled, her soft blue eyes going a little hazy as she gazed off into space—"it gives me pleasure to think of helping any art student achieve his dreams, no matter the recipient's gender."

"Tell her the rest," Juliana prompted.

"Ah, yes." Lady A nodded, coming back from wherever she'd drifted off. "Next month I shall hold an afternoon reception in my home, to which I shall invite the members of the Summer Exhibition Selection Committee. Thanks to my generous patronage, I'm certain they'll all feel obligated to attend. And, of course, I shall invite you too, Lady Corinna, giving you the opportunity to show them some of your work and, more important, charm them and sway their decisions."

Corinna swallowed hard. The idea that her future might depend on her ability to "charm" anyone made her feel queasy. Charm was Juliana's department—Juliana *oozed* charm. And even Alexandra could be charming when necessary, when it helped her to achieve some end. But Corinna had never been much good at hiding her true feelings or keeping up a smooth, polished social grace. She wasn't the type of person who could enter a room full of perfect strangers and instantly captivate the whole place.

Now, if Lady A were looking for someone who could enter the room and blurt out the first thing that popped into her head, she'd have come to the right girl.

But as Corinna was an unknown artist—and that would be a mark against her in the judging—she knew she should be thrilled to have an opportunity to meet the committee. And she *was* grateful and astonished that Lady A would go to such lengths to help her.

"Thank you so much!" she gushed. "I shall do everything I can to make the most of this chance."

"I must give credit where credit is due," Lady A said. "The whole scheme was your sister's idea."

"It was *your* money," Juliana hastened to point out. "And your decision where it should be allocated."

"I was pleased to do it. My dear daughter would have approved. I shall be even more pleased when your sister becomes the first female elected to the Royal Academy in more than fifty years, and honored to have had a hand in it." Taking a sip of her orange brandy, she looked back to Corinna. "Of course, your talent will be the determining factor, my dear. I've no doubt you'll eventually find yourself elected with or without my help."

Corinna wished she could be so confident.

"Have you need of any planning assistance?" Juliana asked Lady A.

"I could use a hand with the invitations," the older woman admitted. "My penmanship isn't what it used to be."

"I'd be pleased to help," Juliana assured her—no surprise, since Juliana lived to have her hand in everything. "Perhaps we can have a little invitation party here next week. Friday afternoon would work well. I'll invite Alexandra and our cousins. You remember Rachael, Claire, and Elizabeth?"

"Of course," Lady A said. "It was a pleasure chatting with them during your many sewing parties." Last year, Juliana had offered to make baby clothes for the Foundling Hospital, and she'd needed a *lot* of assistance. "I would be grateful for your cousins' help. And now..." Lady A gestured to the new Lady C. "I must congratulate my sister before the wedding supper."

She ambled off, and Juliana drew Corinna toward their Chase cousins standing nearby. At sixteen and seventeen, Elizabeth and Claire were both dark-haired and pretty as pictures. Their tall, equally dark-haired brother, Noah, the Earl of Greystone, was twenty and would have been pretty, too, but for a small scar that slashed through his left eyebrow.

He flashed a smile as Corinna and Juliana approached. "I'm going to find Rachael," he said, referring to his elder sister. "If you'll excuse me."

As he strode away, Juliana looked to Elizabeth and Claire. "We're helping Lady Avonleigh with the reception she's planning to help launch Corinna's art career. I'm hoping you'll both come to a little invitation-making party here next Friday. And I hope Rachael will come as well, of course. Where has she gone off to?"

"The terrace. She's just staring out over Green Park." Claire looked fretful. "She hasn't been herself for a long while."

"I've noticed," Juliana said. All the time Corinna's brother, Griffin, had been busy trying to marry off his three sisters, Juliana had been trying to match him with Rachael. But Rachael had been acting sad and withdrawn these past months, which put a damper on Juliana's efforts. "Rachael has always been so good-humored. What do you suppose is the matter?"

"She's not yet got over finding that letter," Elizabeth said.

Claire elbowed her younger sister in the ribs.

"What?" Juliana looked between them. "What letter?"

"Now you've done it, Elizabeth." Claire's unusual amethyst eyes glared into her sister's green ones. "Rachael's kept mum on the subject deliberately, you know."

Elizabeth's hands flew up to slap her own cheeks. "Oh, fiddlesticks!"

"What letter?" Juliana repeated.

Although the Painted Room was filled with the babel of conversation, Claire and Elizabeth's silence was noticeable. "Whatever it is," Corinna said for them, "Rachael wants it kept a secret."

"Surely she didn't mean from us," Juliana said. "We're her cousins."

"No, you aren't," Elizabeth said, then clapped a hand over her mouth.

"What?" Juliana and Corinna burst out together.

Claire glared at her sister again, then sighed. "When Rachael cleared out our parents' suite at Greystone for Noah, she found a letter that revealed she had a different father than ours. It seems our mother was married before and carrying Rachael when she was widowed. Then she married our father before giving birth."

Juliana looked astonished. "Who was her real father, then?"

"She doesn't know." Claire shook her head. "The letter didn't say, and there's no one to ask. We have no living grandparents, and Mama's only sister died when we were young. Rachael went through all of our mother's belongings, searching for clues to who her first husband might have been, but she found nothing."

"Is she still looking?" Corinna asked, concerned.

"She cannot think of anywhere else to look," Elizabeth said. "Griffin even helped her go through everything again last year, in case she missed something."

Now Juliana looked intrigued. "Griffin knows about this?"

"He's the only one besides us," Claire said. "Please don't tell Rachael you know now, too. She'd be mortified."

"Why?" Corinna asked. "Does she think so little of us that she believes we'd feel differently toward her, just because we're not cousins by blood?"

"I fear she's not thinking at all these days." Claire crossed her arms over her violet satin bodice and leveled another glare at her sister. "Much like Elizabeth."

"I'm sorry," Elizabeth squeaked.

Claire sighed again. "I don't think Rachael even realizes you're not her cousins. She's so upset at not knowing who her real father is that she hasn't thought past that. Or maybe she's blocked the truth from her mind, because she can't stand the thought of losing all the family she knows."

"She still has you two," Corinna said. "And Noah. You all shared a mother."

"But that's all. Please just let her work it out for herself in her own good time. I don't think she could take hearing anything more now."

"We promise not to tell a soul." Corinna turned to Juliana. "Don't we?"

"Of course we do." Juliana reached to squeeze both her cousins' hands. "I'm sorry to hear Rachael is so upset, and I promise that no one—including her—will hear about it from either of us. We love Rachael, no matter what."

Corinna nodded agreement, but she knew Juliana well enough to hear the barely concealed glee in her sister's voice.

Oh, Juliana sympathized with Rachael, of course—but far more important was the fact that Rachael's main objection to marrying Griffin had always been their shared ancestry, and that obstacle was now gone. Not to mention, Rachael had chosen to confide in Griffin, and Griffin had tried to help her *and* kept her secret.

Add all of that together, and it seemed another of Juliana's incessant projects was well on its way to success. And if she actually managed to pull it off, she was going to be smug beyond belief.

Corinna couldn't hold back a groan.

FIVE

EW PEOPLE were strolling in Green Park this Thursday evening. The undulating landscape was shadowed by the setting sun, and the gardens were very tranquil.

But Rachael wasn't.

Gripping the terrace's rail, she stared out over grassland and trees, telling herself it was time to let go of these feelings. She was never going to learn who her father was, and she had to come to grips with that. She'd allowed Griffin to help her as he'd wanted, and they'd found nothing—just as she'd expected. That had been months ago, months spent in a melancholy haze.

The man who had raised her had cared for her, so it shouldn't matter that they hadn't shared a blood bond, should it? And how long could she remain cross with her mother for withholding the facts? The woman was dead, for heaven's sake. The anger was pointless, and she had to get on with her life.

"Rachael."

Turning to see her brother step out on the terrace, she forced a smile. "Noah. You arrived so late I had no chance to chat with you before the wedding." His priorities never had been with family or responsibility. "Did you get the new racehorse settled in at Greystone?"

"Horses," he corrected. "I bought two. And they're both doing well, yes. I'm hoping for a good showing at Ascot. While I was home I asked for an inventory to be taken—"

"An inventory of what?" Since when did Noah care about anything at Greystone Castle?

"Of everything. While dining there alone, I noticed that old portrait of the first earl over the fireplace and got to thinking about what might have accumulated in the hundred and fifty years since he was granted the title and lands. The servants aren't finished yet—I expect it will take them weeks to catalog everything they find. But one thing they discovered was an old trunk in the attic with Mama's wedding dress and a few other items. Nothing important—"

"I want to see it."

"I knew you would," he said with a wry smile. "That's why I'm telling you they found it. I had it brought down and put in my room so you can go through it after the season."

"I want to see it now. Can we go to Greystone tomorrow?"

"I've just returned from Greystone, and the Jockey Club meets tomorrow. Besides, I told you nothing in it is important. You can wait a few weeks."

"No, I can't, Noah." He didn't know what was important. The trunk might have something in it that would reveal her father's identity. "I'm going tomorrow."

"I'm not going with you, and you cannot travel that far alone or with Claire or Elizabeth. It wouldn't be safe."

"I know that." But she knew another gentleman who might be willing to accompany her in his place. "When you go back inside, will you ask Griffin to step out here a moment?"

~

"*C*AN YOU COME for me at seven?" Rachael asked, a few loose tendrils of her hair blowing in the breeze that crossed the terrace.

"That anxious, are you?" Griffin's sisters were never ready to leave the house so early in the morning. But then, none of them were nearly as focused as Rachael. "That will be fine. Will one or both of your sisters come along, too?"

"I think not."

"Hmm. Aunt Frances is too far gone with child, so I guess I'll ask one of my sisters to drag herself out of bed and join us."

"Why?"

"As a chaperone, of course."

"We don't need a chaperone, Griffin."

He sipped orange brandy, watching her warily over the rim of the glass. "It's a long journey."

"Only half a day each direction. We won't be gone overnight. Other than you and my siblings, no one knows about my true parentage, and I want to keep it that way, at least for now. Besides," she added, "you're my cousin. Would I require a chaperone to travel half a day with Noah?"

"I'm not Noah," Griffin pointed out. "A cousin isn't the same as a brother." But he didn't point out that he wasn't, in the strictest sense, her cousin. Not by blood anyway, not since it had been established that John Chase hadn't been her father. He didn't want to upset her, and more to the point, he'd just as soon have her think of him as a cousin.

"You're *practically* my brother," she insisted.

Maybe having her think of him as a brother was even better. "Very well," he said. "I'll come for you at seven."

"Thank you!" she exclaimed, looking happier than he'd seen her since that disappointing day when they'd gone through her mother's belongings and found nothing.

As he watched her glide back into Stafford House, gracefully swaying as she went, he clenched his jaw.

Griffin remembered Rachael as an awkward adolescent, a tomboyish playmate, all skinny arms and gangly legs. At fourteen, she'd had a funny dent in her chin, wild, curly dark hair, and rather bulbous blue eyes. But then he'd left home for Oxford and later joined the cavalry. And during the years he'd spent away, the tomboy had become a lady.

A very sultry one.

Those cerulean eyes were now alluring, those limbs long and graceful, that figure anything but awkward. The dented chin made her face distinctive and fetching. Her hair was sleek and tamed, excepting those few tendrils that always seemed to come loose. Or maybe she left them loose deliberately. Either way, they looked soft and silky and tickled the sides of her smooth, sculpted cheeks.

In short, Rachael Chase was spectacularly attractive. Too much so for Griffin's comfort. Which was why he was happy she thought of him as nothing more than a cousin.

Although cousins often wed, Rachael's aunt had married a cousin, then sadly given birth to a crippled, feebleminded child. A doctor had said the family relationship might be to blame, and as a result, Rachael was dead-set against marrying any cousin, no matter how distant. And that suited Griffin just fine, since he had no intention of marrying her.

He had no intention of marrying anyone.

At least, not anytime soon.

His sisters and Cainewood kept him occupied quite enough, thank you very much. The last thing he needed was an additional distraction, or yet another responsibility. After all, he was only twenty-six, he thought as he downed the rest of the orange brandy and went back inside.

There were years and years left before he'd have to worry about taking on a wife.

SIX

*T*HE HOMES ON the east and west sides of Berkeley Square were close to the street and built cheek by jowl against one another, but Lincolnshire House stood alone on the north end, behind a high imposing wall.

On Friday morning, the guard at the massive wooden gate scowled at the portmanteau Sean carried. "Peddlers aren't welcome."

Sean's hand clenched on the handle of the simple leather bag. "I'm the earl's nephew," he said, all but choking on the words.

A little gasp burst from the man's mouth. "Pardon me, Mr. Hamilton, I'm sorry, truly I am." Babbling, he swung open the gate. "Do come in, and please accept my sincerest apologies."

Sean was more than willing to do so, but he was struck dumb at sight of the house.

His own house in Hampstead was sizable and impressive. Originally built in the seventeenth century, it had been extended and remodeled some fifty years ago by the notable architect Robert Adam, for a chief justice who worked in the City but wanted to live in the suburbs. It sat in acres of gardens and ancient woodland, with a stunning view out over London. Deirdre had gasped the first time she saw it.

But it seemed a hovel in comparison to the Earl of Lincolnshire's enormous mansion in Berkeley Square.

A rather plain Palladian-style brick building, it was quite simply the largest house Sean had ever seen. Five gardeners labored industriously in the lavishly landscaped courtyard. After banging the knocker, he shifted uncomfortably on the front steps beneath the portico, wishing he could be anywhere else but here, doing anything else but this.

Deirdre certainly hadn't agreed that going along with Hamilton's plan was worthwhile to secure her divorce. Last night's disbelieving cry—"You promised to do *what*?"—still rang in his head. "That's ridiculous!" she'd railed—and Irishwomen were nothing if not expert railers. "You fool! You knothead! I don't need you to play the martyr for me. I'll be happy together with Daniel whether we're married or not."

Well, maybe *she* would be happy, but Sean wouldn't. And although he'd been tempted to tell her of her husband's threat to make her move back in with him, he'd resisted that temptation. He didn't want to be the martyr; he didn't want her to feel indebted or burdened with guilt. Better she think her brother a knotheaded fool.

That was nothing new, anyway.

A butler opened the door. His dark suit was starched and pressed. His expression looked as rigid as his clothing.

"May I help you, sir?"

"I've come to see my uncle, the Earl of Lincolnshire."

"Your uncle? You must be Mr. Hamilton, then." As though he'd suddenly melted, the man's entire demeanor changed. "Come in, come in," he said, ushering Sean through the door. "I'm Quincy, and the earl is going to be so pleased to hear you've arrived. I shall inform Mr. Higginbotham, his house steward, that you are here so he can make certain your room is ready." He eyed the portmanteau. "That cannot be all you brought along."

"My manservant will bring in my trunks after he sees to my curricle."

"Good, good. I shall send an underfootman to assist him. The earl has been asking after you since he opened his eyes this morning. In truth, since last night when he received your note. He's abed, so I shall fetch a maid to show you upstairs posthaste."

The butler closed the door and promptly disappeared down a corridor. Sean waited, anxious to get this introduction over with. How much time would he be forced to spend with the mean old brute?

Unpleasant as the earl himself might be, he certainly had a nice house. In contrast to the building's simple facade, its interior was absolutely sumptuous. The grand, pillared entrance led to a wide, sweeping curved staircase with broad steps made of purest white marble. Grecian-style couches lined the perimeter, plushly upholstered in light-colored velvet with darker trim. Gold and crystal glittered everywhere, and there was lots of Oriental pottery scattered about. Paintings hung everywhere, too —enormous gilt-framed paintings that Sean imagined were probably famous, though knowing nothing of art, he couldn't identify a single artist.

"Fancy, ain't it?"

Wondering if his mouth had been hanging open, he turned to see a little bird of a middle-aged woman wearing a dark dress with a starched white apron. "It's impressive."

"The most impressive house in London," she declared, leading him across the stone floor toward the steps. "Which is only fair, considering Lord Lincolnshire is the most wonderful man in all of England."

Wonderful? The earl was wonderful?

That couldn't be right. This maid was obviously just being a dutiful employee.

The staircase's newel post looked to be fashioned of solid crystal. Atop balusters of gilded ironwork, the handrail was crystal, too. As Sean climbed, he nodded at two more servants on their way down. "What exactly is wrong with his lordship's health?"

"Such a tragedy." The maid sighed. "He complained of chest pain that lasted a few hours. Before the doctor could arrive, he fell into a dead faint, and when he woke, his legs began swelling horribly. A dreadful sight, I tell you. And he's short of breath, the poor man. Dropsy, the doctor said."

"Dropsy." Sean knew little about the disease, but it sounded bad. "He can talk, though, yes?"

"Aye, that he can." At the top of the stairs, she turned down a corridor that had more paintings on the walls and more Oriental pottery on marble hall tables. She skirted around a woman polishing the already spotless inlaid floor. "And he cannot wait to see you."

Sean was waved through a door to find Lincolnshire in a huge state bed hung with dark damask trimmed with pale silk. His face hidden from Sean's sight by a sturdy nurse dressed in white, the earl sat propped against four or five pillows. The nurse finished plumping them and stepped away.

"John!" the man exclaimed as Sean came into view. He had light-colored eyes, thinning gray hair combed forward, and an altogether dignified, pleasant appearance.

And he didn't look nearly as ill as Hamilton had indicated.

"I'm so pleased you agreed to keep me company in my final days," he enthused. "Come here, nephew. Let me have a look at you."

Sean approached warily. "You seem far stronger than I feared, my lord."

"My lord? Please call me Uncle. But I'm afraid I *am* quite ill.

Began with massive pain—a great, squeezing pressure in the vicinity of my heart. As though a man were sitting on my chest." He paused. And then, "No," he corrected himself, "as though the *Prince Regent* were sitting on my chest."

Lincolnshire smiled at his own joke; the Prince Regent was grossly overweight. Although Sean had never run in court circles, even he knew that. Scurrilous cartoons were often printed in the papers, and a recent one had featured the fat prince picking his teeth following an enormous meal.

"The doctors say I won't last two weeks," Lincolnshire added, sounding a bit out of breath. "I need all these pillows because I cannot breathe lying down. I have to stay upright even to sleep, so I can breathe. Sit down, sit down." Looking much more chipper than a man with a death sentence rightly should, he indicated a tufted velvet chair close by the bed. "It's dropsy, they tell me."

"What causes it?"

"That they *haven't* told me. Or perhaps they don't know. Sit, John, sit."

"You seem so cheerful," Sean commented as he lowered himself.

"I'm happy to see you. After all these years, John—"

"Sean," he interrupted.

"Eh?"

"Call me Sean, please." He couldn't stand being called by the weasel's name, not to mention he would likely forget to answer to it. "Sean is the same name as John in Ireland, you see, so I've been called Sean since I was a lad. I'm still called Sean by all my friends and family."

"You haven't any family left other than me, have you? Or only on your mother's side?" The old man cocked his head. "You've an Irish accent, too. How is that?"

Sean had forgotten Hamilton's parents were dead and he'd had no siblings. He'd have to tread more carefully.

Sweet mercy, whatever had made him think he could pull this off?

He ignored the first questions and answered the last. "Surely you know I was raised in Ireland."

"But you're an Englishman, after all. I made certain you always had English tutors. Paid the enormous bills myself."

Sean shrugged—casually, he hoped. "Everyone else around me was Irish. I expect I picked up a bit of an accent anyway."

"A bit?"

In all honesty, Sean had thought he'd lost most of it. Or at least he'd tried to. He was very careful to always say *yes* rather than *aye*, and *my* rather than *me*. *Yes, that's my best suit,* instead of *Aye, that's me best suit.*

He knew London wasn't overly fond of the Irish.

"Ah, well, I suppose it doesn't signify," Lincolnshire added kindly. "I'll call you Sean if that pleases you. I'm just glad to have you here. Been lonely since your aunt passed on."

"You must miss her." Hamilton's aunt, Lincolnshire's wife. So the earl had cared for his wife—and for his nephew enough to see to the boy's education. He sure didn't *seem* like a heartless beast.

"I still do miss her. After all our children died, at least we still had each other. Rather disconcerting to find oneself alone."

"You seem to be surrounded by staff, sir. Uncle." An under-statement of great proportions. The nurse still puttered in the shadows, and two more maids had come and gone in the past few minutes, delivering a glass of water, fussing with the curtains, seeing to the man's comfort.

"Ah, yes, that I am." The earl smiled a bit sheepishly, revealing straight but tea-stained teeth. "Mrs. Skeffington takes excellent care of me," he said, indicating the nurse, "but she does have some help." He shook his head. "More than a hundred servants altogether, and I cannot bring myself to dismiss a single one. My family has employed all of them for years."

"*All* of them?"

"And their folk before them, generations back. My forebears housed many relations, you see. As did I, in the past." A sigh escaped his lips, a wheezy sort of sound. "While my family shrank, the families of the servants continued to grow. After so many years of loyal service, I cannot find it in myself to turn them out. It's no simple matter to find good positions these days, even with a letter of good character."

While keeping such an overlarge staff bordered on the absurd, Sean found the sentiment admirable—and baffling. Where was the cruel, miserly man Sean had heard about all his life? The distant master of Kilburton who lived to spite others?

Come to think of it, had he ever heard those stories from anyone but the weasel and his parents?

As Sean looked on the earl's open, smiling face, his breakfast felt as though it were congealing in his gut. An iron collar seemed to be squeezing around his throat. Clearly Lincolnshire wasn't the brute Hamilton had described. And neither was he "incapacitated." Perhaps he was knocking on death's door, but for now, at least, he was fully alert.

How could Sean deceive such a nice man?

Lincolnshire leaned to pat Sean's hand. "I'm so glad you're here, John," he repeated gratefully.

"Sean," Sean choked out.

"Sean, yes. I shall have to grow accustomed to that." He smiled again, a fond smile that spiked Sean's guilt. "Lady Partridge is holding a ball tomorrow night. I've already sent my regrets, but I've a sudden hankering to see all my friends one last time. To show off my famous nephew. I'll have my secretary send her a note, if it wouldn't be too much trouble for you to accompany me."

Trouble?

Guilt transformed to a panic that *trouble* didn't even begin to describe.

Sean couldn't appear in public as Lincolnshire's nephew—when the real Hamilton came forward later to claim his earldom, all of society would learn of the hoax. And then where would they all be? Hamilton would lose his art career if not his inheritance. He'd kill Sean, or, at the very least, refuse Deirdre her divorce. Sean's sister would go on to live in sin, or worse, in subjugation to her hateful husband.

And it would all be Sean's fault.

"I'd prefer not to be 'shown off,'" he explained carefully. "I'm rather a mystery to the public. That secrecy adds to my cachet, and—"

"Your mysterious ways are legend. Very well, then." Lincolnshire looked resigned, and Sean was relieved—for approximately two seconds. "I won't tell anyone you're John Hamilton. I'll simply introduce you as my nephew Sean."

"Surely people know who your heir is..."

"I'll tell them you're my long-lost *other* nephew. For now. They'll learn the truth, of course, when you inherit. It will be our little secret." For a moment the earl's eyes danced with merry amusement, but he quickly sobered. "I'd...well..." The old man cleared his throat, looking embarrassed. "I'd given up living, Sean. I didn't want to see anyone. But now... having you here... it makes me want to live again. I've a short time left. With you by my side, I wish to say my goodbyes." A sheen of tears glazed his eyes. "Please, nephew, do me this favor."

How could Sean possibly deny such a heart-rending request? How could he disappoint the most wonderful man in all of England?

He gazed up at the exquisite painted ceiling, where the Goddess of Dawn chased the Goddess of Night. Hamilton had been so wrong about his uncle, in so very many ways. And being introduced as Lincolnshire's *other* nephew should carry no risk. Their ruse would never come to light. Sean had no connections with high society. Before Lincolnshire, he'd never met any member of the *ton*. No one should suspect he was anything but what Lincolnshire said, and after all of this was over, he'd never see any of them ever again.

"Very well," he said at last, lowering his gaze to meet the earl's eyes. "I'll accompany you. Just remember to call me Sean."

The old man's obvious delight did nothing to ease Sean's guilt.

SEVEN

*G*RIFFIN SPENT all of Friday morning seated across from Rachael in his carriage, smelling her heady, floral scent and watching her lick her lips so many times his jaw ached from clenching his teeth.

He talked of parties, books and politics, family and property and plans for the future...anything to keep his mind off that sultry mouth. It was difficult to speak with his teeth clenched, so he was thankful Rachael kept up her end of the conversation. She'd always been easy to talk to, especially for a girl.

At long last, in the early afternoon, the carriage rattled over the drawbridge and into a modest courtyard before the small castle that was Rachael's home at Greystone. Spring rain pelted him when he shoved open the door and leapt to the circular drive. He breathed a sigh of relief.

When he reached to help Rachael out, he discovered she wasn't wearing gloves. The warmth of her hand seemed to spread throughout his body, especially up his neck to heat his face. Maddeningly, she left her hand in his while they made their way down a short, covered passageway and entered through the unassuming oak door. Her fingers trembled, either from the chill or from nervousness at what they might find; he wasn't sure which.

He was thankful she dropped his hand when the butler, Smithson, approached. "Lady Rachael. Lord Cainewood." Tall and lean with gray hair and piercing gray eyes that seemed to match the old castle, Smithson was too mannerly to show dismay at their unexpected arrival. "What a pleasant surprise."

"We'll be here but a short while," Rachael assured him. "No need for any great fuss."

He glanced at the tall-case clock that stood in the square, stone-floored entry. "I'll ask Cook to prepare a luncheon. Will you be wanting anything more?"

"No, thank you. I wish only to fetch something of my mother's, and Lord Cainewood was kind enough to accompany me." She headed toward the oak staircase that marched up the wall opposite the entrance. "Please don't trouble yourself or anyone else."

Griffin followed her up the steps, past two of her mother's watercolor paintings and along the corridor that led to what used to be her parents' bedroom. The chamber's walls were covered in pale green paper with gold tracery, the bedding green velvet of a deeper hue, the furniture light and slender, of the style popularized by Sheraton.

"Wasn't this room decorated in red?" he asked. "And the furnishings of dark oak?"

"I changed it all for Noah." Her younger brother had finally taken responsibility for the earldom—a responsibility Rachael had borne herself since their parents died four years ago, when she was seventeen. "To make it his, not Papa and Mama's."

How thoughtful. How Rachael. "But some of your mother's things are in here now?"

"In that chest." She gestured toward the one heavy, dark piece of furniture, a large carved trunk set in a corner. "Noah had it brought down from the attic." Her voice sounded thin. "He said nothing in it is important."

"He could be wrong," he said, hoping that was the case. "Let's have a look."

"Yes, let's." She crossed to the trunk and removed an embroidered covering and a lamp someone had set on top. Then she knelt and took a deep breath before reverently opening the lid. A musty scent wafted out, starch and aged leather mixed with hints of her mother's gardenia perfume.

Griffin knelt beside her. "Pretty," he murmured, lifting a straw hat from atop the contents.

"I remember her wearing it when I was a child." Rachael removed a few more old-fashioned items of clothing, then shook out a white gown. "This must be the wedding dress Noah mentioned. I recognize it from their wedding portrait."

Though clearly out of fashion, the gown was lacy and beautiful. Rachael's mother had been slender like her daughter, all willowy, graceful curves, and she obviously hadn't been pregnant long when she married John Chase. The dress looked like it would fit Rachael perfectly. "Will you wear it for your own wedding someday, too, now that you've found it?"

"I'd love to, but..." Her eyes grew misty as she gazed into the trunk. "Thunderation. I'm not going to cry."

Rachael could cuss as colorfully as a cavalryman, but that didn't bother Griffin. He considered it part of her charm. It reminded him she'd spent years as the Earl of Greystone in all but name, and he admired her for that.

"But what?" he prompted.

"She wore it for her wedding to him. Lord Greystone. Not my father."

"Balderdash." Griffin sought her gaze. "Lord Greystone was your father in every way that counted. I'm sure he would have wanted you to wear it. He would have been honored, as a matter of fact."

She nodded and swallowed hard. "I'm not sure I'll ever marry, anyway."

"Of course you will. What gentleman in his right mind wouldn't want you? I'm surprised Noah hasn't already found you a match."

"Noah?" Her eyes cleared, and she laughed, turning back to the trunk. "Who would run his household if I wed? He won't be matching me anytime soon."

Though Noah was only eighteen months her junior, he'd always seemed far less mature. Had it not occurred to the boy that seeing his three sisters settled was now his responsibility? Perhaps Griffin would have to set him straight.

A few old books lay beneath the clothes, all inscribed, *To Georgiana with love from Mama*. Georgiana had been Rachael's mother's name, but the inscriptions were all dated with her early birthdays, and the books contained no clues. There were no diaries or anything else of a personal nature. A stack of letters tied with a ribbon held no relevant information, either. They were all written in the years following Rachael's birth.

When the trunk was otherwise empty, Rachael found a tiny box in the bottom and pulled it out. It held a narrow, plain gold band.

"Her wedding ring?" Griffin guessed.

"She was buried wearing her wedding ring. Unless…" She glanced up at him, wonder in her eyes. "This must be from her marriage to my father." She looked inside, turning the band to catch the light. "No engraving. No clues." Sighing, she slipped it onto the fourth finger of her right hand. "It fits."

"I'm not surprised." Griffin's knees creaked when he stood and stretched. "That's it, then, is it?"

"Everything in here was old, things she didn't use anymore, things it made sense to have put away." Leaving the ring on her finger, she began putting everything else back. "I guess she didn't have a lot to keep. Mama led a quiet life."

He nodded. "I remember she was always home with you. My parents often left us with our governesses, but your mother never did."

"She never went up to London. She said the air there was bad for her lungs." Another dismal sigh escaped her lips as she replaced the last few items and shut the trunk. "Noah was right. There was nothing important here. I'm sorry I wasted your time."

"It wasn't a waste, Rachael." He watched her spread the embroidered cloth, the narrow gold ring glinting as she moved. "Did your mother have no other jewels?"

She lifted the lamp. "Yes, of course she did. She may have been quiet, but she liked pretty things. She willed all her jewels to me. Claire and Elizabeth each chose a few pieces, but the rest are in my room."

He took the lamp from her and set it down decisively, then reached a hand to help her up. "We should have looked at them last time. Maybe something will be engraved—"

"Nothing is. I would have noticed."

Yes, she probably would have. Rachael was nothing if not observant. "Let's have a look anyway, though, shall we?"

Rachael's chamber was deep rose and rich green and dark blue, a combination as classic and sophisticated as Rachael herself. Another of her mother's watercolors hung over her washstand. Fetching a mahogany box off her dressing table, she brought it with her to sit on the bed and patted the spot beside her in invitation, apparently not at all troubled to have him, an unmarried gentleman, in her room.

Griffin wished he could say the same.

He sat, though, when she opened the box. Filled to the brim, it sparkled with gold and diamonds, colorful gems and lustrous pearls. Griffin didn't know much about jewelry, but he recognized a fortune when he saw it.

His eyes must have widened, because Rachael laughed at the

look on his face. "This family is descended from jewelers," she reminded him. "My great-great-grandmother, or some such."

"I think you need a few more *greats*," he said, remembering now. "Her father's shop burned in the Great Fire, didn't it? Way back in the 1660s?"

"Something like that. Some cousins own another shop in London. I believe it was opened by one of her sons. In any case, there are many more jewels, including some very old ones, in the safe in Claire's workshop." Her sister Claire had taken up the old family hobby. "These were Mama's personal items. Some family heirlooms given to her by my father—Lord Greystone, I mean—and some newer things. But nothing I could identify as coming from her first husband."

Griffin sifted through the treasure trove, rings and bracelets glittering as they slipped through his fingers. He recognized a diamond necklace as one Rachael had worn to a ball at Cainewood two summers earlier. A brooch he thought he could recall Aunt Georgiana wearing often, pinned to her dress.

A locket made him momentarily hopeful, but it held a swatch of hair, not a miniature or a note. No dates or names were engraved on anything.

Then another brooch caught his eye. "The Prince of Wales's Feathers," he murmured, pulling it from the pile.

Three silver plumes rose from a gold coronet of alternate crosses and fleurs-de-lis, studded with rubies and emeralds. Along the bottom, a gold ribbon bore a motto.

"What does it say?" Rachael asked.

"'*Ich Dien*.' I serve." He looked at her. "Your father...I mean, John Chase, Lord Greystone...was he ever in the cavalry?"

"Of course not. His younger brother served in the army, but Grandfather would never have allowed his heir to risk his life."

"I thought not. This may be our clue."

She blinked. "It's a national symbol of Wales, isn't it? I assumed it was a souvenir from a visit."

"It's a military badge. From the Tenth Hussars. My regiment."

Hope leapt into her sky blue eyes. "Do you think it was given to my mother by a member?"

"An officer, from the looks of this piece. Gold and gemstones. An enlisted man would wear a much less expensive version." The metal felt cool in his fingers as he turned it over. Nothing was engraved on the back.

"No more clues," she said with a sigh.

"This alone may be enough. Would you mind if I keep it a while?"

"Of course not. But how can it help you find my father?"

He slipped it into his pocket. "He died in 1795, sometime in the months after you were conceived but before you were born—that much we know. Napoleon didn't come to power until 'ninety-nine. There shouldn't have been many deaths that year; the Tenth would have been at home; in peacetime, there are few casualties. I'll go to regimental headquarters and ask to see the records."

It would take two days to get there, a day to search the records, and another two days to ride home. Five days during which Corinna wouldn't meet any suitable men. But much as he wanted his sister married and off his hands, he didn't mind.

Rachael's happiness was important, too.

Although another girl might have made a token protest, Rachael wasn't that sort. "Thank you," she said instead, two simple, grateful words. "Do you expect you can find something that could tell us who he was?"

He shrugged, not wanting to get her hopes up. "I can try. I'll take you back to London now, and I'd like to take Corinna to Lady Partridge's ball tomorrow night. I'll leave for regimental headquarters first thing Sunday morning. With luck, I'll have an answer for you by Thursday."

"An officer," she breathed. "Someone important."

A bark of a laugh burst out of him. "It doesn't take importance to buy a commission. Only money."

Her eyes shone. "You were important. You led campaigns in the Peninsular War. Your patrol brought news of the Prussian retreat at Wavre, thus influencing the Duke of Wellington to fight at Waterloo."

"How do you know all that?"

"Your sisters. They're proud of you. You'd have been at Waterloo had your brother not died."

"Well, he did," he said flatly, keeping the bitterness out of his voice.

He'd never wanted to be a marquess. It seemed a frivolous career next to the vital work of the army. But here, now, was a chance to use his military connections to advantage. To help someone.

To help Rachael.

And that thought made him far too pleased.

EIGHT

"**Y**OU'RE NOT going to stay up till all hours again, are you?"

In a haze of concentration, Corinna turned from her easel and blinked at her brother in the drawing room's doorway. It was close to midnight, and she hadn't realized he'd returned home. "I'm starting a new painting."

"You didn't answer my question. I've had a long day, and I'm off to bed. Will you also be retiring soon?"

"I don't know." Irritated, she set down her palette. "It depends upon how this goes."

Griffin walked closer. "Doesn't look like much."

"Yet." All she'd done was layer the pale gray ground that she used as the undertint for her paintings, with a rough white oval in the upper middle.

"What is it going to be?"

"I'm not sure," she hedged.

But she knew what she wanted it to be: a portrait. That was why she'd laid the white oval where she planned to paint the face. Flesh tones would appear brighter over white than gray, and she wanted the face to be luminous.

And she wanted it to be a *good* portrait. That was why she'd sketched the Elgin Marbles.

"I want you to get a good night's sleep," Griffin pressed. "I've several men I want you to meet at Lady Partridge's ball tomorrow evening."

Not that again. *Your turn will come next,* she remembered Juliana saying. All she wanted was to concentrate on her art, but everyone wanted to marry her off.

Like paint swiped with turpentine, her creative haze had dissipated. "Well, then, I shall certainly need my beauty rest," she said tartly.

She may as well go to bed, though. She hadn't decided whom to paint anyway.

"I'm glad you agree," Griffin said, apparently missing her tone. "By the way, I need to leave Sunday morning, and I probably won't be back until Thursday. I won't be able to take you to Almack's on Wednesday night."

"What a terrible pity." Day after day of painting without interruptions, while he was off dealing with some problem at Cainewood or whatever?

What more could a girl like Corinna ask for?

Though she vaguely wondered what he was going to do, she didn't want to prolong this discussion. "That's really too bad, Griffin," she said with a straight face. "Good night."

Looking forward to the week ahead, she hummed as she cleaned up and put everything away. Then she went upstairs to her room, lit a candle from the fireplace, and ducked into her dressing room to grab a nightgown.

And there she stopped short, pulling a face.

In the corner were dozens of paintings stacked leaning against the wall. Her paintings. Portrait after portrait, none of them quite right.

They taunted her.

She'd spent nearly a decade learning to paint still lifes and landscapes. Practicing, persevering, perfecting. Eventually she'd begun putting people into her scenes, figures strolling or laboring or simply lounging in the background. But that hadn't been enough to satisfy her.

She'd always wanted to paint real portraits, detailed studies of people. She all but *burned* to paint portraits, and last year she'd put all other sorts of subjects behind her.

She walked closer and flipped canvases, moving the candle near to scrutinize the year's many efforts. Her maid. Alexandra and Juliana. Alexandra and baby Harry. Juliana alone, her shoulders bare, her skirts hiked up to show one scandalous, exposed knee.

Juliana, the dear, had obligingly posed for Corinna in the nude. Rigidly, self-consciously nude. Unfortunately, Corinna had been unable to *paint* her sister nude, as the sight of such a work of art would make poor Griffin's head explode.

And still, none of the paintings were good enough.

Sighing, she leaned them back against the wall. She knew she had it in her to produce a fine portrait. She'd long since mastered all the things she could easily study—the face, the hair, the clothing, the hands—and she'd been told she portrayed her subjects' expressions well.

But when it came to the body, she found herself frustrated every time. The people looked stiff and unnatural, not altogether surprising, given they'd looked stiff and unnatural when they'd posed. Corinna's maid and sisters could never seem to sit still for long, and sketching them had never proved as helpful as she'd hoped.

Not to mention her maid and sisters were all female. Men were formed differently, and since half the world's population was male, Corinna wanted to paint them, too. But barring her spectacularly unwilling brother—yes, she'd asked him—where on earth was a gently bred girl supposed to find a male model?

Well, perhaps sketching the Elgin Marbles had done the trick, she reminded herself, lifting her chin. At least *they* knew how to hold still.

Squaring her shoulders, she returned to her room and summoned her maid to help ready her for bed. But then she found she couldn't retire. She rarely rose before noon, because she stayed up late as a habit. Although painting by candlelight rather than sunlight could sometimes prove challenging, the night hours were quiet, almost mystical, the very best time for creativity.

It was too early to fall asleep.

She pulled out a small book tucked under her bed, the second volume of *Celia in Search of a Husband* by Medora Gordon Byron. Smiling, she cradled it in her hands. It was a Minerva Press novel, a torrid romance, bound as always in cheap marble-patterned paper.

Other than painting, Minerva Press novels were Corinna's favorite, most secret escape.

She bought them in secret, too. Fortunately, a bookseller's shop sat next door to the colorman's shop where she purchased her art supplies. Her maid or a footman usually accompanied her on these errands, since no one in the family had the patience to wait for hours while she chose the perfect oils and tints. Which was a good thing, since that meant they never saw her go into the bookshop afterward, either.

The last thing she wanted was her family discovering she reveled in such unseemly literature. Her sisters would be properly scandalized—or else they would tease her mercilessly. And Griffin would probably be smug; he'd consider it proof that, deep down, she pined for love and a husband.

She could do without any of those reactions, thank you very much.

To make doubly sure there was no risk of discovery, after reading a Minerva Press novel she always donated it to the circulating library. That way other girls could enjoy them. She had no need to ever reread them herself, since she was afflicted—yes, *afflicted*—with the ability to remember everything she'd ever read, word for word. She could see the printed pages in her mind, and they had a tendency to pop into her head at the oddest, most inconvenient moments. It was rather a nuisance. Almost annoying enough to make her stop reading.

But only almost. She set the candle on her bedside table and opened *Celia in Search of a Husband* with a happy sigh.

Celia was quite amusing. Though the heroine proclaimed loudly and often that she wanted a husband, she discarded men left and right as though they were so many used handkerchiefs.

On page 183, Celia sighed, "mentally," according to the author—Corinna often sighed mentally, too!—wondering, *Am I rigid? What woman of real feeling would trust her peace to the keeping of a libertine? It may prove the vanity of love to believe that we could fix the heart hitherto unprincipled, but a trusting woman must meet, in the creature of her choice, either the idol of her hopes or certain disappointment in her connubial happiness—for here is no medium.*

Exactly, Corinna thought with another sigh. A mental one, of course.

If a flawed fellow couldn't be fixed—no matter how much one might love him—then what were her chances of finding marital happiness, anyway? Corinna would have to meet her "idol," and how improbable was *that*?

Certain disappointment was a much more likely outcome, which was why she, a woman of real feeling, was far better off putting her faith in her art.

NINE

$\mathcal{L}$ADY PARTRIDGE lived in a small mansion at the edge of Mayfair. On Saturday night, the line of carriages stretched past several streets. Sean figured he could have negotiated two contracts and plowed through the entire mountain of paperwork on his desk in the time it took him and his "uncle" to make their way to the front.

Two footmen reached in for Lincolnshire, who had spent most of the wait dozing. As he emerged, supported by the two men, he eyed Sean. "You look a bit sober, eh?"

"I beg your pardon, sir? I should think so." Sean watched the footmen settle the earl in a curious vehicle. A typical dining room chair with a caned back and an upholstered seat, it had two huge wheels attached to its sides and a smaller wheel centered behind. "I'm not an inveterate drinker."

To the contrary—and to Deirdre's screaming amusement— Sean seemed the only Irishman alive who couldn't hold his liquor.

"Downed a toddy myself before leaving," the earl said as one of the men lifted his feet while the other unfolded a small, upholstered shelf for them to rest upon. "A swallow of spirits never hurt a man, should you ask me. But that wasn't what I meant by sober. I plan to stick around long enough to get to know you, yet you appear to be dressed for a funeral. Not mine, I hope."

"Certainly not yours, sir." Sean shook out a blanket and settled it on the earl's lap to hide his swollen legs. Though Lincolnshire was on the whole a slight fellow, his lower extremities would fit a man thrice his size. Earlier this evening, when Sean had seen them uncovered, he'd choked back a gasp. "But I fear that I haven't spent much time at balls." Actually, he'd *never* been to a ball. "Am I wearing the wrong thing?"

"Not wrong, no. Just a bit drab for a festive occasion." Lincolnshire himself was decked out in peacock blue and gold. "Some color wouldn't be amiss, my boy."

"Ah, yes," Sean said as he moved around to push the chair. "I usually prefer black and white."

Actually, he *always* wore black and white. He'd learned early on that attempting anything more adventurous would inevitably lead to some hilarious mismatch (hilarious to everyone but Sean, that was). Since he had nothing but black and white in his wardrobe, he was relieved to find his choice suitable if not stylish.

As he wheeled the earl toward the door, a tall proper butler opened it. Sounds of music drifted out. "Your name, sir?"

"Lincolnshire," Lincolnshire declared. "And my nephew, Mr. Hamilton."

"My lord Lincolnshire, do please come in," the butler said in reverent tones. "Lady Partridge left instructions to be notified the very moment you arrived. This way, if you will," he added, motioning to Sean.

But Sean couldn't push the chair along behind the butler. In fact, he couldn't push it anywhere at all—because people had begun steaming into the foyer, forming a crush around the earl in his wheeled chair. Sean was trapped.

It seemed Lord Lincolnshire had declared his name a little too loudly.

"Lord Lincolnshire!" An aging matron took the old man's hands. "It's positively delightful to see you!"

"I'm delighted as well, Lady Fotherington. May I introduce my long-lost nephew, Mr. Sean Hamilton? He's become like a son to me."

Sean tensed, waiting to be called a fraud, but the woman focused on him only briefly. "I'm pleased to make your acquaintance," she said politely, displaying no interest in him at all. Or no more than was required by good manners, anyway.

Apparently his secret was safe. He didn't know any members of the *ton*, he reminded himself, glancing around at the still-gathering crowd. And none of these people knew him.

There was absolutely nothing to worry about.

"Lord Lincolnshire, how are you feeling?" the woman asked.

"As well as can be expected. And how is your son?" Lincolnshire squeezed her hands. "Well as well, I hope?"

"Oh, he's very well indeed, thanks in no small part to your assistance."

"It was but a trifle, my lady, I assure you."

A burly young man gave a bark of laughter, shaking his head. "You always say so, my lord, and it's never yet been true."

An older, taller gentleman sighed. "Who will provide toys this Christmas for the children at the Foundling Hospital?"

"*We* will," said a commanding woman, apparently the man's wife. "It's the least we can do to honor *you*, Lord Lincolnshire."

Someone else put in, "We'll miss you, Lord Lincolnshire!"

"Yes, mightily!"

"However will we go on without you?"

As Sean watched them all clamoring to voice their sorrow and their gratitude, an icy feeling of horror was slowly creeping over him.

This was *much* worse than he'd thought.

"We would do anything for you, my lord!"

"Anything to make you more comfortable."

"Anything at all..."

Lincolnshire wasn't just a pleasant man. A nice man. A generous man.

"Too right, we would." The commanding woman now had tear-tracks down her stern face. "Though it could hardly begin to repay all you've done for us. London shall never see your equal again."

Sweet mercy.

The man was a blasted saint.

More people crowded in. It was a maelstrom of affection and tears and lamentations. Men and women, young and old alike, sharing their memories and paying their respects and, most of all, expressing their fervent hopes that the dying Earl of Lincolnshire would spend his last days in ease and contentment, in the company of those who loved him.

But he wouldn't.

No, sir!

Instead, the sainted man would be spending his last days in a tangle of petty lies, in the company of some backwoods Irish nobody.

Sean was, without a doubt, the most despicable person on the face of the earth.

~

CORINNA WAS dancing with a thoroughly boring young man—the latest in a string that proved Griffin hadn't the slightest idea of her type—when she noticed her old neighbor Lord Lincolnshire enter the ballroom.

Well, *try* to enter, anyway. He was making excruciatingly slow progress, surrounded as he was by adoring people, all vying for his attention at once.

Propped up in a cane-backed wheelchair, he looked happier than she'd ever imagined a dying man could be. The sight warmed her heart. If anyone in the world deserved happiness, it was Lord Lincolnshire. She smiled when she saw him turn to aim an elated grin at whoever was pushing the chair. She craned —rather gracelessly—to see who it was.

And she sucked in a breath.

Crisp black hair. Emerald eyes. Angular, sculpted face.

Holy Hannah, it was her Greek god!

She'd tried to paint him this very morning—she'd decided she wanted him in her portrait—but that day in the Elgin Gallery, he'd vanished before she had a chance to finish drawing him. With no sketch to work from, she'd found herself unable to recall enough detail. Eventually she'd resigned herself to choosing another subject and glumly painted over her efforts before dressing for tonight's ball.

Her canvas once more had a plain white oval where there should be a face. And now her fingers itched for a pencil.

What was he doing here? She hadn't expected to ever see him again. He'd certainly never appeared at a society event before this. How had he come to be with Lord Lincolnshire, pushing the dear old earl in a wheelchair?

"At whom are you staring?" her partner asked.

She snapped to attention, surprised to find she was still dancing. Her feet seemed to know what to do all by themselves. Perhaps she should have thanked Mama for all those dance lessons instead of throwing a fit every time she was dragged away from her easel.

Then again, maybe it was just that she was letting Lord Snooze-Basket lead, and repeating the same three steps over and over seemed to be all the excitement he could manage.

She shook her head. "I was watching Lord Lincolnshire. I'm glad he managed to attend tonight. Might you know that gentleman with him? I'm wondering if he could be the artist John Hamilton."

"I haven't seen him before, but I seriously doubt he's John Hamilton. The man never appears in public." The music came to an end, and her partner bowed. "Thank you for the dance, Lady Corinna."

"My pleasure," she said with a straight face.

Thinking Juliana knew everyone, Corinna looked around and found her sister conversing with her mother-in-law, the new Lady Cavanaugh.

"Might either of you know that young man accompanying Lord Lincolnshire?" she asked, barging right in.

Juliana shook her head. "Handsome though, isn't he?"

A vast understatement. "I met him the other day at the British Museum. When you and Alexandra went off, remember? Another gentleman introduced him as John Hamilton."

"John Hamilton, the artist? I remember you claimed you'd met him, but—"

"Yes, the artist. But then everything became very confusing, because this fellow claimed he *wasn't* John Hamilton, but the other fellow was instead. And why would John Hamilton be with Lord Lincolnshire?"

"Lord Lincolnshire collects art," Juliana reminded her. "Ming vases and paintings."

"More to the point," Lady Cavanaugh said, "John Hamilton is Lord Lincolnshire's nephew. And his heir."

Corinna hadn't known that. But if John Hamilton was Lord Lincolnshire's nephew, that explained why the two were together. Suddenly everything made perfect sense. The Greek god *was* the elusive John Hamilton! Being a recluse, he must have claimed otherwise in order to preserve his anonymity.

But Corinna knew the truth now.

Rising excitement fluttered in her chest. Her pulse pounded in her ears. She'd actually met John Hamilton.

The John Hamilton, a member of the Summer Exhibition Selection Committee.

The John Hamilton who could help her dreams come true.

Now all she had to do was *charm* him.

Before she could think better of it, she grabbed her sister's hand. "Come along," she said, motioning to Lady Cavanaugh. "I'll introduce you both."

TEN

*L*ORD LINCOLNSHIRE held up a hand, interrupting an outpouring of affection from yet another of Lady Partridge's guests. "Nephew."

"Do you need something, Uncle?" Concerned (and guilty), Sean moved around the front of the wheelchair, wedging himself between two older, portly gentlemen. "Are your limbs paining you? Would you care for some laudanum?" He reached into his pocket for the vial the nurse had pressed into his hands.

"No laudanum. I'd as soon not dull my senses." The earl smoothed the lap robe that covered his legs, looking amused. "That pretty young lady is calling you."

"What pretty young lady?"

"That one." Lincolnshire motioned with his head. "Lady Corinna."

Corinna. Though London was certainly home to more than one Corinna, when Sean turned to look, he already knew what he would see: shining dark hair and stunning blue eyes.

Begorrah, he'd met another member of the aristocracy, after all!

"Mr. Hamilton!" she gushed as she approached, making him

realize she'd already called out "Mr. Hamilton!" several times. He'd known he would forget to answer to the weasel's name. "What a pleasure it is to see you again!"

"Again?" Lincolnshire asked.

"I met your illustrious nephew in the British Museum," she enthused. "But when I went to introduce him to my sisters, he was gone!" She turned to a girl and a woman who had followed her. "Here he is at last, the talented and reclusive John Hamilton. Mr. Hamilton, this is my sister, Lady Stafford, and her mother-in-law, Lady Cavanaugh."

Both ladies curtsied. Lady Cavanaugh looked kind and motherly. Lady Stafford was pretty like her sister, but she was petite where Corinna was shapely.

"I'm sorry, but I'm not Mr. Hamilton." Sean turned to Lord Lincolnshire. "Tell them, Uncle."

The earl's eyes danced; clearly he was enjoying this bit of subterfuge. "Of course you're Mr. Hamilton." His papery lips curved into a smile as he focused on the three ladies, making Sean imagine he must have been a bit of a flirt back in the day. "But he's *Sean* Hamilton," he told the ladies. "Sean, not John. My *other* nephew."

Sean had never in his life heard anything less convincing.

Lady Cavanaugh gave Lincolnshire's shoulder a sympathetic pat. "I know you're not feeling yourself these days, my lord, but you've only one nephew."

"I may have lost the use of my legs, but I assure you, dear lady, I haven't lost my mind along with them." He turned to Sean with an unapologetic grin. "I'm afraid our ruse didn't work."

"I knew it!" Corinna exclaimed loudly enough to wake the dead. Heads snapped round to hear. "You *are* John Hamilton!"

Whispers ricocheted about the room.

"John Hamilton?"

"*The* John Hamilton?"

The whispers became a buzz. "John Hamilton!"

"It's John Hamilton!"

Moving behind Lincolnshire where the earl couldn't see him, Sean looked straight at Corinna and shook his head wildly. But she only frowned in confusion, and he was too late anyway. A matron was already waddling over, dragging a shy, marriage-aged daughter by the hand.

"Lord Lincolnshire, may I beg an introduction to your esteemed nephew?"

Another matron seemed to appear from nowhere. "Is this your heir, Lord Lincolnshire?"

A third matron shoved in front of her. "Mr. Hamilton, my Matilda is a diamond of the first water."

Lincolnshire seemed to puff up like a peacock, albeit a seated one. "Our secret is out." Pride was obvious in his tone. "I'm pleased to have you all meet the next Lord Lincolnshire. My nephew, Mr. John Hamilton."

Sean cringed as more matchmaking mamas came out of the woodwork, their eligible daughters in tow. Corinna disappeared, or maybe she was swept away by the rush. He was surrounded, pinned to Lincolnshire's side, engulfed in a sea of beady eyes, ingratiating smiles, and fancy, fluttering silk fans.

He'd never endured so much giggling in all his life.

Or so much small talk. The endless parade of young misses talked at him for hours (at least it *felt* like hours), while he help-lessly cast about for some means of escape. If only he could stick his fingers in his ears and sing at the top of his lungs like he used to when Deirdre wouldn't shut up…

"Sean."

Feeling a tug on his tailcoat, he leaned down with a sigh of relief. "Uncle, you must be exhausted. I'll take you home."

"Balderdash. I haven't felt so energetic in weeks. I wish to see you dance with one of these lovelies."

The mercenary mamas started shoving their charges Sean's way.

"I couldn't choose," he protested politely. But he wasn't feeling polite at all. What he felt instead was a rising panic in his chest.

He didn't know how to dance. Not like the English, anyway.

His mother had dragged him to many a village *ceili*. *A vicar's family should be social*, she'd always say. But he'd never enjoyed dancing. And more to the point, Irish dance parties featured jigs and reels. No *ceili* band ever played a waltz.

And Lady Partridge seemed quite partial to waltzes. The last dance had been a waltz, a waltz was playing now, and Sean would lay odds a waltz would come next.

He tried for a winning smile. "Besides, I should stay with you, Uncle."

"I think not." One of the earl's grizzled brows went up. "I've a mind to see you settled before I die."

Settled? Posing as Lincolnshire's nephew was bad enough— Sean would go only so far to placate the man. And a wedding went rather beyond that boundary.

Miles beyond that boundary.

And then he remembered.

"I'm settled already. Didn't you know I'm married?" The real Hamilton was married, after all. Had he *not* been married—to Deirdre—Sean wouldn't have been in this mess in the first place. "I've been settled for eight long years now."

A chorus of feminine sighs drowned out most of the earl's response. Sean caught only the tail end: "—forgetting, considering I've never seen your wife in all that time."

Lincolnshire hadn't seen his nephew in all that time, either, but Sean wouldn't be the one to remind him. Instead, he said, " Deirdre is a wonderful girl."

The earl's forehead furrowed. "I seem to recall rumor has it you two don't rub along."

"To the contrary," Sean assured him. "The two of us rub along grandly."

Someone snorted, and a few other bystanders murmured, evidently recalling the same rumors. Or, more likely, rumors of the weasel's many adulterous affairs.

"Where *is* your wife?" Lincolnshire asked.

"In the countryside," Sean told him, not actually stretching the truth. Though Hampstead lay only a few miles northwest of Charing Cross, many Londoners did consider it "way out in the countryside." Which was precisely why he liked living there. He had a preference for wide open spaces—they reminded him of home.

"In the countryside." Lincolnshire let out a long, disappointed sigh, his gaze turning wistful. "I do understand. But since I can no longer dance myself, I was so hoping to see you dance in my stead."

The current waltz ended, and sudden silence seemed to fill the ballroom.

"Dance for him," a woman urged.

Her daughter nodded. "Make him happy."

The music—another waltz, naturally—restarted. "It's just a dance," someone else called out.

The crowd seemed to press closer. "Lord Lincolnshire wants to see you dance."

"Humor him, will you?"

Although attempting a waltz was sure to prove humorous indeed, Sean felt his resolve crumbling. The old, ailing earl was making eager puppy-dog eyes, practically bouncing in his chair.

One of the young misses flapped her fan at Sean. "Don't you *want* to make Lord Lincolnshire happy?"

Saints preserve me.

"Oh, very well," he gritted out. "One dance."

Then he turned on his heel and headed straight for Corinna.

As he elbowed his way through the crowd, Corinna's startled

blue gaze met his, and it seemed as though a fist grabbed him in the gut. He couldn't wait to get his hands on the maddening girl. Part of him felt like wringing her neck.

But instead he seized her hand and hauled her off to the dance floor.

He threaded their way to the center, tripping over other dancers in the process. It was rather ungentlemanly, but he was determined to be in the middle, where he wouldn't be on display.

He turned her to face him. "I hope you can lead."

"I beg your pardon?" She stood still, gazing at all the people moving around them, and bit her lip.

He swallowed hard. "Thanks to you, I've been commanded to dance. And I've never waltzed in my life."

"Oh." Her mouth curved into a sheepish smile. "I confess I've been accused of leading before. I fear it's one of my bad habits."

"It's glad I am to hear it."

Mimicking the other dancers, he wrapped an arm about her waist and held her gloved right hand. She began to move, keeping her frame rigid so that he moved with her.

Not very gracefully, but they moved.

"May I sketch you?" she asked.

"Sketch me?" he echoed absently, marveling at finding himself swirling among the other dancers. "I don't think so."

"Never?"

He tread on her toes.

A wee "Eek!" escaped her lips, but then she gave him another smile. An understanding one this time.

"Very well," she said on a sigh. "I suppose you're too busy with your own art to sit for someone else."

She was exasperating. "You're ruining my life."

"How so?" she asked. "I've done you a favor, Mr. Hamilton. Society is all aflutter to finally meet Lord Lincolnshire's famous, mysterious nephew. They'll pay even more for your paintings."

He leaned improperly close, catching a trace of a light, floral scent with something peculiar—paint?—layered beneath it. "I'm not an artist," he hissed in her ear. "I'm Sean Delaney, not John Hamilton."

When he drew back, making them lurch, he was dismayed to find her latest smile closer to a smirk. "I haven't heard you say that in front of your uncle."

"For his sake." Revealing the truth would probably destroy the kindly old earl, not to mention infuriate Hamilton and jeopardize Deirdre's divorce. "I'll not to embarrass the poor fellow by correcting him in front of his friends."

"I understand you value your privacy, Mr. Hamilton. But as the real Mr. Delaney said in the museum, you are much too self-effacing. You'll get used to being famous, and it's long past time you met your adoring admirers."

He considered stepping on her foot again, on purpose. "They wouldn't adore me if they knew the truth."

"Of course they would. They all love Lord Lincolnshire and will transfer that affection to you. In fact, they already have. I was squeezed right out of the earl's circle by all the girls who want to marry you."

So she hadn't heard he was married. Or rather, that Hamilton was married. Well, he wasn't going to inform her. That would only serve to reinforce her conviction that he was Hamilton.

"Lincolnshire *is* well loved," he muttered instead in disgust. Had the earl been the beast Hamilton had described, he wouldn't have been welcome at this ball. And Corinna would never have introduced Sean as his *famous nephew.* "Everyone seems utterly devastated to lose him."

"Of course we are," she said, pulling his hand back to keep him from ramming into someone. "Lord Lincolnshire is the most compassionate person you'll ever meet. He supports half the charities in London, and he's just as generous with his time. He's helped practically every *ton* family at one point or another."

"You exaggerate."

"Not by much."

"Everyone says they'll do anything for him."

"Anything but the one thing we cannot," she said mournfully, "which is to save his life."

"Then why didn't you believe him?" When he stumbled, her hand gripped his shoulder to keep him upright. "He told you I was Sean, not John, but you disagreed with him. Loudly."

The look she gave him said he was a complete idiot. "He was obviously fooling! Do you not know your own uncle? It seems as if you only met him today."

Well, yesterday.

She went on, "And Sean is the same name as John in Ireland anyway, isn't it? You sound like you come from Ireland."

That he couldn't deny. Not without looking like an even bigger idiot. Luckily for him, just then the music stopped. The dance had come to an end. Corinna curtsied, thanked him politely, and quit the dance floor.

He'd survived his first waltz. But as her intriguing, paint-tinged scent wafted away, he found himself wishing it had lasted longer.

And wasn't that absurd? He was lucky he had come out alive.

ELEVEN

$\mathcal{S}$HORTLY AFTER noon on Monday, Sean paced outside the gate in front of Lincolnshire House, planning his day as he waited for his curricle to be brought round.

Thanks to a long breakfast with Lincolnshire, he was getting a very late start on his very full agenda. Besides all the work that had piled up in his absence—contracts to review, sales to negotiate, properties to inspect—he needed to talk to Deirdre, which meant a drive all the way out to Hampstead and back. He hadn't a moment to spare.

Making himself stand still, he stared impatiently out across the street. Berkeley Square hummed with activity. From his vantage point at the north end, he watched people traipse in and out of the fenced, grassy park in the middle. In the row of houses along the west side, a blue door opened, catching his eye. Two footmen emerged, burdened with boxes and an easel. As they headed across the street toward the park, a girl came out and followed, her shapely figure clad in a pale blue gown with a white apron tied over it, her glossy dark hair worn unfashionably loose.

As his curricle pulled up, he blinked, suddenly recognizing Corinna.

"Just a moment," he told the stableman before dashing out into the square.

By the time he reached her, the servants had positioned her easel beneath a giant plane tree and were setting a canvas upon it—one covered with blotches of gray and white. She riffled through a box filled with little pots of paint, her gaze focused, her bottom lip caught between her teeth.

"Good day to you, Lady Corinna."

Startled, she looked up, narrowing her blue eyes.

To Sean, most everyone's eyes (including his own) were brown. Green, hazel, brown...they all appeared brown. Only shades of blue looked different, and Corinna's eyes were the clearest, most brilliant blue he'd ever seen. They were bottomless.

He gave his head a little shake to clear it.

"Have you decided to let me sketch you?" she asked.

"No," he said. "I was waiting there for my curricle"—he gestured toward Lincolnshire House—"when I noticed you entering the square. I came over to convince you I'm not Hamilton. I'm not Lincolnshire's nephew."

She lifted a dull knife. "So you keep saying." Using it to scoop brown (or maybe red or green) paint onto a palette, she slanted him a glance. "Yet you're living in Lincolnshire House."

"I am. I can explain. Hamilton is my brother-in-law, and—"

"You said that in the museum."

"Because it's true."

She seemed to be staring at his mouth. When he raised an eyebrow, she quickly looked away, wiping the knife on her splotched apron and using it to add a smidge of a lighter color. "I don't believe you." My, she was rather blunt for a lady. "I understand that you've enjoyed your anonymity in the past, but your secret is out now. You're going to have to get used to the fact that everyone knows you're John Hamilton."

She glanced at his mouth again, making Sean suddenly think about kissing her—though really, what he wanted to do was throttle her. "But I'm *not* John Hamilton."

"And I'm not here in Berkeley Square." With a cheeky smile, she picked up a brush and turned to her canvas. "I expect you should get to your own painting, Mr. Hamilton. I wish you a successful day."

Clearly he was dismissed. He marched back to his curricle, bunching his fists.

With Corinna living across the street, he feared his hands might become permanently clenched.

~

WITH GRIFFIN gone, Corinna had been looking forward to a few peaceful days to work on her portrait. But she wandered the drawing room Tuesday, still pondering whom to paint.

She'd decided her picture would be set outdoors. She was an accomplished landscape artist, after all, and it was important that her backdrop be as impressive as her central subject. She wanted the play of light and shadow, the varied greens of grass and trees, the bright hues of blooming flowers. She'd started painting all of that yesterday in the square, and she was happy enough with how it was coming along. But she couldn't make up her mind whom she wanted in the foreground and what, exactly, he or she should be doing.

She didn't care for formal portraits where the sitter just stared at the viewer. She preferred to see subjects in context. Conversation portraits, they were called. Quite popular in the previous century, they often featured whole families or groups of friends posed casually, as though caught in some everyday action.

Although it wasn't common to do the same with a single subject, she wanted to give it a try. She hoped it would make her painting a little different—and therefore more noteworthy.

If the painting turned out well, it would not only be the first work she submitted to the Summer Exhibition, but also the first portrait she put on public view. She wanted to choose someone who would be memorable. Someone whose personality would shine from the canvas. Someone she knew well enough to portray in such a manner that the viewer would feel he or she was a close, personal friend.

That was why she'd painted family members over and over.

She stopped and scanned all the many old Chase family portraits on the wall, settling on one dated 1670. The gentleman wore a long surcoat and a lace-trimmed cravat, the lady a full, heavy brocade gown with an old-fashioned stomacher fronting the bodice. A small engraved metal plate on the frame read:

JASON AND CAITHREN
6TH MARQUESS AND MARCHIONESS OF CAINEWOOD

She'd never known this couple, of course. They'd both died long before she was born. But unlike the ancient, more sober portraits, which invariably featured stern, unsmiling subjects, this pair looked happy. They looked like they were in love.

And they looked more than a little familiar.

Juliana resembled Caithren, sharing her ancestor's warm hazel eyes and straight, streaky blond hair. Griffin had inherited Jason's dark hair, square jaw, and deep green eyes.

But they weren't as startling a green as the eyes Corinna really wanted to paint.

She groaned and turned her back on the portrait. It was infuriating, the way Mr. Hamilton kept lying to her—and even more so the way he kept popping into her head at odd moments. Lately, whenever she picked up a Minerva Press novel, she pictured him as the hero. No matter if the author described the hero as having fair hair and blue eyes; in her head his hair was dark, his eyes that startling green. Whenever the dark-haired, green-eyed hero touched the heroine, she felt a tiny shiver. And whenever the hero and heroine kissed, she imagined Mr. Hamilton kissing her, and her lips tingled.

But in real life, she was about as likely to kiss him as she was to paint him—which was to say, *very* unlikely. He'd already twice refused to sit for her.

She could have had a Summer Exhibition portrait that revealed, for the first time ever, the elusive face of a famed artistic genius and future peer of the realm. Now, *that* would have been noteworthy.

But, *noooo*. That face was *far* too busy and self-important to sit for even one measly little sketch.

She sighed—out loud, not mentally—knowing it was hopeless. His cachet was more important to him than her ambitions, and honestly, who could blame him for it? They barely knew each other, after all.

But she didn't want to spend her career updating the family portrait collection. She couldn't keep painting her poor, patient sisters over and over. She'd been doing that for nearly a year, and none of her pictures had turned out good enough to add to the collection, anyway. She needed new experiences, new challenges, if she hoped to improve and grow as an artist.

She collected her art supplies and summoned two footmen to accompany her into the square. Until she found a subject, she'd continue working on her setting. Carrying her box of paints, she followed the servants out the door and across the street.

Or at least she *tried* to cross the street. Rounding the curve from Lincolnshire House, a curricle drew to a halt in her path. The driver looked down from his high perch.

"I'm not Hamilton," he said coldly.

She shrugged blithely, to cover her agitation. Apparently he hated her. And since he wasn't going to let her sketch him—let alone paint him—she wished he'd just leave her alone. If he'd cease popping into her life, perhaps she'd be able to concentrate on finding someone else to kiss.

To *paint*, she mentally amended. She didn't want to kiss him; she only wanted to paint him.

Holy Hannah, she was a liar.

And was there anything worse than lying to oneself?

"Fine," she snapped. "You're not Hamilton. Now will you please drive on so I can get back to work?"

A bark of laughter burst from his throat. Or maybe it was a noise of derision. Whichever, he flicked his reins and drove off, leaving her to her painting and her thoughts.

But mostly her thoughts.

At this rate, she'd be lucky to finish a new portrait before *next* year's Summer Exhibition.

TWELVE

"**N**EPHEW?"

"Hmm?"

Sean looked up from reading the *Morning Chronicle* at the breakfast table, thinking it was way too late for breakfast.

By this hour on a normal morning, he'd have already risen, eaten, and driven into town. On a normal morning, he'd have already gone through the day's mail, taken several meetings, and directed his staff. On a normal morning, he'd be elbow-deep in work by now, expanding his operation and increasing his fortune. On a normal morning…

This wasn't a normal morning.

No morning had been normal since he'd agreed to this blasted scheme. Lincolnshire had trouble falling asleep and consequently stayed abed late. And then he wanted his *dear* nephew to keep him company at breakfast. He ate very little and very slowly and it all took a very long time.

Now the old man gave him a sunny smile. "I wish to see your studio today."

Sean folded and set aside the newspaper. "My studio is private," he said carefully.

"From me?" The earl looked hurt. "I'm your uncle. You're my heir."

"I have work to do—"

"I know. Work that makes me mighty proud, work that rivals the very best." He gestured to all the old masters on his dining room walls. "I want to see where you work. I shall sit and watch quietly; I promise. It's not as though I could move around much even if I wanted to," he added with his usual good humor.

But Sean's smile was regretful, not amused. "I'm sorry, but I wouldn't be able to concentrate—"

"You won't even know I'm there."

Sean shook his head. He *did* want to make the sainted fellow happy. Lincolnshire's condition was worsening by the day, and he was a nice man who deserved a happy ending. Sean hated to see him disappointed.

But he couldn't allow the earl into his "studio."

At least, not in its current state.

No more than an hour after leaving the British Museum, Hamilton had fetched a few paintings and stuck them in an empty garret in one of Sean's buildings. He'd even included a half-finished canvas and propped it on an easel, so it would appear as though Sean were in the middle of a project.

But after that, he'd run off to Wales. Immediately and without a backward glance. Other than the pictures and a few well-used sketchbooks, he'd provided nothing.

No paint. No brushes. No...whatever else it was that painters needed.

The earl would expect to find more than art, wouldn't he? He'd expect to find art *supplies*.

So Sean was forced to twist the truth once again.

"Unfortunately," he improvised, "I find it impossible to paint with anyone watching over my shoulder. And I'm in the middle of something I fear I'm quite anxious to finish today. Will tomorrow be soon enough? I should be done then, and I'll be happy to take you to the studio. Not to watch me paint, mind you, but to see the space. And to view the latest Hamilton canvases."

He hated lying. This whole business was mentally exhausting. For the umpteenth time, he silently cursed himself for allowing the weasel to drag him into it.

"Very well," Lincolnshire finally conceded. "I shall look forward to visiting tomorrow."

Sean thanked him and finished breakfast, then went off to work. Or rather—abandoning his own responsibilities once again—he went off to purchase art supplies.

He wouldn't have had a clue where to buy anything related to art, but he'd noticed Hamilton's sketchbooks all had REEVES & SONS stamped on them. Recalling a tenant by that name in one of his buildings in the center of town, he drove straight there.

It took him a good while to choose the supplies, particularly the colors. At a complete loss, he finally consulted one of the Reeveses—father or son, he knew not—who selected the proper pigments for him. Listening to the fellow rattle on about tone harmony, warmer and cooler variants, transparent as opposed to opaque, and the benefits versus the drawbacks of a broad palette compared to a more limited one—this particular "palette" apparently referring to a list of colors, not a thing one put the colors on —Sean was again tempted to stick his fingers in his ears.

When at long last he came out of the shop (a "colorman's shop," he'd learned it was called) more than half his day had slipped away.

He was in a hurry. So much so that, on his way back to his curricle, he glanced twice at a girl in the bookshop next door before realizing she was Corinna.

A footman in Chase livery stood outside the shop, looking bored. Corinna stood on the other side of the window, her nose buried in a book. A bell on the door jangled when Sean opened it, but she didn't look up at the noise. Nodding at the bookseller's muted, "Good afternoon," Sean walked past the front desk and right up to her. She didn't acknowledge him.

"I'm not Hamilton," he said.

She jumped. Then slammed the book shut and fixed him with a seething look. "I don't believe you."

"So you keep saying. But I'm no artist."

Her blue, blue eyes focused on the bulky package in his hands. Wrapped in brown paper and tied with string, it had REEVES & SONS stamped on it in smudged black ink.

She smirked. "Then what did you buy at the colorman's shop?"

He had no answer to that. The truth would only dig him in deeper. But he was tired of lying. He'd been fighting to *correct* a lie. He didn't want to try to fabricate some elaborate cover story.

So instead he said, "What are you reading?"

Her reaction was peculiar. She blushed and stuttered and quickly shoved the book onto the nearest shelf. When he bent to see the title, she grabbed his upper arm and maneuvered him down a row of bookcases. And around a corner and down a second row. She didn't stop until she'd backed him into a dead end.

What an odd girl she was. Pretty and stubborn and odd. He smiled down at her in bewilderment. She looked quite fetching with her cheeks flushed. And when she finally released him, he felt rather sorry for it.

A small part of him still wondered what she'd been reading. A very small part of him. The rest of him was busy noticing that the two of them were alone, tucked away between the quiet bookshop's tall, dusty shelves. There didn't seem to be any other customers, the bookseller was miles away at the till, and Corinna's footman was certainly still woolgathering outside.

Sean set the package on a high, empty shelf.

The shop smelled like paper and old leather, but Corinna smelled of flowers and paint. Silence seemed to blanket the store along with the dust, making her breathing sound loud by comparison. She bit her lip.

Without thought, he leaned in to kiss her.

He knew he shouldn't, but he couldn't help himself—or he didn't *want* to help himself. He'd been imagining this kiss since the first time he'd seen her bite that full, pillowy lower lip, that day in the British Museum. He grasped her shoulders, half expecting her to pull back in protest.

But she didn't.

She kissed him back.

For one long, sublime moment, he let himself sink into her warmth. She was soft, boneless, embracing. Her lips were softest of all, even softer than he'd imagined.

It took a massive effort to wrench himself back to earth.

When they pulled apart, her cheeks were even more flushed than before. Her eyes looked twice as wide as usual. She spoke slowly, her voice a wee bit hoarse. "Why did you do that?"

He wasn't sure why. "I suppose because I wanted to."

"But you hate me!"

"Obviously, I don't. Although I'll admit to finding you some-what exasperating." He narrowed his eyes. "Why did you *let* me do it?"

Her eyes went even wider. "Are you jesting? What girl—most especially if she's an *artist*—wouldn't let John Hamilton kiss her?"

For once he didn't protest that he wasn't John Hamilton. He was too stunned. "So it was a trophy kiss?"

"I beg your pardon?"

"You kiss artists? You thought to add me to your collection? A particularly shiny prize?"

She planted her hands on her hips. "I've *never* kissed an artist before!"

She had not, he noted, claimed she'd never kissed *anyone* before. Most intriguing.

Although it hardly changed the fact that he had no business kissing her. He wasn't John Hamilton. He wasn't Lincolnshire's nephew. He wasn't an English lord, or a soon-to-be English lord, or remotely related to any English lord at all.

He wasn't even English.

He was an Irish nobody with lots of money but little social status—and not a lick of sense. Aristocratic young misses like Corinna were off-limits to a fellow like him.

"I'm sorry," he said.

"I'm not."

She was very blunt, he thought, not for the first time. "I won't kiss you again."

"I hope you will." She smiled. "I rather enjoyed kissing you."

"You may find you enjoyed it less than you think," he informed her, "when you realize I'm not John Hamilton."

"Not that again." Reaching up to the shelf, she shoved his package toward him. "Don't forget your art supplies," she called over her shoulder as she strutted away. "You're going to need them the next time you paint."

He was still standing there when the bell jangled and the door shut behind her.

THIRTEEN

*C*ORINNA STOOD before her easel in Berkeley Square the next day, painting.

Oh, very well, daydreaming.

Or—since she was determined to stop lying to herself—reliving the kiss.

For at least the hundredth time.

She'd been kissed before, of course, but never like *that*. She could have sworn her legs had turned to water. Not only her lips, but her entire body had seemed to tingle. She was surprised her pounding heart hadn't cracked a rib.

She'd never expected to experience such a kiss—ever—though she'd certainly read enough of them in Minerva Press novels. In fact, just before Mr. Hamilton had entered the bookshop, as she'd flipped through *Children of the Abbey*, Lord Mortimer had clutched Amanda close and, *straining her to his beating heart, he imprinted a kiss on her tremulous lips.*

Which was a fairly spot on description of what had happened to Corinna yesterday.

Children of the Abbey had seemed an excellent novel, and

she'd had every intention of buying it. Until Mr. Hamilton had *imprinted a kiss on her lips* and left her head spinning like a top. She'd forgotten herself completely, and forgotten all about buying the book.

"Lady Corinna." A familiar voice interrupted her musings.

It sounded weaker and shorter of breath than she'd like. Lord Lincolnshire wasn't doing well. Her heart sinking, Corinna turned to see him sitting in his wheelchair outside the fence that enclosed the park.

Setting her palette down on a bench, she walked over to greet him, feeling a bit better as she got closer. He looked red and swollen...but happy. Happier than she'd seen him in ages.

Mr. Hamilton stood behind him, his hands on the back of the chair. She remembered how yesterday those hands had gripped her shoulders and pulled her against him.

"My nephew is taking me to his studio," Lord Lincolnshire informed her brightly, snapping her attention back to him. "I'm going to see his newest paintings."

"We really must be on our way," Mr. Hamilton said without meeting Corinna's eyes. "I have much to do today after this."

Lord Lincolnshire smiled up at her. "Would you like to come along?"

"No," Mr. Hamilton shot out at the same time Corinna exclaimed, "Oh, yes!"

"Thank you for the invitation," she added. "I'd love to come along!"

"No," Mr. Hamilton repeated more forcefully, finally looking at her. "My workspace is private. There's a reason I'm known as a recluse."

"Come now, nephew," Lord Lincolnshire chided. "You're about to be an earl. Your days as a recluse have come to an end."

"Uncle—"

"Mr. Hamilton," Corinna interrupted, never one to hold her

tongue. "Your uncle would like me to accompany you. Will you disappoint such a kindly man?"

Mr. Hamilton opened his mouth as if to argue, but then apparently had second thoughts, because he closed it. Into a very straight line. And he glared at her.

She'd won.

Remembering that sulky mouth *imprinting a kiss on her lips*, she couldn't help but smile. "I'll be but a moment. I'll meet you gentlemen at the gate."

After dashing back to her easel and instructing the footman to take it home, she removed her apron, smoothed her pink dress, and joined the two Hamiltons outside the fence.

It was a short walk to Piccadilly Street, where the studio was located. Mr. Hamilton remained grim and silent as they went. Lord Lincolnshire chattered breathlessly, talking about this and that, until he said…

"I've been thinking, nephew, that I'd like to meet your wife."

Corinna nearly fell over her own feet.

Mr. Hamilton had a wife?

She'd kissed a married man?

She was so shocked—and instantly guilty—she didn't even hear whatever Mr. Hamilton said in response to Lord Lincolnshire's request. While artists were supposed to be free spirits, living at the whim of their passions, Corinna had too much respect for marriage and sympathy for poor Mrs. Hamilton—whoever and wherever she was—to feel anything less than deep shame for her own actions.

And yet…that didn't change the fact that the kiss had been glorious. Breathtaking. The most exciting thing that had ever happened to her. Though she couldn't let it happen again, she knew she wouldn't be able to help reliving the experience over and over, as she'd been doing since it happened. And surely the kiss hadn't been her fault.

She'd simply been a victim of Mr. Hamilton's unseemly advances.

Hadn't she?

Still, she was ashamed to think she'd been so blind. Mr. Hamilton was obviously well practiced at charming young women. *Very* well practiced. Far more practiced, Corinna realized, than any honorable, respectful young man could hope to become. His very experience should have been a clue. She sighed, thinking that much as she'd never expected to be kissed like that kiss in the bookshop in real life, it was even more unlikely she'd ever be kissed like that again.

Which seemed the greatest shame of all.

"We're here," Mr. Hamilton said, jarring her out of her panic and back into the real world.

She drew a deep breath and pushed those thoughts from her mind, suddenly impatient to see the studio, to see new Hamilton paintings before anyone else. To see exactly where the artist worked, and what sorts of supplies he used, and maybe, if she was lucky, a canvas or two that wasn't finished yet, so she could study his technique.

And she was also pleased to think how after she'd visited his private space—his secret, reclusive hideaway—he'd no longer be able to keep claiming he wasn't John Hamilton. Because honestly, enough was enough.

She looked forward to watching him eat his own words.

The studio was in a very nice building. Shops filled the ground floor, and the two floors above were divided into large flats. Unfortunately, the studio was in a windowed garret above those, and it was no small feat helping Lord Lincolnshire up the many stairs.

Even though Mr. Hamilton took most of his uncle's weight, they went very slowly, and Corinna found the man much heavier than she expected.

The minute they got inside, Lord Lincolnshire shuffled to a

threadbare sofa and plopped down, wheezing. Corinna would have sat, too, but he was sprawled right in its center. And the studio had no other sofa or any chairs.

In fact, it hadn't much of anything.

Six pictures rested on the floor, leaning against the bare walls. An easel held one more work of art in progress. Clearly it would be a lovely scene once it was finished, a beautiful meadow bordered by trees more realistic than any she'd ever seen rendered in paint. Tiny, individual leaves seemed to be rustling in the wind, casting shadows on the grass below. She looked forward to studying it, to figuring out how Mr. Hamilton had managed such incredible detail.

A small table sat beside it, with a few sketchbooks piled on top. But no pencils.

Odd, that.

Mr. Hamilton's supplies were on the table, too. All of them. There was no cupboard, no shelves in the room, no place for anything to be hiding. She walked over to have a look and found a selection of various pigments, a big bottle of linseed oil, a pristine palette, and two—only two!—seemingly brand-new brushes. Neither of them was nearly fine enough to paint the tiny leaves she'd seen on the trees.

And that was it. There was nothing else. No extra jars to hold leftover mixed paint. No turpentine, no varnish.

No rags, no blank canvases, no knives.

No little spots of paint on the wooden floor.

When Corinna painted in her family's drawing room, she always spread a large tarpaulin to prevent spotting, but the floor here was bare and clean. And no folded tarp was in sight.

"Where do you make your paints?" she asked.

Mr. Hamilton shifted uneasily. "Right here. Where else?"

"What do you use, then? What surface do you grind them against?"

"I make them directly on the palette," he said, slanting a glance to his uncle.

She frowned. "Isn't that too porous? I've always used glass. And a glass muller."

"A muller?" Lord Lincolnshire asked.

"It's sort of like a flat pestle," she explained. "One has to grind the pigment into the oil in order to completely combine them."

He looked to his nephew. Mr. Hamilton lifted a shoulder. "With enough elbow grease, one has no need of a muller."

There were, she acknowledged, different methods. "I suppose a palette knife would do if one worked the mediums well," she conceded.

Lord Lincolnshire nodded approvingly. "He's very talented, you know."

"*Extremely* talented," she agreed. But there were no palette knives. And she still wondered how he could grind against a surface as permeable as wood. She wandered to the painting on the easel, admiring its incredibly detailed trees. "Which pigment do you use as the base for your greens?" she asked.

"The green one."

"Hmm?" He had no green pigment. She turned and glanced back to the table to verify. Black, white, yellows, blues, reds, and earth tones. Other pigments were available for purchase, of course, but these were the basics, the same ones she used herself. With these colors, one could mix any other color one might want. Greens were created from blues and yellows.

When she'd asked which pigment was his base, she'd meant which blue. Ultramarine, Prussian, cerulean? "I'm partial to cobalt," she said, "even though it's the most expensive."

"I can afford it," he said haughtily. "I'm partial to cobalt green, too."

Cobalt was *blue*. Transparent, neutral blue. The truest of all the blues, which was why she preferred it.

She thought a moment. And then she smoothed her pink skirts, moving closer to Mr. Hamilton so Lord Lincolnshire, who'd lain back on the sofa and closed his eyes for a spell, wouldn't overhear. Walking right up to Mr. Hamilton, she rose to her toes and placed her mouth close by his ear.

"Do you like my new green dress?" she whispered.

FOURTEEN

"*I*T'S A LOVELY dress," Sean murmured, though he'd glanced away from it quickly. Her neckline wasn't particularly low, but from this vantage point, close as she was, he could see a little ways down the front.

Sweet mercy. He stood tensely still, trying to keep his eyes locked on her face.

"But do you like the hue?" she asked.

"Oh, yes. It's, um, a very flattering green."

"Thank you," she said, and stepped back.

He released the breath he didn't know he'd been holding.

And after that, she miraculously stopped asking questions.

Over on the sofa, Lincolnshire was gingerly moving to sit up. "May I see your paintings, Sean?" he asked, wheezing only a little.

"Of course, Uncle," Sean said. Corinna helped the earl to a sitting position while Sean went to bring the paintings over, one by one.

The earl examined each picture minutely, making thoughtful and considered comments. John Hamilton might have argued or agreed, but Sean was only confused. His feeble responses earned one or two curious looks from Lincolnshire (or maybe suspicious looks?). Sean found the whole business exhausting. He was an entrepreneur, blast it, not an actor!

But at least Corinna had quit making things more difficult. He hadn't heard a peep out of her in several minutes, for which he was thankful. She was just standing by the easel, watching him with the earl, a rather dumbstruck look on her face.

Huh. And all he'd done was say he liked her dress.

With her, apparently, flattery *could* get you anywhere.

After Lincolnshire finished rhapsodizing over the paintings, Corinna remained quiet while they assisted him back down the steps, a slow and painful process even with her help. She didn't say much as they wheeled the chair home, and her farewell at Lincolnshire's door was uncharacteristically reserved and polite.

Mystified by the change in her, Sean saw the wheezing, exhausted earl upstairs and into bed. With that accomplished, he stepped out into the corridor, closed the door, and slumped against it, shutting his eyes and willing his tense muscles to relax.

Begorrah, that had been the longest afternoon of his life.

This won't interrupt your routine, Hamilton had promised. *It shan't affect Delaney and Company at all.*

The weasel had been lying through his teeth.

Sean was seriously considering ending the whole thing now. Not only because he was constantly neglecting his work—which was no small nuisance—but also because the guilt of deceiving a saint was constantly weighing down on him. It felt like...

Like the Prince Regent was sitting on his chest.

With effort, he opened his eyes and straightened, telling himself he was at least free for the moment. Maybe he could finally attend to his own responsibilities. He tramped down the stairs, asked a footman to have his curricle brought round, and headed out of the house.

Then stopped dead on the doorstep.

"You're not Hamilton," Corinna said.

"Saints preserve us." Sean blinked. "What are you doing here?"

"Waiting to talk to you. You're color-blind. Which means you cannot be Hamilton—or any painter at all. At least not a good one."

Once the shock subsided, he cracked a smile. "I take exception to that. I expect I could paint a decently good brown scene. Assuming I had an artistic bone in my body, that is." A stableman arrived with his curricle, but he ignored it. "What was the telltale sign, then?"

"My dress is pink, not green."

"Ah." It looked pale brown. (And so much for flattery getting him anywhere.) "After you figured that out, you didn't say anything. Why did you keep the truth from Lincolnshire?"

"Are you jesting? The truth would destroy the poor man. He loves you."

"He does seem to."

"And he'd be crushed to learn you're not his nephew." She bit her lip.

He remembered how full and soft it had been.

"Who are you?" she asked.

"Sean Delaney. Hamilton's brother-in-law. As I've been telling you all along."

"If you're not an artist, what do you do?"

"I own property. I buy and sell buildings. Among other things." He shifted uneasily. "I should explain. Not about that, but about how I ended up here. Will you walk with me in the square?"

She seemed to consider that for a moment. "Will you buy me an ice from Gunter's?"

"You're overwarm?" It wasn't a particularly hot day.

"No, but Gunter's Tea Shop is probably the only place in

London where a girl can be seen alone with a gentleman without ruining her reputation."

"Agreed, then," he said when he stopped laughing.

She was a clever one.

Leaving the curricle in front of Lincolnshire House, they made their way across the square to Gunter's, where he ordered a lemon ice for himself and a strawberry ice for Corinna. They took them back into the square.

"This is such a relief," he said as they walked.

"The other fellow in the museum was really Hamilton, then. I'm guessing this was his plan?"

Sean nodded. "I didn't want to go along with it."

"But you did it anyway."

"For my sister." Sean sighed. "Hamilton's wife."

By the time he explained, both their dishes were empty. They sat on a bench beneath a large London plane tree.

"So you're not married, then?" she asked. "You don't have a wife?"

"No," he said vaguely, not really listening. He was watching Corinna lick her spoon. When it was spotless, she let it clatter into her bowl.

"Well, I don't blame you for what you're doing," she declared. "I'd have done the same to save my sister from being unhappy all her days."

"I feel terrible tricking Lincolnshire, though. I'm going to tell him the truth."

"You cannot!" She turned to him urgently. "You'll ruin your sister's life, and—"

"I fear I've failed Deirdre already. When Hamilton learns I appeared as him in public, he'll be furious. Think of the damage to his reputation."

"But if you give up now, you'll ruin the rest of Lord Lincolnshire's life, too! He's the most incredible man in the world, and he's tragically lost everyone he loves, and he's so thrilled to have his nephew with him in his final days. How can you even think of depriving him of his last chance at happiness?"

"It's sorry I am for that. But I cannot go on lying to the poor fellow." Sean thought of telling her how the guilt weighed on him, but that wasn't really the point. "It just isn't right—"

"It's kind, and what's so wrong about that? How is it hurting him? He'd be much more hurt to learn his real nephew is so very selfish, and there'd be nothing he could do about it anyway. The law is the law. John Hamilton is his nearest blood relative, his legal heir. He'll inherit no matter what Lord Lincolnshire might prefer."

"True he'd inherit the title and any entailed property. But Lincolnshire could will everything else to anyone he wanted."

"I suppose he could, Mr. Delaney. But—"

"Sean."

"I beg your pardon?"

"My name is Sean. And I'm thinking we should have leave to call each other by our given names."

He already called her Corinna in his head. He'd thought of her as Corinna ever since he'd heard her name called out in the British Museum. And having never spent much time around the peerage, he would probably forget to add the *Lady*.

"I don't know," she said slowly. "That seems rather...intimate."

"You're the only one who knows my secret," he pointed out. "That's a rather intimate thing, don't you think? *And* we've kissed."

Her blue eyes went wide and inscrutable.

"Not that that's happening again," he quickly added.

"But you're not married," she said just as quickly, and then, "Yes, of course that's not happening again." A charming little smile tugged at the corner of her mouth. "Now where were we... Sean?" She sobered. "Oh, yes. You'd said that if Lord

Lincolnshire learned the truth, he'd be able to will most of his property to anyone he wanted. But at what cost? He'd be disappointed and unhappy the rest of his days, and once he's gone, will it really matter whether Mr. Hamilton does or doesn't inherit? Lord Lincolnshire deserves happiness," she concluded with a decisive nod. "That's the most important thing." She looked thoughtful. "And at least there's still a chance for your sister. If you abandon the plan on purpose, we *know* she'll be lost."

Corinna had a point. A lot of points, actually. Lincolnshire's happiness was more important than depriving the weasel of his inheritance. But... "He's going to find out anyway. You just saw for yourself how obvious it is that I'm not an artist. The earl may be wasting away physically, but his mind is sharp as a knife. He's already growing suspicious. And how will he feel when he uncovers the truth? Wouldn't it be better for me to break it to him gently?"

"*I'm* an artist. I can cover for you. I can help you keep up the act."

"You're not around enough to do that."

"I can *be* around enough. I'll visit Lord Lincolnshire every day. I'll stay close. You won't mind that, will you?"

Would he mind? Sean wanted to laugh. Whyever should he mind spending hours and hours every single day with a girl he couldn't stop thinking about, couldn't help wanting, and couldn't ever have for his own?

Of course he wouldn't mind—he *loved* torturing himself.

"I won't mind," he muttered, only adding to his legion of lies.

FIFTEEN

TEA BUNS

Mix a lot of Flower with some Sugar and a little Salt in a bowl, then put in Egges, Butter, halfe

a cup of Milk and a measure of Yeast to make a thick dough. Allow to rise, then flatten and

make rounde buns and allow to rise again before you bake.

A most genteel addition to afternoon tea, these buns encourage serenity.

—Georgiana, Countess of Greystone, 1806

*Y*ESTERDAY'S discovery that John Hamilton was really Sean Delaney—well, that and constantly reliving the kiss—had kept Corinna too distracted to take notice of the calendar. But today she'd realized it was May. The second of May, to be precise. Lady A's reception was on the fourteenth, and Summer Exhibition submissions were due on the nineteenth.

It usually took her at least two weeks to complete a painting. And for this one, she hadn't even chosen a subject.

Griffin had been gone a day longer than he'd said he would, yet with all the peace and quiet, she still wasn't making progress. Her anxiety had kept her mind buzzing the entire afternoon at

Juliana's home. Family and friends had assembled there, in Stafford House's beautiful Palm Room, to pen the invitations to the reception Lady A was planning to introduce Corinna to the art world.

All of Corinna's female relations had come. Alexandra and Juliana, and their three cousins, Rachael, Claire, and Elizabeth. A hugely pregnant Aunt Frances. Lady Avonleigh, of course, and her two sisters, Lady Balmforth and Lady Cavanaugh, who was also Juliana's mother-in-law.

It was touching. Corinna had never been the sentimental type, but the thought of all of them helping her made her throat feel tight.

And the thought of all their generous hard work going to waste if she didn't finish her portrait in time made her stomach feel like rebelling.

"It was so kind of you all to come," Lady A said now as she stacked the last of the completed invitations. "I was dreading this task, but with all you ladies here, it was nothing!"

Juliana piled the leftover tea buns she'd served into a basket. "Have you need of any more assistance, Lady Avonleigh? With anything else at all?"

"Just encourage everyone to attend, please, all of you. Royal Academicians in particular, but anyone else influential as well. You all know the wording for the invitations now, so feel free to write out more should you think of anyone else who might be able to further Corinna's career. Above all, we must make certain the committee members all attend." She rose to fetch her pelisse, saying to Corinna, "I'm sure John Hamilton will accept, as he's your personal acquaintance—"

"I wouldn't call him that," Corinna interrupted. Her nervousness about *charming* the committee had suddenly returned, causing a fluttering in her stomach that mixed oh-so-nicely with the nausea.

"You've danced with him, my dear."

"He's very busy," Corinna insisted. Sean couldn't attend the reception—the Academy members would surely expose him as a fraud. "And you know he doesn't like to appear in public."

"Now that he's inheriting Lord Lincolnshire's title, I'm certain that will change. Don't fret, my dear; he shall attend." Lady A came close and kissed Corinna's cheek, enveloping her in a cloud of gardenia and camphor scent. Corinna quickly stepped away under the guise of retrieving her reticule; the unappealing fragrance had nearly been enough to bring her luncheon back up.

Luckily, Lady A didn't seem to notice. "Should you run into Mr. Hamilton," she went on, buttoning her pelisse, "you might encourage him to see that the other committee members accept as well."

"Maybe...." Corinna said between taking deep, calming breaths.

Shrugging into her own light pelisse, Rachael paused. "Are you all right?"

"I'm fine," Corinna fibbed. "Perfectly fine."

She couldn't help wondering if she'd done the right thing encouraging Sean to continue deceiving Lord Lincolnshire. In fact, it seemed she could think about little else. Besides the kiss. And the reception. And her looming deadline to finish her portrait.

But she was fine. Perfectly fine.

And there she went, lying to herself again.

Rachael patted her shoulder. "Don't get yourself in a dither. I know this reception is important to you, but we shall all contrive to make certain it's a wild success."

Alexandra lifted baby Harry out of his pram. "Yes, we will." The other ladies made noises of agreement.

Aunt Frances pushed slowly to her feet. "Yes, we will," she echoed, sounding a bit out of breath.

Juliana laid a hand on the woman's arm. "Are *you* all right, Aunty?"

"Yes, just fat and ugly and winded. My friend Lady Mabel swears this city isn't good for the lungs once a lady reaches a certain age, but then again, she has asthma." Frances gave a wheezy laugh. "I'm only with child."

Elizabeth grabbed her cloak, but as it was a warm day she laid it over her arm. "Our mother always said that about the London air, too. But I don't remember her ever having any trouble breathing."

"That's because Mama refused to come to London," Claire said, and turned to Juliana. "I hope you put those extra tea buns in the basket for us."

Juliana nodded. "I noticed the recipe in our family cookbook was your mother's."

Claire smiled, taking the offered basket. "She used to make them for us all the time, but we haven't had any in years."

"I hope you'll enjoy them." Leaving her two sisters behind, Juliana started walking the rest of her guests toward the door. "Your mother wrote that the tea buns encourage serenity."

"Is that why you made them?" Rachael asked. "Do you think Corinna is in need of serenity?"

Before Corinna could go after them and speak for herself, Juliana answered. "Of course she's in need of serenity. Her entire future hangs in the balance!"

Corinna heard everyone laugh before they said their good-byes. Then she heard the door shut, and Juliana returned to the Palm Room.

Going to a sideboard that had gilt legs carved to look like palm trees, Juliana poured three glasses of sherry before joining her sisters on one of the many sofas covered in palm tree-themed satin fabric. "Here," she said, handing Corinna a glass. "I expect you'll find this encourages serenity much more than tea buns."

Corinna sipped gratefully.

"It's natural to be nervous about the reception," Alexandra said, shifting Harry on her lap to take a sip.

"And you're nervous about something else, too." Juliana crossed her legs. "I can tell. Out with it, Corinna."

They knew her too well; there was no sense pretending. She sighed. "I have a secret."

Her sisters exchanged meaningful glances. "Well?" Alexandra asked.

"Lord Lincolnshire's nephew isn't John Hamilton," Corinna confessed in a rush. "I mean, John Hamilton *is* his nephew, but the gentleman you met at Lady Partridge's ball isn't. He's his brother-in-law. He wanted to tell Lord Lincolnshire the truth, but I convinced him not to, and now I'm not sure that was right."

"Whoa." Juliana's sip of sherry was more like a gulp. "Explain that again. Slowly, and with more detail."

Corinna did so, telling the whole long complicated story. Then she held her breath before asking, "Was I wrong? Should he tell Lord Lincolnshire the truth?"

Juliana shook her head. "Absolutely not."

"I agree." Alexandra patted the baby's back. "Lord Lincolnshire deserves a happy ending."

Corinna blew the breath out. "You're right. I love Lord Lincolnshire."

"So do we," Alexandra assured her.

"I'm going to visit him more often. I promised Mr. Delaney I would, to help him keep up the pretense that he's an artist."

"You'll get to see more of Mr. Delaney that way too, hmm?" Juliana wiggled her eyebrows.

Corinna looked to Alexandra. "She's meddling again, isn't she?"

"Doesn't she always?"

"I can tell you like him," Juliana said defensively. "And I cannot say I blame you. He's quite good-looking—"

"You're a married woman!" Corinna interrupted.

"A very happy one," her sister agreed. "But a lady doesn't go blind when she takes her marriage vows. Or deaf, either. That accent—"

"You make him sound like a pretty box. You know nothing about the person inside." Neither did she, for that matter.

"I know he's being very nice to Lord Lincolnshire. And that his sister is married to John Hamilton, which means he's connected to the right people."

"He's not a peer, Juliana. He owns property."

"Doesn't every gentleman own property?"

"Gentlemen *inherit* property. Mr. Delaney buys and sells it for a living. Among other things." She wondered what the other things were.

"Well, that seems a very lucrative sort of career. And an impressive accomplishment for a young man his age. He must have quite the work ethic."

Corinna rolled her eyes. "And there's the fact that he's Irish." With that accent. She'd gone back to the bookstore to buy *Children of the Abbey* this morning, and she was already up to page 43, where she'd thought of Sean instead of Lord Mortimer while reading about how *the harmony of his voice imparted a charm that seldom failed of being irresistible.*

"Does his being Irish bother you?" Juliana asked.

"Of course not. But it might bother Griffin."

"Griffin would be a hypocrite if it did," Juliana scoffed. "His own name comes from an Irish ancestor."

"That's right," Alexandra put in. "Our sixth or seventh great-grandfather, wasn't he? Aidan Griffin, Baron Kilcullen from Ballygriffin, Ireland."

"How do you remember such things?" Corinna asked.

"Family is important to me." She smiled at little Harry, who was named after her husband's uncle. "Besides, you remember every word you've ever read."

"That's different. And far more irritating than it is helpful.

My brain is always filled with all those stupid lines." She sighed. "In any case, I'm not interested in Mr. Delaney that way."

She wouldn't say no to another kiss—now that she knew he wasn't really married. But if she knew her sister, Juliana would stop at nothing to get him married now.

To Corinna.

She fixed Juliana with a serious stare. "I have only seventeen days left to finish my portrait, *and* call on Lincolnshire House to make sure the earl's last days go smoothly. I don't have time for your matchmaking schemes."

"Matchmaking schemes? I've no idea what you're on about." Juliana's eyes were wide and innocent. "I happen to think it's very kind of you to look after dear Lord Lincolnshire. You should take him a sweet to comfort him in his illness."

"Corinna doesn't bake," Alexandra reminded her.

Corinna *couldn't* bake. The ladies of their family were famed for their sweets, and she was the only Chase lady in history with no talent in the kitchen. She couldn't measure anything properly; she couldn't mix without creating lumps. If she so much as looked at the oven, biscuits burned and cakes collapsed.

"I didn't say she should make it," Juliana pointed out. "I only said she should take it. *I* shall do the baking for her."

"Thank you," Corinna said sweetly. It wasn't so bad being a bungler in the kitchen, really. In truth, she'd much rather paint.

SIXTEEN

"**I** WONDER WHY Corinna's so nervous," Rachael said to her sisters during the ride home in their carriage. "There's the reception, of course, but she seems to be worrying about more than that."

Corinna had been very far from calm and collected. As a person who wasn't quite herself these days, Rachael recognized the signs. Griffin was supposed to have returned yesterday, and she was on pins and needles waiting to hear what he might have discovered.

"I don't know what's bothering Corinna." Elizabeth shrugged. "But I've been thinking."

"That's a novelty," Claire chimed in.

Elizabeth stuck out her tongue. "I meant I've been thinking about something else. I've been thinking about how Mama never wheezed like Lady Mabel."

"I told you, that's because she refused to come to London." Claire fiddled with a new amethyst ring she'd made, twirling it on her finger. "She knew it wasn't good for her."

"But Mama was very quiet," Elizabeth pointed out. "I'm

wondering if she even had asthma at all. Maybe she just didn't want to socialize, so she used that as an excuse."

Claire stopped twirling. "You think Mama *lied*?"

"I didn't say she lied. I said she might have made up an excuse."

"That's the same as a lie! And she would never—"

"Mama wasn't perfect," Rachael interrupted. An understatement, considering she'd hidden the truth of Rachael's parentage all her life. "It's possible Elizabeth could be right." Thinking back, she couldn't remember her mother ever having difficulty breathing. "Mama never attended large social gatherings. She always preferred to stay home with her needlework and her watercolors and us."

"She went to Cainewood," Claire argued. "Often."

"But only to visit with family. Never for a ball or any other grand occasion."

"I don't believe it," Claire said, looking pouty.

"Well, it doesn't signify anyway, does it?" Rachael sighed. "We'll never know for sure."

They all rode in thoughtful silence until the carriage came to a stop before their town house in Lincoln's Inn Fields. Elizabeth climbed down first, then let out a little yelp.

"What are you doing here?" she cried.

Rachael followed Claire out to find Griffin standing in the courtyard.

"Good afternoon, ladies," he said with the crooked smile that always made her feel flustered. But when his gaze swung to meet hers, his expression grew more serious. "I've been waiting for you. I have news."

"What news?" Claire demanded.

"I'll explain later," Rachael told her sisters. She didn't want an audience when she heard what Griffin had learned. "Go inside. Griffin and I will talk in the square."

Grumbling all the way, her sisters entered the house while

Rachael and Griffin crossed the street and went through the gate to the private park in the center of the square. It was a nice day, sunny but not hot, and Lincoln's Inn Fields was filled with people enjoying the fine weather.

Choosing a bench beneath a large tree, where the shade would hide them from view of the houses all around, she sat and smoothed her pelisse's lavender skirt. "You took longer than I expected."

Angled toward her, he pulled her father's jeweled badge from his pocket and placed it in her palm, folding her fingers around it. "Rachael...I know who he was."

"Was," she repeated. "He's dead, then."

In a cousinly, concerned way, he took one of her hands in both of his. "You knew that, didn't you?"

"Yes. Yes, of course." But apparently part of her had hoped that wasn't true, because a pang of disappointment seemed to spear her heart.

"There's more," he said, squeezing her fingers. "Not all of it good."

She nodded and pulled her hand free, staring down at the badge she held. She couldn't think straight with him touching her. "Start at the beginning. Please."

He took a deep breath. "I searched all the records for the time in question and found a member of the Tenth who took leave to wed a woman the month before you were conceived. An officer, a lieutenant. His name was Thomas Grimbald."

"Grimbald," she echoed, testing the word on her tongue. She should have been Rachael Grimbald, but that sounded so very wrong. "Are you sure he was the right man?"

Griffin nodded. "He married a woman who was thereafter known as Lady Georgiana Grimbald."

Startled, she looked up at him. "He was titled, then?"

"No. She must have been a peer's daughter."

"But my mother was a commoner. She was born plain Georgiana Woodby. She wasn't a lady until she wed my fa—I mean, the Earl of Greystone. You found the wrong man."

"I also thought so at first. That's why I was gone the extra day. I combed the records going back years, in case your mother married long before conceiving you. But very few men from the Tenth wed in the correct time frame, and no one else married a woman named Georgiana."

"You're sure it was her, then?"

"There's no other explanation. Your mother must have lied about being a commoner. She always acted like a true lady, didn't she? And the timing of Grimbald's wedding is perfect. It cannot be a coincidence that his wife had the same given name. He had to have been your father."

"Maybe." The name sounded wrong, but she still couldn't seem to think straight. She focused on a wooden stand in the distance, where lemonade was sold in the square. "This Grimbald...did the records say how he died?"

"They did."

She waited, but no more information seemed to be forthcoming. She waited some more. When she finally looked back to Griffin, his green eyes were flooded with sympathy.

She didn't want sympathy; she wanted the truth.

"What?" she asked, but still he didn't answer. She clenched her hand around the badge. "What in blazes are you hiding from me? I've already learned that my mother lied to me all of my life, came from a different family than she claimed, and my name should be Rachael Grimbald." Grimbald, for pity's sake! It wasn't a cold day, and she was wearing a pelisse in any case, but she wrapped her arms around herself as though she might ward off a chill. "What could you possibly have to tell me that would be more upsetting than all of that?"

Griffin blew out a breath. "He was executed, Rachael. For treason."

She opened her mouth to respond, but suddenly all the air

seemed to have been sucked right out of her. The birds in the tree overhead sounded entirely too cheerful. The people strolling by, chatting and drinking lemonade, sounded too cheerful, too.

"Treason?" she finally managed to say, her voice thin and the opposite of cheerful. "What did he do?"

"That I don't know; the records of the court-martial must be elsewhere. But he joined the Tenth in 1782—transferred from a disbanded regiment—and there was a notation of his family's address at that time. In Yorkshire. I've hired a man to see whether they still live there. I'll let you know when I find out. Then take you to meet them."

Treason. She hugged herself tighter, the edges of the hard metal badge digging into her clenched fist. "I'm not sure I want to. Meet them, I mean. Not if their son committed treason."

"You don't have to, of course. It will be up to you. They're your family, but I'm willing to wager they don't know of your existence. Perhaps that's why your mother used another name. So they couldn't find you."

"That makes sense." As much sense as anything else he'd said to her today. "Treason," she murmured. "My father was executed for treason."

"I'm sorry." He began to reach for her, then apparently thought better of it and crossed his arms instead. "It doesn't change who you are, Rachael, or make you any less good than you are."

"No," she said, "it doesn't."

But she must not have sounded convincing.

"'Fathers shall not be put to death for their children,'" he quoted solemnly, "'nor children put to death for their fathers; each is to die for his own sins.'"

That dredged up a tiny smile. "Griffin Chase, referencing a Bible passage? There may be hope for you yet."

"I live for your approval," he said, his crooked smile reappearing in return.

"Thank you for finding my fa—Grimbald." She rose and smoothed her pelisse. "I do appreciate your going out of your way to do me this favor. I'm sorry it proved so difficult." She cleared her throat and started back home, taking a little comfort when he fell into step beside her. "My sisters must be half dead of curiosity by now."

She wasn't looking forward to telling them the awful truth.

SEVENTEEN

GINGERBREAD CAKES

Take four pints of Flower with Ginger and Nutmeg and rub Butter into it. Add to it Brandy and

Treacle and mix it altogether. Let it lay till it grows stiffe then pinch pieces and make into little

balls. Flatten cakes on a tin and add a Sweetmeat if you please and bake.

These spicy little cakes are known to raise the spirits. Not ghosts, that is, but spirits of the

emotional variety. Excellent to take along when paying visits to the ill.

—Anne, Marchioness of Cainewood, 1775

*U*PON ARRIVING at Lincolnshire House the next afternoon, Corinna was shown to a drawing room. She dragged her feet, not caring that it was unladylike. She felt creaky and headachy from being up all night trying to work on the portrait—but stupidly letting her worries distract her instead. A whole day wasted.

When she entered the room, Sean sat holding a book that he'd apparently been reading to Lord Lincolnshire.

He rose immediately. "I waited for you all yesterday. Where were you?"

He'd waited *all day*? "I was helping Lady Avonleigh make

invitations for a reception. And I was painting. And earlier I went back to the colorman's shop." Well, really to the bookstore to buy *Children of the Abbey*. "What were you doing here all day? Didn't you need to...ah"—she slanted a glance to Lord Lincolnshire—"paint?"

"Yes, I would have loved to paint. But my uncle is my priority," he said pointedly.

"Of course." Now she felt guilty on top of everything else. One might even say that, like the heroine of *Pamela or Virtue and Reward*, Corinna's *poor mind was all topsy-turv—*

Oh, hang it! She shoved stupid Pamela from her mind. She simply couldn't cope with that today.

Nor could she bring herself to face Sean's crossness, so she turned to the earl instead. "Good afternoon, Lord Lincolnshire. I brought you some gingerbread cakes. They're supposed to raise one's spirits."

"Says who?" Sean asked, taking the basket.

"Says my family's heirloom cookbook. Each lady in the family adds a recipe every year, and they all have legends attached. Not that I believe such nonsense," she hastened to add. "My sister Juliana baked these. I'm hopeless in the kitchen."

"I didn't think any Mayfair ladies ever entered a kitchen."

"The Chase ladies do," Lord Lincolnshire said, pausing for a breath. "They're famous for their sweets."

"All except me," Corinna said.

Sean handed Lord Lincolnshire a sweet and took one for himself. "Please, have a seat."

Corinna looked around the room, which she'd never been in before. The butler, Quincy, had called it the "yellow drawing room" when he'd shown her in here. The walls were covered with yellow silk printed with pink roses, green leaves, and some blue flowers she couldn't name. All the sofas, chairs, and footstools were upholstered in yellow brocade. Part of Lord Lincolnshire's extensive Ming vase collection was in here, and there were several excellent paintings on the walls, including two Rembrandts.

She wished to study them, but Sean had asked her to sit. Ignoring his request might irritate him further, and that simply wouldn't do.

Mostly because she'd decided she wanted another kiss.

Once she chose the seat with the best view of the Rembrandts, Sean reseated himself too. "This gingerbread is delicious," he said.

"I'll tell Juliana." She turned to Lord Lincolnshire. He was covered to the waist with a heavy blanket, making her wonder what might be concealed underneath. His hands looked a little puffy, and he'd taken only a tiny bite of the cake. "How are you feeling today, my lord?"

"Better than one might expect, thanks to my nephew." He smiled at Sean, apparently waiting to catch his breath before continuing. "I'm still thinking, nephew"—pause—"that I'd like to meet your wife."

Sean exchanged a panicked look with Corinna. "I'm afraid my wife prefers to stay in the countryside, Uncle. She likes the quiet life."

Lord Lincolnshire looked disappointed but seemed to accept the state of affairs, since his response was, "Very well." But then he added, "As I was saying when Lady Corinna arrived—"

"Shall I continue reading?" Sean interrupted.

"Not now, nephew. We have a lovely...young lady visiting. And as I...was saying—"

"Would you care for another sweet, Uncle?"

"I haven't finished this one." Pause. "I've been—"

"Have you need of another pillow?"

"No." The poor man was already leaning against at least five of them. "I've—"

"Are you certain—"

"Would you let a man finish a sentence?" Corinna snapped.

Tearing her gaze from one of the Rembrandts, she turned to the earl and spoke in a kindlier tone. "What did you want to say, Lord Lincolnshire?"

"I wanted to say...that I've been thinking I'd like Sean...to paint a portrait of me. One last portrait...before I depart this fine world."

Sean glared at her. Apparently he'd realized this was coming. But how was she supposed to have known?

"I don't think he can do that, Lord Lincolnshire," she said carefully. "Mr. Hamilton paints only landscapes."

"Surely he can paint...one portrait."

Sean shook his head. "I've never painted a portrait."

Truer words were never spoken, Corinna thought.

"You're a skilled artist, nephew. One of the very best...in the land." Lord Lincolnshire gasped and waited a moment. Corinna wracked her brain for a way to help Sean, as she'd promised she would. Chases always kept their promises. "Surely—"

"May *I* paint you, Lord Lincolnshire?" she cut him off. "Please? I'd be truly honored if you'd allow me. I've been dying to paint a portrait to submit to the Royal Academy for the Summer Exhibition. If it turns out well, perhaps it will be selected. A subject of your stature could make my career."

"Me?" Lord Lincolnshire wheezed. "In the Summer Exhibition?"

"Possibly," she reiterated. "None of my portraits have turned out great so far, since I haven't had any anatomy lessons. But lately I've been sketching the Elgin Marbles for practice, and I shall try my best—"

"I'm certain," Lord Lincolnshire interrupted, "it will turn out brilliant." He smiled at her as though she'd brought the sun. "But my days are...numbered. Tomorrow being Sunday, I'm hoping...my dear nephew...will take me to church. May we begin Monday?"

"I think we should start now." Her painting was due to the

Royal Academy a scant sixteen days hence, and she hoped to show it at Lady A's reception five days before that. "If you've some paper, I can begin sketching you immediately."

"Excellent." Lord Lincolnshire lifted a silver bell from a table beside him. "I shall have a footman...fetch paper...posthaste."

While he rang the bell, Corinna glanced rather triumphantly to Sean. His answering smile was far warmer than she'd expected. Warm enough to make *her* feel warm. She had to look away.

It seemed he'd forgiven her.

Well, good. Now when was he going to kiss her?

She frowned, suddenly realizing he hadn't even tried to kiss her since that day in the bookshop. Not once. Whatever could that mean? Had he not enjoyed kissing her?

He couldn't have *meant* it when he said he'd never kiss her again, could he?

Holy Hannah, she hoped not.

A footman handed her a pencil and some paper. She blinked and looked back to Lord Lincolnshire. "What would you like to be doing?"

"Doing?"

"In your portrait. I don't care for portraits where the subject simply stands there and stares at the viewer. I'd prefer for you to be doing something."

"Well, I cannot...simply stand there...in any case." With a faint but good-natured smile, Lord Lincolnshire gestured to his covered legs. "I shall...have to be sitting." His expression turned contemplative. "I've always...enjoyed a good book. Perhaps I can be...reading a book."

While she'd been hoping for something a bit more active, she decided that would have to do. If the man had always loved to read, it was suitable, after all. Thinking Sean had pleased the earl by reading aloud, she glanced back to him.

He was still smiling that same warm, dreamy smile.

Oh, very well, maybe it wasn't dreamy; maybe it was only grateful that she'd managed to save his behind. But it *was* warm. And it was a smile. He was happy with her, at least for the moment.

She'd get him to kiss her one way or another.

She smiled back. "Would you care to read while I sketch, Mr. Hamilton?"

He nodded and opened the book.

Letting his harmonious voice wash over her, she settled back and put pencil to paper. And even though Sean wasn't reading a romantic novel, she kept smiling as she listened and sketched.

EIGHTEEN

"THANK YOU," Sean said simply as he walked Corinna toward the door later. "You saved my skin by offering to paint him."

"I told you that you could count on me. May I look in here?" she asked, indicating another drawing room. Lincolnshire House seemed to have a surplus of drawing rooms. "I'd like to see if there are any more Rembrandts."

"I can't think why not." He walked in with her. "What color is this room?"

"Mostly green. The walls are lined with bright green silk damask, and the draperies are green silk trimmed with black velvet. The furniture is all covered in golden and dark red brocade. It's beautiful. I'm sorry you cannot see it."

"I can see it," he told her. "It just looks different to me. The color I can see best is blue. All the rooms in my house are blue, except for Deirdre's."

"Where is your house?"

"In Hampstead. Who painted that landscape you're staring at?"

"John Hamilton." She gave a merry laugh. "All the paintings

in this room are Hamiltons. It seems Lord Lincolnshire truly is quite proud of his nephew."

"Figures," Sean muttered in disgust. "It's good to know that, though. I imagine I'd make a holy show of myself if he took me in here and I didn't recognize my own paintings."

"A holy show?"

"A great fool of myself," he translated. "A massive embarrassment." Somehow, being around her seemed to bring out his Irishness. "Thank you again. I really do appreciate your help."

"I'm glad to hear that," she said. Moving to a fine Kent fireplace, she leaned against the mantel and glanced over her shoulder rather flirtatiously. Or not precisely flirtatiously, because she wasn't a flirtatious girl. She seemed much more straightforward than that.

Was she meaning to flirt with him? On purpose?

His question was answered immediately, when she aimed another inviting look over her shoulder and said softly, "I think you owe me a kiss."

He laughed. What else could he do? "I'm not John Hamilton, remember? I'm no longer a trophy. Why should you want to kiss me again?"

"Maybe I liked it the first time." Her tone was casual, but Sean could tell it was an act to cover her embarrassment—her cheeks were reddening. Well, they were coloring, anyway, and he assumed the color was red. In any case, he felt sorry for laughing at her.

And he hoped she was telling the truth.

He peered into her blue, blue eyes, trying to figure out if she was indeed being truthful. Those eyes...they could make a fellow feel grateful for being color-blind. (What was he supposed to be figuring out, again...?) And then there was her voice. It was a low voice, sweet but not at all girlish. It had a tart edge when she was being cheeky, which was most of the time. He liked that, the way she said whatever she was thinking. He also liked watching her lips move when she talked. But he shouldn't look at her lips, because whenever he did, it made him want to kiss her, which he couldn't do because…

He looked at her lips.

"I told my sisters your secret," said the lips. Full, beautiful, soft-looking—

Wait a second.

"You did *what*?" he roared, shaking his head to clear it. Thinking that this time, he *really* might strangle her.

He definitely wasn't kissing her.

"I had to share it with someone," she said defensively, pushing away from the mantle. "I had to. I feared I'd done wrong encouraging you to keep it up, and—"

"What did they say?"

"They heartily approved. They told me I'd done exactly the right thing. I'm not at all sorry I told them."

"Don't tell anyone else."

"But—"

"*Don't.*"

She hesitated, then nodded. "I won't."

"I want your promise."

"I promise. And a Chase promise is never given lightly," she added, her eyes wide and solemn.

"All right, then." It seemed disaster had been averted. But that didn't mean all was forgiven, no matter how wide she made her eyes. She wasn't getting that kiss. "You'll be back Monday to start the actual painting? Early, I hope?"

"First thing in the morning."

"Excellent." Maybe he'd be able to escape and get something done. "I—"

"Of course, *morning* for me starts at noon."

"Noon?"

"At the earliest. I like to paint through the wee hours, so I sleep late." She walked closer. Right up to him. So close he could see her blue irises were rimmed in a darker, midnight shade. So close he could smell her floral scent with that hint of paint underneath it.

She wasn't getting that kiss.

"Do you know what else my sisters said?" she asked. Not-quite-flirtatiously.

"No, but I'm sure you'll tell me."

"Juliana said she was impressed by your connections. And the fact that you've made a success of yourself at such a young age."

"She doesn't know how successful I am," he pointed out. "And neither do you."

She waved that away. "Houses in Hampstead aren't cheap. And Alexandra reminded me that our brother, Griffin, is named for our ancestor, Aidan Griffin, Baron Kilcullen from Ballygriffin, Ireland."

He narrowed his eyes. "And the significance of all this is...?"

"They think it's all right for you to kiss me." She stepped even closer. "Are you certain you don't want to? I might get up earlier in the morning for a kiss."

He resolutely looked away from her lips. He needed to think. Not that he could think clearly anyway, with her standing so close and daring to make such an offer. He had to admit it was tempting. He *did* need to get to work earlier on Monday. And she *had* just eliminated every reason he'd considered her off-limits.

He sized her up shrewdly. "How much earlier?"

"Ten o'clock."

"Eight."

"Nine."

He yanked her to him.

He would have cursed his weakness, but he was too busy enjoying himself. Or rather, enjoying *her*—her warmth, her hands drifting up to thread her fingers into his hair, her heart pounding like a drum against his own. Even though he'd been expecting it, he was still stunned by the unimaginable softness of her lips. Carefully, gingerly, he drew the bottom one between his teeth and, just as he'd watched her do a hundred times, bit down.

She gasped and pulled away, and for a panicked second he thought he'd hurt her.

But she was laughing, her lovely eyes sparkling up at him. He laughed along in relief.

She pressed two fingers to her bottom lip, as if she could still feel the bite. "I'll see you Monday at nine," she said in her cheeky way, and quit the room.

He heard her footsteps cross the stone floor in the entrance hall, heard the door open, heard Quincy bid her a polite farewell. By the time the door closed, he'd gathered his wits.

Somewhat.

He went back to the other drawing room, where Lincolnshire was dozing, propped on his many pillows. Sean touched the earl gently on the shoulder and smiled when his eyes fluttered open. "Would you like me to see you to bed, Uncle? I think you could use the rest. And I could use a few hours to paint."

"Very well," Lincolnshire said. "But I really do...wish to meet your wife."

Sean winced. He'd thought they'd dropped the subject. "It's truly sorry I am, but as I told you, she prefers to stay in the countryside."

"She can make an exception...just this once? She'll be the next countess...and the mother of my eventual heirs. I wish to... get to know her." The earl paused for a much-needed breath. And another. "Please, Sean." His eyes shone with hope.

Saints preserve us.

Sean couldn't refuse.

∼

"*N*O." IN HER lovely floral-painted bedroom, the only room in Sean's house that wasn't blue—in fact, he wasn't sure *what* color it was—Deirdre tossed a pile of shifts into the trunk she was filling. "I've told you twice already, no."

It felt like days since Sean had been home. Begorrah, it *had* been days since he'd been home. He'd neglected his work yet again to come talk to his sister, and this wasn't the welcome he'd hoped for. "Why are you packing your things, then?"

"I'm moving to Daniel's house tomorrow. I'm bored out of my mind here alone in Hampstead. I'm going to live in the middle of London, where I can see another face once in a while."

Oh, no, she wasn't.

"You'll live in London, all right, but with Lincolnshire." He was shirking his own duties in order to obtain her precious divorce, and she couldn't even wait to see this thing through? "I want you to arrive early Monday evening. That will make it believable that you had to come in from the countryside. You owe me, Deirdre. I'm doing a favor for you. Now you'll do this favor for me."

"I didn't ask for any favors. I don't *want* any favors." She pulled three dresses out of her clothespress. Brown, brown, and brown. "I still cannot believe you allowed John to talk you into this ridiculous scheme."

"Well, I did." And didn't he regret it even more than she? "And now Lincolnshire is insisting he meet Hamilton's wife. Which is *you*, in case you don't remember."

"I remember, little brother," Deirdre said dryly. "But I don't care." The dresses clenched in her hands, she turned to him. "What is the old man going to do, after all, if you fail to produce a wife?"

"He'll be disappointed."

"I've news for you, Sean: We're all disappointed sometimes. The old man will survive."

"He won't survive, no. Either way. And he deserves happiness in his final days. He's a nice man, Deirdre."

"John never thought so."

"John is an idiot."

"You've a point there." She folded the dresses, then sighed and went back for more. "But I don't want to play your wife."

Sean echoed her own words back to her. "I've news for you, Deirdre: We're all forced to do things we'd rather not sometimes."

"Sometimes, maybe. But not this time."

"If I don't fulfill his wishes," he argued, "Lincolnshire may retaliate by withholding his fortune from your husband."

"John deserves that. Nothing would make me happier."

"Think again, dear sister. If your husband isn't satisfied with my performance—if he loses his inheritance as a result—I'd lay odds he won't grant you your divorce."

She shrugged. "I don't care. I told you not to do this in the first place. I'll be happy living with Daniel whether I'm married to him or not."

Sean kept silent a moment, deliberating. And then, "You won't be living with Daniel Raleigh," he said quietly.

"I will. Is something wrong with your ears, Sean? I told you, I'm moving to Daniel's house tomorrow. And there's nothing you can do about it!"

"No, you're not. You're moving to Lincolnshire House on Monday."

"Something *is* wrong with your ears!"

He hesitated. He hadn't wanted her to hear the whole truth, to know the worst of what might befall her. She'd only panic, or throw a fit, or feel guilty. He didn't want any of that.

But he didn't see where he had a choice.

As Deirdre flounced past, he caught her by the arm and made her look at him. "Listen to me. Whether he inherits Lincolnshire's fortune or not, Hamilton is going to be an earl.

He's going to need an heir. If he doesn't divorce you, he'll force you back into his house until you bear him a son."

She wrenched her arm out of his grasp. "He wouldn't."

"He told me so himself."

She rolled her eyes and continued on her way. "You're making this up to get me to do what you want."

"I'm not making anything up." He blocked her path as she turned back from the clothespress, a blue dress and a brown one clutched tight to her middle. "He threatened you, Deirdre, because I wouldn't go along with his plan. He knew I'd have to agree. And *you* know what the law says on the matter. He's your husband. If he demands you back"—he nearly choked on the next words—"in his bed…"

"I'd have no choice," she whispered, her face stark white.

She didn't resist when Sean lifted the dresses from her arms. Nor when he led her to the bed and pushed her down to sit. All her usual spirit and fire had left her.

He hated to see his big sister like this.

If they failed, she might look like this for the rest of her life.

He sighed and sat beside her. "You're already packed. Come play Mrs. Hamilton at Lincolnshire House. With any luck, it will be for the last time."

She was staring down at her hands, folded demurely in her lap in a most un-Deirdre-like manner. "You win," she said in a small voice.

But he didn't feel like a winner.

NINETEEN

$\mathcal{E}$ARLY MONDAY evening at Lincolnshire House, Corinna was cleaning her palette when she felt her hair swept aside. Felt warm lips pressed to the nape of her neck. A little thrill rippling through her, she whirled around to see Sean

"I had a good day," he said. "A productive day. Thank you."

His eyes were so green, so genuine. She was suddenly aware of how comfortable she felt looking into them—just looking. She met most people's eyes with a challenge or a jest. It felt strange and nice to be just looking.

He'd greeted her at the door at nine o'clock this morning, walked her into this salon, and laid a kiss on her that could have melted the Arctic.

"Was that worth getting up for?" he'd asked.

She'd nodded, having temporarily lost her powers of speech. And he'd laughed, then left to do whatever it was he did while she spent the whole day painting.

She felt melty again now, just looking into his eyes. She hoped he would kiss her again—on the lips instead of her neck —but instead he shifted his gaze past her. "I'm impressed."

For a moment she thought he was impressed with the salon.

It was a most unlikely room to use for painting, by far the most grandiose room in London's most grandiose house.

The salon was mostly blue, so she knew Sean could see just how gorgeous it was. Designed for lavish entertainments, it was decorated in the Italian style. Splendid blue and gold furniture matched ornate blue and gold curtaining that hung from gilt rods. The coved ceiling was painted in the palazzo manner, and the walls were broken up by alternating silk panels and mirrors in highly ornamental frames, their surfaces reflecting the room's sparkling gold and crystal chandeliers.

Though she'd laid down a tarpaulin, all day Corinna had feared she'd splatter paint and ruin something. But of all the rooms in the house, this one had the largest north-facing windows, so Lord Lincolnshire had insisted it was the best place to sit for his portrait.

Then her head cleared, and she realized Sean wasn't impressed with the salon. He was looking at her painting.

"I'm glad you like it," she said, turning to see it herself. She resumed wiping her palette. "But I've only just started, really."

"You started this morning, before I left. You've been working all day."

"Time flies when I'm involved in a painting. But I think I wore out poor Lord Lincolnshire. Two footmen helped him up to bed a couple of hours ago." She set the palette on the mosaic table she'd covered for her use. "Do you think it would be all right for me to leave everything here overnight?"

"I'm sure it will be fine. The man's unlikely to host a party anytime soon." He walked closer to the painting, peering at it. "You've laid in the basics of him already. And the background is amazing. So detailed. How did you do that so quickly?"

"Oh, that was already done." She began cleaning her brushes. "I've been working on it for days in the square. I just hadn't decided who to put into it."

He paused for a significant beat before he turned to her. "So you *wanted* to paint Lincolnshire. You didn't offer only to save my skin."

"You've caught me out." Swirling three brushes in turpentine, she grinned. "I think I'm finally going to complete a good portrait. One fine enough to put on display. I've always wanted to, but…"

"But what?"

"Girls don't usually, you know? Paint portraits, I mean. It's not considered very ladylike. We're supposed to paint only scenes and still lifes." Setting the brushes aside, she sighed. "I'm tired of painting apples and bottles and trees."

"You paint very good trees," he pointed out, gesturing toward her picture.

"I've had lots of practice," she said dryly.

"You have goals," he said. "I admire that."

"Everyone has goals. Of some sort."

"But your goals go beyond what's expected of a lady—of any woman. You'll have to overcome great odds to achieve them, and you're not letting that stop you. That's very admirable."

"Thank you," Corinna said softly, feeling her face heat. She'd never had a fellow say he admired her goals, let alone act like he believed she might actually achieve them.

Griffin was supportive, of course, but that was his job. He was her brother. And while she was sure he wished her the best —while she knew he wanted her happy—she'd never felt he truly expected her dreams to come to fruition.

Griffin believed her art was a hobby, something to keep her occupied until she married.

Sean, on the other hand, seemed to believe in *her*. And for that she felt overflowing gratitude. In fact, *her heart felt he was one of the most amiable, most pleasing of men,* just as Amanda's had in *Children of the Abbey.* Corinna feared she was staring in a most embarrassing, moony-eyed fashion, but she couldn't seem to help herself.

Holy Hannah, what was she doing?

She was letting this go too far. Sean was a nice young man—and a spectacular kisser—but he couldn't be anything more to her. She knew he wasn't the sort of husband Griffin wanted for her, no matter what her sisters said. And Corinna wasn't looking for a husband, anyway. Her art came first.

But she *really* wasn't ready to give up the kissing yet. They could still do that, she decided, as long as there were no more moony eyes.

Excellent.

That settled, she cleared her throat. "Thank you," she repeated. "I'm finished here and expected home for dinner. I'll be back tomorrow morning."

"At nine?"

"For another kiss, I'll be here at nine."

He laughed. "You aren't anything like I expected a marquess's daughter would be, do you know that?"

"I'm an artist," she said.

And he laughed again. "I'll walk you to the door."

Unusually for this mansion full of servants, the entrance hall was empty. Quincy wasn't there, and there were no footmen, no maids scurrying from one side of the house to the other.

"My sister will be here soon," Sean said quietly. "She's going to live here until this is all over."

"Will she?" Corinna asked, surprised.

"Lincolnshire's insisting upon meeting my wife. And she's Hamilton's actual wife, so..."

"So at least that one thing won't be a lie?"

"Exactly." Reaching the front door, he opened it. "But I'm afraid something will slip now that Deirdre's getting involved."

"You're not having second thoughts, are you?"

He shrugged, making it obvious he was.

She touched his arm. "*Please* don't reveal the secret. It might be easier, but it won't be best. I don't like keeping secrets either, you know. I feel terribly guilty keeping my brother in the dark."

"Don't tell him," he warned under his breath. "You promised."

"I remember. And that's why I haven't told him. But my sisters think we're doing the right thing, and I'm certain he would, too—"

"He wouldn't. He'd expose me posthaste; I'm sure of it."

"You don't know Griffin—"

"He's a marquess, isn't he? That's all I need to know. I'm everything the *ton* despises." Standing there in the open doorway, he raised a hand and began ticking off all the marks against him. "I'm Irish—"

"I told you, we're part Irish, too."

"What, a quarter?"

"Probably a tenth," she admitted, thinking it was probably even less than that.

He rolled his eyes and ticked off more fingers. "I'm untitled, I'm in trade, I earn more in a month than most of them earn in a year—"

"Really?" She'd had no idea he had *that* much money.

He looked mortified. Apparently he hadn't meant to let that slip.

She opened her mouth to question him further, but just then the wooden gate opened outside, and a young woman entered the courtyard.

Looking quite sure of herself, the woman crossed to the portico and mounted the steps. She was blond, green-eyed, and very pretty. Or at least, she looked like she'd be very pretty if she weren't scowling.

"Corinna, this is my sis—" Sean started, then stopped when the woman gave him a discreet little smack on the shoulder.

He turned to see Quincy approaching from inside the house.

"My wife has arrived," he said loudly instead.

TWENTY

*A*FTER INTRODUCING his "wife" to Corinna, who then took her leave, Sean marched Deirdre straight up to Lincolnshire's bedroom. He couldn't wait to get this farce over with.

"Uncle," he said, "this is Mrs. Hamilton. Deirdre, the Earl of Lincolnshire."

Deirdre curtsied. "It's pleased I am to meet you, Lord Lincolnshire."

"I'm so very pleased you've come." Struggling to sit taller against his mountain of pillows, Lincolnshire blinked and yawned. "Please excuse me. I sat all...day for a portrait, and I fear that...left me exhausted."

To Sean's relief, Deirdre didn't seem fazed by the man's shortness of breath. Nor did she seem repulsed by his ever-swelling body. "I understand that you're ill, my lord."

"I'm dying," Lincolnshire said in his plainspoken way.

"That, too. And it's sorry I am to hear it."

"No fault of...yours." The old man cocked his head. "You're Irish."

She exchanged a wary glance with Sean. "Born and raised in

Kilburton, sir. Your nephew married me while he was living in Ireland."

Lincolnshire nodded. "Kilburton is a pretty place."

"And how would you know that?" Deirdre raised a brow. "I don't recall your ever visiting."

Sean flinched. Deirdre never had been one to mince words. But Lincolnshire only laughed—a laugh that ended in a wheeze. "Haven't been there...since before you were born," he told her, and then added to Sean, "I like her."

Releasing a breath, Sean smiled and moved closer to his sister, wrapping an arm about her shoulders. "I like her, too."

"You should, considering...she's your wife. Whyever did you leave her in the countryside? She's...lovely." He grinned at Deirdre, the old flirt. "What a handsome couple you...two make. Give her a kiss!"

Sister and brother exchanged another look. One of panic.

"Go on," Lincolnshire urged, his eyes dancing.

Sean leaned down to Deirdre and gave her a peck on the cheek.

"Hmmph, that will never do," the earl said in disgust. "Word is you two...don't get along. Rumor has it you live apart."

Was that why Lincolnshire had insisted on meeting Hamilton's wife? Was he determined to see a reconciliation? "You've said that before," Sean reminded him. "Wherever did you hear it?"

"Everywhere. I'm dying, not deaf. And I won't countenance...such a relationship in Lincolnshire House." He paused, all but gasping for air, but when Deirdre went to open her mouth, he waved a hand to stop her. "All the Lincolnshire earls have been happily...married, and I mean to see...that tradition continue."

"You shouldn't listen to rumors," Sean protested. "I love Deirdre."

Which wasn't exactly a lie. Maybe not in *that* way, but he did love her.

"Then...kiss her...like a man," the old earl wheezed.

There was nothing for it.

Slowly, mournfully, Sean turned to face his doom. Deirdre looked as ill as he felt. She squeezed her eyes shut. He wished he could do the same, but he feared missing the target. Even worse than kissing his sister on the lips would be accidentally kissing her on the nostril...

He shuddered.

All right, man, just get it done. Sucking in a breath, he leaned down, fighting the nausea rising in his throat as he drew closer... and closer...until finally, with the lightest possible impact, and for the shortest possible instant, he touched his lips to hers.

When it was all over, Lincolnshire shook his head. "Before I expire...I want to see better than that."

Saints preserve us. Sean and Deirdre studiously avoided eye contact with each other. Sean felt a strong urge to gargle with whiskey.

If there was anything on earth that could drive him to drink, *this* would be it.

"And I've a favor...to ask of you," the earl went on.

"Anything, Uncle," Sean said. "Anything at all." So long as it didn't involve kissing his sister.

A weak smile twitched on the man's lips. "Were I you...I'd wait to hear it first." He paused for a breath, and then another. "I wish you to...keep this house—"

"I will. You have my word." Arrogant Hamilton wouldn't be selling the most impressive house in all of London. "You won't mind living here, will you, Deirdre?"

She glanced around in patent disbelief, taking in the towering damask-hung bed, the scenes painted on the ceiling, the gold-stamped leather wallcoverings. "What sort of knothead would mind living here?"

That prompted another smile. But Lincolnshire wasn't finished. "And all of my staff...in perpetuity."

Sean was tempted to agree for the sake of the old man's peace of mind, but he couldn't bring himself to add another lie to the heap. He glanced at Deirdre, murmuring, "The property has more than a hundred servants."

Her eyes widened. They both knew her husband didn't keep many servants. He was a fellow who valued his privacy. Even considering the grandness of the house, he would probably dismiss well above half—without blinking an eye, of course.

The weasel.

"Oh, Lord Lincolnshire," Deirdre said regretfully, "my husband doesn't like spending much time in London. The scenes he paints are all in the countryside—"

"And as I've told you many times, Uncle," Sean cut in, "my wife prefers the country as well." He threw his sister a significant look.

She caught on. "Yes, that's right. I'm just a country girl at heart. So you see, we won't be needing so many servants when we're not in residence here."

"Won't you keep them on anyway? For me, my dear. I cannot stand to think...these loyal people...*my* people...will be left out in the cold."

Exchanging a glance with his sister, Sean pulled a face.

"I need to know...this house will remain in your hands. And my staff...will retain their employment."

"I'll keep the house," Sean promised, "as I've said, although it's overly large for just Mrs. Hamilton and myself." Indeed, it would have been overly large for the entire village of Kilburton. "But as to the other—"

"Sean," Lincolnshire cut in gently. Beseechingly. "Did you not say...you would do anything for me?"

In the long silence that stretched between them, Sean's mind raced. Once the earl passed on, there was simply no way to force

Hamilton's hand. And they couldn't hope to appeal to his better nature, since he hadn't one to speak of. Was there another option? "What if I could find new employment for them all instead? Better employment?"

Lincolnshire gave a wee snort. "Better than working...for me?"

"Very well, I misspoke," Sean conceded. "I agree there's no kinder, more thoughtful employer. But—"

"There *are* humbler ones," Deirdre chimed in, earning a chortle from the earl.

Sean shot her a warning look. "But more prestigious positions exist. And..."

"And I won't...be here."

Sean nodded.

"How can you find them all...employment? You're an artist, not...a man of business."

"I know people. Trust me."

"I do," Lincolnshire said sincerely, making Sean writhe inside with guilt. "But I want...I need to know they're settled. That... they'll be happy."

"You will. I'll find them all employment."

"Better positions?"

"Better positions than they have now."

"Before I'm gone?"

"Before you're gone, Uncle. This I promise."

One promise he could keep. One promise he *would* keep.

The man nodded, apparently satisfied. "Now, as to you two."

Deirdre's eyes widened again. "What now?"

"I want to see you dance...at the Billingsgate ball...on Saturday."

TWENTY-ONE

APPLE PUFFS

Pare the fruit and bake them. When cold, mixe the pulp of the Apple with Sugar and lemon-peel shred fine, taking as little of the Apple-juice as you can. Orange marmalade is a great improvement. Put in paste with a little Sugar inside and on top. Bake in a quick oven a quarter hour until browne.

The homely apple is always dependable. Serve at family gatherings to assure harmony.
—Helena, Countess of Greystone, 1776

"A LOVELY first vintage." Lamplight glinted off deep ruby as Alexandra held up her glass on Tuesday night, toasting her brother during their family dinner at his Berkeley Square town house. "You did it, Griffin."

Her husband smiled. "A toast to England's newest wine producer."

"I don't know that *wine producer* is an appropriate description." Griffin grinned at his brother-in-law. Tristan had helped him save Cainewood's ailing vineyard. "Doesn't that imply producing enough wine that we could actually sell some of it?

We'll probably polish off this year's entire production within a week. Perhaps tonight."

Alexandra laughed. "You'll make more next year, and still more the year after that. Eventually there will be enough to sell."

"Charles would be proud," Juliana said.

Charles, their eldest brother, had planted the vines when he was the marquess. But he hadn't lived to see them bear fruit. Two years ago, when Charles died of consumption, Griffin had been forced to leave the cavalry. To come home to take Charles's place. To accept Charles's title. He'd also found himself saddled with the care of three unmarried sisters, a hodgepodge of mainly unprofitable properties, and a field full of dying grapevines.

Today the vines were thriving, he'd overhauled the family estate, and two of his sisters were happily wed. Not bad, Griffin thought, relishing a sip of the wine he'd helped create.

One by one, all of the pieces of his life were falling into place. Now he had only to find a husband for Corinna and puzzle out the mystery of Rachael's parenthood. He was making good progress on the latter. Having heard from his man today, he looked forward to giving Rachael the news when he saw her at the Billingsgate ball on Saturday.

Corinna, however, was another matter altogether.

Paint, paint, paint...all she ever wanted to do was paint. She clearly had little interest in finding a husband. He'd introduced her to countless fine young men, and though on the surface she seemed to cooperate, she always danced and smiled and moved on, never giving any of them a second thought.

All he wanted was her happiness. And girls were happier married, weren't they? But lately it seemed Corinna paid attention to just one gentleman. He'd be decent husband material, Griffin supposed—a little old, but wealthy, single, and kind...

If only he were expected to last out the week.

"Corinna has been spending a lot of time with Lord

Lincolnshire," he commented as Juliana served the apple puffs Alexandra had brought for dessert.

"I'm painting Lord Lincolnshire's portrait. I hope to submit it for the Summer Exhibition."

Juliana put another puff on a plate and moved to take it to her husband, James. "How is the poor dear?" she asked.

"Well enough, under the circumstances. He seems to be holding his own." Corinna paused for a sip of wine. "He's very happy to have his nephew keeping him company."

"His nephew?" James asked.

"Yes, his *nephew*," Corinna said pointedly.

"Hmm?" James frowned, but then his face cleared. "Oh, you mean Mr. Delaney."

Griffin cocked his head. "Who is Mr. Delaney?"

Juliana paused with the plate hovering over James, apparently torn between setting it before him or dropping it on his head. "That was a secret," she said between gritted teeth.

"Oh." He winced. "You didn't tell me."

Corinna glared daggers at her sister. "Why on earth did you tell *him*?"

"We don't keep secrets." Juliana wrung her hands with remorse. "We promised before our wedding."

"Well, when you tell a secret, you could at least tell that it *is* a secret!"

"I'm sorry," Juliana squeaked.

"Who is Mr. Delaney?" Griffin demanded.

Everyone else exchanged glances with each other, their expressions showing various levels of panic.

Corinna looked most anxious of all, so Griffin settled on her. "What the devil is this about?"

She gulped. "Well...the gentleman you met at Lady Partridge's ball—the one introduced to you as John Hamilton—is actually Mr. Hamilton's brother-in-law, Sean Delaney. Mr. Hamilton asked him—"

"Blackmailed him," Alexandra interrupted.

"Well, yes. He blackmailed him into posing as himself. As John Hamilton, I mean. Lord Lincolnshire's nephew. But now he's having second thoughts, even though it's the right thing, and—"

"I beg your pardon?" Griffin cut in.

None of this made sense. The name, Sean Delaney, seemed familiar. Yet the gentleman introduced as John Hamilton at Lady Partridge's ball hadn't seemed familiar at all. In fact, Griffin was certain he'd never set eyes on that fellow before in his life.

More confused than ever, he swung toward his old friend Tristan. "Did you know about this, too?"

"Not all of it." Looking down, Tristan speared a bite. "And only for a short while."

"A short while," Griffin growled.

"*You* told your husband, too?" Corinna turned her glare on Alexandra.

Alexandra released an exasperated sigh. "The apple puffs aren't working."

"Come again?" Tristan asked.

"They're supposed to assure harmonious family gatherings."

Tristan and James both looked amused. Griffin wasn't. "Would someone *please* explain—"

"Excuse me a moment," Juliana interrupted. "And don't you dare discuss anything in my absence. I'll be right back."

While she was visiting the water closet, or wherever else she might have rushed off to—Juliana was a girl, so her brother didn't dare inquire—Griffin shoveled apple puff into his mouth and fumed.

Everyone seemed to know what was going on except for him.

"Explain," he demanded when she returned. "And don't leave anything out."

Between them, with much jumbled back-and-forthness, his three sisters explained.

And explained.

And explained.

A quarter hour later, when they finally finished, Corinna paused for a breath. "You won't give away Mr. Delaney's secret, will you? Not only would it threaten his sister's divorce, but it would also upset poor Lord Lincolnshire."

"I don't know," Griffin grated out. His sisters' hearts seemed in the right place, but none of this sat quite right with him. "I don't like tricking that kindly old man."

"You're not the one tricking him," Juliana said. "You're only allowing someone *else* to trick him."

"Which is nearly as bad. And certainly not honorable."

Alexandra shook her head. "Caring for Lord Lincolnshire's happiness is the very definition of honor."

"It's lying," Griffin said flatly.

Now Corinna shook her head. "It's only failing to reveal the truth."

Girls and their illogical logic.

Griffin was opening his mouth to say as much when a footman stepped into the dining room. "A caller, my lord. A Mr. Sean Delaney."

"What a coincidence," Griffin said. "Show him in."

Corinna snorted. "It's not a coincidence."

"I sent a message to Lincolnshire House," Juliana explained. "I told Mr. Delaney that you're aware of his true identity and there's something we need to discuss."

"So that's what you were doing when you went off." Tristan said. "I wondered."

James shrugged. "I thought she was visiting the water closet."

"We should have guessed," Griffin muttered. "It's Juliana, after all."

Both his brothers-in-law nodded in agreement. They well knew Juliana.

When Mr. Delaney walked in, Corinna motioned to a footman to fetch him a chair, then scooted over so it could be placed beside her own.

A tall young man, Delaney looked like he spent all his free hours in Gentleman Jackson's boxing salon. Griffin wouldn't care to challenge him to a match. And he was even more certain they weren't acquainted. "Had we already met?" he asked him. "Before Lady Partridge's ball?"

Delaney gave a little bow before he sat. "Not that I recall, my lord."

The fellow had a distinct Irish accent, and Griffin hadn't come across many Irishmen. "Yet your name seems familiar."

"Is it?" Although he took the glass of wine Corinna handed him, Delaney didn't drink from it as he seemed to consider. "I think I may have bought a piece of property from you. Last year, through your solicitor, which explains why we never met."

"Ah." Now Griffin remembered seeing the name on the contract. "A tumbledown boardinghouse near Lincoln's Inn Fields, it was. Cannot imagine why my father and brother held on to it for so long. I was pleased to get rid of it."

"I take it you haven't been by there of late." A corner of Delaney's mouth twitched as though he were holding back a grin. Or a smirk. "That *tumbledown boardinghouse* is now a beautifully restored four-story building with sixteen tenants. Shops and offices on the ground floor, residential above." He looked to Corinna. "I received your note. What is it you feel we need to discuss?"

"It was *my* note," Juliana said. "And you've been summoned in order to persuade both you and my brother that your posing as John Hamilton is the very best thing."

Which she proceeded to do, of course, with the help of her sisters.

Though Griffin didn't know Delaney, he thought him a quick-witted fellow. Together they put up a good fight. In the end, however, they both reluctantly agreed to preserve Lincolnshire's happiness for his final few days.

It was inevitable, Griffin supposed.

Three stubborn Chase ladies against two hapless gentlemen was nowhere near a fair match.

TWENTY-TWO

"*V*ERY HANDSOME gentleman," Juliana commented as Corinna came off the Billingsgates' dance floor Saturday night. "Who is he? Have you kissed him?"

"I cannot remember his name. Lord Stonehurst, or maybe Lord Brickhaven? Something to do with building materials." Corinna watched the young man walk away, expecting Griffin to bring another one by at any moment. "And no, I didn't kiss him," she added. "I just met him, for heaven's sake."

"Tonight?" Juliana's smile was a tad too innocent. "Then I expect you'll make him wait a week?"

"At least," Corinna confirmed, tilting her chin up. She'd once told her sister she never let gentlemen kiss her right after meeting them; she made them wait at least a week. But the awful truth was that since she'd started kissing Sean, she hadn't wanted to kiss anyone else.

Which meant that for the last three days, she'd been rudely deprived of kissing altogether. Lord Lincolnshire was so anxious to see his portrait finished before he passed on that he'd been ready and waiting when she arrived each morning at nine, thwarting her usual morning kiss. And although the earl tired easily and went up to bed every afternoon, Sean never returned before it was time for Corinna to go home.

Lord Lincolnshire had taken his rest extra early today, because he was bringing Sean and Deirdre here tonight. He'd told Corinna he wanted to see his nephew "dance with his lovely wife." Corinna was very much looking forward to their arrival, not least because she hoped to get Sean alone and make up for lost time.

The odd thing was, normally when one of her favorites was making himself scarce, she'd lose interest and move on to someone else. But tonight she couldn't seem to muster even a thimbleful of admiration for any other gentleman. It seemed she belonged to Sean in a sense, or he to her.

For now.

It was just a bit of harmless fun, after all.

But perhaps that was what made it so thrilling—the illicit and fleeting nature of their relationship made her feel like a true, free-spirited artist. All this passion and yearning was sure to enhance her work! Hopefully it was already serving to improve Lord Lincolnshire's portrait.

Although, she couldn't say she'd been feeling particularly passionate while painting it. But maybe it wasn't a conscious thing?

In any case, she felt just like a Minerva Press heroine caught up in a torrid affair, and she was enjoying herself immensely. Especially now that the danger of the moony eyes had passed. She hadn't mooned even once since that day in the salon. She was completely in control.

And even if she wasn't...

Well, yesterday she'd casually—just out of curiosity—asked Griffin what he thought of Mr. Delaney, and he'd said he was impressed with the fellow's business sense and was hoping to buttonhole him sometime soon to ask him for advice regarding property management.

In other words, he hadn't sounded at all disapproving.

Which didn't mean she wanted to marry Sean. She didn't. It just meant that she maybe *could*. If, one day—after she'd accomplished everything she'd set out to do with her art—she happened to change her mind.

It was just nice to have options, that was all.

Thinking of her brother made her realize he seemed to have abandoned the Billingsgate ballroom. For now, at least, he wasn't shoving any potential suitors at her. She relaxed a little bit. "Do you know where Griffin went off to?" she asked her sister.

"I don't. Who is that woman?" Juliana gestured with a flick of her dark blond head. "The one who just came in with Lord Lincolnshire and Mr. Del—um...Mr. Hamilton."

They were here! And fortunately no one was nearby to hear Juliana's stumble. "That's Deirdre," Corinna whispered. "His sister. We were introduced earlier this week, but I haven't found a chance to actually talk to her. She never seems to be around in the daytimes when I'm at Lincolnshire House painting."

"Let's talk to her now," Juliana said.

Corinna wasn't sure that was a good idea, since Sean feared his sister might slip up and give them away in front of Lord Lincolnshire. But she had no choice. In her usual decisive manner, Juliana was already heading their way.

"Lady Corinna!" he wheezed when they arrived, grinning up at her from his wheelchair. "And Lady Stafford. Please...allow me to introduce Mrs. Hamilton, the next...Countess of Lincolnshire."

Behind him, Sean shifted uncomfortably. But Deirdre *was* Mrs. Hamilton, after all. And she *would* be the next Countess of Lincolnshire—at least until she managed to secure her divorce.

"It's a pleasure to meet you," Juliana told Deirdre.

"It's my pleasure to meet you. I've been hearing so much about your family, especially your sister."

Corinna flushed, wondering what Sean might have told his

sister about her. But then she realized it was probably Lord Lincolnshire who'd done the talking. She was painting him, after all, and he was rather thrilled about that.

"Mr. Hamilton!" Lady Ainsworth, a tall woman who looked even taller wearing a golden turban, bustled over. "What a delight to see you again! What are you painting these days, if I might ask?"

"A landscape," Sean said.

"A landscape!" Lady Ainsworth's loud guffaw drew more people to their circle. Apparently Sean's celebrity had yet to wear off. "Have you ever painted anything that *wasn't* a land-scape, Mr. Hamilton?"

"I suppose I haven't."

"You suppose?" Lady Ainsworth's laugh was really quite annoying. "What is it a landscape *of?*" she asked.

"It's a meadow scene," Corinna said.

Lady Hartshorn turned to her. She was a short, round woman who had very arched brows at the moment. "You've *seen* it?"

"I have." Corinna smiled at Lady Hartshorn's obvious envy. "The trees are exquisite, their shadows most intriguing."

"Speaking of intriguing shadows," a gentleman said, looking to Sean, "I've been wondering about *Allegory of Shadow.*"

"I beg your pardon?"

"*Allegory of Shadow.* Your most famous painting?"

"Oh, yes." Sean's own laugh sounded rather forced. "Of course. I was still thinking about my new painting, I fear. Once I finish a piece, I tend to put it out of my mind."

"May I ask what inspired you? What made you decide to focus so on the shadows?"

"The, ah...the trees. I've always found trees very inspiring. Lush trees of the English countryside that grow from wee acorns to cast large shadows—"

"But Mr. Hamilton," Lady Ainsworth interrupted, her turban bobbing indignantly. "I don't recall seeing any trees in *Allegory of*

Shadow. Its central subject is a stone circle, isn't it? And not in England, but in Ireland, I do believe?"

"Well, I was raised in Ireland—"

"Exactly," Corinna cut in. "Allegories are symbolic representations, as you know. If one looks closely, one will see that the shadows cast by the standing stones resemble trees. English trees."

"Oh," the woman said.

"I cannot believe you didn't know that," Lady Hartshorn scoffed. "It's brilliant, Mr. Hamilton. Simply brilliant. How long did you take to paint it?"

"Three days, my lady."

"Three *days*? The thing is the size of a drawing room wall! The largest painting in the history of the Summer Exhibition, wasn't it?"

"When one is inspired," Corinna said, "the image simply flows from the hand through the brush. I myself have completed a painting in a single day." Once. One tiny painting, no more than eight inches square. *Allegory of Shadow* was eight feet by sixteen, at the very least. "Have you ever painted, Lady Hartshorn?"

"No. No, I haven't."

"I thought not," Corinna said in a superior tone of voice that shut her up.

Just then Lord Lincolnshire coughed. And coughed again.

"Do you need something to drink, Uncle?" Sean took the back of his chair, looking not at all upset to have a route of escaping this conversation. "Let me take you to the refreshment room."

Without the celebrated Mr. Hamilton as a point of focus, the gathering quickly dispersed. Shifting uneasily, Deirdre watched her brother wheel the earl off.

"Would you like to go outside, Mrs. Hamilton?" Juliana asked her kindly. "Lord Billingsgate has a lovely garden."

"Oh, yes," Deirdre said, sounding grateful. "I would like that very much."

"Why don't you take her?" Juliana suggested to Corinna, her gaze straying to where her husband stood in a circle of men engaged in a heated argument. All members of Parliament, no doubt. "I think I shall rescue James by asking him for a dance."

Corinna nodded, taking Deirdre's arm to steer her around the perimeter of the dance floor, toward French doors that opened to the terrace. "Thank you," Sean's sister breathed when they finally made it outside. "I'm thinking I don't really belong in there, do I?"

Corinna led her down a path where twinkling lanterns hung overhead. "Whyever would you say that?"

"I'm a vicar's daughter from a tiny village in Ireland. I've no place in London society."

"You're married to John Hamilton."

"In name only," Deirdre said darkly. "He hasn't paid me any mind since…well, for a long time."

In all the time since Deirdre lost their baby, Corinna knew. Although Sean had told her little about himself, he'd spent much time explaining Deirdre's situation and how it had led to the mess they were in now. She wasn't surprised Deirdre didn't wish to speak of it. "You have every right to be here. And at least you probably know more about art than your brother."

"I know less about my husband's art than you might think. You did a grand job deflecting those questions. I can see why Sean admires you."

Sean had told her that? Corinna's heart skipped at the thought. "I'm surprised to hear he said so."

"Not in so many words, mind you. But he told me all about you, and I know my little brother."

"He likes my paintings."

Deirdre laughed. "He doesn't care a fig about art. But he likes that you aren't afraid to have big dreams and work hard to achieve them. He's the same himself, you know. Everyone in Kilburton thought he was daft to come to London. He told us all —this skinny sixteen-year-old who could barely even grow a mustache—he told us all he was going to 'build an empire.' And that's exactly what he did."

Corinna was impressed. She'd had no idea Sean began his operation at sixteen. Why, he'd been younger than she was now! She hadn't brought Deirdre out here for an interrogation, but since the topic had been introduced...

"However did he manage it?" Corinna asked eagerly.

Deirdre shrugged. "He says he has a knack."

"A knack?"

"I don't know what he means, exactly. All I can tell you is that right after I wed John, Sean left our village, Kilburton, with a small inheritance he'd received from our uncle."

"And?"

"The next time I saw him, he owned several properties, including his own house. Eighteen years old, and he had his own house." She shook her head disbelievingly. "I didn't get to see Sean often, since John hates London. Once a year, maybe, if that. But the next time I saw Sean, he owned more property, and some manufactories, and any number of other businesses. Ships, too. And a bigger house. And, a couple of years later, a bigger one still."

"Holy Hannah, he owns all of that? No wonder he's so busy! He must work very hard," Corinna marveled. "Tell me more."

Deirdre looked her up and down, her lips stretching into a wide, knowing smile. "I think you should ask him yourself."

TWENTY-THREE

"**G**RIFFIN," RACHAEL said. "What are you doing here?"

In his cousins' Lincoln's Inn Fields town house, Griffin stopped pacing the drawing room and turned to see her leaning against the doorjamb. Even in a simple day dress, she looked utterly, unmistakably sultry. Her lips had a rosy-red sheen. Her dark hair fell in soft waves around her face. Her eyes looked large and luminous.

And sad.

"I'm waiting for you, as I suspect your butler told you. Why aren't you at the Billingsgate ball?"

"I didn't feel like going," she said.

The look on her face was gut-wrenching, but Griffin welcomed the anxiety it sparked in him. Concern was much safer than lust. "You cannot withdraw from life, Rachael."

"I'm not." She took in his evening clothes. "Why did you *leave* the Billingsgate ball?"

"To fetch you."

"What if I don't want to be fetched?"

He shrugged and said nonchalantly, "Then I won't tell you my news."

"What news?" she demanded, straightening and coming toward him. "Tell me."

"I'll tell you on the way to the ball," he promised her with a smile—the charming smile that worked on everyone.

But it didn't work on Rachael. Not tonight. "I don't want to go to the ball."

"Then I don't want to tell you my news. I'll stop by again tomorrow."

"Griffin!" Moving closer, she laughingly punched him on the shoulder. "You cannot do this to me!"

He was happy to see her more animated, but that wasn't enough. He wanted her joyful. He wanted her socializing. He wanted to see her dancing with eligible gentlemen and getting on with her life.

"Would you care to bet?" he asked, starting from the room.

She grabbed his arm. "All right, I'll go to the ball."

"Excellent." With any luck, she'd meet a fellow this very night. Then it wouldn't matter that she wasn't his cousin, because she'd be taken anyway. "I'll wait here while you change."

"Oh, no, you won't." Still holding his arm, she pulled him toward a sofa. "Tell me what you learned. Now." With both hands, she pushed him to sit. "What in blazes are you waiting for?"

"Has anyone ever told you you're demanding?"

"Most everyone." She sat beside him and licked her lips. "Did the man you hired find my father's parents?"

"Hmm? Oh, right, the news." He cleared his throat. "Grimbald's mother is dead, but my man found his father. His name is Thomas, same as his son. Colonel Thomas Grimbald—he was a military man, too."

She nodded, looking vulnerable in a way that made him want to hug her. "Is he still living in Yorkshire?"

"Not anymore. He's living at the Royal Hospital in Chelsea."

"So close," she murmured. The Royal Hospital wasn't a hospital for the ill, but rather a government-funded home for pensioned soldiers. "I have a grandfather so close, and I never knew it." She licked her lips again, making Griffin clench his teeth. "I want to see him. I want to meet him and find out if my father really committed treason."

"I'm glad," he said. It was better to know than to stay in denial. "I'll take you Monday. No, Tuesday. I've got a meeting with my solicitor on Monday. I'm sorry."

"You're entitled to live your own life. I can wait. I've waited twenty-one years already."

"I guess you have. Now *I'll* wait while you change for the ball."

She sighed. "You're not really going to hold me to that, are you? I don't want to dance, so what's the point in going? I don't feel up to having men paw me."

"They wouldn't dare. I'd issue a challenge on the spot."

"To a duel? Just what I need…your death on my head."

"You think I would lose? You wound me." He playfully clutched his heart. "Get changed. You can dance with me," he offered, vaguely wondering why on earth he was doing this to himself. "Nothing but innocent, cousinly dances."

And more teeth clenching.

TWENTY-FOUR

*T*HE BILLINGSGATES had a rather impressive art collection, one Corinna had spent several happy hours viewing during the Billingsgates' ball last season. But this year, although she once again found herself stationed in their picture gallery, she hadn't the time to look at any paintings.

She was too busy trying to keep Sean afloat.

A pack of eager Hamilton admirers had managed to herd the poor fellow in here over many polite protests. To say he was unhappy with this turn of events would be an understatement—from the look on his face, you'd think he was having his teeth pulled out one by one. Corinna was frankly astonished he hadn't yet bolted for the door.

And she wasn't enjoying herself any more than he was. All she'd wanted was a few minutes alone with Sean—and his lips. She wanted to talk to him without everyone's eyes on the two of them. She wanted him to look at her without it being a look of panic. Was that so much to ask?

Apparently, it was, because they'd been stuck here for over an hour with no end in sight. Every excuse for escape that Sean and Corinna could think of had been brushed aside by his hang-ers-on. And Lord Lincolnshire was being equally uncooperative.

"Wouldn't you care for some air, Uncle?" Sean asked for the third time.

"Oh, no. I'm…enjoying this conversation."

No doubt he was basking in the reflected glow of his nephew's greatness. Well, good for him. But Corinna was begin-ning to run out of creative interpretations for Sean's brilliant "insights." Among other blunders, he'd mistaken a watercolor for an oil painting and described a William Hogarth piece as a "groundbreaking new work."

When Hogarth had been dead since 1764.

"It was groundbreaking when it *was* a new work," Corinna explained. Everyone nodded, their faces arranged into intelli-gent-looking expressions, as if they'd got his meaning all along and, incidentally, quite agreed.

"Oh, I do adore mythology as the subject for a painting," Lady Trevelyan said as they moved on to the next piece of art. "What do you think of this one by Kauffmann, Mr. Hamilton?"

"Very detailed," Sean said—a safe enough comment. But then he added, "I admire his—"

"His?"

"Joshua Reynolds, he means," Corinna rushed to say. "Am I right, Mr. Hamilton? You were referring to Sir Joshua Reynolds, since *Angelica* Kauffmann was one of his protégées?"

"Joshua Reynolds, yes." He sent her a grateful smile. "As I was saying, I admire Reynolds for being open-minded enough to recognize a talented female artist."

"Indeed." Corinna nodded, wondering if he might be talking about her. "Although, of course, Kauffmann was widely recog-nized as one of the founders of the Royal Academy. One of only two female Academicians in its history, in fact."

Sean's smile widened. "I look forward to your being the third."

He really *did* want to see her succeed. She held his gaze. "I appreciate your support," she said softly.

Drat. She was moony-eyed again, wasn't she?

She blinked the expression away fiercely.

A gentleman cleared his throat. "Speaking of Reynolds," he said, moving along to stand before two large portraits. "What do you think, Mr. Hamilton, of Reynolds's work as compared to Gainsborough's?"

"Hmm." Corinna saw Sean glance at the artists' signatures. "This Gainsborough is rather sentimental, is it not, while the Reynolds here is, ah, more grand. Establishing the importance of the man portrayed rather than sympathy with the subject."

Though Sean looked rather proud of his analysis, the questioner frowned. "I meant in *general*, Mr. Hamilton, not these particular portraits. One man's body of work juxtaposed against the other."

"I do not judge entire bodies of work, sir. I never seek signatures prior to evaluating a painting. Each work should stand on its own—the artist's identity shouldn't influence my opinion of any specific picture."

The gentleman was clearly taken aback. "I thought all artists studied the masters' techniques."

Corinna didn't quite know what to say to that, so she was relieved when Juliana stepped in. "Ah, there is your mistake, Lord Prescott," she called out charmingly. "You suppose there are conventions that *all* artists conform to. But seeing as they're known to be unconventional creatures, wouldn't it be rather safer to suppose that whenever a particular approach becomes a convention, the artist will instantly cease employing it?"

A round of laughter followed this speech, and the original question was quite forgotten.

Thank goodness for sisters, Corinna thought. She smiled at Lord Lincolnshire, who was laughing as heartily as anyone. He blinked madly. And then he coughed. And coughed again. A bit of froth appeared on his lips.

The laughter died down as, looking anxious, Sean dug out a handkerchief and dabbed at the earl's mouth. "I really think you need some air, Uncle. I insist."

"Take me to the...doors, then. And...let me see...you dance" —gasping, he looked to Deirdre—"with your wife."

Corinna was anxious, too. "He cannot even get three syllables out before needing a breath," she said to Juliana as they followed Sean, Deirdre, and Lord Lincolnshire into the ballroom. "Maybe you should ask James to have a look at him." Besides being an earl, Juliana's husband was also a physician.

"I'm sure Lord Lincolnshire has his own doctors."

"But he's getting worse."

"He's dying," her sister reminded her gently.

"But he might die before I finish his portrait, and he really wants to see it completed."

Juliana sighed. "All right. I'll ask James."

"Thank you," Corinna said.

They watched Sean wheel Lord Lincolnshire over to the open French doors, then turn to Deirdre and reluctantly escort her to the dance floor. The musicians struck up a country tune.

Corinna breathed a sigh of relief. "Thank goodness it isn't a waltz."

"Why is that?" Juliana asked.

"Sean cannot waltz to save his life."

"Sean?"

"Mr. Delaney," Corinna corrected quickly. "And thank you for stepping in to save him. With any luck, that was the last in our long series of close calls."

A slow smile curved her sister's lips. "*Our*, hmm?"

"Yes, our. You, me, Mr. Delaney, Alexandra, Griffin. We're all in this together. All of us who know the secret."

Juliana's smile remained. "*Our* could also mean just you and

Sean—I mean, Mr. Delaney." Now her smile widened at her own deliberate mistake. "The two of you belong together, you know. Anyone can see it."

"We do not." The last thing Corinna wanted was her meddlesome sister interfering. "He's not from our world, Juliana. Griffin would never agree."

"Griffin has nothing against the gentleman. In fact, he said he admires him. I asked him what he thought of Mr. Delaney earlier this evening, before he left and came back with Rachael."

Rachael and Griffin were dancing together now. Of course, Juliana was looking rather smug about *that* relationship's progress. And Corinna wasn't at all surprised to hear her sister had questioned Griffin about Sean, either. "Mr. Delaney is colorblind. He cannot even appreciate my paintings."

"There's something between the two of you," Juliana insisted.

"A mutual desire to see Lord Lincolnshire happily through his last days, that's all."

Her sister shrugged. "If you say so," she said agreeably, without sounding like she really agreed at all.

"Holy Hannah," Corinna muttered. "Go dance with your husband, will you? And don't forget to ask him to have a look at Lord Lincolnshire."

TWENTY-FIVE

*S*EAN HAD decided that the day he'd brought Lincolnshire to Hamilton's studio hadn't been the longest one of his life, after all.

This blasted ball felt at least a week longer.

Escorting Deirdre off the dance floor, he noticed Corinna standing by the open French doors. She caught his eye, motioning her head toward the Billingsgates' garden before slipping outside.

Sean brought Deirdre in the same direction, walking her back to Lincolnshire. "Are you enjoying the fresh air, Uncle?"

"Very much. And…I enjoyed…seeing you dance."

"We enjoyed the dance, too." For the earl's benefit, Sean smiled at his sister and kissed her on the cheek. "I'm feeling a wee bit overheated, though. Would you mind keeping my wife company while I step outdoors for a moment?"

"Not at all," Lincolnshire said, reaching for Deirdre's hand.

Leaving the two of them, Sean entered the garden, knowing he definitely shouldn't, and immediately spotted Corinna on a path lit with twinkling lanterns. Beckoning for him to follow, she disappeared.

He considered turning back, but having come this far, he didn't think it fair to leave her waiting. Following the sound of her light, running footsteps, he found her quite a distance down the path and off to the side, in the darkness of a small stand of trees. Though the area was shadowed, he could see the outline of a familiar, shapely figure in a slim, high-waisted dress. He walked closer, telling himself he shouldn't touch her, knowing he would anyway.

Her scent drifted to him through the starlit night, flowery and sweet, with that barest trace of astringent that reminded him she wasn't just a normal girl. She was an artist, a talented young woman who went her own way. But beneath that, she was also an aristocrat, sheltered and immaculate, a girl who had never wanted for anything. Like a bright, shiny new coin, her perfection drew him. She was part of a world that was so high above him, so out of reach.

A world where he'd never belong.

He knew that, and it was the reason he'd done his best to stay away from her the past few days. He'd kissed her three times already—four if he counted kissing her neck—and he knew that was three or four times times too many.

He also knew she didn't feel the same hesitation. She was impulsive and eager. When he drew close and she playfully reached out to run a fingertip along his jaw, he wasn't the least bit surprised. She smiled warmly, impishly, and that made him smile too, drawing him even closer. She went straight into his arms.

It was overwhelming, almost frightening, the effect her nearness had on him. But the fear didn't stop him from giving in and taking what he wanted. It didn't stop him from running his hands down her back to feel the warmth of her skin through the thin material of her dress, from wrapping her in his arms and dragging her body against him, from slanting his mouth so he could press her even closer.

When they broke apart, they were both breathless. She stayed near and laid her head upon his chest. "I've missed you these past three days," she said softly.

"It's sorry I am for that." He *was* sorry for disappointing her, and also for letting things get to the point where she'd miss him. But weak-willed as he was, he couldn't stop his arms from stealing around her anyway. "I've had things I've had to do."

"What things?" She pulled back far enough to gaze up at him, her blue eyes looking black in the darkness. "What do you do, Sean, exactly?"

"Lately, very little of what I *should* be doing. Now Lincolnshire has asked me to find new positions for all of his many servants. Well, actually he asked me to keep all his servants after he passed, but Hamilton isn't going to do that, so I told him I'd find positions for them instead. So that's what I've been doing. Finding placements for them all." He smiled down at her, and because he couldn't help himself, he gave her another kiss. A short, gentle one. "Thank you for keeping him busy and making that possible."

"It sounds like a horrible imposition. You'll be glad when this is all over, won't you?"

"Very glad." Although he wondered if he would ever see her again. How he possibly could. And how he would bear it if he couldn't. "I'll miss seeing you, though, when it's over," he admitted.

She sighed and laid her head back down. Her arms stole back around him. "I think we'll see each other again. My brother wants to talk to you. He wants to ask your advice about property management."

"Does he now?"

"He likes you. He's impressed with your business sense."

"I didn't think marquesses were interested in business."

"They're not, mostly, but Griffin's a little different. He never wanted to be the marquess. He likes keeping busy. He was in the cavalry, you know, before our older brother died. An officer. He led campaigns in the Peninsular War. And he complains about the burden of a marquess's responsibilities, but I think the truth is he feels a bit useless now. He'd much rather be challenged, be doing something that feels important."

"Managing property can be very challenging." Cainewood sounded like a fellow he might get along with. And if the fellow got along with him as well, then…

There was no sense thinking in that direction. There were other obstacles to consider besides Cainewood's approval. Many obstacles. "We'd best get back," he said reluctantly, pulling away and taking her hand to lead her out of the trees. "Or people will come looking for us."

"That wouldn't be good," she agreed, trailing along without resistance. "Juliana would come looking for us first, and then who knows what would happen." While he was wondering what she meant by that, they turned onto the path. "I liked what you said in the picture gallery."

"In the picture gallery? Saints preserve us. You liked the part where I was blathering like an idiot or the part where I was tongue-tied like an idiot?"

"The part where you said that an artist's work should stand on its own, that his identity—or hers—shouldn't dictate the viewer's opinion of any particular piece." Her small hand soft and warm in his, she looked up at him and smiled. "Wherever did you come up with that?"

"Hamilton," he admitted, not bothering to hide his disgust. "Hamilton said something very like that, and I remembered it. In my desperation to sound artistic, I just blurted it out."

"I know he's a despicable human being, but I'm so very glad to hear that. It makes it so much more likely that he'll vote for my painting."

Sean didn't think so. She didn't know the rest of what Hamilton had said—the part about girls never painting good portraits. But he wasn't going to tell her that, not now. He wasn't going to ruin whatever time they had left together.

"He should be back by now," he told her instead, pulling his hand from hers as the house came into sight. Faint snatches of music floated to them from the open French doors. "He said he'd be gone two weeks, and it was two weeks on Thursday. But instead of coming home to deal with the mess he caused, he sent a letter."

She clasped her hands before her, as if to make sure she kept them to herself. "That's just as well. If he came home now, he might ruin his uncle's last days. What did the letter say?"

"He's painting the Lady of the Waterfall, and he doesn't want to leave. But I'm suspecting the lady he doesn't want to leave is the lady of the house." The weasel. "He told me not to worry; he'll be home well before the Summer Exhibition vote."

"I don't expect you were worrying," Corinna said. "You obviously cannot do the voting for him. Just like you cannot come to Lady Avonleigh's reception next week in his place. Ten days," she added with a sigh as they approached the open French doors, instinctively moving to put an appropriate amount of distance between them. "In ten days my painting will be turned in and Mr. Hamilton will come home."

"He should return before that. He said he'd be here well before the vote."

"Then in fewer than ten days, you'll be free."

Sean wouldn't be free until Lincolnshire passed, whether or not Hamilton had arrived.

But he didn't want to say so. He didn't want to think about losing the dear, sainted old earl. He would miss him.

But not as much as he'd miss Corinna.

TWENTY-SIX

"*H*OW DOES LORD Lincolnshire fare today?" Sean asked as he returned to the earl's house late Monday afternoon.

Quincy sighed mournfully. "I know not. Perhaps you should ask his new physician."

"New physician?"

"He's with him now. Second doctor to visit today."

Alarmed, Sean headed for the crystal staircase. Glimpsing Corinna inside the salon as he passed, he was tempted to stop. But her back was to him, and she looked absorbed, humming tunelessly while dabbing at her canvas.

And the earl's health took precedence anyway.

Sean took the steps two at a time, wincing at the sound of Lincolnshire's cough. Apparently hearing her brother's footsteps, Deirdre hurried out into the corridor. "You're back early today," she whispered.

"He wasn't doing well this morning."

"That's why I decided to stay home with him. He was sitting for Lady Corinna when he started coughing blood. Just a wee bit, but..."

"A wee bit is too much."

She nodded. "Lady Corinna sent him upstairs. Nurse Skeffington summoned his doctor, and then Lord Stafford arrived, too. Dr. Dalton was livid." Her eyes were wide. "He packed up his leeches and left."

"His leeches?" Sean pulled a face before registering the rest of Deirdre's words. "Lord Stafford? Corinna's brother-in-law?"

She nodded again. "Lady Corinna sent him a note. He's in with Lord Lincolnshire now." She ushered Sean into the room.

"My recommendation is that the leeches and bleeding and blistering be stopped," Lord Stafford was telling the earl as they walked in. "It's your choice, of course, but I don't believe those treatments will accomplish anything, except to make you even more uncomfortable."

Lincolnshire's nod set off another fit of coughing.

"There now." Lifting a cup off the earl's bedside table, Lord Stafford leaned closer and held it to his lips. "Have a little sip for me, will you? It will soothe your throat, and the warmth will ease your lungs." He straightened and looked to Sean. "Good afternoon, Mr. Hamilton."

Considering the gentleman knew he wasn't Hamilton, he'd said that smoothly, Sean thought. "Thank you for attending him. I thought you ran a smallpox facility?"

"I do spend most days vaccinating. But I also see a few very special patients." He looked back to Lincolnshire with a kind smile. "Another sip for me, as a favor?"

The earl took a very tiny one.

"He doesn't have but a wee appetite," Deirdre said.

"He's sure to be nauseous," Stafford explained. "Although we cannot see it, of course, his internal organs will be swelling along with those parts we can see. He won't be wanting to eat much, but you should encourage him to take what he can. Especially the tea."

"We will," Sean said. "And we shouldn't allow Dr. Dalton to apply more leeches, then?"

Stafford shook his head. "In my opinion, they're ineffective at best."

"And at worst?"

"They'd only bring on the end faster," he said grimly. "Better to let things progress naturally and do what we can to keep the patient comfortable. But I don't expect Dr. Dalton will be returning in any case." Stafford set a gentle hand on the earl's shoulder. "I'll be attending Lord Lincolnshire now."

Lincolnshire gave him a fatigued smile. "Thank you," he whispered, closing his eyes.

"Think nothing of it. I'd do anything for you—just like everyone else who's had the good fortune to be part of your life."

Not Hamilton, Sean thought darkly, watching the earl's breathing even out as he drifted off to sleep. His head lolled against the pillows. Despite his show of good cheer, Lincolnshire was weakening. He wouldn't last much longer. Though Sean regretted spending the day out of the house, he'd needed to talk to his people, to figure out where more of Lincolnshire's servants could be placed. He wanted to fulfill the earl's wishes before he passed.

Stafford dropped his stethoscope into his black leather bag and fastened it with a *snap*. "I'll return in the morning. I trust Nurse Skeffington to take good care of him in the meantime."

Deirdre nodded at the sturdy woman hovering nearby. "Sure, and she will. And Sean and I will be caring for him, too."

Lord Lincolnshire's actual niece by marriage, Deirdre was proving more devoted than Sean had expected. More trustworthy than he'd expected. Perhaps his big sister had grown up more than he'd thought. He gave her a faint smile of approval before following Stafford downstairs.

The two gentleman paused at the salon door. Corinna still

had her back turned, but she wasn't painting anymore. She wasn't humming, either. She just stood there, gazing at her canvas.

Her hair was swept up, and the nape of her neck looked exposed. Vulnerable. Sean couldn't seem to tear his eyes away from the sight.

As though she could sense his gaze on her, she turned. "Sean. And James." Joining them in the entry hall, she looked to her brother-in-law with a question in her eyes.

"Lord Lincolnshire has fallen asleep. I put a drop of laudanum in his tea. He's resting easily for now."

"Might he get better, then, do you think?"

"I fear not," Lord Stafford said gently. "It is, of course, difficult to predict the path of an illness. He could have an hour or a day when he seems better, but overall he'll continue to decline." He leaned in to kiss her on the cheek. "You were right to send for me. Juliana suggested I see him, but I didn't realize the situation was so urgent."

"Thank you for coming." She walked him to the front door, which the competent Quincy was already holding open. "I know Lord Lincolnshire is in the best of hands," she added.

Watching him go down the steps, then waiting for Quincy to close the door, she finally turned to Sean. "When did you get home?"

This wasn't home, but he didn't correct her. "A while ago. You looked very busy."

"I'm finished."

"Leaving for the evening, then?"

"I'm *finished*. With the painting."

"Oh." He blinked. "May I have a look?"

"Yes, I was hoping you would." She hesitated a moment before heading back to the salon, motioning him to follow. As they drew near the canvas, she seemed to hold her breath. "What do you think?"

"It looks just like Lincolnshire. A much healthier Lincolnshire." The man who'd sat for her, blended together with the younger Lincolnshire of her memories, Sean guessed.

It was a full-body portrait, a natural pose in lieu of the typical head-and-torso formality. The painting showed the earl seated on a bench beneath a plane tree in Berkeley Square—perhaps the same bench where Sean had explained the truth to Corinna. Lincolnshire wasn't eating a Gunter's ice, though; instead he held a weighty, leather-bound book. Rather than reading it, he looked like he'd just glanced up, distracted by the viewer walking by. He seemed relaxed and contemplative. And very much alive.

"It's good," Sean said simply.

She exhaled in a rush. "You know nothing about art."

He snorted, knowing better than to take offense—it was true, after all. "I know what I like, and it looks very well done to me. You'll submit it for the Summer Exhibition, won't you?"

"I hope to. But first I'm going to show it at Lady Avonleigh's reception on Wednesday." She'd have it delivered, along with a selection of her other paintings, to Lady A's house tomorrow. "I want to see what the artists think of it."

"The judges."

"Yes." Corinna bit her lip and met his gaze, nerves suddenly jumping in her stomach. "I hope they'll like it."

Her voice quavered, and she wondered if he'd heard it. He didn't say anything, so she couldn't tell. He only looked at her for a moment. Just looked at her, while she stood there wishing she hadn't eaten any luncheon, because she felt like the cold meat and fruit she'd nibbled on was about to come back up.

Abruptly he turned and walked back to the salon's huge carved and gilded door. Shut it with a heavy *thump*. Then turned to face her. "You're nervous," he said in that melodic voice that made everything shift inside her. "Come here, Corinna."

She rushed into his arms, lifting her chin for a kiss. The kiss was short and fiercely sweet, and then he only held her. He only held her tight, swaying slightly, murmuring comforting words she didn't recognize, perhaps Irish words or perhaps just nonsense ones—she didn't know. But just at that moment, she fell in love.

The realization made her heart stutter. Then it raced. She slid her hands beneath his tailcoat, wrapping her arms around him as if she could keep him here. Squeezing him as he was squeezing her, as hard as she could.

"There's nothing to be nervous about," he said soothingly, skimming his hands up and down her back. "It's a beautiful painting."

She turned her head to lay her cheek against his warm, comforting chest. "I know."

"And you've many more paintings at home, don't you? So if the judges don't agree, they could choose another one."

He smelled like starch and soap and something else. "I know." Something she couldn't put a name to.

"And if they don't choose another one, there's always next year. You won't give up. I know you."

She knew him, too. And she loved him. She didn't think she could tell him now—there was so much happening around them, so much complicating their lives. But she loved him. She lifted her chin, wanting to tell him without words.

She hoped he'd get the message.

It was different from their other kisses—different from any kiss she'd shared with anyone. It wasn't urgent or forceful. It was slow and tranquil and lingering, as though they had all the time in the world. As though they were getting to know each other. She didn't feel the same desperate excitement she'd felt the other times they'd kissed, but she felt something better. Something that made her skin prickle from head to toe. Something that made her feel as if she were floating.

She heard a low sort of moan escape her throat, but she was

floating too high to get embarrassed. It just seemed natural and right. Or maybe it was just that nothing could embarrass her or bother her, not here. Not now that she knew she loved him.

A knock came at the door, and they jerked apart. Sean whirled and opened it. "Deirdre."

His sister blinked, looking between them. "I'm sorry. I wasn't meaning to interrupt."

"No, no." He drew her inside. "Lady Corinna was just showing me her finished picture."

Corinna feared Deirdre could see the truth on her face—or rather her lips, which felt puffy and thoroughly kissed. But if Deirdre could tell, she didn't let on. Her attention was on the painting, her face lighting up as she walked forward.

"Oh, Lady Corinna, it's absolutely stunning. Tell me about it, will you?"

Behind Deirdre's back, Corinna shared one last look with Sean. His eyes were unreadable, but she was sure her own were moonier than ever. She wasn't worried about that anymore. Nor about the reception. She felt so much better about everything. She was in love, and she knew that mattered more than any painting. She *could* always try again next year.

Hugging her new secret to herself, she went to join his sister.

TWENTY-SEVEN

ALMOND CAKES

Grinde halfe a pound of Almonds and mixe with halfe a pound of Sugar and Orange or Lemon
Water. To this add ten Yolks of Egges beaten and the boiled skins of two Oranges or Lemons
grounde fine. Mixe together with stiff Egge Whites and melted Butter gone cold and bake it all
in a good Crust.

Good for nibbling during nervous occasions, such as when my daughter brought my first
grandchild into the world earlier this year. Oh, my, what a day and night. I think I'd much
rather give birth myself!
—Elizabeth, Countess of Greystone, 1736

$\mathcal{A}$S WAS customary, the furniture in Aunt Frances's
Hanover Square home had been rearranged to prepare
for the birth of her child.

On the ground floor of Malmsey House, a room had been
designated as the lying-in chamber, and a portable folding bed
had been brought in for the occasion. A larger connecting room
provided a gathering place for relations during the labor, and
more rooms across the corridor had been outfitted to house the
accoucheur—the obstetrical doctor—and the monthly nurse,

called such because she not only assisted the accoucheur and attended the mother during the birth, but stayed for a month afterward to care for the baby.

The accoucheur and monthly nurse had arrived yesterday in anticipation of Aunt Frances's due date a week hence. But apparently Dr. Holmes had reckoned incorrectly, because today, while Corinna and her family nibbled on the almond cakes Juliana had brought, Frances was laboring in the inner chamber.

As she had been for half a day already.

Corinna had been forced to rush this morning to get her paintings sent to Lady A's house before coming here to be with Aunt Frances. Along with the portrait, she'd chosen all her best landscapes and a few of her favorite still lifes. At least waiting for the birth was stopping her from fretting over whether she'd made the right selections.

Well, it was slowing her down, anyway.

Hearing more moans and murmurs through the door, she winced. "How long is this going to take?"

"It hasn't been that long." Alexandra smiled down at Harry, settled in her lap. "If you'd attended my son's birth, you'd know that."

Alexandra had delivered in the wintertime, at Hawkridge House in the countryside. Two weeks early, a full week before her sisters had planned to arrive. Her accoucheur had miscalculated, too, and at the moment, Corinna was grateful for that. The thought of Alexandra wailing like poor Aunt Frances made her want to wail herself.

"Oh, hang it," Griffin suddenly said.

"What is it?" Corinna asked, her heart jumping into her throat. Did he know something she didn't about their aunt's condition? Something bad? Something dire?

"It's nothing," he said. "I just forgot something." He rose and went over to a little desk in a corner of the room, where he started pulling drawers open. "I need to send a message."

Juliana rose, too, and found paper and quill for him. "It seems this is taking forever," she said, looking rather pale as she returned to her seat. "James, maybe you should help."

James rolled his eyes. "I don't deliver babies," he said for the fifth time. "But there's no need to fret. Dr. Holmes is the very best."

"He could take some measures," Griffin muttered as he scribbled.

"It's usually better not to intervene as long as the labor is making progress. What would you have him do?"

"Bloodletting, perhaps."

"James doesn't believe in bleeding," Juliana said quickly. Juliana couldn't stand the sight of blood. She said it made her sick to her stomach.

Griffin folded his letter and began scribbling again, adding the direction to the outside. "Then maybe forceps."

"Using forceps," James said, "can result in tearing the mother."

"I don't want to hear this," Corinna said, jumping out of her seat and going to the window. The sight of blood didn't bother her, but all of this talk—labor pains, bloodletting, forceps, tearing—coupled with Aunt Frances's intermittent cries…

Well, it was enough to make a girl keep her legs crossed for the rest of her life.

"Are you all right?" Juliana asked her.

"I'm fine. I just never, ever want to give birth."

Everyone laughed. But this was no laughing matter. She was never going to tell Sean she loved him, because what if he wanted to get married? And though Griffin probably wouldn't assent, what if he did? She could end up wedded and bedded and howling behind a birthing room door herself.

A particularly piercing scream came from the lying-in chamber, and she felt the blood drain from her face.

"It's worth it," Alexandra said softly, still smiling down at her child.

"I think I'll stick to making pictures," Corinna muttered.

"Your husband may have something to say about that," Griffin said, rising from the desk. He strode toward the room's door. "I'll be right back. I need to pass this off to a footman."

I believe all men are deceitful, Corinna remembered Amanda saying in *Children of the Abbey.* But Griffin wasn't deceitful. Oh, no, *he* was perfectly straightforward. He was determined to marry her off even if it meant she'd suffer like Aunt Frances was suffering. And he wasn't afraid to tell her so right to her face.

Your husband may have something to say about that.

Her blood boiling, Corinna waited impatiently for her brother's return, knowing exactly what she would yell right in his face make it clear to him, once and for all, that she wasn't looking for a husband in the first place, and wouldn't accept one who didn't support her art career in any case—when the wailing and screaming suddenly stopped.

Corinna's breathing stopped, too. "Is Aunt Frances…?"

She couldn't bring herself to finish the sentence. And evidently no one else could, either, because a tense silence flooded the room.

And then a thin cry came through the closed door.

"Of course not, you goose." Juliana grinned, though she'd looked just as anxious a second ago. "She's had her baby."

"Thank goodness." Corinna bit off a hunk of almond cake, suddenly ravenous. The ordeal was over. "When can we see it?"

"Not for a while," Alexandra told her. "The baby will be covered in mucus and blood, so it will need to be cleaned up first, and Aunt Frances will need to deliver the afterbirth—"

"Stop." Griffin walked back in, looking rather green. "I don't think Corinna needs to hear this."

Corinna giggled. She was feeling better already, if a little hysterical. Her stomach fluttered with excitement as they all waited to be called inside. The baby stopped crying, and the murmurs that came through the door sounded contented rather than distressed. She heard Frances's familiar laugh and knew everything was going to be all right.

At last the connecting door opened. From the bed Frances smiled, propped comfortably against her pillows. Lord Malmsey came out of the room, a short man with a receding hairline, a wide smile, and a pink bundle cradled in his arms.

"It's a girl," he said, sounding bemused.

Everyone seemed to sigh in unison.

Slowly he unwrapped the blanket, revealing a little heart-shaped face, a shock of straight dark hair, and large, unfocused blue eyes.

Corinna rose and walked toward him.

"What are you calling her?" she asked.

"Belinda," he said quietly.

"Oh, my." Frances's older sister's name. Corinna's mother's. "May I hold her?"

Griffin laughed. "I thought you didn't want a baby."

"There's a big difference between having one and holding one," she retorted, opening her arms.

Lord Malmsey reluctantly handed his daughter over. Belinda felt warm and impossibly tiny. And holding her squirmy little body close, Corinna fell in love for the second time in two days.

TWENTY-EIGHT

Hanover Square, Tuesday 13 May

My dear Cousin,

I regret that I shall be unable to accompany you to Chelsea today, as my Aunt Frances is most inconveniently delivering a child. I shall take you tomorrow if that agrees with you.

> *Fondly,*
> *Cainewood*

~

"A USEFUL SKILL indeed, miss." Sean made a notation in his notebook. "Perhaps I can find a position for you cleaning Delaney and Company's main offices."

"Offices?" the maid squealed, her cracked and work-reddened hands flying up to her cheeks. Cleaning offices was a huge step up from the scullery. "A place of business? Not a kitchen?"

"I cannot make any promises, since decisions have yet to be made. But you won't be working in a kitchen." One business he *wasn't* involved in was food service. He stood, and when she stood too, he stuck out his hand. "Whatever your final assignment, you should expect to begin the Monday following Lord Lincolnshire's passing." He'd had enough practice saying it that his voice no longer cracked on the last word.

"Will I still live here?"

"I'm afraid not." Sean was certain Hamilton would never allow it. "But have no fear, miss. I shall arrange lodging in a boardinghouse for you until you can find a situation of your own."

She clutched his hand in both of hers, her eyes filled with awe. "Thank you, my lord. You cannot imagine—"

"I'm not a lord," he interrupted. "Merely a mister."

"You'll be a lord soon—"

"And you're very welcome. Before you return to the kitchens, please ask Mr. Higginbotham to step in."

Sean sat and made a few more notes while she all but danced out of the room. When the house steward entered, he rose again. "Was she the last one then, Mr. Higginbotham?"

A tall, thin man with a gaze that didn't miss anything, Higginbotham ran Lincolnshire's household like clockwork. "Other than Eugene Scott, one of the gardeners, yes. I allowed him the day off to sit with his ailing mother."

"A gardener." Sean nodded and made another note. Perhaps Mr. Scott could be assigned to work with the crews that landscaped new buildings following construction. "Please sit down, Mr. Higginbotham."

The steward did so, smoothing his palms on his striped trousers. "I must tell you, sir, that everyone, from the basement of this house to the attics, is extremely grateful for your seeing to their continued employment."

"Think nothing of it. They're remarkably loyal employees, and as such, will surely be assets to their new employers."

Now that Sean had interviewed them all—mostly in the evening hours over more than a week—he would assess their relative strengths so he could place them strategically among the different businesses he owned. Some would be involved in property management, others in import or export, manufacturing, construction, and many other of his endeavors.

"I hope everyone will be pleased with their final assignments," he said.

"I'm certain they will be pleased to have any employment at all. Although they wish to remain with Lord Lincolnshire until he's gone, of course."

"Of course. I wouldn't have it any other way."

Higginbotham hesitated. "If you don't mind my asking, Mr. Hamilton..." He cleared his throat. "How is it you've come to know of enough available positions? And come by the authority to hire—"

"I know a lot of people," Sean interrupted firmly.

"I expect as a well-known artist you've had commissions from all the best—"

"Something like that." He tapped his quill on the notebook. "As for *your* future, Mr. Higginbotham..."

The man sat forward, apprehension crossing his long face. "I assumed I'd remain here. If I may say so, Mr. Hamilton, you're going to require a minimum of staff at the least."

Sean wouldn't think of leaving such a fine man at the mercy of the weasel. "I've been impressed by your efficiency. I know of a factory in Surrey in need of a foreman. If you're willing, I'd like to see you in that position."

Higginbotham's eyes widened. "A factory?"

"They manufacture lamps, the new gaslights. As it's a growing industry, it's a very large factory, with upwards of three hundred employees."

The steward squared his shoulders. "I have managed a sizable staff here."

"More than a hundred, by my estimate." Sean felt like he'd interviewed a thousand. "You'll have to relocate outside London, of course, but compensation will include a foreman's house and the staff to manage it, leaving you free to focus on the factory's needs."

"I'm to have my own servants?"

"You'll need them. The factory is a major responsibility."

Higginbotham's face set with determination—and perhaps a touch of excitement. A house steward was a respectable position, but managing a factory was something else altogether. Rather than a glorified servant, he'd be a man of industry, a man of business. "I'm up to it, sir, I assure you."

"I've no doubt." Sean snapped the notebook closed. "We're agreed, then, and I'm finished here. Let Lord Lincolnshire know, if you please. I'm off to…paint."

Lincoln's Inn Fields, Tuesday 13 May

My dear Cousin,

It should have been better had you notified me of your delay sooner than four hours after I expected you. You seem to have forgotten that Lady A is holding her reception tomorrow, possibly the most important day of your sister's life. As I plan to attend, Thursday afternoon will be more agreeable for Chelsea.

Yours very sincerely,
Rachael

P.S. I wish Lady Malmsey the best.

TWENTY-NINE

ROUT CAKES

Take Flour and mix with Butter and Sugar and Currants clean and dry. Make into a paste with Eggs and Orange Flower Water, Rose-water, sweet Wine, and Brandy. Drop on a floured tin-plate and bake them for a very short time.

My mother said these cakes bring luck, and indeed, I fed them to my husband the day he proposed! Serve to ensure the success of your rout or any other event you'd like to see turn out well.

—Katherine, Countess of Greystone, 1765

INALLY, THE day of the reception dawned. Corinna arrived at Lady Avonleigh's town house, where an ancient butler ushered her inside. Her knees were shaking. Lady Balmforth, who shared the house with her sister, came to greet her and take her to the drawing room.

"Welcome, my dear. Where is Mr. Hamilton?"

"He…ah…he couldn't come," she said, which was the truth. Mr. Hamilton couldn't come, as he was in Wales, and Sean couldn't come in his place, either. "I haven't seen him the past few days, Lady B. Apparently he's very busy."

That was true, too. She hadn't seen Sean since she'd finished the portrait.

"Well." The older woman huffed, sucking in her already thin cheeks. Lady B was as skinny as Lady A was plump. "My sister is not going to be happy about this."

Some of the ladies' friends were already there, exclaiming over Corinna's paintings. Lady A and Lady B had taken all the other pictures off their peach-painted walls and hung Corinna's art there instead.

Everything in their house seemed to be peach. The color unfortunately clashed with some of Corinna's work, but there was nothing she could do about that. Nothing but cross her fingers and hope that the artists would like what they saw when they arrived.

And hope that they would like *her*.

Alexandra showed up next, a platter in her hands. "Rout cakes," she explained. "They're supposed to ensure the success of your rout."

"It isn't *my* rout. In fact, it isn't a rout at all. It's a reception."

"It's a fashionable gathering, and as Lady A's home isn't overly large, it's bound to be a crush. That's a rout in my book." Alexandra leaned to kiss her sister's cheek. "You look nervous."

A sarcastic retort hung on the tip of Corinna's tongue, but she felt too on edge to make jests. "I am," she admitted instead. She abruptly realized that, other than the rout cakes, Alexandra held…nothing. And there was a decided lack of squeaky wheels. "You left Harry at home."

"Babies don't belong at routs." Alexandra set the platter on a side table of mahogany inlaid with lighter, peach-colored wood. "Show me your newest painting."

But before Corinna could do so, Juliana walked in. Then Rachael and Claire and Elizabeth. Then more of Lady A's and B's friends, and their other sister, Lady Cavanaugh, and the first of the Exhibition judges.

Suddenly, it was a rout.

Corinna could barely move among all the people. Lady A pushed through the crowd to give her a hug. Corinna held her breath as she was enveloped in camphor and gardenias. "Our honored guest! Where is Mr. Hamilton, my dear?"

"He couldn't come."

"Well. I...well. I never—" More guests were arriving, cramming the drawing room. Her plump cheeks quivering with indignation, she turned to the nearest new arrival. "Have you heard, Mr. West, that Mr. Hamilton isn't coming?"

Benjamin West! The president of the Royal Academy! Corinna found herself speechless with terror.

"I'm sorry to hear that, madam, but it's hardly a surprise, considering he's currently in Wales."

"When did he leave for Wales?"

"Last month, I do believe."

"Last month? I think not." Lady A looked confused. "Lady Rachael," she called, motioning her over. "Did we not see Mr. Hamilton last Saturday at the Billingsgate ball?"

"Why—"

"No," Corinna cut in, sending her cousin a pitiful, pleading look. Although Rachael didn't know the truth, surely she'd respond to such obvious silent begging. "That was *Sean* Hamilton, remember? Sean, not John." Before Rachael could disagree or Lady A could protest further, Corinna clutched Mr. West's arm and began pulling him toward her painting of Lord Lincolnshire.

Though she was no shrinking violet, she surprised herself with her boldness. But she didn't see where she had much of a choice. She had to get Mr. West out of there before—as Rachael would put it—everything went to blazes.

"Will you have a look at my newest painting, Mr. West?" she asked, coming to a stop before the portrait and flashing what she hoped was a charming smile. "As I'm considering submitting it to the Summer Exhibition, I'd surely appreciate your thoughts."

Before commenting, he studied the picture quite a while. Corinna studied him. He was balding, what was left of his hair was gray, and he looked rather solemn overall. But not really unkind, she decided with some relief.

Mr. West was famous for his paintings of recent battles that depicted their heroes wearing modern dress rather than traditional, classical garb. Since Corinna thought it rather silly to paint contemporary men sporting flowing Roman robes, she heartily approved—and she hoped his willingness to take the less traveled road meant he was more open-minded than most.

"It's very nice, Lady...Corinna, is it?" he said at last in his disarming American accent. "Your basic techniques demonstrate fine skills. But I'm not certain your model's form looks quite realistic."

"His form?"

"His body, under his clothing. Not quite natural, I'm afraid."

Her heart turned to lead in her chest. She'd done her best, considering the Academy refused girls access to anatomy lessons. Maybe she should point that out to him. As the Academy's president, maybe he would see how unfair that was, how detrimental to a girl's chances, and decide to change the Academy's rules.

No, that would never happen. And he might consider such a request to be very bad form. She'd never get elected to the Academy if its president found her vulgar.

On the other hand, maybe he was wrong. Maybe Lord Lincolnshire's form looked perfectly fine. West was known for painting all of his subjects with large almond-shaped eyes, so maybe he wasn't one to judge. Although his portrait clients thought those eyes most dashing—and surely commissioned him for that reason—it wasn't realistic, after all. Some of them had narrow, squinty eyes, or small round ones.

"Thank you very much for your opinion," she told him as nicely as she could manage. "I quite appreciate it, and I shall take your thoughts under consideration."

Suppressing a sigh, she returned to Rachael after he took leave. "Well, *that* didn't go well."

Rachael's sisters came to join them. "Who was he?" Claire asked.

"Benjamin West, the president of the Royal Academy. He said Lord Lincolnshire's body doesn't look natural beneath his clothing."

Elizabeth glanced over toward the painting and shrugged. "Looks fine to me. Rather more impressive than the earl's *real* body, in fact."

"He did say I have fine skills. And maybe he's wrong about the other, but that doesn't really matter, does it? Either way he won't vote for my painting. Unless I change it."

"His is just one opinion." Rachael touched her arm. "There are other committee members, aren't there? How many in total?"

"Nine. The president plus eight elected Academicians."

"So you have eight more men to influence. Seven if you count Mr. Hamilton as being on your side. And he should be, considering you've become friends with him."

"I'm not sure *friends* is an accurate description of our relationship." But although Rachael didn't know the truth, in a sense she was right. The real Mr. Hamilton *should* be on Corinna's side, considering how hard she'd been working to keep his uncle happy. And he believed each work should stand on its own and not be judged by the gender of its creator. "However, I think he probably will vote for me," she decided.

"So you've already balanced Mr. West's negative opinion with a positive." Rachael smiled; but then her brows drew together in a frown. "Why did you claim you didn't see Mr. Hamilton at the Billingsgate ball on Saturday? That he was Sean Hamilton, not John? I've heard you *call* him Sean, and Lord

Lincolnshire calls him that as well, but I thought it was just a nickname?"

"Mr. West seems to think Mr. Hamilton is in Wales for some reason. I didn't want to argue with the president of the Royal Academy. Better to go along with what he said, I was thinking."

Rachael exchanged dubious glances with her sisters. "I don't know about that."

Corinna gave what she hoped was a casual shrug, then smiled at Lady A, who was approaching with another gentleman trailing her.

"I cannot understand why everyone thinks Mr. Hamilton is in Wales," the older woman muttered darkly. And then more graciously as she drew near, "Mr. Mulready, I'd be pleased for you to meet Lady Corinna Chase. Lady Corinna, this is William Mulready."

Mr. Mulready looked *much* younger than Mr. West, probably not much more than a decade older than Corinna herself. "A pleasure to meet you, my dear," he said in an accent that reminded her of Sean.

That thought made her smile. "Oh, Mr. Mulready, your painting in last year's Summer Exhibition was my absolute favorite!"

She wasn't making that up; the enthusiasm in her voice was genuine. And judging from the man's expression, he rather liked hearing it. "Which one, my dear?" he asked.

Academicians were allowed to display six paintings each— works that were hung without question, without being judged by the committee. "*The Fight Interrupted*. I adore the seventeenth-century Dutch masters, and it reminded me of their work. An updated version, of course."

"I too admire the Dutch masters," he said, sounding like he also admired her for admiring them. "Their work inspired *The Fight Interrupted*."

Encouraged by how much better this was going than her last

conversation, Corinna started inching Mr. Mulready toward her painting of Lord Lincolnshire. "I also much admire your wife's landscapes, Mr. Mulready."

"Elizabeth does lovely work."

"Since you married a female artist, may I assume you don't disapprove of us?"

He laughed, which was a relief. It *had* been a rather saucy question. "A valid assumption. I've had a look at your paintings, my dear. Your own landscapes are quite remarkable."

Oh, this was going *astoundingly* better. "Here is my latest portrait. What do you think?"

"Lord Lincolnshire, isn't it?" Cocking his head, he perused the picture. "I think, Lady Corinna, that you've truly captured the essence of the man."

Corinna couldn't help but grin. She couldn't think of a more glorious compliment than hearing she'd *captured the essence*. That was exactly what she tried to accomplish, not only with this portrait but with all of her paintings.

And the score was now two to one. Mulready and Hamilton on her side, and only Benjamin West on the other. Clearly her chances were good.

She *loved* William Mulready.

Until she heard the next words out of his mouth. "But he seems a wee bit…stiff."

"Stiff?"

"Yes, stiff. I've had the pleasure of meeting Lord Lincolnshire —quite the art collector, isn't he?—and he struck me as a relaxed sort of fellow. It's something about this fellow's frame beneath his clothing that looks stiff, I think…" Smiling, he patted her on the shoulder. "Not to fret, Lady Corinna. Your landscapes are brilliant. I'm sure the committee will be more than pleased to choose one of them."

She didn't want them to choose a landscape. She was no

longer sure she even wanted to submit any. She was going to have to fix Lord Lincolnshire's portrait.

"How is it going?" Alexandra came and asked when Mr. Mulready had walked away.

"He likes my landscapes."

"Well, that's good, isn't it?"

"He's not nearly as impressed with my portrait. He thinks Lord Lincolnshire looks unnatural beneath his clothes. And Benjamin West said the same thing."

"Oh, my. I think you need a rout cake."

Alexandra fetched one from the platter and handed it over. Corinna bit into it morosely, thinking she could use their luck.

No matter that she didn't believe in that nonsense.

"How many works will be chosen?" Alexandra asked.

"There were nearly a thousand in last summer's Exhibition."

"Well, then, I should think your chances will be good."

"But there were more than *eight* thousand submitted. And there are eighty Academicians who get to show six pieces each, which leaves only five hundred twenty for the rest of us."

"*Only* five hundred twenty," Juliana said with a laugh as she joined them. "I should think there'd be room for one of yours in all of that. And I cannot believe you did that calculation that fast."

Juliana never had been very quick with numbers, but that was beside the point. "I've done that calculation a hundred times," Corinna admitted. "At the very least."

"How are the pieces chosen?" Juliana asked.

Shrugging, Corinna was about to confess ignorance when a stranger interrupted her. Giving a little bow, the gentleman said, "I could not help but overhear the lady's question, and I'd be more than happy to provide an explanation." Although he was older and not nearly as handsome as Sean, he too spoke with a similar lilt. She'd had no idea so many Academicians were Irish.

"Martin Archer Shee, at your service," he added with a merry wink.

Martin Archer Shee had studied with the late, great Sir Joshua Reynolds. Corinna was awed to find such a man speaking to her, let alone flirting with her. If only she had Juliana's abilities, she could turn that to her advantage.

But since she was merely Corinna, she said, "I'm Corinna Chase, and it's an honor to meet you, sir. We'd be delighted to hear your account."

"It's very pleased I am to meet *you*, Lady Corinna. The process is a simple one, if a wee bit tedious. The works are marched past the Committee by a chain of human art handlers. The first round cuts the mass of submissions to about two thousand, and the next round is much more rigorous. From the Academy's earliest days, two metal wands have been used to stamp labels attached to each painting. One wand is surmounted by a letter *D*, the other by an *X*. A work which receives the vote of three or more Academicians is awarded a *D* for 'Doubtful' and passes to the next round of selection. Works which get the *X* are eliminated. The rounds are repeated until the paintings that remain are reduced to a reasonable number. Beef tea is always served to keep the Academicians' spirits up during the ordeal." His eyes twinkled. "Which isn't really very much of one, in reality. Hanging the exhibition is a much more arduous affair."

"That takes days," Corinna told her sisters. "More than a week."

"With much politics involved regarding whose picture goes where. All done in a veil of secrecy, to protect the Hanging Committee from being hanged ourselves."

Mr. Shee smiled at his own joke, while the three ladies tittered politely. Corinna laughed loudest of all, hoping she sounded convincing. "Thank you kindly for your insight, sir."

"My pleasure." He winked again. "I'm much impressed by your work, Lady Corinna. Your textures are quite admirable. I wish you the best of luck in the selection process," he added before taking his leave.

Corinna turned to her sisters. "He likes my work!" she squealed. Maybe her prospects weren't so grim, after all. "Martin Archer Shee likes my work. And he studied with none other than Reynolds!"

"Ah, but I wrote *Life of Reynolds*," another stranger said.

This one was accompanied by Lady A, who'd evidently brought him over for an introduction. In fact, when the gentleman joined Corinna's circle directly, without waiting to be introduced, Lady A looked slightly put out. But Corinna couldn't worry about offending the woman's sensibilities when there was such a man as James Northcote in their midst! "Mr. Northcote, it's truly an honor," she gushed. "I read your book four years ago, when it first came out, and I found your recollections of your old master tremendously enlightening."

"He was an enlightening man," Northcote said. "And a discerning one. He'd have been impressed, as I am, with your portrait, Lady Corinna. The subject's suit looks like real velvet, his lace genuinely handmade, the trees in the background wet and glistening. An admirable endeavor, Lady Corinna. Not perfect, of course. The underlying anatomy seems a mite off, and—"

"I'm so pleased you think well of it," Corinna interrupted before she was forced to hear that complaint again. "I realize it's not usual for a woman to paint portraits."

"Half the things that people do not succeed in are through fear of making an attempt," he told her solemnly. "You've an excellent start. I wish you well in proceeding with your portrait career."

"I think you have a good chance," Juliana said as he walked away. "He seemed very impressed with your realism."

Corinna smiled at her sister's use of the latest jargon, wondering where she'd read about realism. But then she sighed. "He didn't think the underlying anatomy looked very real."

"He said you have an excellent start."

"Exactly. One doesn't submit a painting that looks like a *start*. Clearly he was saying I need more practice."

She mentally counted her votes. Against: Benjamin West and James Northcote. For: John Hamilton and Martin Archer Shee. William Mulready would vote for a landscape but not for a portrait.

She wanted to submit a portrait.

Well, maybe Mr. Mulready or Mr. Northcote would vote for her portrait if she fixed it. And there were four other committee members. With either Mulready or Northcote on her side, she needed only two of them to swing the vote.

"How are things going?" Lady A asked, joining their little circle.

"All right," Corinna said. "Mr. West was lukewarm, but Mr. Shee said he was impressed by my work, and so did James Northcote." She wouldn't mention Mr. Northcote's other comments.

"Mr. Hamilton will certainly vote for you, although I'm still miffed with him for not attending. He could have influenced the others positively. What did William Mulready have to say, my dear?"

"He loves my landscapes, but he's not as enthusiastic about the portrait."

"Well, that doesn't signify, now, does it? My daughter painted wonderful landscapes. You should be happy enough to get a landscape into the Summer Exhibition."

Corinna wasn't certain that would make her happy, but she didn't say so. She didn't want to sound ungrateful. She was thankful to Lady A for giving her the opportunity to meet all the committee members, even if things weren't working out quite as she'd hoped.

Besides, things weren't looking all that dreadful, either. She needed only two more artists to love her work, and she had four more chances to find them.

"I spoke with William Beechey," Lady A added. "I'm sorry to tell you, my dear, that it doesn't seem he approves of ladies painting portraits."

Corinna couldn't say she was surprised. Disappointed, but not surprised. A portrait painter himself, Mr. Beechey had painted the royal family and nearly all the most famous and fashionable people. A steady stream of very sober portraits. Obviously he took life seriously and probably didn't relish competition from anyone, let alone from female artists. "Well, then, I don't need to meet him. There are still three committee members I've yet to speak with."

Lady Balmforth threaded her way to them. "I talked to William Owen," she reported. He was principal portrait painter to the Prince Regent.

"And?" her sister asked.

Lady B just shook her head. Woefully.

Another artist to cross off Corinna's list. Now there were just two left...and her stomach felt as though rocks were collecting inside it.

"How about Henry Fuseli?" she asked. "Or John James Chalon? Have either of you talked to either of them?"

"Our sister has one of Mr. Fuseli's pictures in her bedroom," Lady B said. "Let's ask her if she'll introduce you."

Lady A nodded. "That would be good. I'll find Mr. Chalon in the meanwhile."

As Lady B took her to find Lady C, Corinna wondered what sort of picture Juliana's mother-in-law had in her bedroom. That she had a Fuseli at all was rather intriguing. Mr. Fuseli painted weird, haunting images, daring fantasies. His most acclaimed painting, *The Nightmare*, depicted a woman in the throes of a bizarre dream.

Griffin would throw a fit if he knew his innocent little sister had ever even glanced at one of his pieces.

To be honest, she was a bit nervous to meet Mr. Fuseli. Though she admired his creativity, she wasn't sure how she felt about some of his subject matter, and she wasn't at all sure she wanted to encounter the man who'd dreamed it up. She almost hoped Lady Cavanaugh would be too hard to find.

But she wasn't, of course. The peach house simply wasn't large enough to get lost in it. Lady B found her sister very easily, and Lady C was delighted to provide the introduction.

Corinna steeled herself.

Mr. Fuseli had masses of curly white hair and a face that looked oddly like a lion's. He'd apparently already examined Corinna's artwork.

"Your paintings are very well done, Lady Corinna," he told her in a booming voice. "Very accurate."

"Thank you, Mr. Fuseli. I admire your paintings, too. They're so inventive. Very visionary."

"I do believe that a certain amount of exaggeration improves a picture."

Was that a criticism? He'd described her work as *very accurate*. She always did her best to portray the truth or, as William Mulready had put it, to *capture the essence*. There was nothing exaggerated in her pictures at all.

"Our ideas are the offspring of our senses," he continued.

What was *that* supposed to mean?

"It was lovely speaking with you, Lady Corinna," he concluded. "I wish you the best of luck."

That was it? He was done? She hadn't the slightest idea what he'd been talking about, or whether he'd liked her pictures.

Her sisters descended on her immediately. "What did he say?" Alexandra asked.

"I don't know, exactly. He didn't quite make sense. But he did wish me the best of luck."

"Then he goes in the *for* column," Juliana said firmly, being the type to always look on the bright side.

Corinna wished she could be half so optimistic. But maybe Juliana was right, and there was still John James Chalon.

The crowd seemed to be thinning out. Spotting Lady A, who was looking rather flustered, Corinna made her way over, her sisters following in her wake.

"Did you talk to Mr. Chalon? Did he say he was willing to meet me?"

"I couldn't find him," Lady A said. "It seems he's left."

"Oh, no. He was the last committee member." Her final opportunity to convince herself she still had a chance. "Now I won't know if he liked my portrait."

"It's all right, dear." Lady A beamed. "Everyone loved your landscapes. This all went brilliantly, don't you think?"

Corinna nodded, for Lady A's sake.

But that was the best she could manage.

Juliana jumped in to save her once again. "Yes, Aunty, it was an absolute triumph! Well done! Corinna was just telling us how overwhelmed she's feeling. We're all so very grateful to you for taking her under your wing."

Corinna nodded again. She *was* incredibly grateful, and happy to see her kindly benefactress flushed with pride and confidence.

But she feared that if she opened her mouth, all that would come out would be a sob or a scream.

"Have another rout cake," Alexandra said.

THIRTY

*T*HE EARL'S health had taken a decided turn for the worse.

Lord Lincolnshire hadn't left his bedroom in two days...two days during which he wanted his nephew nearby. Stuck in the house for hour upon hour, Sean was at his wit's end. He had so much he should be accomplishing, so much that wasn't getting done.

And he missed Corinna.

He'd become used to having her at Lincolnshire House. For an entire week she'd been there, painting in the salon, morning to evening. Though he hadn't been there with her very often, he'd liked examining her portrait every night, checking her progress. He'd liked thinking that if he wanted to see her, he knew exactly where to find her.

She'd been a fixture. A comfort.

But since she'd finished the portrait, all her time had been spent with her aunt and new baby cousin, or with Lady Avonleigh. Now that he was here at the house, she was gone. He didn't know when he might see her next. And the house felt empty.

Yesterday Sean had finally accepted he wasn't going anywhere anytime soon, and asked Higginbotham to have his art supplies fetched from the studio on Piccadilly Street. Thinking it was what the weasel would do himself, he'd set everything up in the drawing room that had Hamilton's pictures all over the walls. Then he'd summoned his secretary, Mr. Sykes.

Sykes had been working with Sean for nearly seven years. He was a short, dark fellow with round gold spectacles, a quick, precise mind, and an encyclopedic knowledge of Sean's many and varied enterprises. During the hours the earl slept, the two of them worked quietly behind closed doors in the drawing room. The staff had been told that Sykes was Sean's assistant, there to mix paint for him and such. In reality, they were allocating positions for all of Lincolnshire's many servants.

Sean was thankful that was now done. He'd begun notifying each member of the staff of their final assignments. Were it not for the melancholy of Lincolnshire's failing health, he reckoned many of them might be singing as they worked. They were obviously looking forward to what lay ahead. And very relieved overall.

But Sean was neither of those things. In fact, he was the exact opposite.

His life was a disaster. Days—weeks—behind on his work, his affairs were in complete disarray. And it would probably all be for naught, once Hamilton found out Sean had defied his wishes by appearing as him in public. *And* he'd managed to get himself into a truly dreadful romantic quandary, on top of everything else.

Great work, Delaney. Just grand.

After days of not seeing Corinna, he was only just beginning to realize how hard he'd fallen for her. Lately he'd found himself wondering if maybe—somehow—he could stay with her. Marry her. He kept thinking about how Cainewood apparently thought him a decent fellow, and attaching way too much significance to that.

This had to stop.

When she showed up unexpectedly Thursday morning, he was far too happy to see her.

"How is he?" she asked quietly, poking her head into the earl's room.

"The same." Sean waved her to the chair next to him beside the towering bed, where Lincolnshire slumbered upright, his back propped against a dozen pillows. It seemed the only way the earl could sleep these days, the only way he could breathe.

"You look upset."

"It's not pleasant," he said with a shrug, "but it cannot last much longer." He looked closer at her, noticing her tense jaw and a certain wildness in her eyes. "You look upset, too."

Lowering herself to the chair, she sighed. "Lady Avonleigh's reception didn't go well."

"What happened?"

"She kept asking why you weren't there," she said, keeping her voice low. "Or rather, why Mr. Hamilton wasn't there." She winced and flicked a wary glance at Lincolnshire, apparently worried he might have overheard. "Sorry."

"He's asleep. Though we should be careful."

She nodded. "The committee members were mystified, since they believe Mr. Hamilton to be in Wales. Lady A and her sisters and my cousins and others all kept saying he'd been seen at various social events, and the artists kept saying that was impossible..." She clenched her hands together in her lap. "It was a mess, Sean."

"It's sorry I am about that." Not that there was anything he could have done. But it *was* his fault. He tried to put it out of his mind. "How about the rest? Did the committee members like your new painting?"

She sighed again. "A couple of them liked it. The rest, not really."

"Why not?" he demanded, outraged. Who was running that Academy she was so enamored of, anyway? Because whoever they were, they sounded like idiots. "It's brilliant!"

"It isn't." To stifle his protests, she unclenched her hands and laid one on his arm. "They liked Lord Lincolnshire's expression well enough. William Mulready said I captured the essence of the man." A hint of a smile transformed her face; she'd obviously liked hearing that. "And they admired the textures and the techniques."

"But...?" All of that sounded sensational. Which meant there had to be a *but*.

"But they claimed Lord Lincolnshire's form doesn't seem real beneath his clothes. He looks stiff and unnatural."

"Did they?" Sean blinked. He hadn't noticed any such thing. But then, he hadn't known to look for any such thing. He'd been impressed with the quality and detail of Lincolnshire's face, and aye, his clothes and the background. Even color-blind, he could see all of that was exquisite. But he'd paid no attention to the earl's body.

Hurting for her, he tried for a positive angle. "It doesn't sound all that bad. They had lots of good things to say."

"One of them really loved my work—"

"*One?*"

"Yes, one. Or rather, only one had no reservations about it. Martin Archer Shee, that was."

"How about the rest?"

"Benjamin West liked my basic technique but didn't have anything else good to say. William Mulready and James North-cote both think I paint excellent landscapes, but they weren't so enthusiastic about the portrait."

He didn't know any of those names, but he wasn't about to

tell her so. He tried to commit them to memory so he could look them up later. "That's four out of how many?"

"Eight, not counting Mr. Hamilton. Two were hopeless. William Owen and William Beechey. They don't approve of girls painting portraits. I have no idea what the last two thought. I found Henry Fuseli's comments completely indecipherable, and John James Chalon left before I could hear his opinion."

"They might approve, then, the both of them."

"They might. But they might not. Or they might, like some of the others, like my landscapes but not my portrait."

"You can submit landscapes, then, can't you? Or landscapes along with your portrait? How many paintings are you allowed to turn in?"

"Three. Non-Academicians are allowed to submit three..."

She trailed off with yet another sigh, though she looked as if she wanted to say more.

And she looked wretched, which seemed to make his heart squeeze in his chest. He wanted to hold her, but he couldn't do that in Lincolnshire's bedroom. He curled his hands into fists to keep from reaching for her. "What is it, *cuisle mo chroí*?"

Now she looked puzzled instead of wretched. "Cooshla-macree? Whatever does that mean?"

"Nothing," he said quickly. "Just nonsense. It just slipped out." Heat rose in his cheeks.

He shouldn't be calling her that. Not as a slip of the tongue or anything else.

The wretched look had returned to her eyes. "What is it?" he repeated, without the stupid Gaelic this time. "What has you so troubled?"

"I don't know how to explain it," she said slowly, her gaze focused on the canopy above the earl's bed. "I don't quite understand it myself. As the reception wore on, it became more and more obvious that one of my landscapes would surely be accepted. Which has been my goal all these years, hasn't it? Yet it seemed the more they said they liked my landscapes, the more I wanted to submit a portrait. Only a portrait." She lowered her gaze, finally meeting his eyes. "I want to be known as a portrait painter. I'm going to try to fix Lord Lincolnshire's portrait."

"Can you do that?"

"I hope so. I think so. I have four days before the submission is due. I painted him into the scene in a week, so I should be able to fix him in a shorter time."

"That sounds hopeful." It made sense. But she still didn't look very sure of herself. "Well then, is there another problem?"

"There is." The two wee words sounded so despondent. "Even should I fix it, two of the committee members will refuse to vote for it just on the grounds that I'm female. And I cannot count on all six of the other members, either. If it's better—if it's brilliant—I imagine some of them may come around. But others may not. I'm counting on Mr. Hamilton to be the deciding vote, but that will work only if three others besides Mr. Shee vote for me, too. So I was wondering…"

"Wondering what?"

She glanced toward the bed uneasily. "When he gets here, before the vote, do you think you could ask him to talk to the committee?" she whispered in a rush. "I don't want my painting selected if it doesn't merit the honor, but if he could just ask them to seriously reconsider it even though they've seen it before, to give the revised version a fair look even though I haven't made a name for myself yet. Do you expect he might be willing to talk to them, as a favor? After all, you and I have done *him* a big favor by caring for his uncle."

Sean couldn't believe she'd said that in the earl's bedroom, even in a whisper. He slanted a nervous glance toward Lincolnshire, but the man was snoring peacefully. Or at least as peacefully as a dying man could.

Their secret was still safe.

But he wasn't at all sure Hamilton would vote for Corinna's

portrait, let alone encourage others to do the same. *I seriously doubt I will vote for that girl's painting,* he remembered Hamilton saying. *I'm certain her paintings won't be good, because she's never studied anatomy. Sketching statues is not going to help her learn anything.*

"I'm not sure," he said fretfully. "Hamilton isn't known for being cooperative."

"But we saved his inheritance."

Darting another glance toward Lincolnshire, he rose. "Let's discuss this somewhere else, shall we?"

"We cannot leave him alone."

"I told Mrs. Skeffington to take a rest, but I'm sure she wouldn't mind returning."

Fortunately, Mrs. Skeffington was coming down the corridor when Sean peeked out. He thanked his lucky stars she hadn't returned a minute earlier and overheard Corinna. After seeing the nurse settled by Lincolnshire's side, he guided Corinna downstairs and into the salon.

He closed the door behind them both. Took a seat on a blue-and-gold sofa. Smoothed his palms against his thighs.

Cleared his throat.

Corinna settled beside him, closer than he would have liked. Well, he liked it, but he needed to keep a clear head for this conversation.

"I'm sorry I said that out loud," she began. "It was foolish."

"No harm done." He drew and released a breath. "I have an idea."

"For what?"

"For helping you fix the earl's portrait."

"Helping me? How can you possibly help with that? I only want you to have a talk with Mr. Hamilton."

"You need to learn anatomy, don't you? Since you're wanting to make him look more natural?"

She looked perplexed. "That's why I sketched all those Elgin Marbles."

"But that wasn't good enough, was it?"

Begorrah, he couldn't believe what he was about to say. He'd spent the last two days thinking about how he'd let himself get too close to her, and this would make it even harder to keep away. But he saw no other way to help her win Hamilton's vote. No other way to repay her for everything she'd done for him.

He drew another deep breath. "I'm thinking I can pose for you."

"What?"

THIRTY-ONE

*H*OLY HANNAH.

Corinna couldn't seem to close her mouth.

"I can pose for you," Sean repeated. "You'll practice painting me, and that will help you learn anatomy so you can fix the portrait."

There was a long pause, during which Corinna struggled to gather up the pieces of her mind from where they'd splattered all over the walls.

"You want to pose for me," she finally said. "So I can learn anatomy."

His chin jutted out. "I said so, aye."

Aye. Sean never said *aye.* "You do realize..."

Though his green eyes looked apprehensive, a corner of his mouth turned up in a half smile. "That I shall have to take off my clothes?"

She glanced away, heat rushing into her cheeks. It was the most scandalous thing she'd ever heard. But she recognized a good opportunity when she saw one. She needed to fix Lord Lincolnshire's portrait, make his body look more realistic, and sketching marble gods clearly hadn't taught her enough.

And here was the chance to sketch a real Greek god instead.

She would never have asked him to pose for her. Never. Not even after a hundred more kisses. The very idea was unthinkable. But now that he'd offered…

Well, how could she possibly refuse?

She glanced furtively over her shoulder, as if Griffin might somehow be standing there, ready to box her ears for even considering such a thing.

But this could be her one and only chance to study male anatomy. And it was certainly her only chance before this year's Summer Exhibition. There'd be no time for more than a session or two, of course. But if there was any chance it'd be enough to make the difference, how could she not at least try?

Though she was staring through the large windows that overlooked the garden, she wasn't seeing trees and flowers and blue sky. Instead she was imagining the sofa where Lincolnshire had sat for her…with Sean on it instead.

Naked as the day he was born.

She swallowed hard. Her heart thumped unevenly. She flushed even hotter.

Biting her lip, she met his gaze again. "You won't have to take off *all* of your clothes."

"Will I not?" He raised a brow. "Lord Lincolnshire's portrait isn't just head and shoulders. His body wouldn't look 'stiff and unnatural' had it not been shown, would it?"

"But there's no need to sketch all of you at once. I can do parts."

"Parts?" The corners of his eyes crinkled with amusement.

"A part at a time. You can undress just a little bit."

"If you say so." He looked dubious, but also distinctly relieved. "Where shall we do it?"

"Not here. And not in my brother's drawing room."
Heaven forbid.

"In the square, then? Where the painting is set?" At her look of shock, he released a shaky laugh. "I was jesting, *mo chroí*. We can use Hamilton's studio."

Macree again...what did that mean? "That sounds good. When shall we meet?"

"Time is of the essence, is it not?"

"I have four days to fix the painting. I'd best not sketch more than two."

"We shan't delay, then. I'll meet you there in an hour."

"So soon?" Time might be of the essence, but she wasn't at all sure she was ready for this. "Can you leave Lord Lincolnshire? I thought he wanted you to stay here."

"Let's make it in the evening, then. Lincolnshire's been falling asleep early these days. And if he doesn't, I'll come up with an excuse."

"What excuse can I give Griffin to leave the house alone in the evening?" She preferred, of course, to be honest with her brother, but she could hardly tell him she was going out to sketch a nude man.

"Tell him Lincolnshire's invited you for dinner. I'll come for you, and we'll walk to the studio together." Sean grabbed her by the shoulders and pressed a quick kiss to her lips. "It'll be fine, Corinna. Don't worry. This plan is going to work."

THIRTY-TWO

*H*ER GRANDFATHER was here somewhere.

Nervously smoothing the lavender dress she'd chosen to wear—after trying and rejecting six others—Rachael gazed down the length of the Royal Hospital's great hall. The black-and-white marble floor seemed to stretch forever. "Which one is Colonel Thomas Grimbald?" she asked the guard at the door.

It was early evening—dinnertime, to be precise. Covered in spotless white cloth, sixteen long tables crowded the hall, each seating twenty-six pensioners. Every man wore the same outfit: a scarlet coat and tricorn hat based on the service uniform of the Duke of Marlborough's time. They were all sixty-five or older, and they all, to Rachael's eye, looked alike.

Maybe none of them was her grandfather. Maybe Griffin had been wrong.

"I'll show you to Grimbald, milady," the guard said. Griffin offered his arm, and she clutched it tightly as they followed him. Cutlery clinked, and the hall rang with the deep voices of so many men. The chandeliers overhead seemed too few to light the towering chamber, but the last of the day's sunshine streamed through its many tall, arched windows.

The guard stopped at one end of a table. "Colonel Grimbald?"

A gray-haired man glanced up—a man who looked eerily familiar.

Griffin hadn't been wrong.

"This fine lady and gentleman are here to see you," the guard told him and walked off.

The man blinked and rose, standing at attention, his narrow chest puffed out in the smart red coat. He was medium height, with a long nose in a long, pleasant face. He had Rachael's dented chin and, beneath the black tricorn, Rachael's sky blue eyes.

But they were blank.

"Who are you?" he asked, not rudely but not in a welcoming tone, either.

Griffin took Rachael's hand. "I'm the Marquess of Cainewood, and this is my cousin, Lady Rachael Chase. Your son's daughter."

"Hmmph." He reclaimed his seat and picked up his fork, silently dismissing them. "My son has no daughter."

Would he send her away without even listening? Rachael looked to Griffin and back to the man. Her grandfather. "Sir." She swallowed hard. "I know this must come as a shock, since your son—my father—is dead, but—"

"Thomas isn't dead." He lifted a tankard and took a swallow of beer.

"Sir." Rachael felt tears sting her eyes and cursed herself. It would have been nice to be welcomed with open arms, but if that wasn't to be, she at least wanted some answers. "I know your son did something shameful, but I just want to ask you—"

"My son has done nothing wrong." The words weren't said angrily but rather matter-of-factly, his blue gaze unfocused on his dinner. "Thomas will be an important man someday; just you wait and see. He'll be marrying John Cartwright's daughter, he will. *Lord* John Cartwright's daughter. Course, the gel ain't yet born, so I cannot be telling you her name." He glanced back up, cocking his head in apparent confusion. "Who are you?"

Flustered, Rachael freed her hand from Griffin's so she could dig in the beaded reticule that matched her lavender dress. "I'm your granddaughter." She pulled out her father's badge and held it out toward the man. "See, this is your son's badge."

"My son has no badge," he said flatly. "Where would he get such a thing? The lad isn't even a year old."

The man across from him, an aging fellow with big ears and a hooked nose, reached to take the badge and examined it with a low whistle. "Tenth Hussars. Old Grimbald's son must have done well for himself." He handed it back. "He don't mean to be uncivil, milady," he said sympathetically. "Colonel Grimbald, he's not quite here, if you catch my drift. Thinks it's 1760. If you stay long enough, he'll start nattering on about how he just saved some fellow's life and the bloke promised his firstborn daughter to his infant son."

"John Cartwright," Grimbald confirmed with a nod. "A bloomin' a-ris-to-crat." He drew the word out into four distinct syllables and ended it with a chortle. "My name will be connected to nobility."

Rachael dropped the badge back into her reticule. "Thunderation," she muttered under her breath. She stared down the hall toward an old, faded mural of King Charles II on a horse with the Royal Hospital in the background. He'd commissioned these buildings, she suddenly remembered—a disjointed thought that came out of nowhere—but never lived to see them finished.

Like her father hadn't lived to see her.

Disappointment knotted her stomach. She looked back to her grandfather and tried again. "Sir—"

"Yes?" He looked up, appearing startled to find her there,

blinking at her through eyes just like her own. "Who are you?" he asked.

"Our thanks for your time, sir." Griffin curved an arm around her shoulders. "Let's go," he murmured in her ear. "Staying here will accomplish nothing."

She nodded and allowed him to draw her back toward the door. Suddenly the huge room felt close and stifling, making her grateful to step out into the cool evening air. In the center of the deserted courtyard, a grand, bronze statue of King Charles thrust toward the sky, and she sat on its marble base, smoothing her dress over her knees and hugging them to her chest.

"He's gone," she said. "He's there, but he's *gone*."

"I'm sorry." Griffin stood gazing down at her. "I should have come to see him myself before taking you."

"No. I'd have wanted to see him, anyway. Just to convince myself he was my grandfather."

"He has your eyes."

"And my chin. We're related; I've no doubt of that at all." She hugged her knees tighter. "But he'll never be able to tell me what happened to my father."

"No, he won't." Griffin lowered his rangy frame to sit beside her. "He thinks your father is still a child."

A lone hawk circled overhead, looking as solitary as Rachael felt. "I'll never really know who I am."

"Ah, Rachael." He shifted closer, wrapping an arm about her to pull her against him. "What your father did, however awful or not, has nothing to do with who you are."

She dropped her head to his shoulder, taking comfort from his nearness. "I know. I just wanted to *know*. I assure you, even if the truth was terrible, I wouldn't have fallen apart."

"I never thought you would. You're strong, Rachael."

"You think so?"

"I know so."

There was conviction in his voice, and admiration, and a

warmth that helped the knot in her middle loosen a little. It helped to have Griffin here. She'd always considered him a bit of a rascal, and she'd certainly never imagined she'd find herself depending on him. Yet he'd been by her side all through this. Which seemed to lend her the strength she'd been missing. The strength he seemed to believe she had.

It was amazing what a difference it made to have someone believe in her.

THIRTY-THREE

"**H**OW SHALL we work this?" Setting his large case full of art supplies on the table, Sean glanced around the sparsely furnished garret studio. "Will you sit on the sofa?"

"Lord Lincolnshire sat on a sofa for the portrait," Corinna pointed out, "so I think you should pose there. Did he fall asleep?"

"He didn't. I think he might be getting better." Sean had mixed feelings about that. Happy to see the earl looking stronger, sad to think the poor man's suffering would be prolonged. Anxious that it meant his own life would remain on hold. Hopeful that it might give him a few days more with Corinna.

"Then how did you manage to leave him? What excuse did you give?"

"I told him my painting wasn't going well at Lincolnshire House, so I needed to work here instead. That's why I brought along the supplies. I'd have looked a liar otherwise."

He'd brought candles, too, knowing it would grow dark as the evening wore on. He pulled them out of the case and began setting them up around the room.

"Lord Lincolnshire didn't mind, then?"

"I sent for Deirdre to keep him company."

Though his sister was technically living at Lincolnshire House, she spent most of her waking hours at Daniel Raleigh's house. Sean was less than thrilled about that, but he didn't want to fight with his sister. He'd told the earl his wife was very fond of shopping.

Yet another lie, he thought grimly. "She wasn't happy, but she agreed."

"She should. You're doing all this for her benefit."

If only Deirdre saw it that way. "Lincolnshire likes her," he said dryly. "Thinks I chose a fine wife."

"That's good," she said distractedly. "I usually paint standing, but I like to sit when I sketch." She moved his case to the floor and sat herself on the small table. "This should do fine."

He lit the last candle. "I'll get you a chair."

"From where?"

"From one of my tenants." At her blank look, he smiled. "I own this building, Corinna. And half the others on this street."

"Oh." Now she looked impressed, which he couldn't help enjoying. "I thought you said the studio was Mr. Hamilton's. I guess you didn't mean literally."

"Hamilton plans to lease it when he returns. And *I* plan to charge him a small fortune for the privilege. I'll be right back."

He ran downstairs and borrowed a chair from one of the shopkeepers on the ground floor. When he returned, Corinna had her sketchbook open and her bottom lip between her teeth. She'd chewed it puffy and pink.

At least, he assumed it was pink. It definitely looked darker than usual. He had to tear his gaze away from it while he moved the chair before the sofa. If he kissed her now, he knew, this session would get way out of hand.

"Sit," he said, and sat himself, reaching down to pull off his boots.

"No need to undress all the way," she quickly reminded him.

As she settled in her chair he removed his stockings as well. "Will this do?"

She stared at his bare feet as if she'd never seen a pair before. "Lord Lincolnshire's feet aren't in the picture," she finally said. "Just a little more."

Keeping a straight face, he rose and shrugged out of his tail-coat. "Will this do, then?"

She cracked a smile. "A little more."

He unbuttoned and took off his waistcoat.

"More."

He untied and drew off his cravat.

"A little more."

He unfastened the top button on his shirt.

"Wait."

"Wait?" His fingers paused on the second button, he raised an eyebrow. "You're going to draw this wee bit of my throat?"

A nervous laugh escaped her. "Your hands. Lord Lincolnshire's hands are in the picture. I've decided to start with your hands."

"I'm thinking you've sketched hands before. Your sisters', perhaps?"

"Yes, of course. But I need male hands."

"Lincolnshire had two, I believe. Quite naked at the time he sat for you."

"Old hands. I painted him younger."

"Your brother's hands, then. Surely he's sat for you."

"Not without grumbling. And never long enough."

"I don't remember you mentioning that any of the artists criticized Lincolnshire's hands. I'm thinking you've probably mastered the painting of hands."

"It's notoriously difficult to paint hands," she said haughtily. "Will you just sit down and show me your hands?"

He knew she was postponing the rest of the undressing due

to nerves, but perhaps she needed a moment to ease into things. "All right," he said, sitting and placing his hands on his spread knees. "Will this do?"

"That will do fine." She blew out a breath. "Just relax."

"I might suggest you do the same."

"Yes. Of course. Right." She scooted her chair closer and bent over her sketchbook. "However did you come to own half this neighborhood?"

He hesitated. He didn't usually like talking to people about his work or his prosperity. He'd learned that when others discovered someone who looked like him (young, unassuming, *Irish*) was actually one of the wealthiest entrepreneurs in London, they tended to have rather strong reactions.

To say the least.

Some, like Corinna, were just surprised or impressed. But others reacted negatively. They were envious or suspicious or resentful. They didn't see how someone like him could have built something like Delaney & Company. At least, not without resorting to dishonest means.

It was those people Sean feared. Those people he tried to keep in the dark.

But Corinna wasn't one of those people, so he supposed it was high time he stopped dodging her questions.

"I have a knack," he finally said.

Her gaze stayed on her sketch, but a faint smile curved her lips. "Deirdre said you'd say that."

"When was that?"

"At the Billingsgate ball." Focusing on his left hand, she deftly penciled a few lines. "She told me you left Ireland with nothing, and the next time she saw you, you owned a bunch of property."

"I didn't start with nothing," he corrected. "My uncle left me an inheritance."

"How much?"

He laughed. "You surely don't beat about the bush."

She looked up, all wide blue eyes. "I—"

"It's all right. I don't mind. Your bluntness is one of my favorite things about you." As her face melted into a smile, he added, "It's an endless source of amusement."

She stuck her tongue out at him and returned to her sketch.

He laughed again. "It was ten thousand pounds."

She didn't even blink. Not that Sean had expected her to. Ten thousand might be an unimaginable fortune to a vicar's son in Ireland, but to a marquess's daughter in Mayfair?

It might as well be pocket money.

Such different people they were, from such different places. He might be wealthy now, and he might dress like a gentleman, but still, if not for Hamilton's antics, he'd never have crossed paths with a girl like Corinna. They'd never have spoken. Never have danced or shared ices in Berkeley Square.

And they definitely would never have kissed.

He looked down at his hands—the ones she was sketching—thinking he shouldn't be doing this. *Knowing* he shouldn't be doing this. What would her brother say if he knew what his sweet, innocent little sister was doing at this very moment? Just the thought of Cainewood finding out made Sean squirm on the sofa.

She frowned. "Hold still."

He obeyed.

"What happened after you received the inheritance?" she asked.

"I left my family and came to London. I bought a small, run-down building. By myself I fixed it up and sold it for a profit. That's when I discovered I have a knack."

"For buying and selling property?"

"For making money," he told her with a grin.

He couldn't help himself. He was proud of what he'd achieved. The seventh deadly sin, his father would have reminded him had he been alive to see how far his son had risen. But Sean didn't think this was the sort of pride God meant to condemn. Sean worked hard for what he earned, after all, and he never forgot that God had a hand in his success. He still tithed, and he contributed staggering sums to charity besides. He took at least as much satisfaction from using his money to help people as he had from earning it in the first place.

So he grinned, and he didn't feel bad about it, either. "I bought a larger building and did it again," he went on. "And again. After a while, I had enough resources to hire more people to fix up more buildings, so I could buy and sell them faster, and after that, I realized it might be more profitable to keep some of the buildings—certain ones, that fit certain criteria—and make money leasing them out."

"Deirdre said you own more than buildings. Businesses. Manufactories. And also ships, she told me."

His sister had a big mouth. No wonder Corinna had been so curious. "One of the tenants I leased to had a business that was about to fail, and I realized I could fix that up, too. So I bought the business and made it profitable. And then I bought other businesses. And started some. Some of the businesses needed supplies that came from outside the country, and I realized I could make more profit by importing the supplies myself. And importing supplies for other people. And exporting some of the things I was manufacturing, and some other things other people were manufacturing..." He shrugged. "There are all sorts of ways to make money."

Corinna was frozen midsketch, more than a little stunned. All the gentlemen she knew were rich, of course—but their money came from owning land. In most cases, their families had owned the same land for hundreds of years. No one she knew had started with nothing, or even with just ten thousand pounds. No one she knew had built their fortune all by themselves.

She'd never met someone like Sean, someone with a "knack"

for making money. Or a knack for much of anything, come to think of it. Except maybe sitting a horse or tying a perfect cravat.

No, wait. They all had valets to tie their cravats for them.

"How is it coming?" Sean asked.

"I beg your pardon?"

"The hands."

"Oh. They're...they're fine."

"You need to see more than hands, Corinna, if you're going to fix Lincolnshire's portrait."

She nodded slowly, reluctantly, knowing he was right.

He rose immediately and, as if hurrying to get it over with before he could change his mind, finished unbuttoning his shirt. He pulled it off over his head. Then he draped it over the arm of the sofa and...just stood there.

Half naked.

Corinna held her breath. Held herself still. Tried to keep her face blank and unreadable. She didn't want him to know what she was thinking.

Which was that he truly *was* a Greek god.

Or even better, because he was human instead of marble.

She'd never seen a real man without his shirt before. Did they all look like this? Somehow, she thought not. His skin looked young and smooth, encasing all sorts of interesting ridges and planes. Muscles, they were, she supposed. It appeared that men had many more of them than women—or at least men like Sean did. Men who fixed buildings and worked hard instead of leading soft lives of leisure.

His hands moved to the buttons on his trousers.

"No!" She swallowed hard. "That's enough for now." *Plenty* for now. "You need a book."

"A book?"

"In the painting, Lord Lincolnshire is holding a book."

He reached for one of the sketchbooks Mr. Hamilton had left

behind. With fascination, she watched his skin moving over his abdominal muscles. "Will this do?"

"What? Oh, yes. Have a seat. Like Lord Lincolnshire did, if you'll remember."

He sat and held the book, looking nothing like Lord Lincolnshire, although the pose was similar. She sketched a few lines. Shaky lines, since she couldn't seem to take her eyes off him long enough to look down at the paper.

"I fear you don't really look like Lord Lincolnshire."

"You're painting him younger, aren't you?"

"I thought the portrait would be more appealing that way. And more pleasing to Lord Lincolnshire as well. But I seriously doubt he ever looked like you."

Though her thoughts were still a jumble, her fingers began to fly over the page. She felt compelled to capture every detail of what she was seeing, while she had the chance. It was just so unlike anything she'd ever seen or experienced before. To think this was what Sean saw every day when he looked in the mirror...

She laughed at the thought.

"What?" he asked.

"Hmm? Oh, nothing."

He smiled and settled back. "How many sessions do you expect you'll need?"

A thousand. At least. "I've time for only two," she said regretfully. "After that I'll really need to paint. I hope Mr. Hamilton won't return and expect to use this studio before then."

"Don't worry yourself about that." He shook his head. "I got another letter from him yesterday. He's staying longer. Claims he's seeing fairies in the falls or some such blarney," he added with disgust. "But of course he's really lingering with his lover."

His lover. Corinna felt her face heat. Her eyes skimmed Sean's form, her pencil traced the lines on the paper, and her mind imagined kissing him.

Her lips tingled.

She released a tense breath.

"Is something wrong?" he asked.

"I'm just concentrating."

They sat in silence for a while. As time wore on, he slowly shifted position. The book began to droop. He reclined a little to one side. He laid an arm along the back of the sofa. Soon his pose had nothing in common with Lord Lincolnshire's. He looked far too relaxed. She considered asking him to move back, but she didn't want him to. This pose was far more interesting.

She was shifting too, her pencil slowing, slowing, until finally it stopped moving entirely. She just looked at him in the flickering candlelight. Looked at him and thought about kissing him.

Oh, hang it.

This would never do.

"Is something wrong, *a rún?*"

Oh, yes, something was wrong. He kept saying words she didn't understand, for one thing. Words that sounded lovely and melodic and made her want to launch herself at him, even not knowing what they meant. And the way he was looking at her, the way she was looking at him. She wanted to kiss him, and she needed to sketch.

It was all just impossible.

Her sketchbook and pencil both slipped from her hands. "I don't think I can do this anymore. Not tonight."

"Why not?"

She didn't answer. She couldn't tell him. He sat up, looking concerned. "What is it?"

"I cannot concentrate," she said in a small voice. "All I...all I can think of is kissing you."

"Oh. Well, then. I think we can fix that." She thought he might smile, but he didn't. He looked uneasy instead. "Why don't you come over here and give me a kiss, then? Get it out of your system?"

It would have been nice if he'd sounded a bit more eager than that. But, again, she wasn't one to ignore a good opportunity when it came her way. She was out of the chair faster than you could say *shameless*.

He'd intended it to be a brief kiss. A get-it-out-of-your-system kiss. She knew that.

She didn't care. She sprawled herself over him.

His resistance didn't last long.

I am yours whenever you come to claim me. The words from *Ethelinde* rippled through her mind as he gave in and claimed her lips. And then there was, blissfully, nothing in her mind at all. Nothing but warmth and melting and floating. Nothing to hold her back.

Until he pushed her away.

"We cannot," he whispered, taking her hands. Taking them and moving them off him. "I want to, but we mustn't do this." He sat up, lifted her easily, set her down on the sofa. "Not now, not before…this isn't right, Corinna." A strand of her hair had come loose, probably when she'd leapt on top of him, and he reached to tuck it back.

She ducked his hand. "What's not right?" she demanded. "It's only kissing, for heaven's sake. It's innocent."

Sighing, he dragged the hand through his own crisp black hair. "Innocent, is it? With me half-dressed, and the two of us alone up here in the dark?"

She couldn't look at him. She stared at the floor, chewing her lip. Part of her felt mortified. Rejected. But she knew that wasn't fair. It wasn't that he didn't want her. She could tell from the frustration in his voice that he wanted her, even if he was apparently much better able to control himself than she was.

He was just too honorable to let things get out of hand.

Too dratted honorable.

But she'd already known that about him, hadn't she? He'd proved his honor so many times, in so many ways. The way he'd tried to tell her his true identity from the very beginning, and kept at her until she believed him. The way he still felt guilty deceiving Lord Lincolnshire, even though he knew it was best.

And then there was the way he didn't want Deirdre to be with the man she loved until they could marry. She should hardly be surprised that he held himself to the same standard. That his honor wouldn't let them get into a position where they might get carried away.

Sean was the most honorable young man she knew.

That was one of the many reasons she loved him.

And those two little words hadn't escaped her notice: *not now*, he'd said. Meaning there would be a *now* sometime in the future—meaning he was planning a future with her! He hadn't told her yet, just like she hadn't told him she loved him. All of that had to wait until the deception was over, until they could put this mess behind them. She was just going to have to keep her hands to herself until they could be properly wed.

Unfortunately, patience wasn't her primary virtue...or even a secondary one, really. But she would try.

"You're right, of course," she said quietly. "I understand why we mustn't." And then because she couldn't help herself, she added: "I was just surprised that...well...that it was so easy for you to stop."

"You think that was easy?" he burst out, sounding exasperated, sounding like he couldn't believe he had to explain this. "You obviously *don't* understand. It's never easy to keep away from you. It's not easy now, it wasn't easy a minute ago, and it won't be easy a minute from now. Being near you is all I ever think about. The only thing I care about more than being near you, *is you*."

And when those words came out of his mouth, that was when Sean knew.

He loved her.

Yes, he'd fallen hard for her; yes, he admired her ambition; yes, he wished to be near her, always. But it was more than that, much more. Because when he'd pushed her away, he hadn't done it out of some sense of honor or integrity—he'd done it for *her*. Because as much as he wanted her—and he wanted her more than he'd known it was possible to want anything—he wanted what was best for her even more.

And if that wasn't the definition of love, he didn't know what was.

He loved her. He was going to ask her to marry him.

Not now, not until all of this was over. Not until he'd fulfilled his obligations to Lincolnshire, dealt with the aftermath, and settled things between Deirdre and her husband. Not until he had something to offer Corinna besides lies and complications. Not until he could approach her brother with his head held high.

Even then, Cainewood would probably refuse him. But he was going to ask.

And, vicar's son that he was, he was going to pray harder than he ever had that the answer would be *yes*.

He kissed her, because he couldn't tell her he loved her. Not yet. But he kept the kiss chaste, because he really had meant it when he'd said they should wait.

Then he rose and reached for his shirt. "I'm thinking it's a good idea for us to stop, as you said. We'll finish tomorrow afternoon."

THIRTY-FOUR

*T*HE NEXT DAY, Lincolnshire perked up.

When Lord Stafford made his usual early morning call, he was pleased to see his patient more comfortable. "He's more awake than he's been for days," he reported when he came out of the earl's bedroom following his examination. "And he can speak whole sentences—entire paragraphs—without pausing for breaths between words."

Sean had suspected the man might be getting better. "Do you expect all the sleep has revived him?"

"Perhaps, but only temporarily," the doctor reminded him. A gentle warning. "This sort of disease tends to progress and regress in uneven waves, but he's not recovering by any means." His brown eyes met Sean's with sympathy. "You'd best enjoy your uncle's alertness while you can."

Lincolnshire wasn't his uncle, but Sean nodded and thanked Stafford and saw him out. Only to find someone else coming in.

The tall man carried a leather valise. A quite official-looking one. "I'm Mr. Lawrence Lawless," he said by way of introduction. "Lord Lincolnshire's solicitor. Here to consult with him at his request."

Lawless seemed a very sober sort of man, but Sean couldn't suppress a smile at meeting a lawyer named Lawless. He turned away to hide it, allowing Quincy to escort the man upstairs.

It was the last time Sean smiled that day.

The solicitor spent a full hour closeted in Lincolnshire's bedroom, and no sooner had he left than the earl summoned his nephew. On her way out to go to Raleigh, Deirdre turned back and went upstairs with Sean.

"Good day to you, Lord Lincolnshire," she said warmly as they entered his room.

"Good day to *you*, my dear," the earl wheezed. Sean was amused to hear him echo Deirdre's Irish phrasing rather than saying *good morning* in the English way. And pleased that Lincolnshire had managed to complete the sentence without pausing for breath.

But when the earl added, "I'm getting my affairs in order," Sean's good humor vanished.

That sounded so dire. So final. Despite the doctor's warning, despite his need to get on with his own life, Sean must have been holding on to some small hope that Lincolnshire might recover after all, because suddenly he felt an ache in his chest.

"I'm sorry," he mumbled.

"For what?" The older man coughed. "Sit...both of you."

Sean and his sister exchanged a glance. Playacting, or perhaps sensing Sean's distress, Deirdre took his hand as they slowly lowered themselves in unison.

The earl swiped the back of a swollen hand across his face, clearing his mouth of a bit of froth he'd coughed up. When his hand dropped, his lips were curved in a half smile of his own. "I'm pleased to see the two of you holding hands. I cannot imagine why those infidelity rumors persist, when I've seen for myself you've a wonderful marriage. Devoted, close...under-standing."

Sean's guilt spiked to record levels. He'd have dropped

Deirdre's hand like a hot coal, except she sensed that and gripped his tighter.

"Give her a kiss," Lincolnshire coaxed.

Sean turned to his sister and gave her a wee peck on the cheek.

Lincolnshire nodded, still smiling. "Discreet in public, as usual. But I'd wager that behind closed doors—"

"Uncle," Sean cut in. He couldn't take hearing more about his *wonderful marriage* to Deirdre. Not without losing his breakfast. "Was there something else you wished to tell me?"

"Indeed. I wanted you to know that I'm pleased—or shall I say overjoyed—at the success you've had finding new positions for all of my staff."

"It was nothing," Sean muttered.

"It was everything," Lincolnshire disagreed. "My heart sings to know all my holdings will be going to such a worthy young man. My nephew—my blood." Tears sprang to the older man's eyes: not tears of pain, but tears of regret. "I'm so sorry I never came to know you before this. That your undeserved reputation and my unresolved feelings about my brother kept me from seeking you out earlier—"

"There's nothing to be sorry for," Sean interrupted, having had enough of this guilt-inducing affection. "I'm glad we've had this time together. But your brother...this is the first you've mentioned these 'unresolved feelings' concerning him."

Lincolnshire shrugged. "I loved him, of course. He was my twin—"

"Your twin?" This was the first Sean had heard *that*.

"Surely you've noticed your father and I look identical?"

"I hadn't...thought about it." Now *he* was the one pausing between words. "My, uh...father...died years ago. He never mentioned you were twins. What happened between you? What made you banish your twin brother to the backwoods of Ireland?"

"Banish him?" Lincolnshire snorted. "He should have been down on his knees kissing my feet. I *saved* the ungrateful son of a gun." He cocked his head, measuring Sean for a long moment. "He never told you what happened?"

"Never." And Sean would wager that Deirdre's weasel of a husband wasn't aware of the facts, either. "What happened?"

"You honestly don't know?"

Sean shook his head.

Lincolnshire sighed. "When we were young men," he said, settling back against his pillows, "our father died, leaving me the earl. Your father was less than happy I inherited everything and he nothing. He was furious, as a matter of fact. A mere five minutes' difference in our births made me the heir and him the second son."

"It's understandable he might feel that way," Deirdre said, perhaps in leftover deference to her father-in-law.

"I agree. But that's the way our world works. I assured him I'd take care of him, support him and his new child and his young wife—a wife he'd been forced to wed after getting her in the family way, I might add."

"Like father, like son," Sean whispered beneath his breath.

"Why do you say that?" the earl asked, proving his hearing wasn't affected by the dropsy. "My father's marriage was a love match. No one forced him to wed our mother."

"No, of course not," Sean said quickly, thinking back. Hamilton's parents' marriage hadn't been a happy one, from what he remembered. He'd always figured the discord was caused by their misery at being stuck in Ireland, but maybe it had been more than that. "Just a slip of the tongue. Pray, go on."

"Well, promising to support my brother and his family wasn't enough. He wanted more than just a generous allowance. Shortly after I inherited, I went off to Ireland, to Kilburton, to see my steward, meet my villagers and tenants. I returned to a scandal of unimaginable proportions."

"What?" Deirdre breathed.

"In my absence, William had decided to take some of what he considered his due. He'd pretended to be me, and we looked so much alike that people had believed him. He'd lived in this house, worn my clothes, gone to my club. He'd attended dinners and card parties and breakfasts and balls and soirees. He'd even paid my respects to King George at court, and while doing all of this, he'd run up debts that amounted to thousands. The biggest gaming debt in all of London, in my name. He couldn't pay it, of course. And a man's vowels, a debt of honor, is expected to be paid before any other."

"They must have been livid," Deirdre said. "All those men to whom he owed money."

"Oh, they were livid, all right. All the gentlemen and the ladies, too. But not because of the debt. I paid that immediately upon my return."

"Why then?" Sean asked. "Why should they remain angry after having been paid?"

"Because he'd tricked them," the earl said. "Made fools of them, one and all. He'd made them believe he was me, and for that they would never forgive him. Society has a long memory, and they hold a grudge even longer." Lincolnshire's sigh was one of heartache, of sorrow and deepest regret. "Only the gravest misdeeds will warrant the cut direct, but my brother had crossed that line."

"He had to leave," Deirdre concluded. "He couldn't stay any longer in London."

"Indeed, he couldn't. Many wanted him banished to the countryside, to live in poverty and anonymity, or even better, they'd have preferred to have seen him shipped off to America. He hadn't the option of entering the clergy, and I couldn't buy him a commission in the military—the peerage is too well connected to both for him to have held posts in either. So I did what I could. I sent him to Ireland, where no one knew him.

Where he could hold up his head and play the lord in Kilburton. Live in the drafty old castle—"

"He built an enormous new manor house."

"I know that, my dear." Lincolnshire smiled sadly at Deirdre. "He wanted a fancy new house, and I wanted him to be happy. Or at least as happy as possible. He was my brother, after all, my twin. If I never fully forgave him, it wasn't because of what he did, but because I lost him as a result."

"He never forgave you, either," Deirdre said.

"I know that, too. But I also know I did my best." He looked to Sean, who hadn't said anything for quite a while. "I hope you don't blame me for your father's disgrace. Under the circumstances—"

"No," Sean said in a dead tone. It was the only tone he could manage, because he felt dead inside. "I don't blame you."

"You understand, then?" Lincolnshire pressed.

Sean nodded. He understood perfectly.

He understood that the aristocracy wouldn't tolerate deception. He understood they held grudges forever. He understood that, having impersonated Hamilton, Lincolnshire's nephew and heir, he'd soon be earning the cut direct himself.

Once Mayfair learned the truth, no member of society would speak to him ever again. They'd look right through him as though he weren't there. And should he marry Corinna, she and all of her family would be rejected along with him.

How had he not realized this? How had he convinced himself that he, an Irish vicar's son, could ever presume to wed the daughter of an English marquess? He and Corinna had been doomed from the first. If not by his background, then by Hamilton's schemes. Blast the weasel.

Blast him to blazes and beyond.

The fact that Sean would never have met Corinna if not for Hamilton was irrelevant. He'd been happy before he met her, or if not happy, at least content. But now...

How could he ever hope to be either again?

And how was he going to tell her? They'd never discussed marriage, but he wasn't a knothead. He knew that she cared for him—he'd seen the dreamy look she sometimes got in her eyes.

And she had only three days to fix Lincolnshire's portrait. After she sketched Sean this afternoon, she'd have only two days left to paint. The truth could devastate her, break her concentration, destroy any chance she had of achieving her lifelong dream. How could he tell her now?

He couldn't.

He couldn't tell her for three whole days, until after the painting was finished. He was going to have to lie again, for her sake. He hated lying. And lying to the girl he loved seemed the worst lie possible.

His gut felt heavy. Like an anvil was lodged in it.

"Nephew... Sean." The earl was tiring. And clearly struggling to make amends. His eyes were pleading. "I wish I'd... known you all these years. I'm so...sorry—"

"Please, Uncle," Sean ordered himself to focus on the dear old man. "I can't bear to see you in such distress. We've come to know each other now, haven't we? And nothing could make me happier than bringing what cheer I can to you in your time of need."

"Cheer? I am...euphoric. You came running when I asked... you've cared for me like a son. You've found positions...for my servants...seen all my concerns...are alleviated."

Lincolnshire wheezed, then coughed, then placed a hand on his chest. His lids fluttered, then slowly shut. Before he drifted off to sleep, he uttered one last sentence in a ragged whisper.

"You're the best man...I've ever had...the privilege of knowing."

But Sean felt like the worst person who'd ever lived.

THIRTY-FIVE

ICED CAKES

Mix sugar together with butter and rose-water. Mix this together with six eggs leaving out two whites and beat for a quarter of an hour. Put in your flour and mix them together well. Put them in your patty pans in an oven as hot as for manchet. Then make your icing. Put fine sugar in a mortar with rose-water and the white of an egg. When the cakes are cold put them on a tin then dip a feather in the icing and cover them well. Set the cakes back in the oven to harden.

These are sweet as a newborn baby. Eat them for the baby's health.

—Belinda, Marchioness of Cainewood, 1799

"OH, AUNTY, she's beautiful." Balancing Harry on her hip, Alexandra leaned to run a finger down her new cousin's tiny, downy cheek. "Is she a good baby?"

"When she isn't crying." Aunt Frances was reclining on a chaise longue that had been moved to her drawing room, holding Belinda close. She smiled a weary smile at all the visiting ladies seated around her. "Which seems to be most of the time."

"For her first three months, my youngest daughter cried all

the time too," Lady A said. "She nearly drove me to Bedlam. Luckily she soon outgrew that and was a lovely child thereafter."

"I'm certain Belinda will outgrow it, too," Claire said.

Elizabeth nodded. "And you do have the monthly nurse."

Rachael took an iced cake from the plate Juliana offered. "I expect the nurse sees to the baby's needs?"

"True," Aunt Frances said wryly. "The monthly nurse currently sees to her needs, and she's instructing the permanent day nurse and the night nurse. I'm only surprised Theodore hasn't hired a governess to start teaching Belinda her letters and numbers already. Nothing is too much for his daughter."

"As it should be," Lady A said approvingly. "It was the same with mine."

"But *three* nurses? When I'd as soon care for Belinda myself?"

"Alexandra feels the same way." Juliana set down the platter. "I expect I shall be that way, too. May I hold her?"

"Of course." Aunt Frances held out the baby. "Support her head."

"I know," Juliana said, taking Belinda like an expert. "I learned that with little Harry."

Bouncing her son, Alexandra watched her sister and smiled. "Does she make you want one of your own?"

"I'm going to have one of my own," Juliana murmured, gazing down at Belinda's tiny face. "In the winter."

A hush fell over the room. Someone let loose an excited squeal. Then it seemed everyone was talking at once, exclaiming and congratulating and jumping from their seats to rush over and give Juliana hugs.

Except for Corinna, who seemed riveted in place. She was very happy for her sister. But she was also very confused.

Suddenly, despite the horror of little Belinda's birth, she was quite certain she wanted a child after all.

She supposed somewhere in the back of her mind, she'd known all along she would have children someday. Someday unimaginably far away, that was—after she'd made her mark on the art world. And because starting a family seemed such a vague and distant event, because she had no mental picture of her prospective family, it had been easy to dismiss the whole idea when she'd been frightened by Aunt Frances's ordeal. But now her future children didn't seem so vague.

Because she knew who she wanted their father to be.

He had dark hair and perfectly clear, deep green eyes. A charming grin. An irresistible accent.

And Sean Delaney's face.

Sean was exactly what had been missing from the picture. He was honorable and kind and supportive. He would make such an amazing father.

Of course, she'd have to marry him first, but she'd already been thinking about that, hadn't she? And she couldn't imagine having a child with anyone else. No one else had ever made her feel like Sean did. No one else ever would.

And giving birth with him by her side, soothing her and encouraging her the way he had when she was nervous about the reception, suddenly didn't seem so bad.

Oh, very well, it still seemed hideously awful. But she knew she could trust Sean to get her through it.

"Are you all right?" Juliana asked, interrupting her reverie. She waved a hand in front of Corinna's face. She had handed the baby to Rachael at some point. "You look odd."

That made sense, because Corinna felt odd. Or at least different from how she'd ever felt before. She cleared her head with a little shake, and smiled. "I'm sorry, I must have drifted off for a moment. I'm so excited!" She threw her arms around her sister.

It was true. She *was* excited. For Juliana, James, and the whole family. And for this afternoon, when she'd see Sean in the garret again. But there was something—something unpleasant— niggling at her. It wasn't childbirth. She'd put those worries aside for now. It was something more immediate, but she couldn't seem to quite put her finger on it.

She must have tensed up, because Juliana pulled away, looking suspicious. "You're *sure* you're excited?"

"Of course I am." Corinna forced a laugh. "I'm just being selfish as usual. Thinking about my upcoming submissions. I need to take my paintings to Somerset House on Monday."

"Who is going with you?" Lady A asked.

Corinna hadn't thought that far ahead, but of course she couldn't go alone. It wouldn't be proper. Being a girl could be terribly inconvenient at times. "I suppose I'll ask Griffin."

"I'd be honored to accompany you, my dear." Lady A's smile looked wistful. "It would be my pleasure. I'm supposed to assist my nephew at the Institute until four o'clock on Monday, but I can tell him I need to leave at noon." The New Hope Institute was James's facility, where he provided smallpox vaccinations for the poor. Lady B was his assistant today—she and Lady A took turns. "Will that be early enough?"

"That will be fine." Considering all that kind Lady A had done for her, Corinna wouldn't think of denying her wish. "I'll come for you in my brother's carriage at one o'clock. The submission deadline isn't until five."

"Oh, then two o'clock would be better, if you wouldn't mind. That way I'll have time for luncheon first. And there's nothing to worry about." Lady A leaned to give Corinna's hand a pat. "The committee members said lovely things about your paintings. My daughter would have been overjoyed to have such important men admire her work," she added with a sigh.

Corinna didn't know whether Lady A's sigh was a hopeful one or a regretful one. But regardless, she sighed along with her.

"Most of them did say nice things, but they also said my portrait wasn't quite right. I need to fix it before Monday."

"You're not going to skip the Teddington ball tomorrow night, are you?" Juliana asked. "Or Lady Hartley's breakfast on Sunday? It's the event of the season."

"I probably should skip both." Which meant Griffin would be hovering over her all weekend, badgering her to leave the house and meet more gentlemen. "I wish I could find somewhere peaceful to paint."

"Chelsea Physic Garden is very peaceful." Sitting beside Corinna on the sofa, Juliana rubbed her belly, even though it was still flat as a canvas. "Only physicians and apothecaries can usually gain entrance, but James could request a ticket for you."

"I was just in Chelsea yesterday," Rachael commented a bit absently, bouncing Belinda on Corinna's other side. "At the Royal Hospital."

"Why was that?" Corinna asked.

When Rachael hesitated, looking flustered—which was unusual for self-assured Rachael—her younger sister Claire answered for her. "It was a charitable visit. She brought books for the pensioners."

"That was very kind," Lady C said.

A footman came in and set a tray of tea things on a table by the door.

"Would anyone like tea?" Since Aunt Frances wasn't up to acting as hostess, Lady A rose and made her way toward the teapot, saying, "My younger daughter's father-in-law is a Chelsea Pensioner. But I haven't heard from him in years."

While Lady A was across the room, Rachael nudged Corinna. "Lady A seems to take any excuse to mention her younger daughter," she whispered. "I think the poor woman really misses her."

"You don't say," Corinna whispered dryly.

"James told me Lady A's younger daughter took her own

life," Juliana said quietly. "Lady A doesn't have any grandchildren. Her oldest daughter eloped against her father's wishes, and he banished her from their lives. Her middle child, a son, drank too much and accidentally drowned. And her younger daughter was in the family way when she jumped off the London Bridge, taking Lady A's last chance at having a grandchild with her."

"Oh, poor, poor woman!" Rachael sighed. "I really like Lady A. She reminds me of my mother. I think it's the gardenia scent she wears. Mama always loved gardenia perfume." Though she smiled, the expression looked sad. "I think I'll go help her pour tea."

As their cousin went off to return Belinda to Frances and join Lady A, Corinna nudged Juliana. "I think Lady A smells as much of camphor as gardenias."

"I agree." They pulled faces at each other. "But as Rachael's spirits are still low," Juliana added, "I don't think we should say anything to ruin her comforting illusion."

Corinna wished *she* had a comforting illusion. All the way through the rest of the visit, and all the way home, she tried to figure out what it was that could be niggling her. As she went up to her bedroom to ready herself before meeting Sean, she told herself things weren't that bad.

She was in love, and she still had time to fix Lord Lincolnshire's picture. And her life certainly wasn't as tragic as Lady A's. She'd lost her parents and a brother, yes, but to illness, which was sad but not completely unexpected. She hadn't lost anyone to drink, or to suicide, or because they'd eloped without permission and been banished from the family. And someday, she'd start her very own family, and—

She plopped onto her bed, suddenly realizing what was bothering her.

She'd decided she wanted to marry Sean. She wanted to have

children with him. But what if the only way to accomplish that was to elope?

She hoped Griffin would agree to their marriage, but what if he didn't? Sean wasn't anything like the gentlemen her brother pushed on her, and not only because he was Irish. He could certainly support her—after what she'd learned yesterday, she suspected he could support half of London. But he wasn't from their world. He wasn't an aristocrat. Griffin's saying he admired Sean and wanted his advice didn't mean he'd support their marriage.

She was willing to defy her brother's wishes to marry Sean, should it come to that. She was willing to run off to Gretna Green to elope. Her family wasn't the type to banish her. And she was an artist, after all, wasn't she? Freethinking, a rebel, unconventional.

But none of that mattered...because Sean *was* conventional.

He wouldn't elope with her against her brother's wishes. She knew him well enough to be certain of that. He was too honorable.

Too dratted honorable, again! She was beginning to think honor might be overrated.

The niggling feeling grew now that she'd pinpointed its cause. The iced cakes she'd eaten felt like they were congealing in her stomach, the tea she'd sipped sloshing around.

How could she force her brother to give his blessing? She didn't know. This was more Juliana's field of expertise. All Corinna knew was that unless she came up with a plan, her future with Sean was uncertain. This might be the last time they were alone together, ever.

She'd best make the most of it.

She'd work on a plan, she decided as she rose to change and gather her things. But in case she failed, she wanted one last kiss.

And it had better be a good one.

She'd just have to make Sean comfortable so he wouldn't fear things going too far. And she couldn't afford to be nervous about sketching him today, either. If she were to have a prayer of fixing Lord Lincolnshire's portrait, she needed to study Sean. *All* of him.

Her stomach churned with a mixture of anxiety and anticipation and ice cakes. Thinking she might need what she'd sometimes heard referred to as "Dutch courage," she grabbed a bottle of her brother's first vintage on her way out.

THIRTY-SIX

*T*HERE WAS PLENTY of light streaming in through the garret's north-facing windows, so Sean didn't bother lighting candles this time. The atmosphere wasn't nearly as romantic, which suited his intentions perfectly.

Unfortunately, Corinna seemed to have some rather different intentions.

He'd noticed she'd brought two glasses and a bottle of wine, and now she was looking him up and down with that not-quite-flirtatious look on her face. "The light is perfect," she said, confirming his assessment. "I can see *all* of you."

He swallowed hard.

How on earth were they going to get through this session without any impropriety? Or rather, without any *unnecessary* impropriety—taking off his clothes was plenty improper all on its own. But yesterday, he'd only removed his shirt, and today she wanted to see *all* of him.

"This is a business meeting," he reminded her.

"A what?"

"We're here to get sketching done. There won't be any kissing. And I'm thinking you won't need to see all of me at once."

He watched her set out the wine glasses. "I'm remembering you said you wanted to sketch part of me at a time."

"I really need to see all of you if I'm to fix Lord Lincolnshire's portrait." Turning away, Corinna made herself busy pouring the wine. "Male artists get to sketch live models day in and day out. I have only these two sittings to get it right." With an apologetic smile, she turned back and held out a glass filled to the brim. "I brought some of my brother's wine to help us both relax."

Sean accepted the wine reluctantly. He needed to keep a clear head. He took a tiny sip, just to be polite.

She took a much larger gulp. "Don't you like the wine?"

"I like it fine. But I don't drink very much, so it goes straight to my head."

"Now I'm remembering you drank only a little that night you were summoned to our family dinner. Just a couple of sips."

"I watched my mother's father drink himself into the grave. An effective advertisement for moderation."

She touched his hand, a brief contact that still gave him a jolt. "I'm sorry."

He'd felt the warmth of her fingers, and now he smelled her sweet floral fragrance and the hint of paint underneath. He loved that hint of paint, because it was uniquely Corinna and he loved *her*.

But he couldn't kiss her. They couldn't end up together, so it would be wrong.

He couldn't kiss her. Kissing her would be wrong.

He'd just have to keep repeating that to himself until he accepted it.

He moved toward the sofa as an excuse to put more distance between them. "Grandpapa was a happy drunk, but he never made anything of himself," he said, taking another polite sip before sitting down.

"You've made a lot of yourself," she said, moving to sit across from him. After another big gulp, she set her glass on the floor. It was already half empty. "You're the best person I know."

She was the second person to tell him that today, which served to remind him of the first, and then the rest of what Lincolnshire had revealed. He tried to shove it all from his mind. He couldn't stand to think of it right now, of losing her, of—

He took a more generous sip of wine.

Her blue, blue eyes locked on his, she opened the sketchbook. "You can undress now. I'm ready."

He wasn't ready—he didn't think he'd ever be ready—but there was nothing for it. He'd offered to pose for her, and he wanted her painting to be a success. He took another swallow of wine and put his glass down carefully, then stood and tugged off his boots and stockings, his cravat, his coat, his waistcoat. Feeling her gaze on him, he unbuttoned his shirt and stripped it off over his head.

Like last night, his hands moved to the buttons on his trousers. But this time she didn't stop him.

He stopped himself instead.

Gulping air, he wished it were wine. So he reached for his glass and took one more sip.

"Sean?" she whispered, then bit her lip. She looked as tense as he felt. And as full of…well, to be perfectly honest, lust. Her cheeks were flushed, her eyes wide and dreamy…

The sight devastated him.

Their gazes were locked together, and it could be only a matter of time before *they* were locked together, too. The pull between them was uncanny. Overwhelming. Even preposterous…he almost wanted to laugh. He couldn't cope with these feelings—was there any human who could? It was extraordinary. It was a nightmare. He was breaking apart at the seams.

But somehow they had to keep it together. Or was it that they needed to stay apart? He couldn't seem to think straight. (How much wine had he drunk?) Maybe he should just tell her the truth right now. Tell her they had no future together. Cut this off before he completely lost his head.

No, he couldn't tell her, not until she'd finished the portrait. Telling her wouldn't just cut this off; it would devastate her. He was devastated already, so he knew exactly how she would feel. Completely, utterly devastated.

And she wouldn't be able to paint...

THIRTY-SEVEN

CORINNA COULDN'T sketch.

She could only stare. At Sean. It was taking everything she had to stop herself from leaping across the space between them.

It seemed the wine was going to *her* head instead of his. She gnawed her bottom lip, feeling a bit woozy. He'd said he wouldn't kiss her, but she wouldn't settle for that. What if this was the last time they were ever alone together? This could be their last chance to kiss. Ever.

How could she get him to kiss her?

Again, this was Juliana's sphere. Juliana was the beguiling sister. What would she do?

As soon as Corinna asked the question, she knew the answer.

Juliana would use *the look*.

Yuck. Corinna cringed just thinking about it. *The look* was a sort of choreographed flirtation that Juliana swore by. She said it would make men fall at one's feet. And Corinna *had* seen it work, more than once. But still, she'd never imagined trying it herself. She'd always found it too laughably contrived.

Maybe it was the Dutch courage or the desperation—or both—but suddenly she didn't care.

Remembering her sister's instructions, she glanced down, letting her lashes flutter, and then swept her gaze up, looking Sean dead in the eye as she curved her lips very slowly in a seductive smile. At least she hoped it was seductive...

His pupils dilated, and he sucked in his breath.

Huh. Perhaps she could be beguiling, after all.

Or perhaps it was just Sean. He was so beguiling himself that any girl would feel beguiling around him. Every word he said in that lyrical Irish voice seeped right into her, melting her insides. She hadn't even touched him yet, nor had he touched her, but her body was already humming.

Soft light slanted through the north-facing windows, highlighting his sculpted cheek, his crisp hair, the faint dark stubble on his chin. She wondered what the stubble felt like.

She breathed slowly in and out, watching Sean's face. He was watching her too, *watching her with the most impassioned look*, just like Lord Mortimer in *Children of the Abbey*.

It was a look more potent than any wine...

~

*S*EAN STOOD riveted, transfixed, waiting for Corinna to do something. To start sketching or try to kiss him, so he could tell her to stop. Because he had to tell her to stop.

He couldn't kiss her. Kissing her would be wrong.

But he couldn't stop it until it started, and the waiting was excruciating. The waiting and the wondering and the wanting. With an effort he tore his gaze away and turned to squint into the afternoon sun, as if perhaps he could burn the image of her off his retinas.

It didn't work. All he could see was that devastating look in her eyes.

"Sean," she said finally, her voice coming out a little hoarse. She rose, and he heard the sketchbook slide from her lap to the floor. She stepped over it and right up to him, so close he could feel the heat shimmering off her skin. Lifting a hand to his cheek, she turned his head to face her. "Are you all right, Sean?"

He wasn't all right, no. His heart hurt. He was devastated.

"Sean," she whispered, brushing her fingers on his face so gently he wondered that he could feel it. But he did feel it, so strongly the feeling seemed to spread all through him. She leaned closer. "Sean, will you kiss me? Please?"

Saints preserve us.

It was so forthright, so Corinna. It reminded him of everything he loved about her. He saw fathomless blue, and he smelled paint, and he heard her low, sweet voice, which right now was hoarse with emotion and need. How could he push her away when she needed him so much?

But he couldn't kiss her. Kissing her would be wrong.

He kissed her.

It was a defensive move, because he couldn't look into her eyes a moment longer without the devastation ripping him apart. But the instant his lips touched hers, he lost his head completely.

Somehow they made it down to the sofa, and she was pushing him back and crawling over him. Time slowed, or maybe it sped, or maybe it ceased to have any meaning at all. His world was reduced to the softness of her mouth, and the sensation of her fingers on his bare skin, and the warmth of her body pressing him into the sofa.

And though none of it felt wrong, he was devastated.

But he couldn't stop, couldn't let go of her. He knew that once he let go, he'd never touch her again. They kissed their lips raw, and when they couldn't kiss anymore, they just lay together on the sofa, her head on his chest, his hands in her hair, saying nothing, scarcely moving.

They stayed like that for a long time. When Sean opened his eyes, the sun was beginning to dip.

"Are you awake, *críona*?"

She nodded without lifting her cheek from his chest.

"I'm sorry." He wrapped his arms around her, still not ready to let her go, and pressed his sore lips to the top of her head. "I'm so sorry," he murmured against her hair.

"I'm not sorry," she said. "I know you think this is wrong, but I don't. I think it's exactly right. I feel like I've been waiting for you forever."

Hearing her say those words, he discovered he still had a wee shred of clarity. The wispiest shred, the barest fog, but just enough to bring him back to the real world. The world where he couldn't be with her, not forever, not for a moment, not at all.

"I'm sorry," he said again, and sat up, moving her off him. His throat felt tight, making it difficult to breathe.

He was devastated.

They had no future together.

But he couldn't tell her, not now, not until her painting was finished.

And he still had to help her fix the painting. She hadn't sketched yet, and she needed to sketch. He couldn't marry her, he would never be with her, but he could still do what he'd come here to do. Three days from now, when he told her the truth, when he devastated her, at least she would have her art. She'd have fixed her painting, and when it was accepted for the Summer Exhibition, she would still have her dreams, and they would help console her.

That thought in mind, he rose from the sofa and pulled her up, too. He gripped her shoulders and turned her around. "Go sit in the chair, Corinna."

She looked back at him. "What?"

"It's time to sketch now." He started unbuttoning the left side of the falls on his trousers.

"I feel hazy now." She turned to face him. "I think we should do this tomorrow."

"We came here so you can sketch," he said, unbuttoning the right side. "This is a business meeting, remember? Go sit down."

She backed up, watching him shuck his trousers. When her legs hit the chair, she dropped onto it, her eyes as wide as he'd ever seen them. Thank goodness he'd remembered to wear short drawers, he thought, because like many a fellow, he often went without. Tucking one's shirt tails under and over was generally much more comfortable.

"This is all I'm taking off," he said, grabbing a used sketch-book off the table. "I trust it will be enough. Sketch, Corinna." He sat, holding the book as the earl had in her picture, arranging himself in a similar pose. "I want you to sketch."

Her gaze wandered over him. Wandered everywhere. That dreamy look returned to her eyes.

She devastated him.

But he hadn't the luxury of being devastated, not now. "Start sketching."

"I really don't think I can concentrate. I drank too much wine. We'll have to do this again tomorrow."

"We're not doing this again, Corinna. I'm not leaving here until you've sketched enough anatomy to fix Lincolnshire's portrait. And I'm not kissing you again, that I promise...so sketch."

THIRTY-EIGHT

*C*ORINNA HAD never painted so fast in her life.

As she swept her brush along the canvas, she remembered all the hours she'd spent sketching earlier tonight. Intense hours. She hadn't thought she'd be able to concentrate, but she'd found herself focusing, fascinated, sinking into the experience. After sketching a full hour and realizing that wasn't nearly enough, she'd sent home a note, and Sean had lit candles, and she'd kept sketching.

She'd captured him, all of him, head to bare toe. Captured his essence, she was sure of it. Her painting instructors had spoken of this, but studying a real, live man had made the difference. Finally, after months and years of trying, it had all clicked into place. She'd come home with page after page of sketches that she knew would help her fix Lincolnshire's body beneath his clothes.

She wouldn't see Sean again until the portrait was finished. He'd made it clear, very clear, that he expected her to spend the entire weekend painting. Knowing she needed that time, she hadn't argued. Much as she would miss seeing him, she had but two days left to paint.

Three hours ago, in the darkness, Sean had walked her to her doorstep, kissed her forehead, and sent her inside to fix the portrait. Instead, without conscious thought, she'd grabbed a blank canvas. In the quiet house, while Griffin and his staff slumbered upstairs, she'd surrounded it with lanterns.

And started another portrait, more vivid than any she'd ever painted before.

Now, in the middle of the night, the picture was pouring out of her, the brush flying over the canvas. Hour by hour, stroke by stroke, the portrait was taking form, coming to life.

Unlike most of the portraits she'd ever seen, this portrait wasn't posed; it wasn't contrived; it wasn't meant to convey the importance of its subject. The gentleman's clothing wasn't carefully chosen to indicate his level of status or wealth. He wasn't meticulously groomed, nor did he hold objects imbued with significance. His gaze didn't issue a challenge. It didn't say: *Look at me. I'm superior and distinguished.*

Instead, the subject reclined half-clothed, sprawled with casual abandon on a sofa upholstered in sumptuous velvet. He held nothing, one arm relaxed along the back edge of the furniture, the other on a bent knee. His shirt had been removed and draped negligently on the sofa, revealing a toned chest and smooth skin that gleamed in the candlelight. His feet were bare, his legs clad in form-fitting trousers. His gaze was focused off-canvas, lost in contemplation. It didn't say anything direct at all, allowing the viewer to draw his own conclusions.

It was Sean, of course. Sean in a richer version of the garret studio, Sean in Corinna's mind's eye. Young, taut golden skin. Crisp black hair. Eyes of the deepest emerald green edging toward black, a shadowed hint of stubble on his chin. All she'd touched, all she'd experienced, all her emotions, all she wanted...

Exposed for all to see.

As she created, snatches of prose tumbled through her mind.

...a passion which virtue cannot sanction or reason justify...

...the soul-soothing certainty of being beloved by him...

...life, without him, would lose far more than half of its charms...

She painted without thinking, only feeling. Flesh tones, candlelight and shade, starched white linen, velvet-dark fabric. The sofa, ruby red and decadent. Richly paneled walls in the background, an exotic carpet underfoot.

Her brush followed the ridge of a thigh, the slope of a shoulder. The jaw, the cheek, the flexed and bended knee. Her insides were melting again. Melting right onto the canvas.

She was going to marry him.

She had a plan now, a solution, something to guarantee Griffin's cooperation.

This painting.

An hour ago, well into painting it, she'd suddenly realized that all she needed to ensure Griffin's blessing was to tell him the truth—and prove it. If he knew that Sean had posed for her half-naked in the garret, he'd have to agree to their marriage. If he saw this portrait, he'd *insist* on it.

He'd insisted Tristan marry Alexandra after they were caught together in her chamber, even though they'd both sworn nothing had happened in her bed. The sight of this portrait would make Griffin think she and Sean had shared a bed, too.

And if she didn't correct that assumption, well, it would serve him right for jumping to conclusions.

She stepped back and examined her work.

It was spectacular. The portrait looked breathtaking in the lanternlight, like a window into another world. Though still quite unfinished, she had no doubt it would be the most inspired thing she'd ever painted. It was provocative and scandalous and altogether brilliant.

It would be the talk of the Summer Exhibition.

No!

Blinking, she took another step back.

She couldn't.

If it were selected, it would be hung for all to see. Sean would be mortified. And everyone—*Griffin!*—would know that he had posed for her half-undressed. It would be like announcing to the world that she and Sean were...

Unless...

Unless nobody knew it was Sean.

What if she were to change the hair color, the eyes? Then no one would recognize him. There might be whispered speculation about the artist's love interest, but she could laugh it off, because no one would find a young man who looked like him anywhere.

That was an idea. She held her breath, thinking it over.

Was she bold enough to actually go through with it?

As soon as she asked the question, she knew the answer. Or rather, she knew that she'd asked herself the wrong question.

The right question was: Did she want to be an artist, or not?

She was going to forget Lincolnshire's portrait. Forget her landscapes and still lifes. *This* would be the painting she submitted for the Summer Exhibition.

The one she wanted to be known for, the one that would launch her career.

~

SEAN WAS IN a beastly mood when he joined Deirdre for breakfast the next morning. A cup of coffee was waiting on the table, strong and black the way he liked it, and she pushed it toward him after he slammed into his chair.

"You look upset," she said mildly, sipping her tea.

Upset didn't begin to describe his feelings. It didn't so much as scratch the surface. Allowing wine and weakness to overcome him last night, he'd kissed Corinna again when he'd promised himself he wouldn't. And keeping the truth from her was tearing him up inside, like coarse gravel tumbling around in his gut.

He'd been fooling himself all along, of course. There'd never been a chance for him and Corinna. And Deirdre wasn't going to get her divorce, either. The moment Sean had appeared as Hamilton in public, he'd sealed his sister's fate. All that was left was seeing Lincolnshire through his last days. There was nothing else of worth he could do.

But he wasn't going to tell Deirdre any of that.

"Lincolnshire's sliding downhill again," he said instead, taking a gulp of the hot, bracing coffee. "He's too tired to come down and join us."

"Someone to see you, Mr. Hamilton." A footman appeared in the doorway. "Your assistant, Mr. Sykes."

"Mr. Sykes? Send him in. At once. Please," he added as an afterthought.

"By all means," the man said, and left.

"Just what I need," Sean muttered.

Deirdre frowned. "What could he want?"

"I haven't a clue. But it's Saturday. Sykes doesn't work on Saturday. Which means whatever it is can't be good."

"You can't know that. It might not be bad."

"Maybe it isn't."

And maybe the sun would fail to rise tomorrow. Maybe it wouldn't rain in London for the whole of the summer. Maybe a marquess's daughter would marry a backwoods Irish nobody.

"Will you shut the door?" he requested when Sykes walked in.

The secretary obliged. "I apologize for the interruption."

"I'm certain you've a good reason. Do sit down."

After pulling out a chair, Sykes wasted no time coming to the point. "All of your concerns are being investigated. Inquiries are being made." He pushed up on his round spectacles. "Not only at your main offices, but at your factories, your shipyards, your—"

"I get the picture," Sean interrupted.

The timing was awful, but he wasn't all that surprised.

It was one of those *people Sean feared*, probably someone he'd done business with. Perhaps someone whose failing enterprise he'd purchased for next to nothing and turned into a success. Or someone whose property he'd bought and improved and made profitable. Or someone whose employees he'd hired and paid better, or…

The possibilities were endless.

He liked to think he was a likable person, if maybe a bit driven. All of his business dealings were honest and straightforward, and, even more important, they were fair. He didn't cheat people, he didn't try to wring every penny he could get from them.

But this wasn't the first time someone had tried to ruin him, and he knew it wouldn't be the last.

"I'll get on it." Downing the rest of his coffee, he pushed back from the table. "If Lincolnshire needs me," he told Deirdre, "send for me. You know where I'll be."

He was out the door, on his way to Delaney & Company's main offices, before the cup stopped rattling in its saucer.

THIRTY-NINE

Berkeley Square, Saturday 17 May

My dear Cousin,

I have an idea I wish to discuss with you. As I'll be taking Corinna to the Teddington ball tonight, I hope you will also be attending.

Fondly,
Cainewood

❧

*a*RRIVING AT the Teddington Ball on Saturday night, Rachael waved to Lady A and looked around for Griffin. She found him in the refreshment room, talking to Juliana.

Or rather, complaining to Juliana.

"I cannot believe she refused to come tonight. How on earth am I supposed to find her a husband?"

"Corinna's submissions are due on Monday, Griffin. This is important to her."

"Well, she said she doesn't want to go to Lady Hartley's breakfast tomorrow, either, but I won't hear of it. It's the event of the season, and I've already lined up three young men for her to meet."

Juliana looked ready to argue, but then she noticed Rachael standing there. "Good evening, Rachael."

Griffin turned and looked at Rachael, too. Or rather, he skimmed her from her toes on up, his gaze taking in her sky blue silk dress before it reached her face. The rascal. "What are you doing here?"

"You sent me a note," she said, confused. "You asked me to come." What kind of a fool would ask her to come and then ask her why she was here?

"Well, I didn't ask you to wear a dress like that."

"It's a ballgown. This is a ball." What else was she supposed to wear? "Your note sounded important." She glanced around at the crush of people. "Is it something we should talk about privately?"

"Let's go to Lord Teddington's library."

"All right." They'd gone to the library during the Teddingtons' ball last year, too—in fact, it was where she'd first asked Griffin if he might help her find her father—so she knew exactly where to find it. Slipping inside, she walked over to a leather sofa and sat, irritated that she'd responded to his note. "What did you want to discuss with me?"

Leaving the door open, Griffin joined her on the sofa, sitting sideways to face her. "I thought of something," he said quietly. "Maybe your grandfather wasn't the last chance to learn what became of your father. If we can find your mother's family, perhaps they will know the truth."

She stared at him. "We cannot find her family."

"We have a name now. John Cartwright. If we can believe your grandfather's ramblings, he saved John Cartwright's life and Cartwright promised his daughter in return. I know your mother called herself Georgiana Woodby, but she must have been Georgiana Cartwright."

Rachael could see the sense in Griffin's reasoning. "But even if she was Georgiana Cartwright, she had no family left. There's no family to find."

"Maybe that's not the case. If she gave a false name, she might have told other untruths. She might have had living family, after all."

"Maybe." Though the implications made her reel, she was willing to concede the possibility. "But how would you find them with just a name, and such a common one at that?" The man who'd raised her had also been called John, as were many other gentlemen of her acquaintance. John Hamilton, for instance. "There must be a hundred John Cartwrights." Maybe more.

"But how many of them are titled? At the time of her marriage, your mother was Lady Georgiana, which means her father was an earl at the very least. We can look him up in *Debrett's Peerage*. Even if he did die young, the succession will be listed in the pedigree. If you have any living relations, I can find them."

Of course he could. "I'm a blazing idiot." It was so simple. "Why didn't I think of that?"

He shrugged. "I expect your mind was on other things. Your life has been rather traumatic lately. Besides," he added artlessly, "I'm here to think for you."

She preferred to think for herself, but she had to admit—if *only* to herself—that it was comforting to have Griffin's support. And surprising. Never in a million years had she thought she'd lean on Griffin.

A fellow dumb enough to ask her to a ball and then ask her why she'd come wearing a ballgown.

"I'm going to go home right now and consult *Debrett's*," she said. "Do you want to come with me?"

"There's no need to go anywhere," he said, rising from the sofa. "Why do you think I suggested we discuss this in Lord Teddington's library?"

She *was* a blazing idiot. Everyone had a copy of *Debrett's*. It didn't take long for Griffin to find the Teddingtons'. He drew it off a shelf and came back with it in his hands, a small but very fat volume bound in deep green leather.

"Here," he said, handing it to her as he reclaimed his seat by her side. "You look it up."

With shaking fingers she opened the cover and turned to the table of contents. All they had to go on was a last name.

"There," Griffin said. "'Surnames and the Superior Titles of the Peers and Peeresses of the United Kingdom of Great Britain and Ireland.' That's the section you want."

"I know," she said dryly. "I've looked in *Debrett's* before." She turned to that section and flipped to the second page, where the Cs were listed. "Cartwright—Avonleigh."

There was a little *e* by the listing, indicating Cartwright was an earl. "Your mother's father was the Earl of Avonleigh," Griffin said.

"Maybe." She wouldn't believe it until she saw her mother's name in the Earl of Avonleigh's pedigree. She simply couldn't make herself believe it.

Although the earls were all listed in one section, they were in no particular order that she'd ever been able to discern, so she went back to the front, where all the titles were indexed.

"Avonleigh," Griffin said. "There it is. Page two thirty-three."

"I can read, Griffin." He may have done all the research up until now, but she could do *this*. She turned to page 233. "'Robert Cartwright, Earl of Avonleigh...'" She scanned down past the current earl's birth and marriage dates. "'... succeeded his uncle, John, the late earl, born 1739, married 1765 to Aurelia Egerton, daughter of William, Earl of Wilton, by whom he has issue Alice, born 1767, married 1785 to George Egerton, youngest son of

John, Earl of Wilton, died 1799; Harold, born 1770, died 1791; Georgiana—'"

She broke off.

"There she is," Griffin said softly.

"Yes." There it was, in black and white, her mother's name.

"What does it say about her?" he prompted.

She swallowed hard and refocused on the tiny print. "'Georgiana, born 1777, married 1795 to Thomas Grimbald, died 1796.'"

"The year you were born," he said.

"Yes. She didn't die. She married my father—Lord Greystone —and had me." Something seemed to be tugging at her mind. Something significant. Confused again, she glanced up at Griffin.

His green gaze was unfocused, as though he were deep in thought. "Everyone believed she'd died, obviously. She was officially dead. Then she married Greystone and hid herself in the countryside."

"She pretended she had asthma and couldn't go to London because the air here was bad for her. She never liked to socialize."

"Are you sure?" Griffin asked. "I'm thinking she never came to London because someone here might have recognized her. Someone here would have realized she wasn't actually dead."

"Maybe," she said. "That does make sense. Maybe her family was here in London. John Cartwright, the Earl of Avonleigh, my grandfather. And his wife"—she glanced back to the pedigree to find the name—"Aurelia…"

When she trailed off, Griffin laid a gentle hand on her arm. "What?"

"Aurelia, Lady Avonleigh. I don't believe it." That was what had been tugging at her mind. "We know her, Griffin! She's Juliana's aunt by marriage, one of the ABC sisters. She hosted the art reception for Corinna. She smells of gardenias, like my mother. Lady Avonleigh is my grandmother!"

～

*A*T TEN O'CLOCK, Sean arrived back at Lincolnshire House, exhausted. Deirdre met him at the door and hurried him into what he thought of as the Hamilton drawing room. "What did you learn?" she asked, closing the door.

He shut his eyes, not wanting to see all of Hamilton's blasted pictures. "Nothing."

"Nothing?"

"I spoke with dozens of my people around London and learned nothing helpful," he told her, opening his eyes. "Whoever is making inquiries is going about it very discreetly. Asking who owns each place and what sort of fellow I am—but nothing else. Nothing to help me figure out what he's actually looking for. Or so my people told me."

"They haven't any reason to lie to you, have they?"

"I wouldn't think so, but even good people sometimes do wrong." Another lesson he'd learned. "They could have been bribed, or...oh, I don't know. Nothing surprises me anymore." He wandered to an armchair and dropped onto it.

"What happens now?"

"I've asked for reports from the operations farther out, but I won't be hearing anything back until tomorrow, at the earliest. More likely Monday and later in the week. I'd go interview them myself, but I cannot leave Lincolnshire."

"You cannot, no." She patted his shoulder sympathetically. "I'm sorry, little brother."

It was a chilly night, and someone had laid a fire on the hearth. He stared at the dancing flames for a while, wondering how Corinna was doing with the painting. Wishing she were here. She'd be far more of a comfort to him than Deirdre (though Deirdre was doing her best).

But he didn't deserve Corinna's comfort, he reminded himself. He'd be breaking her heart any day now.

"You didn't send for me," he said finally. "How is Lincolnshire? I suppose I should go up and talk to him."

"He's with Mr. Lawless. His solicitor."

"Again? This late at night?"

"The man's been here for hours. I cannot imagine what the two of them are doing in there."

"Getting Lincolnshire's affairs in order." Wishing he could get *his* affairs in order, Sean sighed and rose. "I'm after going up to bed."

"Good night. I hope tomorrow will be a better day."

"I hope so, too," he said.

But hoping, he knew, never accomplished anything. He was a doer, not a hoper...but there seemed nothing he could do these days to make things right.

FORTY

"*I* SAW HER here earlier," Rachael said, wandering the Teddington ballroom for the second time.

Griffin walked with her, keeping his eyes off her accursed clingy dress. Or at least trying to. "I saw her here as well, I think." He wasn't exactly sure which woman was the Dowager Countess of Avonleigh. He realized she was one of the ABC sisters, but Lady C, Juliana's mother-in-law, was the only one of them he knew at all well. He'd always thought of Lady A and Lady B sort of lumped together. One was plump and one was skinny, but he wasn't sure which was which. "Has she got some meat on her bones, or is she a stick?"

"Really, Griffin. She's a perfectly lovely, kind, healthy-looking woman."

The plump one, then. The other one looked like she hadn't eaten in a week, which couldn't possibly be healthy. "Let's check the refreshment room again. And then you can check the ladies' retiring room again."

"And we should check the garden again, too." Rachael turned toward the refreshment room, then turned back. "There's Lady C. I bet she'll know where her sister went. Lady

Cavanaugh!" She waved, and Lady C started walking toward them.

They met her halfway. "You look lovely tonight, dear," Lady C told her. "That's a stunning ballgown, and it matches your eyes, which are sparkling like diamonds."

"Thank you," Rachael said, her eyes sparkling even more. "I'm looking for your sister, Lady Avonleigh. Do you know where she might have gone off to?"

"I'm afraid she went home, dear."

"Oh, no. Is she unwell?"

"Not at all. But my sisters are older and don't stay out as late as they used to, especially since they began helping my son run his Institute. I expect she's sound asleep by now." Lady C put a hand on Rachael's arm. "What did you want with her? Is it something I can help you with?"

"No. I...well, I just need to talk to her. Do you think she'd mind my paying a call on her tomorrow?"

"I'm sure she wouldn't mind at all," Lady C said, looking curious but obviously much too polite to press. She pulled her reticule off her wrist and opened it, fishing out a scrap of paper and a pencil. "She lives just off Oxford Street. I'll write down her direction for you."

"I know where she lives. I was at her house for Corinna's art reception."

"How could I have forgotten that?" With a charming laugh, Lady C dropped the items back into her fancy little purse. "I'm sure she'll be happy to see you again."

"Thank you so much," Rachael said, and waited patiently while Lady C walked off. Or at least, she *looked* patient. No sooner had the woman got out of earshot than she whirled to Griffin. "Lady Cavanaugh is my aunt—can you believe it? She's such a nice lady. The wait is going to kill me. Can we visit Lady Avonleigh first thing tomorrow? You'll come with me, won't you?"

"I need to take Corinna to Lady Hartley's breakfast."

"That doesn't start until half past one. The best people won't get there until three o'clock. It isn't fashionable to arrive at parties on time."

He'd never understand why a garden party that started after one o'clock was called a breakfast. He ate breakfast every morning at eight. And why on earth was it *fashionable* to arrive late? But maybe Corinna would be more cooperative if he allowed her to paint until three. "Very well, then. We'll go see Lady Avonleigh right after church."

"How about before church?"

"You can't wake up an old lady to give her this news, Rachael. Or interrupt her toilette. And then no doubt *she'll* be in church, and then she'll want luncheon." Lady A was the one who liked to eat, after all, and Lady Hartley wouldn't be serving "breakfast" until the fashionable people arrived. "I'll pick you up at one o'clock."

"Then we won't get to Lady A's until half past one. What if she's left for Lady Hartley's house already?"

"You just told me people won't arrive until three. Half past noon, then. That ought to be safe."

"I cannot wait that long."

"You've already waited twenty-one years, remember? I expect you'll survive."

"All right," Rachael muttered, sounding more than disgruntled. But her eyes were still sparkling. She looked better than she had in months, as though she were blossoming, as though a weight had lifted off her shoulders. Not that she'd looked bad before…

She licked her lips.

Hang it, he would really be in trouble now.

∿

"*H*OW IS IT going?" Griffin asked.

Startled, Corinna jumped, then quickly stepped from behind her easel, struggling out of the fog she'd been working in all day.

"All right," she said, though the painting was going brilliantly.

Although it was faced away from him, she raised her palette before it like a shield. She couldn't risk Griffin's seeing it before she'd changed Sean's hair and eyes—she didn't want him to know Sean was her model unless he had to know. Unless she had no choice but to tell him. With any luck, Griffin might decide she could marry Sean without ever learning about her "anatomy lessons."

"I don't want you to see it until it's finished."

He only shrugged. He'd never cared overmuch about her art. "I'm glad to hear it's going well. I want you to attend Lady Hartley's breakfast tomorrow."

"I'm not going, Griffin. I already told you that. How was the Teddington ball?"

"It went well. I lined up four gentlemen there for you to meet tomorrow. You should go up to bed now, so you'll be fresh."

She glanced toward the clock on the drawing room's mantel. "It's only one in the morning, and you know I rarely stop painting before three. And I don't need to be fresh tomorrow, because I'm not going to the breakfast."

"How about if we compromise and you paint until three o'clock tomorrow afternoon? That sounds fair, doesn't it? It's the event of the season."

"The Summer Exhibition is the event of my *life*." He was such a brother. And a bother. She decided to change the subject. "Have you asked Mr. Delaney's advice yet regarding property management?"

"I've been too busy. And why do you care?" His eyes

narrowed. "Juliana asked me about Mr. Delaney, too. You're not interested in him, are you?"

She wondered whether he would consider that a good thing or a bad one. "Interested in what way?"

"As a suitor. A potential husband."

She still couldn't tell what he was thinking. Better to play it safe, she decided; better he should get to know Sean before she admitted anything. "Of course not. I just remembered you'd said you wanted to talk to him, and I wondered if you had yet, that's all." She hoped that when he *did* talk to Sean he'd be impressed. "Now leave me alone, Griffin. I need to paint. And I'm not going to Lady Hartley's breakfast."

"I'll send our regrets," he gritted out, and then, as he walked off, Corinna heard him mutter, "Why do girls always seem to get the best of me?"

Fog-free for the first time all day, she returned to her easel to examine her progress. It really was coming along brilliantly, she thought, smiling. Just brilliantly.

But oh, my.

This was one extremely sensual painting.

It wasn't due to the model's state of undress—after all, artists had been depicting the human form for thousands of years, and besides, he was only uncovered from the waist up. No, what made the picture shocking wasn't the bare skin…it was the emotions laid bare on the canvas.

It was obvious—in fact, the painting positively screamed—that the artist was in love with her subject. Wildly, passionately in love. The painting was a moony-eyed vision of the world.

She decided no one besides the committee should see it before it was hung. Yes, it was her best work ever, and yes, nudity in art was nothing new, but regardless, showing the portrait to her friends and family would be risky. Even though they were lovely,, *relatively* broad-minded people, she felt certain they'd have trouble supporting her in this. Society was barely beginning to tolerate ladies painting regular, fully-clothed portraits, let alone sensual, half-nude ones! And even though he wouldn't recognize Sean, she shuddered to think how Griffin would react…

But after all was said and done, after her work had been honored by the Selection Committee, it would be a different story. Surely he would be proud of her then.

Wouldn't he?

Thanks heavens Lady A had offered to go with her to deliver it. She'd have to cover it up so the dear woman wouldn't be able to inspect it in the carriage. Then somehow get through the submission process without her ever seeing it.

How she'd manage that, she couldn't imagine, but she'd worry about that later. After the painting was finished, after she'd changed Sean's hair and eyes.

Until then, she wanted him just as he looked now, she thought, raising her brush to the canvas and letting the fog close in again.

FORTY-ONE

"*D*ID YOU NOT sleep well?" Deirdre asked when Sean slammed into the breakfast room again Sunday morning.

"I didn't sleep at all."

He'd spent the entire night alternating between worrying about Delaney & Company and arguing with himself over whether to devastate Corinna now or let her paint in peace.

There was nothing he could do about the former that he wasn't already doing. He knew that. As for the latter, he also knew what was kinder to Corinna. But it didn't feel kind to himself.

The gravel had torn his insides to a pulp.

Still deliberating, he gulped down coffee and little else, then stomped upstairs to play nephew to Lincolnshire.

Coming to a halt in the earl's doorway, he listened to the man's ragged snores for a long minute. "How is he doing?" he finally asked Mrs. Skeffington quietly.

Sadness etched on her face, the nurse shook her head.

The ragged snores ceased, making them both turn. "Cainewood?" Lincolnshire croaked.

"I'm here, Uncle." Sean walked closer and touched the man's hand, wincing when his fingers left indentations in the swollen flesh. "It's Sean."

Lincolnshire slitted his eyes, but just for a bare moment. "Cainewood?"

"He's not here, Uncle. But I am."

"Wake me...when...Cainewood...arrives," he wheezed again, and drifted off.

Sean looked to Mrs. Skeffington. "He thought I was Cainewood. Is he delirious, then?"

"Not delirious, but very tired. He was up quite late last night, closeted with his solicitor. And I fear..." She sighed and shook her head again. "I cannot say it."

Sean also feared the earl's time was short. "I cannot say it, either," he muttered. "Why would he want to see Cainewood?"

She shrugged. "Lord Lincolnshire asked for the marquess last night. Instructed Mr. Lawless to summon him first thing in the morning. I expect he wants to say goodbye. They've been neighbors for twenty-six years, after all, since the marquess was born." She forced a smile and patted Sean's hand with her own sturdy one. "I'll watch your uncle, Mr. Hamilton. You go paint. There's nothing you can do for him now."

He hesitated, then nodded. "Perhaps I will." The earl didn't seem to want or need him right at the moment. He wouldn't paint, of course, but he might go talk to Corinna or return to his offices. See if any reports had come in yet from outside London. "Please ask my wife to send for me if my uncle has need of me. She'll know where to find me."

He went downstairs and asked a footman to see that his curricle was brought round. As he headed for the door, the knocker banged, and Quincy opened it to reveal Corinna's brother.

Cainewood stood stiffly, his arms folded behind him. He looked impatient, or maybe furious. Sean didn't know him well enough to be sure which, but he was worn down and muddled from sleeplessness and guilt—guilt over lying to (and sneaking around with) Cainewood's sister. Had the marquess somehow found out?

For one wild moment, he expected Cainewood was hiding a pistol behind his back.

"It won't happen again," he blurted out.

As Cainewood raised his hands, Sean's last thought was: *She was worth it.*

Until he saw that the hands were, of course, empty. Then he thought: *I'm an idiot.*

Cainewood frowned down at the watch fob he'd lifted in order to check the time. "I beg your pardon?" he said absently.

Sean blew out a breath, remembering Lincolnshire. "The earl has been asking for you."

"Yes, his solicitor summoned me. I don't know why. But I've another appointment this morning, so I'm hoping this won't take long."

"I think he just wants to say goodbye," Sean assured him, moving past him.

On the street, waiting for his curricle, he found his gaze drifting to the town house with the blue door on the west side of the square. As though drawn by unseen cords, he walked toward it, stopping on the pavement in front of the large window that fronted the drawing room.

Corinna wasn't in the drawing room, of course. It wasn't even ten o'clock, and she slept until noon unless someone offered her a kiss for getting up early. Her easel was visible, though, so he walked closer to have a look at how Lincolnshire's portrait was coming along. But it sat sideways, and the painting was covered by a crisp white sheet.

And it wasn't finished. He knew that. She'd use every minute she had left before it was due. It wouldn't be finished before tomorrow, which meant he couldn't devastate her until then. He couldn't wake her—that wouldn't be fair.

He needed to see this thing through the right way, he lectured himself, heading back to where his curricle waited. He'd known that all along. There had been no use losing sleep over a decision so obvious.

❧

*L*ADY AVONLEIGH'S town house was near all of Oxford Street's many shops. As Griffin banged the knocker, Rachael couldn't help hoping that Lady A might invite her to visit often. They could go shopping and get to know each other. It would be such fun. She'd never had any living grandparents to spend time with—at least, not any she'd known of.

The butler who answered the door looked as old as Lady A and Lady B put together. "Yes?" he croaked.

"I've come to call on Lady Avonleigh," Rachael said.

He cleared his throat. "She's not here. She's left for Lady Hartley's breakfast."

"But it's not even one o'clock."

He shrugged his bony shoulders. "She doesn't like to be late, my lady."

Her heart sinking, she swiveled to Griffin. "I told you we should have come first thing in the morning."

When he also shrugged, she couldn't help noticing his shoulders were much wider than the butler's. "I don't mind waiting," he said.

"Lady Hartley's breakfast will probably last until midnight! It's the event of the season."

"We'll change our clothes, then, and go to the breakfast."

"I've already sent my regrets. And it's in a garden, under a tent. There will be no place to talk privately."

"We could walk with Lady Avonleigh in the garden."

"Any number of people might be walking as well and over-hear us."

"Then we could take her into Lady Hartley's house."

"You cannot go into someone's house during a garden party, Griffin. It's not polite to go where you're not invited."

"Juliana went into Lady Hartley's house during last year's breakfast," he pointed out.

"And look what happened! It was the scandal of the season!" When it came to the social niceties, men didn't know anything. She sighed. "We'll come back tomorrow. In the *morning*."

FORTY-TWO

$\mathscr{a}$S THE CLOCK on the mantel struck ten on Sunday night, Corinna dipped her smallest brush in coffee-colored paint and carefully covered the green irises on her canvas. Over the next quarter hour, she added black pupils, curvature, depth and highlights, and glints where the flame of a candle reflected.

Blowing out a breath, she stepped back.

Sean's eyes were brown now, and the portrait was done.

She'd already changed his dark hair to a streaky blond, made it a little wavier and a little longer, made it positively glow in the candlelight. The rest of the picture remained the same—the informal pose; the sculpted, faintly stubbled face; the gorgeous body; the heart-stopping gaze—but she was sure no one would recognize Sean now.

The painting was going to be a sensation.

Blond or black-haired, brown-eyed or green, the portrait looked compelling. Captivating. Spellbinding. Seductive. Like Sean himself.

She'd never completed such a large painting in only two days before, and she could hardly believe she was finished. The hours had sped by in such a frenzy since late Friday night. But done was done, and there was no sense in fiddling with it any longer. She'd be as likely to ruin it as she was to improve it.

Although she couldn't show it to Sean, of course—she wasn't yet ready for anyone, including him, to learn he was her portrait's inspiration—she couldn't wait to tell him it was complete. He'd be so surprised to hear she'd finished half a day early. Bursting with happiness and excitement and energy, she hefted the canvas off her easel and started upstairs, holding it at arm's length, where she could smile at it as she went.

She was hauling it down the corridor toward her bedroom when the door to Griffin's study opened. Whirling to face him, she watched him raise his hands to grip the jamb on either side of his head. Such a casual pose, when she was feeling her heart pound in her throat.

"What are you doing, Corinna?"

"Taking this to my room. I'm finished."

"Are you?" He looked pleased. Probably because he could get back to shoving men at her now. "Let's see it," he said, moving into the corridor.

"No!" In reaction, she pulled the canvas closer to her body, nearly smearing paint against her apron. She'd have killed him if that had happened, just *killed* him. "Not yet. It isn't varnished yet."

Artists rarely varnished their paintings before submitting them to the Summer Exhibition. There was a tradition called Varnishing Day, after the selected pictures were hung but before the Exhibition opened, when all the artists came to make last minute changes and coat their works in varnish.

"I don't want anyone to see it until after it's varnished," she added. "If it's accepted, you can see it in the Exhibition."

"Well, that's just silly."

She shrugged. "I'm an artist, temperamental and all that."

She began backing down the corridor. "I'm going to put this in my room now, and you'd better not go looking at it."

It was his turn to shrug, as though he couldn't be bothered to walk that far to look at a silly painting. He backed into his study, and she backed into her room and closed the door behind her. After leaning the painting against a wall, facing in, she covered it with a sheet. Then she balanced a hairpin precariously on the top edge, where it would be knocked off if anyone disturbed it.

There, she thought with a grin.

Impatient to see Sean, she ripped off her apron, smoothed her dress, left her room, and poked her head into Griffin's study. "I'm going to tell Lord Lincolnshire his portrait is finished," she said, although, of course, it wasn't.

Scribbling on some paperwork, Griffin didn't look up. "Lincolnshire will be sleeping now, Corinna."

"Maybe, but maybe not. I won't wake him. If he's sleeping, I'll go back in the morning."

"Take a footman with you. I won't have you walking alone in Berkeley Square in the middle of the night."

She rolled her eyes. "I'm not the ninnyhammer you seem to think I am," she informed him. "I won't be long." Then she all but ran down the stairs, pausing just long enough to request a footman before running all the way to Lincolnshire House. Leaving the footman panting at Lincolnshire's gate, she lifted her skirts, raced up the portico steps, and banged the knocker.

Quincy answered. "Good evening."

"I wish a word with Mr. Hamilton."

"I'm sorry, but he's not at home, milady."

"He isn't? Oh." Disappointment was a sudden ache in her middle. *How many hours must intervene ere she could press him to her throbbing heart, as the sweet partner of her future days?* She gave her head a little shake to dispel *Children of the Abbey.* "I'll return tomorrow then, I guess."

She had just started to turn away when Deirdre came to the door. "Lady Corinna?"

Turning back, she dredged up a smile. "I was hoping to see your...your husband, Mrs. Hamilton. I have something exciting to tell him."

"He's been gone all day. A wee bit of trouble with his, ah... his latest painting." Deirdre slanted a look at Quincy. "Would you care to come in?"

"Is Lord Lincolnshire awake?"

"I fear not." Sean's sister sighed. "He spent the morning closeted with his solicitor yet again. Then he complained of some pain—claimed the Regent was sitting on his chest again or some such thing. He passed out for a moment, then woke and fell asleep. He's been sleeping ever since."

"That doesn't sound good," Corinna said, the ache of disappointment growing sharper. "I'll return tomorrow, when I hope he'll be better."

Deirdre nodded and took a step back to allow Quincy to shut the door.

"Wait," Corinna said, remembering something. "I've a question, if you wouldn't mind. About a word or a phrase I'm thinking might be Irish."

"Is that so?" Coming forward again, Deirdre looked curious. "What is it, then?"

"Cooshla-macree. Does that mean something? Or is it only a few syllables of nonsense?"

Sean's sister frowned a moment before her expression cleared. "*Cuisle mo chroí,*" she repeated, the words sounding a bit different as they rolled off her tongue. "It means 'pulse of my heart.' Or 'sweetheart,' I suppose you might say."

"Sweetheart," Corinna breathed. "How about creena?"

"*Críona,* 'my heart.'"

"Ahroon?"

"*A rún,* 'my love.'" Sean's sister cocked her pretty blond

head. "I find myself wondering where you heard these words, I do confess."

"I expect you know." Bursting with happiness once more, Corinna gave a startled Deirdre an impulsive hug before she ran back home.

FORTY-THREE

SEAN DIDN'T slam into the breakfast room Monday morning. He was much too drained, much too discouraged for so much emotion. At half past seven, he simply walked in and slowly sat down, feeling brittle, as though his bones might crack in the process.

Deirdre slid his cup of coffee toward him just as slowly. "No good news?"

"No news at all." He reached for the cup but didn't drink from it, just cradled its warmth between his palms. "No helpful news, at any rate. Maybe today."

She sipped her tea, watching him. "Lady Corinna came by to see you last night before you returned. Late, but I hadn't yet gone up to bed. She seemed rather…excited. Out of breath. She must have run all the way here from her house. She said she had something to tell you."

"Her painting must be finished," he said glumly. She'd completed it half a day early, which meant it must have gone well. But it also meant it was time to explain the facts.

"You don't sound happy for her. It's a good thing, isn't it?"

"Sure, and it's excellent." Now he could devastate the love of his life.

They both glanced over as the door opened. "Mr. Hamilton?"

A maid entered. The one who'd shown Sean upstairs the first day he arrived, the little bird of a middle-aged woman who'd informed him Lincolnshire was the most wonderful man in all of England.

Today she looked like an old woman, her face drawn in tight lines. "Nurse Skeffington asked me to fetch you," she said. "Your uncle is dying."

~

ON HER FAMILY'S Lincoln's Inn Fields town house, Rachael was going downstairs to have breakfast when her brother started up. "Oh, there you are," Noah said. "I was coming to look for you."

"You're up and about early." Pausing on the steps, she noted he was wearing shoes rather than boots, and a double-breasted tailcoat rather than a riding coat. "And isn't it Monday morning, Noah?"

"Of course it is, yes."

"I thought all you horse-mad young bucks met at Tattersall's on Mondays to settle your accounts. Or is Monday an auction day? Either way, you always seem to head for Tattersall's every Monday, but you're not dressed for that."

"Maybe I'm not horse-mad anymore," he suggested, a challenge in his blue eyes.

Hearing a challenge in his voice, too, she wondered if he could possibly be serious. "You're off to your club, then, I expect?"

"No, I'm not." Noah lifted his square chin. "I was hoping you'd come with me to Oxford Street. To Robert Gillow and Company, to be more precise, to pick out a new desk."

"Did you say a desk?" She must have heard him wrong. "What kind of a desk?"

"An oak one, I'm thinking. Something sturdy, in any case, with many drawers. The one in the study seems to be growing rather rickety."

"I imagine it's a hundred years old, at the very least. But however did you come to notice it's rickety?"

He rolled his eyes. "I *used* it, Rachael. Is that such a surprise?"

"Frankly, yes." *Surprise* seemed too mild a word—she was positively shocked. First he'd asked for an inventory at Greystone, and now this. Could it be her little brother was growing up? At twenty, he was looking like a man, but was he actually becoming one?

"Well?" he asked, still looking like a man, but one who was rather annoyed. "Will you come with me or not?"

"Oh, I wish I could." The sight of Noah inspecting desks rather than horseflesh was bound to be a spectacle. But she expected Griffin to arrive in half an hour. "I've other plans for today, I'm afraid, but let me talk to Claire and Elizabeth about going with you to Gillow's instead."

∿

"*L*ORD LINCOLNSHIRE!" Corinna called excitedly. "Mr. and Mrs. Hamilton!"

She hurried toward Lord Lincolnshire's bedroom, having been told at the front door that Sean and Deirdre were with him. She'd risen at the crack of dawn this morning and come before even eating breakfast, because she couldn't wait a moment longer to share her news.

"I finished my portrait!" she announced, stopping in the doorway. "I'm going to submit it this…"

The sentence trailed off when she saw her brother-in-law

James by the bed, leaning over the earl with his stethoscope. All her excitement dissipated along with the words.

"… afternoon," she finished in a small voice. "How is he?"

Sean rose from where he sat by Deirdre. "I think Lord Stafford is just about finished and ready to tell us."

"I am, yes." James drew the covers up to the earl's chin and straightened, looking grim. "I fear the end is imminent. He may last the night, but not any longer. I don't believe he'll wake, either. He'll likely just continue like this until his breathing and his heart simply stop. I'm sorry," he concluded with a sigh. "We'll all miss him."

Corinna looked back to the huge crimson-draped bed where Lord Lincolnshire slumbered, propped upright against a dozen pillows. When the covers were down, she'd noticed his belly appeared swollen now, along with the rest of him. His skin looked tight and wet, as though it were weeping fluid. Gurgling noises came from his throat.

Her heart sank even lower. "That sounds dreadful. He must be suffering so."

"He sounds like that because his lungs are filling," James explained gently. "But he's sleeping. I don't think he's really suffering in the sense you imagine." He dropped the stethoscope in his leather bag and snapped it closed, looking to Sean. "I can stay if you wish, but there isn't anything I can do. It's only a matter of time now."

"I understand," Sean said. "We won't be needing you to stay, though I appreciate the offer. I'll be with him."

"I'll stay with him, too," Deirdre added softly. "And Nurse Skeffington will be back within the hour."

"All right, then." James moved to Corinna and lightly kissed her cheek. "I'm sorry," he said again, and left.

For a moment, Corinna just gazed at Lord Lincolnshire. Hot tears pricked her eyes. Deirdre rose and came to place a hand on her shoulder. "I'm sure he knows you finished his portrait."

Guilt flooded her. She *hadn't* finished it. But she would. She'd promised to paint his final portrait, and she'd follow through with that. She had only to fix the underlying anatomy, and she knew how to do that now. His portrait wouldn't be exhibited at the Royal Academy, but it would hang here at Lincolnshire House.

Which would be John Hamilton's house, unfortunately. At that thought, a rush of anger tempered her guilt. But it would be Deirdre's house, too, at least until she got her divorce, and that helped a little.

She raised a hand to touch Deirdre's where it rested on her shoulder. "Thank you for saying that."

"Which other pictures will you submit along with the portrait today?" Sean asked.

"I'm not submitting any other pictures," she told him, turning to him. "I've decided to submit the portrait alone." She neglected to mention it wasn't the one he expected. "It's my best work, the painting I wish to exhibit as my debut. If it isn't chosen, I'll try again next year."

"It's pleased I am to hear you're that happy with the way it turned out," he said.

But he didn't look pleased. Or sound pleased.

At all.

"I'm sorry you're losing Lord Lincolnshire," she said, her heart breaking for him. "I know you've grown close."

He nodded. "I need to talk to you about something. Something important. Not here, though," he said, slanting a glance to his sister. "Later."

"Take her out of the room," Deirdre said. "I'll stay with Lord Lincolnshire." When he hesitated, she added, "Go," and waved a hand. "Lord Stafford said he might last the whole night. Nothing will be happening in a few minutes."

After hesitating a moment more, Sean took Corinna's arm and drew her out and down the corridor. But when he turned to her, he didn't say anything. He just looked at her, his heart in his deep green eyes.

"What is it?" she asked. Remembering he'd called her *sweetheart* and *my heart* and *my love*, she raised a hand to his cheek. "You look so sad."

"I am sad." Turning his face, he raised his own hand to hold hers to his mouth and pressed a warm kiss to her palm before releasing it. "I'm very sad, Corinna. I cannot do this standing outside Lincolnshire's bedroom. Will you meet me at Hamilton's studio one last time?"

"Of course." She'd soothe his sadness then, show him how much she loved him. She'd kiss him and…he was right: None of that could happen here. "What time?"

"In an hour," he said, and then: "No. I need to stay with Lincolnshire right now. I'd never forgive myself if he—"

"I understand." He looked tortured. "James said Lord Lincolnshire wouldn't last the night, and you need to be with him until then. And I need to submit my portrait later this afternoon. How about tomorrow?"

"That's too long…but all right."

"I don't want to wait that long, either." It seemed so very long since they'd last been together. Only two and a half days, but it felt like forever.

"Shall we say ten o'clock?" he asked.

"All the ladies are visiting Aunt Frances tomorrow at eleven, but I can—"

"Let's make it in the afternoon, then." He shut his eyes briefly, then opened them with a sigh. "This will probably be best," he said as though trying to convince himself. "I'll spend the morning making arrangements for Lincolnshire's funeral."

"But you won't need to play his nephew once he's gone," she said, then clapped a hand over her mouth.

He glanced quickly around, but fortunately no servants had overheard. Looking relieved, he ran his hands slowly down her arms, then linked his fingers with hers, lacing them together. "I owe him that, at least," he said softly. "And who else is going to do it?"

He was so good. And he looked even more upset. She didn't want to wait until tomorrow afternoon to comfort him. She couldn't kiss him here outside Lincolnshire's bedroom, but she slipped her arms around him, squeezing him tight. "This will all be over soon," she murmured against his chest, thinking much better times lay ahead.

"Yes," he said in a flat tone. "It will."

FORTY-FOUR

ALF AN HOUR later, Griffin found himself on Lady
Avonleigh's doorstep again. In the *morning*.

The ancient butler opened the door. "Yes?" he croaked.

"I've come to call on Lady Avonleigh," Rachael said.

He cleared his throat. "She's left the house, milady."

"I don't believe this!" She turned to Griffin. "We should have
come earlier."

He'd picked her up at nine o'clock, and now it was half past.
"How much earlier could we have come?" He'd been sure they'd
be dragging poor Lady A from her bed. In his experience, ladies
slept until at least ten. Except Corinna, who slept until at least
noon. "What time does Lady Avonleigh rise?" he asked the old
geezer at the door.

"Six o'clock," Lady Balmforth said, apparently having overheard them and come to see what was up. She looked curious.
"When you get to a certain age, dear, you won't sleep late in the
morning, either."

"Good morning, Lady Balmforth," Rachael said before
swinging to Griffin again. "I told you we should have come
earlier."

"We'll come earlier tomorrow." With any luck, he wouldn't receive another surprise summons from Lincolnshire.

"I'm not waiting until tomorrow. We'll wait here today."

Yesterday he'd been willing to wait, and she hadn't wanted to. Today he'd assumed she wanted to leave, but she wanted to wait. He would never understand women. "Fine," he said, "we'll wait."

"Well, maybe we shouldn't wait." She turned to Lady B. "When will Lady Avonleigh be back?"

"Aurelia is assisting our James today at his Institute," Lady B said. "Then she's accompanying Lady Corinna to the Royal Academy this afternoon."

"Thunderation," Rachael said softly, making the older woman's eyes widen at her language. "I'd forgotten about that. The two of them planned that right in front of me, too, when we were visiting Lady Malmsey and the new baby."

Lady B briefly touched Rachael's hand. "My sister will be at home for a short while in between. She told our nephew she had to leave before luncheon." The skinny lady leaned closer. "Aurelia never likes to miss her luncheon."

Griffin stifled a snort of laughter.

"What did you want to talk to my sister about?" Lady B asked, looking very curious. "Is it important?"

Rachael nodded. "Very. But I...well...you're welcome to listen, but I'd rather wait until Lady Avonleigh is here to talk about it."

Lady Balmforth looked even more curious. "If it's that important, perhaps you ought to send Lady Corinna a note, saying she should find someone else to accompany her to Somerset House."

"That's an excellent idea," Rachael said, "but I think *you* need to write the note. That way Corinna won't be suspicious about what I'm doing with Lady Avonleigh."

"She's not going to be suspicious," Griffin said.

"Yes, she is. Your sisters aren't stupid, Griffin."

"Why don't you just tell them the truth?"

"I'm still not ready," Rachael said.

And Lady Balmforth looked very, very curious. "I think we'd better send for Cornelia, too," she said.

◇

*A*T ONE O'CLOCK, Corinna came downstairs with a footman carrying her painting, which she'd framed—by borrowing one off a family portrait—and wrapped in brown paper. "I need a hackney coach," she told Adamson, their butler. "My brother took the carriage, and I must pick up Lady Avonleigh."

Though Adamson was a very short man, he prided himself on being quite dignified and proper. "I don't know if that's wise, Lady Corinna."

"It's necessary. Please hail a hackney."

"Lord Cainewood has been gone since the morning. He's likely to be home soon."

She was early, true. It wouldn't take an hour to reach Lady A's house, and the woman had said two o'clock. But she was too anxious to wait. "Hail a hackney," she repeated, and paused before adding, "now."

He hemmed and hawed and clucked his tongue, clearly reluctant to put Lord Cainewood's sister in a hackney coach. Corinna crossed her arms, knowing he would eventually comply. But before that happened, the knocker banged, and Adamson opened the door to reveal a messenger with a letter.

"Ah," the butler said, looking not at all displeased to have an excuse to put off hailing a cab. "It's directed to you, Lady Corinna."

She grabbed it and broke the seal, swiftly scanning the missive.

My Dear Lady Corinna,

I am sorry to inform you that circumstances prevent my sister, Lady Avonleigh, from accompanying you to the Royal Academy this afternoon. Unfortunately, I cannot do so in her place. Please accept my sincerest apologies.

Yours sincerely,
Lady Balmforth

"Circumstances? What's that supposed to mean?" Corinna sighed. "It seems I need paper instead of a hackney. I must send a note to Alexandra."

FORTY-FIVE

"**I** DON'T KNOW where to begin, Lady Avonleigh."

Rachael hadn't expected to be nervous. But now that Lady A was finally home and they were all seated in her peach drawing room, she didn't know what to say.

Sitting across from her in a peach wing chair, Lady A gave her a kind smile. "Through the years I've learned what's important. Both of my sisters are here, and I just came from seeing James, which means all the people I love most are healthy. I cannot imagine anything you could tell me that could be so terribly bad."

"Oh, it isn't bad." Rachael clenched her hands in her lap. "At least, I'm hoping you won't think it's bad. I'm hoping you'll think—"

"Say it already," Griffin interjected, sitting on the sofa beside her. He'd seemed a bit annoyed that they'd had to wait so long, but that was his fault; if they'd come early, as she'd wanted to, they wouldn't have had to wait at all. "Good gracious, I've never seen you so flustered. You're always so levelheaded and composed."

Was that what he thought? She'd never felt like that inside.

But she rather liked him seeing her that way. And he was right: She needed to just say it.

"You're my grandmother," she told Lady Avonleigh in a rush. "I'm Georgiana's daughter."

Lady A looked at her. Her face went white, and from across the room she just looked at Rachael, staring at her in a way that made her feel very uneasy. It was terribly awkward. She'd been picturing Lady Avonleigh welcoming her with open arms. She'd been picturing them shopping together.

Griffin leaned closer. "Maybe she's a bit peeved because she hasn't had her luncheon yet," he whispered.

What a stupid comment. Rachael was about to elbow him when Lady Balmforth finally broke the silence. "You cannot be Georgiana's daughter," she said, not unkindly. "Our Georgiana jumped off the London Bridge."

"She must have pretended to jump off the London Bridge and then run away and married my father. I mean, not my real father, but the man who raised me."

The awkward silence resumed. Rachael glanced back to Lady A, but her grandmother was still just looking at her. No matter how much she wanted to be welcomed with open arms, it was clear that wasn't going to happen. Griffin wrapped one of his own arms around her shoulders, and she leaned into him, taking the comfort he offered, forgiving him for being annoyed and saying the stupid things he often said.

"Who is that, dear?" Lady Cavanaugh asked. "Who was the father who raised you?"

"John Chase," Rachael replied. "The Earl of Greystone."

And Lady Avonleigh suddenly came to life. "What did you say?"

"John Chase, the Earl—"

"Oh, my goodness!" she squealed, and then she leapt from her chair and rushed over to the sofa and welcomed Rachael with open arms. Probably the most welcoming arms Rachael had ever felt. They clung together, and Rachael inhaled her grand-mother's gardenia perfume, remembering her mother smelling the same.

Griffin moved to Lady A's chair so she could share the sofa with her granddaughter. Tears ran down both their faces, and they just held on to each other for a good long while. Until Lady B leaned over and tapped her older sister on the shoulder.

"What convinced you?" she demanded.

"My daughter was in love with John Chase," Lady A said tearily. At last she released Rachael and held her hand tightly instead. "My husband and I wouldn't let her marry him."

"That's right!" Lady C exclaimed. "I'd forgotten."

The whole story came out.

John Cartwright had been a second son. While a young man in the army before his marriage, a soldier named Thomas Grim-bald had saved his life on a battlefield in Germany during the Seven Years' War. Cartwright had granted the man a boon, and Grimbald wanted his newborn son married to the aristocrat's firstborn daughter. After Cartwright's older brother died, he'd sold out of the military and become the Earl of Avonleigh and married Aurelia. They'd had a daughter, Alice, who was promised to Grimbald's son. And a son, who'd sadly drowned at twenty-one, and another daughter, Georgiana.

"How did Georgiana end up married to Grimbald," Griffin asked, "if Alice was promised to him?"

"Alice fell in love with her cousin," Lady A explained. "Her father forbade her to marry him, but they eloped to Gretna Green. Then my husband cut her out of our lives. I've heard she eventually died, but I've never really known what happened to her—"

"I know!" Rachael said. "I knew Aunt Alice. We saw her all the time. I know what happened to her. She had a child before she died, a little boy named Edmund." She wouldn't tell Lady A that the child had been crippled and unable to talk. Not now, at least. "After that, Mama raised Edmund, but he, too, died a few years later."

Her grandmother's eyes glazed with tears. "Was she happy in her marriage, my Alice?"

"I think so. I was young when she passed away, but she never seemed unhappy to me." Even though having Edmund must have been heartbreaking. "She and Mama visited often. They loved each other very much. And I loved Aunt Alice, too." She squeezed her grandmother's hand. "Go on, please."

But it seemed Lady A couldn't. "I'm so happy to know Alice and Georgiana were together," she whispered, and waved her free hand toward her sisters.

With a teary smile, Lady C took over the story. "After Alice failed to follow through with the betrothal, Georgiana was next in line. When she turned sixteen, she begged for one London season before marrying Grimbald—"

"I never had been able to deny her anything," Lady A interrupted. "Georgiana was the sweetest child."

"I'm sure she was," Rachael said. Maybe Mama had lied to her—a lie by omission—but she'd loved Rachael and her siblings dearly. She'd been a wonderful mother. In the past months, it seemed she'd forgotten that. "She loved you, too, Lady Avon—"

"Grandmama. Please call me Grandmama."

Rachael's heart swelled. "She loved you, too, Grandmama. She always wore gardenia perfume. I think that must have been because she missed you. Did she meet my father that season?"

Her grandmother waved a hand again, overtaken by emotion.

"That's when she met John Chase, yes," Lady B said. "She begged to marry him, but my sister's husband wouldn't hear of it. He'd made a promise and had no other daughters left to satisfy his debt to the man who had saved his life. Georgiana hadn't seen her sister in seven years, and she didn't want to disobey her parents and end up estranged like Alice. So she reluctantly agreed to go through with the ceremony."

"That sounds like Mama," Rachael said. "What happened then?"

Her grandmother was recovered enough to continue. "Like his father, Grimbald was an army man. He took a leave of absence to wed Georgiana and got her with child right away. Then he went back to his regiment, and she came home to London to live with us." Her voice dropped. "She didn't love him, so she didn't mind, really, and she was so looking forward to having her baby."

"Me," Rachael whispered.

"Yes. And then she received a letter saying her husband had been executed for treason. No details. She was furious with us, I'm afraid, for making her abandon her love and wed a traitor. She wrote a suicide note and jumped off the London Bridge, taking her baby with her. Her body was never found."

"Because she didn't jump off the London Bridge," Griffin said, "no matter that the note said she would. She ran to the countryside and married John Chase instead."

They could only guess what had happened after that. She hadn't wanted her baby to grow up as the child of a traitor. She'd claimed she was Georgiana Woodby, a commoner, and stayed far away from London in order to avoid ever seeing her parents. Far away from any social situation, to avoid running into anyone she might have known in her previous life.

"Did she have asthma?" Rachael asked.

"Not at all," Lady Avonleigh said. "She was the healthiest of all my children."

"I thought so," Rachael said with a sigh. "So no one ever learned what had become of my real father. How he came to be labeled a traitor." She sighed again, but supposed it wasn't all that important. She'd been making much too much of the whole thing. Her mother had only wanted to protect her from being tainted by her father's shame, and she had new family now, and—

"Oh, I know what happened," her grandmother said. "After my younger daughter's death, I paid a visit to Grimbald's father."

"My grandfather? I met him at the Royal Hospital. But—"

"He's lost his mind, poor man, yes. But I talked to him a long time before that." Lady Avonleigh—Grandmama—shifted on the sofa to face Rachael and took her other hand. "It wasn't all that bad, my dear. If Georgiana had known, she might have forgiven him. Although I suspect she would never have loved him. She was in love with the Earl of Greystone."

Rachael's parents—the two she'd grown up with—had been very much in love. No matter how cross she'd been with her mother, she'd never forgotten that. "What did Grimbald do?" she asked. "What did he do that wasn't so bad?"

"It was during the war against the colonies in North America, just three years after Georgiana was born. He was much older than she was, you see—probably another reason she preferred the earl. In any event, he and a fellow soldier, one William Smith, killed a British officer to keep him from murdering a number of American civilians. They managed to convince the authorities that the man was shot by a revolutionary. And all was well for fifteen years, until Smith fell ill in 1795 and revealed in a deathbed confession that the two of them had killed the officer."

"But if they killed him to save innocent people," Rachael said, looking to Griffin, "the officer might have been a bad man. They might have done a good thing."

"That officer probably was a bad man," Griffin said sympathetically. "But that wouldn't matter. If Grimbald killed a superior, he'd have been arrested, court-martialed, and convicted—regardless of how bad the man had been."

"It doesn't signify," Lady A said. "Not now. Instead of being sorry for everything that happened, let's just be glad we've found each other." She squeezed Rachael's hands, and her smile reminded Rachael of her mother. "I have a granddaughter."

"You have three granddaughters," Rachael said. "Don't forget Claire and Elizabeth. They're Georgiana's daughters, too." Watching her grandmother's soft blue eyes widen, she added, "And you've a grandson as well. Our brother, Noah."

Lady A was holding Rachael's hands so tightly, her own were beginning to hurt. But she didn't care. Her mother had only wanted to protect her, and her father hadn't really done wrong, and Grandmama had welcomed her with open arms.

"I cannot wait to see your sisters and brother again." Lady B's smile resembled Georgiana's, too. Rachael wondered how she'd never noticed. "I'm their aunt, you know," Lady B added. "And yours. And so is Cornelia."

Lady C, being the youngest, looked closest to her mother of all. "I never had a daughter until Juliana," she said. "I'm so happy that now I'll have nieces again. And a nephew, too. Oh, my."

"My sisters are out with Noah at present," Rachael told her new family. "They're helping him choose a new desk. But they should be at home later, so we can go tell them our good news."

There were numerous murmurs of agreement to that plan.

"Maybe we'll all go shopping," Grandmama suggested. "I want to spoil my grandchildren. But first, let's have luncheon."

FORTY-SIX

*C*ORINNA PACED the foyer, watching the clock tick toward the hour when it would be too late to submit her painting. Two hours earlier, the messenger she'd dispatched to Alexandra's house had returned with the news that her eldest sister wasn't at home. Corinna had then sent a desperate note to Juliana and another to Rachael, Claire, and Elizabeth.

Since then she'd heard nothing. Nothing. Nothing at all.

"What is taking them all so long?"

"Pardon, my lady?"

"Nothing, Adamson." She paused midpace. "No, not nothing," she revised, glancing at the tall-case clock once again. It was four o'clock, and she had to get to Somerset House by five, or she'd have to wait a whole year for another chance to submit to the Summer Exhibition. "Hail a hackney now, please. I shall have to take a footman. I cannot wait any longer."

Adamson opened his mouth to protest, but the knocker banged once again. He opened the door to reveal another messenger with a note—and Juliana out in the street, just alighting from the Stafford carriage.

"Thank heavens," Corinna breathed. "I won't need a hackney

after all. Adamson, do please see my painting put in the Stafford carriage immediately. And carefully. The paper shouldn't be allowed to touch the paint, because it isn't dry yet."

The butler handed her the note. "It's for you, Lady Corinna. Surely you want to read it?"

"Oh, very well." She broke the seal and scanned it as Juliana joined her on the doorstep. "None of the cousins are at home, either," she reported with little surprise.

"Either?" Juliana echoed.

"Alexandra wasn't home, and neither is Griffin. And Lady A and Lady B are both busy this afternoon. And apparently Rachael, Claire, and Elizabeth are all busy, too. I'm grateful you could accompany me. Let's go."

"Everyone else was busy? *Everyone?* Dear heavens, what are the odds of such a coincidence?"

"I don't know, but I can't think about that now. We'll find out what everyone was doing tomorrow when we all visit Aunt Frances and the baby." She ushered her sister toward the carriage, where the painting was already tucked inside. "I must get to the Royal Academy before five o'clock."

They settled against the squabs, side by side facing forward, with the painting leaning against the other seat. As the carriage lurched into traffic, Juliana patted her sister's knee. "You aren't nervous, are you?"

"No," Corinna lied. "Just rushed. I feared no one would get here in time to accompany me. You weren't arriving, and the cousins live all the way in Lincoln's Inn—"

"Mr. Delaney is right nearby, along with his sister. Did you think to ask them?"

"I couldn't."

"Why is that?"

"Lord Lincolnshire is fading, and they have to stay with him. And besides, I couldn't let them see the painting."

"Why is that?"

Holy Hannah, Corinna thought, why had she blurted that out? She really needed to practice thinking before she spoke.

"Why?" Juliana demanded. "You're hiding something, Corinna; I can tell."

There was nothing for it. Her sister would never give up badgering her, and if her painting was accepted, everyone was going to see it in the Summer Exhibition, anyway.

Corinna drew and held a breath. "Have a look," she finally said, reaching across to tear off the brown paper. But she paused mid-tear. She couldn't do it.

"It's not varnished," she hedged.

Juliana shrugged. "All right."

"If it's accepted—if it's hung—I'll get a chance to make last minute changes and then varnish it right there on the wall."

"All right," Juliana repeated, and then, when Corinna failed to respond, she added, "So...?"

"Very well," Corinna said, and ripped the rest of the paper off, quickly, before she could change her mind.

Juliana's eyes widened. "Oh, my goodness."

"Is that all you have to say?"

"It's...well, it's different." She stared at the painting. "I've heard of men painting nude women, but never..."

"He's not nude," Corinna pointed out, feeling a bit queasy. "He's wearing trousers."

"True," her sister agreed. "He's absolutely..." She blinked. "Faith, don't you just want to take a bite out of him?"

Well, yes, as a matter of fact...but Corinna wasn't sure she liked to hear her sister speaking speaking that way about Sean. Not that Juliana *knew* it was Sean she was speaking of.

"He's compelling," Juliana murmured. "I cannot seem to take my eyes off of him." But she did, finally, meeting Corinna's. "It's magnificent. You've always been good, but this time you've outdone yourself."

Corinna's breath went out in a rush. "Do you really think so?"

"I know so. It's remarkable." She shifted her gaze back to the painting. "Why didn't you want Mr. Delaney to see it?"

"Does it perhaps...remind you of anyone you know?"

Juliana tilted her head. "Blond hair and brown eyes. That's an unusual combination, isn't it? I don't think so."

Corinna had counted on no one looking past the coloring, but she must not have been completely confident, because relief flooded through her now. "I feared Mr. Delaney would find it shocking, that's all. His father was a vicar, you know."

"Really? I suppose I know very little about him."

"I don't know much about him, either," Corinna said, averting her gaze.

FORTY-SEVEN

$\mathcal{I}$N THE WEE hours, the earl died.

He slipped off peacefully, leaving the world in his sleep as Lord Stafford had said he would. One instant his breathing rattled noisily; the next he went eerily silent.

Sean and Deirdre both held their breaths for a tense moment, then turned to each other, embracing and holding tight. Deirdre's tears wet her brother's shirtfront, but they were quiet tears. Tears born of grief mixed with relief.

Sean felt exactly the same.

He sat by the earl's side the balance of the night, because it seemed like the right thing to do. And because he wasn't ready to begin what he needed to do next. Because eventually he would finish with that.

And then...

Dawn was a faint glow through the bedroom window when the household stirred to life. Mrs. Skeffington appeared on the threshold, holding an ewer of fresh water. "Is he...?"

"With the angels," Sean said quietly.

A sound of sorrow escaped her throat, and she turned and fled, returning a few minutes later with Higginbotham.

"My lord," the steward said, "what shall we do?"

For a moment Sean was nonplussed. He wasn't a lord; he didn't belong here. But Higginbotham didn't know that, of course, and no one else at Lincolnshire House did, either. The lot of them wandered at loose ends, passing by the earl's chamber as though they were all ghosts themselves.

When Sean failed to respond, Higginbotham released a shuddering breath. "There must needs be funeral arrangements, and—"

"I'll see to everything," Sean assured him.

It would be a busy morning.

And then...

"Thank you, my lord earl." Higginbotham forced a wan half smile of gratitude. "I fear I am...numb."

Sean wished he could say the same. He wasn't numb. He was in agony. He had to force himself to move, to do what needed to be done.

And then...

Then his empty life stretched ahead.

Seemingly forever.

FORTY-EIGHT

ORANGE CUSTARD

Boil a pint of Cream with a little sack. When it be cold, take four Yolks and two whites of

Eggs, a little juice of Orange and peel of Orange and Sugar to your palate. Mix them well

together, and bake them in cups. Before serving, put your cups on ice.

This custard tastes lovely, and it brings love as well. My sisters and I each made this when we

were looking for love, and we all found it.

—Anne, Marchioness of Cainewood, 1772

*E*XCITEMENT still simmered in Corinna on Tuesday when she arrived to visit Frances and the new baby. Her submission had gone even better than she'd hoped. Though she'd half expected to be asked what made her think she, seventeen-year-old Corinna Chase, was worthy of submitting to the Summer Exhibition, nothing of the like had occurred. No one had looked askance. Not only had her painting been accepted for consideration, but Henry Fuseli, who'd taken possession of it, had exclaimed loudly over its brilliance.

She supposed she shouldn't be surprised that a man who

painted weird, daring fantasies might approve a portrait like hers.

And she was very much looking forward to this afternoon, when she would meet Sean at Hamilton's studio. She wasn't sure whether Lord Lincolnshire had passed away yet or not, but she knew he probably had, and that was the only thing that marred her happiness.

When she entered Aunt Frances's drawing room, Ladies A, B, and C were the only ones there, and they were chattering enthusiastically. Corinna wondered what they were so excited about it, but when they noticed her in the doorway they all fell silent. She saw the three of them exchange meaningful glances before Lady Avonleigh met her gaze.

"Oh, my dear!" she cried. "I'm so sorry I couldn't accompany you to Somerset House yesterday. Did the submission go all right?"

"Yes, it did," Corinna assured her. She was eager to relay Mr. Fuseli's reaction, but then Aunt Frances came slowly downstairs, supported by her maid and a footman, followed by a nurse with the baby. It took quite some time for her to get settled on her chaise longue with Belinda in her arms. Then Alexandra arrived with *her* baby, and Juliana showed up with a huge, flat basket filled with cups of orange custard, which she claimed would assist Corinna in finding love with a "certain someone."

"Which will make my sister's life complete," she added with a smile, handing the basket to a maid so the cups could be taken down to the basement kitchen and put on ice, "because her new portrait, which I have had the pleasure of seeing, is going to be the sensation of the Summer Exhibition."

"I cannot wait to see it," Lady A declared, which made Corinna a little nervous. She was grateful when the talk turned to Belinda's first smile—which Alexandra claimed could be caused only by indigestion—and on to Juliana's burgeoning belly. Not that Juliana's belly was actually protruding yet, but she kept rubbing it as though she could feel the baby inside.

Corinna wondered how long it would be before Griffin talked to Sean, before she could broach the subject of their marriage. Her stomach fluttered at the thought, with both anticipation and a touch of nerves.

Soon Rachael arrived with her sisters, the three of them chattering enthusiastically as they made their way through the foyer. Corinna wondered what they were so excited about, but at the drawing room's doorway they all fell silent. She saw the three of them exchange meaningful glances before Lady A exchanged meaningful glances with *her* sisters...

And even distracted by her own excited and nervous thoughts, Corinna couldn't help thinking something mysterious must be happening under her very nose.

"Good afternoon," Rachael said, breaking the silence.

"Good afternoon," Corinna returned. She watched Claire and Elizabeth make their way to two chairs and sit down, clucking over the new baby. And then she watched Rachael choose a seat on the sofa beside Lady Avonleigh.

Rachael paid no attention to the new baby. Instead she leaned close to embrace Lady A, and she seemed to be breathing in the lady's scent. She closed her eyes momentarily, and a faint smile curved her lips as she sighed a contented sigh, even though that odd mixture of camphor and gardenias couldn't possibly be pleasing.

And odder still, Lady A was smiling a matching smile and sighing an identical contented sigh. Although, Corinna supposed, Rachael's jasmine perfume *was* more pleasant than Lady A's.

Lady C pulled out a handkerchief and dabbed at her eyes and nose. "Oh, dear. I seem to be coming down with the sniffles."

"Me, too," Lady B said, although she looked perfectly fine. In fact, she and Lady C were both smiling. And so were Claire and Elizabeth. And they weren't faint smiles. They were smiles a mile wide.

"Would anyone care for some orange custard?" Juliana asked, rising from her seat. "Corinna, could you come with me to the kitchen to fetch it? And Claire and Elizabeth? I cannot carry ten cups all by myself, and James said that I shouldn't overexert myself in my delicate condition."

Juliana could certainly carry all ten cups in the same basket she'd brought them in, Corinna thought, and she hadn't seemed to overexert herself doing so earlier. But she rose and followed her sister anyway.

With a decided lack of regard for her delicate condition, Juliana hurried Corinna and their cousins from the drawing room and through the foyer. Halfway down the steps to the basement, she stopped and turned to them. "What in heaven's name is going on here? What on earth am I missing? Something has happened between Rachael and Lady Avonleigh. Something significant. I can tell."

"A blind and deaf person would be able to tell," Corinna put in.

Elizabeth coughed a little sniffly cough. "Lady A is Rachael's grandmother."

"What?" Juliana and Corinna burst out together.

Claire nudged her sister in the ribs. "Now you've done it, Elizabeth!" She sighed. "Rachael *is* Lady Avonleigh's grand-daughter. And we're her granddaughters, too. We've discovered our mother was Lady A's younger daughter—the one who jumped off the London Bridge. Only she didn't, not really. She married our father and moved to Greystone instead. And she never went back to London, because she was afraid someone there would recognize her, and her family would know she was alive."

This was what had made the two sets of sisters chatter like that, Corinna realized. And no wonder—the six of them turning out to be related was a positively astounding coincidence. Even more astounding than everyone's being too busy to accompany her to Somerset House at the same time.

"That's why everyone was busy yesterday," Juliana marveled. "You two and Rachael and Ladies A, B, and C were all together, discovering all of this."

"Your mother didn't have asthma, then," Corinna said.

"No, she didn't. That was just an excuse." Claire pulled a handkerchief out of her sleeve and blew her nose—because she was overcome with emotion, *not* because she was coming down with the sniffles. "Please don't tell Rachael you know. She'd be mortified."

"Why?" Corinna asked. "None of this is any fault of hers. Does she think so little of us that she believes Aunt Georgiana's deception would change our feelings towards her?"

"I fear she's not thinking at all right now." Claire crossed her arms over her amethyst bodice and leveled a familiar glare at her sister. "Much like Elizabeth. Again."

Elizabeth sniffled, too. "I'm sorry."

"We promise not to tell a soul." Corinna turned to Juliana. "Don't we?"

Juliana reached to touch both her cousins' arms reassuringly. "We love Rachael, and we're thrilled that she's found more family to love. And do you realize this means James is your first cousin? How amazing is that?"

Juliana *sounded* sincere, but Corinna couldn't help noticing that she hadn't actually promised not to tell. She suspected her sister had her fingers mentally crossed. There was a little thrill in the tone of her voice that made Corinna sure she was already plotting her next move.

Juliana was a born meddler, after all, and no doubt she thought this news splendid for all concerned. For their cousins, of course, and also for Lady A, who'd sorely missed her younger daughter and now had grandchildren at long last. But mostly for Griffin and Rachael, because Rachael's newfound happiness put Juliana that much closer to her goal of seeing the two of them together as a couple.

Corinna had no doubt Juliana would accomplish that goal, because her sister wasn't only a born meddler, she was an obnoxiously good one—and anyone with two eyes in her head could see that Rachael and Griffin *did* belong together.

Just like Corinna belonged with Sean.

Sean, of course, was the "certain someone," because Juliana believed they belonged together, too. She'd made orange custard to bring them love. Though it was a silly superstition that would have no impact whatsoever, it was still a meddlesome thing, and Corinna was certain Juliana had plenty more meddling planned.

But for the very first time in her life, she found herself hoping Juliana's meddling would work.

Juliana would be smug beyond belief, of course, but it would save Corinna from having to reveal that Sean was the model in her portrait.

To avoid Griffin's wrath, Corinna would gladly put up with a whole heap of smugness.

FORTY-NINE

*A*N EARL'S funeral bore little resemblance to the simple ceremonies performed by a country vicar like Sean's father. Lord Lincolnshire was to be buried in Westminster Abbey on Friday, and Sean had also arranged for a reception at Lincolnshire House afterward.

Getting everything in place took the better part of the day, and it was late afternoon by the time he trudged up the steps to the garret studio, hoping Corinna wasn't already waiting. A small part of him couldn't wait to see her, but most of him dreaded her arrival. He wanted a few minutes to prepare himself, to steel himself for what lay ahead.

He didn't have to do this, he knew. There were other, easier ways out. Soon the truth would be revealed, as Hamilton was due in town for the judging and would waste no time claiming his new title. Once that happened, society would make it clear to Corinna that Sean was unacceptable. Or he could allow her brother to explain the facts. But he wasn't the sort of fellow who expected others to do his dirty work. He still picked up a hammer if he saw the need on a construction site, and he wouldn't leave this task to others, either.

And he had to say goodbye. He needed to tell Corinna just how much he wished things were different. He'd brought something to give her to remember him by, and he'd do that first, while she was still clearheaded enough to be capable of understanding what it meant. He wanted one last kiss—even knowing it was wrong—and he wanted, one last time, to have her look at him in that dreamy way, and speak to him in that low, sweet voice.

Reaching the top of the stairway, he opened the door to the garret and heard a harsh voice instead. "Go away!" it barked.

"I beg your pardon?" Thinking for a moment that he must have entered the wrong building, Sean took a step back. Then the voice's owner turned to face him, paintbrush in hand. Sean blinked. "Hamilton? What are you doing here?"

"Working. I'm going to lease this space, if you'll remember, so I consider it mine." He gestured to a large canvas on the easel, where the beginnings of a scene were already taking form. "The falls, with the Lady of the Waterfall visible in the towering gush. Inspired, isn't it? What do you think?"

Sean shut the door behind him. "I think you were due back weeks ago."

The weasel merely shrugged. "I arrived early today, in time to vote on the submissions for the Summer Exhibition this morning." He turned back to his canvas and began adding mist rising at the bottom of the falls. "I told you I would."

"You also told me your uncle would die within days."

"He didn't?"

"Not until this morning."

Sean wasn't surprised to see the weasel display no emotion at the news of his uncle's passing. But Hamilton wouldn't stay calm for long—not once he heard what had gone on since he left the country.

Having long since accepted that it would all come to nothing —Deirdre wasn't getting her divorce—Sean's main regret was that he hadn't managed to speak with Hamilton before the Summer Exhibition selection. He hadn't realized it would take place the very day after the submissions were due. "Did you vote for Lady Corinna Chase's painting?" he asked with a sigh.

"Who the deuce is Corinna Chase?"

"The girl we met in the British Museum. The one who said she wanted to paint portraits."

"I don't remember her. And I haven't the slightest idea. As usual, I voted for my favorites without looking at any signatures." He added more mist. "The whole exercise was very tedious. No less than fourteen rounds before the final selection was decided on, and all the while all I wanted was to work on this picture."

"It was a portrait of Lincolnshire. Seated on a bench in Berkeley Square, holding a book—"

"I don't recall anything like that. Not that I would have recognized the old beast in any case. I haven't set eyes on him since I was a—"

"Sweet mercy, he was your father's identical twin! And she painted him looking younger, probably very much as you remember your own father."

"I didn't see any portraits of my father, Delaney. And I voted for very few portraits altogether—you know I prefer landscapes." Having finished adding the mist, he started on some water splashing back up. "My favorite canvas, however," he mused, "did turn out to be a portrait. I'm not sure whether it made the final cut—it may not have, because it was very unusual. A rather outrageous depiction of a golden-haired young man, half-clothed and bathed in candlelight. Henry Fuseli was quite taken with it as well."

That certainly wasn't Corinna's. Which meant Sean was finished with this discussion. "Nothing went the way you said it would, Hamilton. Nothing went as planned."

The fellow cocked his head, then added a wee smidge of

white to a brown blob on his palette. "What could possibly have gone so wrong?" he asked vaguely, focused on mixing the colors together.

"Everything," Sean snapped. "To begin with, all of London believes I'm you."

"*What?*" His attention finally snagged, Hamilton whirled to face him. "How in blazes did that happen?"

"Lincolnshire asked me to take him to a ball, promising to keep my identity a secret. My identity as you, you understand. Once there, however…"

While he explained everything, Hamilton slowly lowered his palette and dropped heavily to the threadbare sofa, covering his lowered face with his hands.

When Sean finished, the weasel finally, inevitably, exploded, springing off the sofa. "You blasted son of a vicar! You were supposed to keep the mean old brute happy and stay out of public entirely!" He paced here and there, fuming. "Since you didn't keep your end of the bargain, I'll clearly not be keeping mine." Stomping right up to Sean, he growled, "Deirdre will never see her divorce! She'll bear the next Lincolnshire earl if it's the last thing she does—and with any luck, she'll die in childbirth, so it will be."

Hamilton stormed out, leaving Sean standing still, rooted to the spot, his hands clenched into fists. It was a good thing the weasel had left. If he'd stayed, Sean might not have stopped himself from beating the shorter fellow to a pulp.

He told himself he should've expected no less from the weasel, but still, it took him several minutes to calm down. Finally he drew off his coat and draped it over the arm of the sofa, then slowly lowered himself to sit and wait for Corinna to arrive.

FIFTY

"**C**ORINNA," SEAN said when she walked in.

Just *Corinna*. Nothing else. He rose from the battered sofa and walked toward her, and she could see sadness on his face, weariness in his eyes. He looked battered himself, his coat off, his cravat askew, his hair disheveled as though he'd run his hands through it over and over.

"Lord Lincolnshire is gone, isn't he?" she said quietly, but it wasn't really a question. "Did you stay up all night with him before he passed?"

In answer he stepped closer and took her in his arms. They stood there like that for a very long while, Corinna's eyes closed, her ear pressed to his chest where his heart beat steadily through the thin fabric of his shirt.

"I don't know what happened with your painting," he said at last in a bleak tone of voice.

"Something happened?" she asked, confused.

She felt rather than saw him shake his head. "Hamilton voted before I could speak to him, so he didn't speak to any of the other committee members about you, either. And he said he mostly voted for landscapes."

She opened her eyes, her gaze falling on a large canvas propped on the easel, a scene of a waterfall. Proof of Hamilton's return. Unfinished though it was, the painting was impressive... but the selfishness of its creator made it ugly to her.

And she couldn't care how the vote had turned out, not now. Maybe tomorrow it would matter, but right now all that mattered was Sean. And he was hurting.

"It's not important. Whatever happened will be." She sighed and pulled away. "It's all over. I know you're sad that Lord Lincolnshire is gone, and I am, too. But you can get back to your life now, and that's good, isn't it? The sadness will pass, and you'll be able to focus on your work, and..."

She couldn't bring herself to say that now they could be together. Sure as she was that he cared for her, he hadn't asked her to marry him yet.

"Corinna. *Críona.* I need to talk to you. But first I want to give you something," he said, reaching into a pocket. He pulled out a fine link chain with a pendant attached, but she didn't get a chance to see what it looked like before he took her hand and put the necklace in her palm, folding her fingers around it. "It's only silver. My family could never afford anything made of gold. I've the money now to have bought you something fancier, but I wanted you to have this."

He still held her hand with both of his wrapped tightly around it. His hands felt warm, and whatever was inside her fist felt hard but delicate. "This belongs to your family?"

"For a hundred years or more." His lyrical words came slower than usual, and his voice was a bit rough, the sound of it making her heart hitch. "It was my mother's, and my grandmother's before her, and so on going back for generations."

"Oh, then it should be Deirdre's now, shouldn't it?"

"I want you to have it," he repeated, releasing her hand.

Slowly she unfurled her fingers and drew out the necklace,

raising it by the chain so the pendant dangled at the bottom. A symbol. Two hands holding a stone heart, surmounted by a crown studded with a few tiny gems.

"They're not diamonds," he told her, "only marcasite. I cannot tell you what the heart is made from, because I don't know."

"It's green." She smiled. "Like your eyes."

"Is it? I never knew that. But I can assure you it isn't an emerald."

"No, it wouldn't be, because it's opaque. And I don't care what it's made from, anyway. It's beautiful. And it's from you." Anything Sean had given her would have been beautiful to her, of course, but it really was a very pretty charm. "Does the symbol have a special meaning?"

"It does, aye. It's called a claddagh. The hands signify friendship, the crown loyalty, and the heart love. All the things I feel for you, *a rún*."

A rún meant *my love*—she remembered that—and he'd said *love* in English, too. "It's perfect. So much better than diamonds or gold." He loved her. She'd thought so for some time now, but hearing the words made it more real. "I love you, too. I love you so much I feel like I might burst, like I cannot hold it all inside me." Happy tears welled in her eyes. "Will you put this on me?"

She turned around, and he clasped the chain around her neck, his warm fingers brushing her nape. When she turned back, he held her face in his hands and lowered his lips to meet hers. It was a long kiss but a gentle one, heartfelt and tender, the tenderest kiss she'd ever received.

When he drew back, his eyes burned into hers. "We need to talk now," he said. "Let's sit down."

"All right." Suddenly feeling apprehensive, she walked the few feet to the sofa and sat. He sank down beside her, angling himself so he could see her. "What is it?" she asked.

He took both her hands. "Corinna. *Críona.*" She watched him swallow hard. "Lincolnshire told me a story last Friday. That seems so long ago, doesn't it?"

She nodded, her heart pounding with love or trepidation, or maybe a mixture. It was only Tuesday, but last Friday, the night she'd sketched him, seemed a lifetime ago.

"It was a story about his twin brother, John Hamilton's father, and why he sent him to Ireland," he began.

And then it all poured out.

She listened silently, taking it all in, until he finished. Until his hands squeezed hers hard, so hard her own hands hurt. "Corinna. That will happen to me now. Once society finds out I impersonated Hamilton, they will never accept me."

She knew he was right. The *ton* wouldn't look kindly upon someone who had tricked Lord Lincolnshire. "Why didn't I think of that?"

"I didn't think of it, either. I knew all along that Hamilton was risking his reputation as an artist by participating in the hoax. I even warned him of that, and I worried that if the truth came out, he'd retaliate against Deirdre. But I never considered how it would affect *me*. Or maybe I didn't think it would matter. Not being part of society, I didn't care what they thought of me —not until I fell in love with you."

I fell in love with you. She was so thrilled to hear those words that she leapt the small distance between them, wrapping her arms around him, burrowing her nose into the crook of his neck. "I love you, too," she told him again, the words muffled against his skin. "I was waiting to tell you. Everything was so complicated. But now it's over, and we'll work this out. It will be difficult, but—"

"Corinna. You don't understand." He unwrapped her arms and set her away, far enough to meet her eyes. "I cannot marry you. There isn't anything I want more in the world, but it's impossible."

"No." That couldn't be. "This wasn't your fault. You didn't even want to do it. You did it for your sister, and for Lincolnshire —you made him happy. You shouldn't have to suffer—*we* shouldn't have to suffer—because you did the right thing."

"I'm not saying I did the wrong thing. I did the only thing I could. But no one ever promised life would be fair. Your people aren't ever going to forgive me for what I've done."

"I don't care. I don't need those people. I love you. I only need you. If they won't forgive you, if they make our life here too uncomfortable, we'll go to Ireland—"

"Your art would be shunned no matter where you made it. You'd never be admitted to the Royal Academy."

"You're more important to me than the Royal Academy. I don't care about that, either."

"*I* care." He took her hands again. "And if you married me, Corinna, you and I aren't the only ones who would be cut out of society. Your family would be ostracized as well."

A hole seemed to open up inside her.

Alexandra and Juliana, Griffin and Rachael, Frances and the cousins...if she stayed with Sean and bore the consequences, they, too, would be rejected by all of society.

She couldn't do that to them.

She was willing to give up everything she knew for Sean, to start over with him in a place she'd never seen. That would be rather artistic...wild, passionate, romantic. But she couldn't take her family with her.

That would make her more selfish than John Hamilton.

Her heart cracked, and she could see in Sean's eyes that his was already rent. His overwhelming sadness, his weariness, his battered appearance...she understood all of that now. She felt it herself.

He gathered her into his arms, and they clutched each other, held each other close for a long, long time, while sobs racked her body.

And then, when she'd cried herself dry, when there was nothing left inside her but a vast, aching emptiness, he walked her home in silence, careful not to touch her.

FIFTY-ONE

*A*S FRIDAY afternoon slid into evening, Corinna stood alone in Lincolnshire House's yellow drawing room, wearing a black dress that matched her mood.

Excited voices drifted from the crowded salon, where a reception was being held following Lord Lincolnshire's burial. More chatter came from the entrance hall, where the crowd spilled out. Women very rarely attended funerals, so Sean had arranged the reception to allow the ladies a chance to pay their respects.

She'd wager he hadn't anticipated such a crush. He wasn't part of the crush, of course, and she'd been told he hadn't attended the ceremony, either. The reception should have been a polite gathering, the guests soft-spoken and sober rather than excited. But tongues had been wagging ever since this morning, when John Hamilton had shown up at Westminster Abbey and announced he was the next Earl of Lincolnshire.

Being female, Corinna hadn't witnessed that, of course, but she'd already heard all about it. The new Lord Lincolnshire had informed the astonished gentlemen at the funeral that his impostor's name was Sean Delaney, and Sean's reputation had been torn to shreds before the reception even began.

Just as he'd predicted, she thought now with a heavyhearted sigh.

For the past two days, lines from Minerva Press novels had been running through her head annoyingly, unceasingly. Pamela thinking *life is no life without you*, and Ethelinde deciding *hope seemed to be excluded from her heart*, and, in *Children of the Abbey*, Amanda crying, *the hand of fate is against our union, and we must part, never, never more to meet!*

But although she'd known Sean was right and there was no way they could be together, some small part of her must have been holding out hope, because somehow she'd managed to get through those two days without completely falling apart.

She'd locked herself in her room and buried herself in her art. Fixing Lord Lincolnshire's portrait had kept her from thinking too much and from having to face her brother or anyone else. The picture was finished, and she'd brought it over this morning while Griffin was away at the funeral.

Lord Lincolnshire's house steward, Mr. Higginbotham, had praised the portrait mightily and promised to find somewhere to hang it immediately. Unaware at the time of the trouble brewing in Westminster Abbey, he'd also praised "Mr. Hamilton," telling her each of the staff had been thrilled to receive letters that morning with details of their new assignments, to begin Monday.

After she'd left, Mr. Higginbotham had hung the portrait in the yellow drawing room, on the wall behind the armchair where Lord Lincolnshire had been sitting when Corinna first offered to paint it. She gazed at it now, thinking it seemed the right place for it. Above the chair like that, it almost seemed as though the dear earl were still sitting there.

The portrait was mounted beside a Rembrandt, and it should have been a thrill to see one of her own paintings next to an old master. But she hadn't the capacity to feel thrilled when everything else had gone so very wrong.

Even Mr. Higginbotham was scandalized by the news. A few minutes earlier, when she'd asked him where to find the painting, he'd been sputtering with indignation. From this day forward, Sean would be shunned by society, and that meant she could never see him again without ruining her family. That was the only thing that mattered to her now. She didn't know yet whether her picture had been accepted for the Summer Exhibition, but she couldn't bring herself to care.

"Corinna?"

Hearing footsteps behind her, she turned to see Griffin enter the room, holding a glass of liquor the color of raw sienna pigment.

"What are you doing in here all alone?" He came to a stop before her, his gaze drifting up to the painting over her head. "Isn't that the portrait you did of Lord Lincolnshire?" When she didn't answer, he looked back down to her. "I thought you submitted it for the Summer Exhibition."

"I didn't. I submitted something else."

"Really?" Sipping, he looked curious. "What?"

A picture of the love of her life, the love she'd lost. That thought brought a flood of pain. As she couldn't tell her brother she loved Sean, instead she lashed out at him. "Why should you care what I submitted? All you're concerned with is getting me married off!"

He looked hurt. "That's not true, Corinna. All I'm concerned with is your happiness. I want to see you happy."

Seeing his hurt made her hurt even more. "Well, you have an odd way of showing it," she cried, tears flooding her eyes.

She couldn't take this anymore. Not any of it.

Pushing past him, she ran from the room and out into the entrance hall. The grand, pillared area was crowded with people dressed in black—people gossiping—people drinking up the contents of Lord Lincolnshire's liquor cabinet while annihilating Sean's future—and hers.

Their faces blurred as she charged toward the front door, her brother at her heels.

∼

"GRIFFIN!" RACHAEL said as he shoved a glass at her. "Where are you going?"

"After my sister!" Having passed Rachael already, he wove through the mass of guests. "I'm going home," he called back.

Rachael watched him follow Corinna at a run, then just stood there for a moment, feeling a bit dazed. She raised the glass to her lips and took a sip, hoping whatever was in it would be bracing.

Brandy. It burned a path down her throat and felt warm in her stomach.

She sipped again.

Juliana walked up. "Where did Griffin go off to?"

"He went after Corinna. I believe he was concerned for her well-being." She shook her head. "He seems more responsible than I remember."

Her cousin smiled. "You seem to like him much more than you used to."

Rachael shrugged a shoulder—casually, she hoped. "I guess he's changed over the years."

"Yes, he has. He'd make an excellent husband now, don't you think?"

"For someone else," Rachael said warily.

"For you. I think you two would get along splendidly together."

"He's my cousin. You know I won't marry a cousin."

"Rachael…"

Juliana glanced away, her gaze sweeping the thronged entrance hall. Her husband was talking to Alexandra and Tristan, and Rachael's sisters and Noah were in the salon. Apparently satisfied that no one important was watching, she took Rachael's arm and drew her into the room Griffin and Corinna had vacated.

"I know your secret," she said in a low voice.

Feeling blindsided, Rachael struggled to look normal while she sipped more brandy. "What secret?"

"I know John Chase wasn't your father," Juliana said gently. "And I know you're Lady A's granddaughter."

Rachael relaxed a little, and not just due to the brandy. Apparently her cousin *didn't* know her real father had committed treason, or surely she would have mentioned that, too—because if there was one thing Juliana loved, it was a juicy secret like that.

And she supposed it wasn't all that dreadful for people to know the rest. Her mother had been married when Rachael was conceived, after all—it wasn't as though Georgiana had been carrying an illegitimate child when she married the Earl of Greystone. And while not being John Chase's true daughter was a disappointment, being Lady A's granddaughter was a joy.

Still and all, it *had* been a secret. "Who told you?" she asked.

"It doesn't signify. It was an accident, and the person I learned it from wished you no harm. But, Rachael, I...well, I realize you wanted it kept secret, but I thought it best to reveal I know, because there's something you apparently *don't* know. Or haven't realized yet."

Juliana paused for effect, or maybe to give Rachael a moment to absorb what she'd already said. Because what she said next seemed somewhat confusing.

"You're not Griffin's cousin."

Rachael hadn't thought much about that, but it was true, of

course. "I know we're not blood related, since I'm not really a Chase, but..."

"But what?"

"He's still family. Griffin is Griffin. My cousin. We grew up together."

"Why should that matter? There would be no risk of you two conceiving a tragic child like your cousin Edmund, and that was your issue, wasn't it? You wouldn't have to worry about having a child like that with Griffin."

She'd never thought about that, either. Two years ago, when Griffin had first come home from the cavalry, she'd found herself stunned by how much he had changed. He'd fascinated her, she recalled. The reckless, gangly youth she'd remembered had grown tall, dark, and broad-shouldered, and she'd been surprised to find herself attracted to him. But she'd told herself he was her cousin—not knowing any different at the time—and that had been that.

That *wasn't* that, though, was it?

"Oh, drat," she finally said softly. "I've been such a blazing idiot."

"We all are sometimes," Juliana soothed.

But Rachael wasn't listening. She'd shoved the glass at Juliana, her black skirts rustling as she ran from the room.

FIFTY-TWO

"CAN I NOT just be sad over the loss of Lord Lincolnshire?"

"Not this sad. You've been hiding in this room since Tuesday." Griffin gazed down at his sister lying on her bed, her back to him. Her knees were hugged to her chest. He couldn't see her face, but she didn't strike him as sad.

More like devastated.

"I'll miss the earl, too," he added, "but it has to be more than that."

She heaved a sigh so pathetic it broke his heart. "All right, it's more than that," she admitted, tears in her voice. "The Summer Exhibition committee did the judging on Tuesday, and my painting wasn't accepted."

"Have you received a letter saying so?"

"No. Not yet. The Exhibition won't open until the first Monday in June, and until the Hanging Committee has finished arranging all the selections on the walls, a few pieces may be in question. So I wouldn't expect a letter yet."

"That's good news, then," he told her, trying to cheer her.

"Acceptance must at least be a possibility. Surely they'd have sent a letter by now if the answer were a definite no."

"You don't know that. And I've heard that Mr. Hamilton—I mean, *Lord Lincolnshire*"—this pronounced with an abundance of disgust—"didn't vote for any portraits."

"He's not the only man on the committee."

"No, there are eight others, two of whom abhor female painters. Another three didn't like my portrait of Lord Lincolnshire, and two more gave me no opinion at all."

"So you'll try again next year." Griffin sat on the edge of the bed and awkwardly patted her shoulder. "Maybe you should sign a man's name next time."

She rolled over, and the glare she gave him made it clear this had been a poor time to jest.

"I'm sorry," he muttered quickly.

Now that he could see it, her tear-streaked face made him feel like the worst brother on earth. He'd known her art was important to her, but he honestly hadn't known it meant so much that she'd be completely crushed by a temporary setback. He couldn't remember her ever being this upset before, not even the two times he'd come home, taking short leaves from the cavalry, to mourn their father and mother.

"I know this is important to you," he said carefully, "and I'm sorry if I've ignored your art while trying to find you a husband. That wasn't my intention. I've just been a little...focused. *Too* focused, apparently. I promise not to do that from now on, all right? I won't push suitors on you. When you see someone you're interested in, just let me know, and—"

"Leave me alone, Griffin," she snapped.

"But—"

"Now."

"Very well." He rose and backed away, his hands held up defensively. "I'm sorry, Corinna, truly I am. But I wish you would believe me when I say I want to see you happy."

Rolling to face away from him again, she said, "I know that," in a wan little voice.

He supposed it was the best he could expect for now.

He'd done all he could, he told himself as he left, softly closing the door between them. Too bad it wasn't good enough. Turning to face the door, he banged his forehead against the polished wood, pressing hard.

He would never understand girls.

He felt bad that he'd made light of Corinna's art, and he would pay more attention in the future. Make more of an effort to show her he cared and help advance her career, if he could think of a way to do that. But he still felt that finding her a husband to love would make her happier.

Or at the very least, make someone else responsible for her happiness.

He banged his head against the wood again.

"Griffin, are you all right?" said a voice behind him.

A sultry voice.

He straightened and turned to see its owner, standing there in a modest black dress that should have made her look drab, or at least less alluring than usual. But it didn't. It had a wide neckline, and it rustled as she moved closer, the bodice clinging to her figure. Her hair had been done up formally for the reception at Lincolnshire House, leaving just a few loose chestnut tendrils that fell in soft waves around her face.

He swallowed hard and took an uneasy step back, bumping against Corinna's door.

"May I have a word with you?" Rachael glanced around the corridor. "In private?"

He nodded and led the way to his study, aware all the while of her heady, floral scent following behind him. Would she never leave him in peace? He'd found her grandmother, hadn't he? He'd tracked her mysterious origins, discovered what had become of her father. What more did she want from him? Why wasn't she with Lady Avonleigh over at Lincolnshire House, together with her happy new family?

After ushering her into the study, he shut the door and turned to her. "What do you want, Rachael?"

She blinked, no doubt taken aback by his unintended harshness. But she recovered her composure quickly. "I want you to kiss me."

His pulse seemed to stutter. He definitely stopped breathing.

She licked her lips.

"**C**ORINNA?"

A knock sounded on her closed door.

"Are you all right?" Juliana called.

Corinna might have ignored anyone else, but there was no putting off Juliana. "I'll live," she muttered, rolling over and levering herself to sit on the edge of the bed. Realizing she was clutching the claddagh necklace, she shoved it under her pillow, then mopped the last of the tears off her face with the back of her hand. "Come in."

Juliana did, holding up a piece of heavy cream-colored paper with a large, broken red seal. "A letter came for you."

Just what she needed now, the news of her rejection. Well, at least the suspense would be over. "From the Royal Academy?"

"From the former Lord Lincolnshire's solicitor. Addressed to 'The Marquess of Cainewood.' And then inside it says, 'My Lord Marquess and Lady Corinna Chase.'"

"What does the solicitor want?" Not that Corinna really cared.

"You're requested to attend the reading of the late earl's will at Mr. Lawless's Queen Street offices on Monday at noon."

Corinna shrugged. "Lord Lincolnshire probably left us a trinket. One of his four hundred Ming vases or some such. For being kind through his last few days."

"I don't think he'd leave you and Griffin *one* vase. Two, maybe." Juliana smiled, a transparent effort to raise Corinna's spirits. "I'm famished. The reception at Lincolnshire House is winding down, so I walked over here to ask the staff to serve a family dinner before the rest of us go home. Will you come down and join us? And where's Griffin?"

"How should I know?" Corinna paused. "And how did you come to read a letter addressed to Griffin if you haven't seen him?"

"Well, obviously," Juliana said airily, "I opened it."

FIFTY-THREE

*G*RIFFIN HAD kissed Rachael in his study. He'd kissed her *across* his study. He'd kissed her as he'd maneuvered her down to the long leather sofa, and now, a good thirty minutes later, he was lying half on top of her, still kissing her.

She'd been kissed before, but not by anyone who kissed anything like Griffin. He seemed to put his entire heart and soul into a kiss. When Griffin was kissing her, she was wholly convinced his mind was on nothing but that. On nothing but her. Which made it difficult to think about anything but him, either.

In fact, he made it difficult to think at all.

His kisses went from sweet to warm to burning and back again. From gentle to deep, from rushed to unhurried to frantic. Her senses were reeling, swirling with the heat of his mouth and the scent of his skin and the taste of brandy. Her blood coursed through her veins, beating an electrifying rhythm in her ears.

When it was over, when he finally lifted his head, looking utterly disoriented, when he struggled to his elbows and gazed down at her, she still found it hard to think. His eyes were so very intense, his mouth—the same mouth that had just been kissing her senseless—curved into that slightly crooked smile. Hooking a hand behind his neck, she pulled him back down and kissed him some more.

A long while later he lifted his head back up again, and her own head finally cleared.

A little.

"You're not my cousin," she murmured, looking up at him, feeling a little smile tug at her own mouth.

"I know."

"That means we can marry."

He was off of her like a shot. "Oh, no."

"Oh, no?" She raised herself to a sitting position. She'd probably shocked herself as much as him by saying that. But it was true.

She wanted to marry Griffin.

She loved him.

She wasn't sure when she'd fallen in love, because she'd never admitted that to herself before—she hadn't been able to, having never overcome thinking of him as a cousin. But she knew she could lean on Griffin; she knew she could depend on him. He'd always be there for her—he'd shown her that, hadn't he? And wasn't that the most important quality in a husband?

And it certainly didn't hurt that he was so nice to look at. So tall and lean, so broad-shouldered and masculine. His eyes such a gorgeous green, his jaw so strong and square, that crooked smile so irresistible.

"Oh, yes," she said, "I want to marry you."

"You *don't* want to marry me," he said at once, a hint of panic in those green eyes. "You think I'm an irresponsible scapegrace."

"Not anymore." Or not exactly. Yes, he said stupid things, and he did stupid things sometimes, too. He had his flaws. But who didn't? At least she knew Griffin's flaws—she knew what she was getting into with him.

And she'd never felt such a force of attraction with anyone but Griffin.

She loved him just as he was, flaws and all.

"I *do* want to marry you," she disagreed, "and, really, how can you refuse me? You've been kissing me for half an hour."

He shifted on his feet, glancing away from her. "It was only kissing, Rachael. And you invited it. You cannot expect a man to turn down an offer like that."

He hadn't kissed her only because she'd invited him. She might be a blazing idiot for not realizing there was no reason she couldn't marry him, but she wasn't so bird-witted she didn't know when someone wanted her.

Griffin had been wanting her for two years, at the very least. A gentleman didn't look at a lady the way he looked at her—or kiss her the way he just had—unless he wanted her. And he loved her, too. She was sure of it. Look at all the trouble he'd gone to in order to find her family. A fellow didn't go to such trouble for a girl he didn't love.

And she couldn't let him get away with saying it had been *only kissing.* "Are you telling me all that kissing meant nothing?"

He looked back to her. "That's what I just said, isn't it?"

Oh, that had come too easily. She'd asked the wrong question. "You didn't enjoy it, then? Not at all?"

He hadn't an answer for that, which didn't surprise her. He'd be lying if he claimed he hadn't enjoyed himself.

"Tell me, Griffin," she drawled, rather amused by his increasing discomfort, "would you approve of a gentleman kissing Corinna for half an hour if he had no intention of marrying her?"

He couldn't say that without lying, either, of course. To his credit, he didn't. "No, I wouldn't approve. But she's my sister."

"Well, I think I deserve the same respect as your sister." Rising from the sofa, she reached for her reticule. "So unless you change your mind and declare your intentions, I trust you won't ever kiss me again."

She wanted him to kiss her again, of course. But she wasn't worried she wouldn't get what she wanted. Another of Griffin's flaws was resisting change, but he'd come around eventually.

She'd lay odds he'd be kissing her inside of a week.

He jumped out of her way as she headed for the door. Reaching it, she placed her hand on the knob and glanced over her shoulder. "Will you be attending Lady Hammersmithe's ball tomorrow night?"

"I'm planning to take Corinna."

She licked her lips, suppressing a smile when his eyes widened. "I'll see you there, then," she practically purred as she opened the door and waltzed out.

FIFTY-FOUR

THE ATMOSPHERE in Hampstead was very thick that Friday evening. So thick it seemed an effort to breathe. Just drawing air in and out of his lungs seemed to take everything Sean had.

Sitting opposite Deirdre in his dining room, he set down his knife and fork with a sigh. "I'm not hungry." He'd scarcely eaten in three days, but he wasn't hungry.

His sister knew what he'd lost. When he'd asked her where he could find the claddagh necklace, she hadn't asked why. "It's sorry I am for you, Sean," she said quietly, her eyes full of sympathy.

He didn't want sympathy—he wanted the calendar flipped back to April, to before he'd received that blasted letter from Hamilton. Shifting his gaze away, he stared at a blue wall. "I'm not the one who has to go back to a husband I despise."

"At least the man I love isn't forbidden to me forever, as Corinna is to you. I'll give John a son and *then* I'll move in with Daniel."

Skeptical, he looked back to her. "You'd leave your child?"

Her chin in the air was so familiar. "Rather than stay with John, yes."

"If you say so," he murmured. But he knew she wouldn't. Once she had a son or a daughter, she'd change her mind. Hamilton would banish Deirdre and their offspring to the countryside, and she'd live there, bored out of her mind, for the rest of her life.

And even should she find the will to leave her child, would Daniel Raleigh wait a year or two or more while she made a son with Hamilton?

He doubted that as well.

"Two letters, sir." A footman walked in, holding them out. "One for you and one for the lady."

With its large red seal, Sean's letter looked important. As the servant left, he cracked the wax and unfolded the paper.

"Who is it from?" Deirdre asked.

"A solicitor on Queen Street in Cheapside. A Mr. Peregrine Peabody. He's wishing to meet with me Monday at noon."

"Regarding what?"

"He doesn't say." Whatever it was, it couldn't be good. "I assume I will finally learn who's been poking around in my business, and what he's managed to trump up to ruin me or put me in prison. And what it's going to take to prove him wrong." He glanced at the folded paper Deirdre held, recognizing the scrawl on the outside as the same on the blasted letter he'd received back in April. "What does your husband want now? His uncle isn't in the grave even a full day. Is the weasel forcing you back to his house already?"

She broke the seal and scanned it. "He isn't, no. Not yet. He says I'm to attend the reading of the late Lord Lincolnshire's will on Monday. He's sending a carriage to fetch me at eleven o'clock."

"Where is the reading being held?"

"John doesn't say. Just that the carriage will come in the morning." She glanced up from the paper, looking nervous. "Remember that ball Lord Lincolnshire took us to? What if someone who was there recognizes me as the woman introduced as your wife?"

Sean reached to lay his hand over hers on the table. "I don't expect the Billingsgates' guests will be at the reading, Deirdre. It will likely be just you and Hamilton and that lawyer named Lawless."

"I'm not sure that lawyer ever got a good look at me. We were never formally introduced."

"You've nothing to worry yourself about, then." He patted her hand. "Even if Lawless recalls seeing you at Lincolnshire House, you *are* Hamilton's wife. Lincolnshire's niece by marriage. It's not unbelievable you'd be at the man's deathbed."

"That's right." He saw her relax a little. "I wish you could come with me, though."

"I wish I could, too," he said dryly. "I also wasn't formally introduced, but I've no doubt Lawless saw me. And if he doesn't remember me, I'm certain Hamilton would be happy to remind him. And in any case, I cannot go with you because I'll be busy Monday at that time."

Feeling yet more incapable of breathing than earlier, he heaved another sigh. The atmosphere seemed to be getting even thicker.

"The way my luck has been going lately," he added grimly, "I'll probably be busy getting arrested."

~

*W*HEN RACHAEL and her siblings returned home from the reception at Lincolnshire House, their butler handed a folded paper to her brother. "A letter, my lord."

With its large red seal, it looked important. "What does it say?" Rachael asked as the butler closed the door.

Pausing in the foyer, Noah raised the letter to his forehead. "Hmm. I'm getting a vision. I think it says—"

"Noah." She whacked him with her reticule, feeling giddy. She was in love, and she was going to get married. Griffin was going to be kissing her inside of a week. Maybe tomorrow night. "Open it, you fool."

"If you insist." He broke the seal and scanned down the page. "It's from a solicitor in Cheapside, Mr. Lawrence Lawless. He wants us to attend the reading of Lord Lincolnshire's will Monday at noon."

"Us?" Elizabeth slid off her pelisse. "What do you mean by *us*?"

"All of us." Shrugging, Noah looked up. "It's addressed to all four of us."

FIFTY-FIVE

"**Y**OU'RE LATE," Juliana said when Griffin arrived at Lady Hammersmithe's ball Saturday night.

"*Fashionably* late," he corrected, spotting Rachael talking to her sisters. She was wearing another clingy dress, a sapphire blue one with tiny sleeves that left most of her arms bare.

"Where's Corinna?"

"Still in the doldrums." He looked back to Juliana. "You can blame her for making me fashionable. She refused to leave the house."

"Yet you came anyway," she said, appearing speculative. "Why is that?"

He wasn't about to tell her he'd come to see Rachael. Juliana meddled enough without his encouragement. "Am I not allowed to socialize without an agenda?" Since she looked even more speculative, he changed the subject. "I expect tonight's buzz is still all about yesterday's revelations?"

"Mr. Delaney, you mean? Actually, no. The gossip tonight is about how everyone's been invited to the reading of Lord Lincolnshire's will on Monday."

"Everyone?"

"When James and I arrived home last night, there was a letter waiting. Alexandra and Tristan got one, too. As did every other household in Mayfair, if one can believe the talk."

"I've never heard of such a thing."

"The reading is going to be a shocking squeeze." Juliana sounded thrilled at the prospect. "Lord Lincolnshire cannot have left bequests to everyone, so I wonder what could be the reason."

"You'll know soon enough." He looked over toward Rachael, only to find she was gone. "Have you seen Noah or any of his sisters?"

"Last I noticed, Rachael was talking to Claire and Elizabeth." She glanced around. "Oh, Rachael's dancing now. And Noah just walked into the refreshment room." That speculative look came into her eyes again. "Why do you ask?"

"I was just wondering if they received a letter, too," he said casually. "I'll go ask Noah."

Leaving Juliana, he ambled toward the refreshment room— then went right past it. And around to the far side of the ball- room, where she couldn't see him. He couldn't care less whether his cousins had received a letter. But Rachael dancing...

Well, that was another matter altogether.

He shifted uneasily, watching the fellow Rachael was dancing with pull her closer, watching him run a hand slowly down the back of her clingy dress. When the music ended and she curtsied to the son of a gun, Griffin moved quickly to block her path off the dance floor.

"What are you doing, Rachael?"

"What do you mean, what am I doing?"

"Why are you dancing?"

"I'm at a ball, if you haven't noticed. What else should I be doing but dancing?"

"I don't remember you dancing at a ball in the last two

seasons, except with me. You told me you didn't like men pawing you."

"Well, I thought I didn't, at the time." Watching him, she licked her lips. "But a certain experience last night changed my mind."

"I didn't paw you last night," he protested, though he felt an urge to paw her now.

"Maybe I wanted you to paw me," she suggested. "Maybe it crossed my mind that might have been enjoyable."

Clenching his jaw, he looked away. Blast it, she'd accused him of disrespecting her and all he'd done was kiss her for half an hour. After she'd asked. Now he wasn't allowed to kiss her again unless he proposed first, but it was all right if another man pawed her?

In the distance, Juliana caught his eye. Standing in a clutch of jabbering chatterboxes, she glanced between him and Rachael and raised a speculative eyebrow.

"Instead of dancing," he gritted out, "why don't you just gossip like every other girl?"

Rachael followed his gaze. "I'm not Juliana, if you haven't noticed."

Now, *that* he'd noticed. He'd never once been tempted to kiss his sister for half an hour.

"I prefer dancing to gossiping," Rachael informed him archly. "Especially now, since I'm looking for a husband."

"You're doing *what*?"

"You heard me. Since you don't want to marry me, I've decided to find someone who's ready to make me his wife." The lips he'd kissed last night curved into a satisfied smile. "Stop gaping, Griffin. You look better with your mouth closed. Not that I care what you look like anymore," she added, and sailed off.

Three minutes later Griffin was still standing there, and

Rachael was dancing with another man. Another son of a gun. This one seemed to be whispering secrets in her ear.

Ten minutes later, another son of a gun was holding her too close.

Ten minutes after that, another another son of a gun was making her laugh. Had Griffin ever made her laugh? *With* him, that was, not *at* him?

When she came off the dance floor for the third time, he pulled her aside again. "Why all of a sudden do you want to get married?"

"I'm twenty-one years old, Griffin, and I wasted two seasons chasing down my father. I'll be on the shelf if I don't marry soon. That's what decided me."

"You don't just *decide* to find a husband, Rachael."

"Odd statement, coming from you. Is that not what you've decided for Corinna?"

"I've changed my mind. I'm thinking it would be better to wait until she falls in love. I'd suggest you do the same yourself."

"I *have* fallen in love," she informed him. "But since it took twenty-one years to happen, I don't think I can afford to wait for it to happen another time. Your mouth is open again," she added before she turned in a swish of clingy skirts and walked away.

Not a minute later, she was dancing once more.

Griffin's mouth remained open for quite a while.

She loved him? Hardly a word passed her lips that didn't disparage him. And if she loved him, why the deuce was she dancing with yet another son of a gun? One with the gall to put a hand where it didn't belong, no less? Just for a split second, but Griffin had seen it. He wanted to strangle the man.

Juliana sauntered by. "Close your mouth, Griffin," she said as she passed, her voice filled with speculation. She turned to walk backward, a smug smile emerging as she studied him. "You look jealous," she said before turning again and walking away.

Now he wanted to strangle *her*.

Was he jealous? Could he possibly love Rachael? He'd thought what he felt for her was just lust, but mere lust shouldn't incite jealousy. And if this was what jealousy felt like, he didn't care for it one bit.

By the time Rachael curtsied to the son of a gun who'd put a hand where it didn't belong, Griffin was standing next to her. "You must have misunderstood me yesterday, Rachael."

She turned to him. "How is that?"

"It isn't that I don't want to marry you. I just don't want to marry you *now*. I'm not ready to take a wife. At the moment, I've too many other responsibilities. I'm quite concerned about Corinna. Before I even think about settling down myself, I need to concentrate on getting her married. To someone she *loves*."

"I'll tell you what you need to concentrate on, Griffin, and that's growing up. You're twenty-six years old. For heaven's sake, Noah's growing up, and he's only twenty. If I wait until you're ready, I'll be waiting forever."

"I'm not asking for forever, Rachael. Just until Corinna's married."

"Corinna won't be married for another year at least. The season's more than half over, and she hasn't shown interest in anyone yet. In fact, your sister seems rather wed to her art career, which means she may not *ever* marry. Have you considered that?"

He hadn't, and the thought struck terror in his heart.

And Rachael wasn't finished. "If I agree to wait until she's married, I could end up a shriveled old lady, and you'll still be asking for time." She shook her beautiful head. "Thank you for the offer, but no."

"But I love you."

He couldn't believe those words had come out of his mouth, but even more than that, he couldn't believe her response.

"I know that, Griffin. But I want children. I'm going to find someone who's willing to marry me while I'm still young enough to have them." She rose to her toes and kissed him on the cheek. "I'll see you at Lincolnshire's solicitor's office on Monday."

FIFTY-SIX

*W*HEN SEAN arrived in Queen Street on Monday at noon, he found it clogged with traffic and pedestrians. He'd never seen any street in Cheapside so busy. He felt lucky when he found a place to leave his curricle in a mews only two streets away.

Walking back, he fretted over what trouble he might be facing. At the bottom of the three steps that led to the solicitor's office, he stopped to check the plaque mounted by the building's door to make sure he was in the right place.

88 QUEEN STREET
PEABODY & LAWLESS
ATTORNEYS-AT-LAW

Mr. Peregrine Peabody being the solicitor he was supposed to meet, he nodded to himself and started up.

Then stopped again, ignoring a steady stream of people pushing past him up the steps.

Peabody and *Lawless*?

Lincolnshire's solicitor?

His first thought was to slink away. A summons issued by Lincolnshire's solicitor was potentially much worse than being summoned to discuss an accusation against Delaney & Company. He knew all his company's dealings were honest, after all. No matter who accused him of what, he ought to be able to prove his innocence, even if it doing so might be a colossal nuisance. When he'd told Deirdre he might be busy getting arrested today, he hadn't really *meant* it.

But had impersonating John Hamilton been an actual crime?

Had he been summoned here to be arrested?

"Sean!" Coming up the steps, Deirdre looked astonished to see him. "What are you doing here?"

"I wish I knew." He gestured toward the plaque. "These are Peregrine Peabody's offices, too."

A woman mounting the steps did a double take, then turned to face him. "Mr. Delaney, isn't it? You have quite the nerve showing up here. Hmmph," she added, pushing through the door, no doubt to spread the news that he'd arrived.

There was nothing for it. There would be no slinking away. "Come along," he muttered, taking Deirdre's arm and steeling himself to face the fire.

But instead he came face-to-face with Corinna.

~

*A*T FIRST, Corinna thought Sean was a figment of her imagination. She wasn't ever supposed to see him again, and he very especially wasn't supposed to be *here*. But then she met his eyes, and the anguish in them was so poignant that she knew he had to be real.

And it wasn't just anguish she saw. It was a mixture of anguish and love and regret that matched her own feelings.

Seeing him made her happy and sad and excited and apprehensive, all in a single instant. Her hand went up to touch the claddagh necklace, but it wasn't there, of course. She could wear it only in her room at night, where no one would see it and ask questions.

She started toward him.

"You need to come inside now, Corinna." Griffin appeared, took her arm, and began weaving her through the crowded corridor. "Mr. Lawless is about to begin, and you've been directed to sit in the front."

She looked back, but Sean was already lost in the crowd. She could only hope he was following.

When Griffin had told her that everyone they knew had been asked to attend the reading, she'd figured he'd been exaggerating. She'd had no idea just how many people would show up. They crammed the large chamber where the reading was to be held and spilled out into the corridor, filling the building all the way back to the front door. With all the bodies in the way, she and Griffin barely managed to squeeze into the room.

Mr. Lawless was a very tall, very serious-looking man. Over a sea of chattering heads, Corinna could see him from where she was stuck in the back. "Ladies and gentlemen," he called. "I beg your attention! Will the following individuals please make their way to the front row. John Hamilton, the ninth Earl of Lincolnshire. His wife, Deirdre, the ninth Countess of Lincolnshire. Lady Corinna Chase. And Mr. Sean Delaney."

The crowd suddenly parted like the Red Sea, letting Corinna through. Griffin followed and went to stand at the left end of the front row, against the wall. Corinna noticed that the rest of her family already waited there. Four chairs at the front sat empty save for small signs set upon them that said RESERVED. Corinna dropped gratefully onto one of them, and a moment later the new Lord Lincolnshire lowered himself to the chair on her left, and Sean took the seat to her right.

Deirdre sat beside Sean rather than her husband.

"Why were you asked here?" Corinna whispered to Sean.

He looked pale. "I wish I knew. I assumed—"

"Ladies and gentlemen," the solicitor interrupted. "Although the eighth Lord Lincolnshire requested your presence, I feel compelled to inform you at the outset that you did not all receive bequests. Alas, while he was well-known for his generosity, Lord Lincolnshire's largesse did not extend quite that far." He paused while an amused titter ran through the room. "Rather, Lord Lincolnshire asked you here to stand as witnesses to his final wishes."

Now a speculative murmur circulated the room instead. Mr. Lawless waited for that to die down before continuing.

"Let us begin." A suspenseful hush fell as he raised a large document. "'I, Samuel Hamilton, eighth Earl of Lincolnshire, being of sound mind and failing body, declare that this is my last will and testament. I revoke all prior wills and codicils. I wish to thank everyone who has assembled to bear witness to my wishes. I have instructed Mr. Lawrence Lawless not to schedule the reading of this will until my nephew, John Hamilton, has arrived in London and presented himself as my heir, which I hope will prove to be sooner rather than later. I assume that doubtless scandalous event has by now taken place.'"

Shocked whispers buzzed around the room, accompanied by a few more titters. Corinna and Sean exchanged wide-eyed glances.

"'I imagine it came as a surprise that an impostor has been posing as my nephew. It certainly came as a surprise to me. What may come as a larger surprise indeed is that I also discovered my true nephew, John Hamilton, was responsible for the deceit. He demanded another individual impersonate him and made certain said individual did so by means of blackmail.'"

Gasps filled the room, and John Hamilton jumped from his seat. "I object to that slander!"

Griffin stepped forward. "This isn't a trial, you fool. You have no right to object to anything." He shoved the fellow back down.

"Stay, Lincolnshire," he ordered as though the new earl were a misbehaving dog.

Which he wasn't, Corinna thought fiercely. He was much worse than that.

Mr. Lawless cleared his throat and continued. "'Needless to say, I was disappointed to learn my nephew is truly as deplorable as the reputation that precedes him. For him I wish all the censure he deserves. Contrarily, I wish everyone to know that his impostor, whom I am now identifying as Mr. Sean Delaney, proved one of the best young men I've ever had the privilege to meet. He treated me better than an uncle—indeed, better than a father—and were I to be granted one impossible wish, it would be to have had such as him for my son.'"

Corinna's heart had stuttered when Sean's name was read off, and it was racing now. An expectant silence filled the room as Mr. Lawless lowered the document and looked around as though making sure everyone had heard his words. He nodded slowly before raising the will once more.

"'And so, my dear friends, I have summoned you to this event in order to beseech you to treat Mr. Delaney as I believe he deserves to be treated. Rather than persecuting the young man, I beg you to accept him into our circle. I will remind you that you've all claimed numerous times that you'd do anything for me, and *this* is my most fervent request.'"

The solicitor glanced up again, this time looking directly at Corinna and Sean.

"'In addition…'"

At the significant pause, everyone sat up straighter.

"'In addition, although I will not put any conditions in this will stipulating the matter, as I believe such decisions are best left to those whose hearts are involved, I wish to publicly convey my hopes that Mr. Delaney will propose marriage to Lady Corinna Chase.'"

If Corinna thought everyone's gasps were loud before, the

ones they emitted now sounded like nothing less than a roar. And the loudest gasps of all came from her family. Meeting Griffin's eyes first and then those of her sisters, she reached for Sean's hand.

"And now, for the bequests…"

She hardly heard what came next, at least not at first. She felt faint. Her blood was thundering in her ears. Sean's hand felt warm in hers, and when she squeezed it and he squeezed back, she feared her heart might burst.

She glanced back to her family. Griffin's mouth was open in shock, Alexandra nodded approvingly, and Juliana's grin was smug beyond belief.

And the reading wasn't yet finished.

"'… only my title as required by law and the small amount of entailed property that goes along with it,'" Mr. Lawless was saying. Given the indignant huff to Corinna's left, she guessed that was the new Lord Lincolnshire's punishment. "'The balance of my fortune will be held in trust, the income to go to charity. I name Mr. Sean Delaney as trustee to oversee all investments and distribution, because I know him to be a person who has no need for the income himself, a person with an excellent head for business, and most important, a person who is eminently fair and makes decisions for the right reasons.'" The solicitor paused for effect. "'Unless…'"

Skirts rustled and shoes shuffled. Everyone sat on the edge of their seats.

"'Unless,'" he repeated, "'my errant nephew, John Hamilton, grants Deirdre Hamilton a divorce, in which case he shall receive half the income of the trust in perpetuity.'"

John Hamilton stalked out of the room as Deirdre collapsed in a swoon.

FIFTY-SEVEN

STILL HOLDING Corinna's hand, Sean walked with her and Deirdre toward Mr. Lawless, who stood by the door where he'd been busy ushering everyone out. Although Sean's little party was the last to leave the chamber, excited chatter could be heard from the corridor. The reading of Lord Lincolnshire's will would doubtless be talked about for weeks.

"I'll be setting up the trust in the next few days," the solicitor said. "I'll need to meet with you to go over the details. Shall we say next Monday, at the same time?"

Sean nodded. "Agreed. But I've one question I'd like answered today."

"I have *lots* of questions," Corinna said.

"I'm thinking your brother can answer most of them," Sean told her, and looked back to Lawless. "Why did the letter I received requesting my presence here come from your partner rather than yourself?"

"Those were Lord Lincolnshire's instructions. He didn't want my name on the letter. He thought you might not show, fearing arrest."

"Lincolnshire was a clever man," Sean said, as arrest was

exactly what he'd feared on seeing Lawless's name. "My thanks." He held out his free hand, and the solicitor gave it a firm shake. "I shall see you a week from today."

As Sean, Corinna, and Deirdre stepped into the corridor, the chatter ceased. Apparently a nosy lot, most of the people followed them outside, where Corinna's family waited bunched together on the pavement.

Sean tried to drop Corinna's hand as they approached, but she tightened her grip. Lady Stafford, Corinna's middle sister, elbowed their brother when she noticed the two of them walk up.

Cainewood turned. "Ah, there you are, Corinna. Since the atmosphere here on Queen Street is a little tense"—he waved a hand, indicating all the busybodies—"we've decided to discuss these developments at home." He looked to Sean. "If you could follow us there, I'd appreciate your participation in the discussion."

"I'm riding home with Sean," Corinna announced.

"*Sean?* Since when do you call the fellow Sean?" Glancing down to their clasped hands, her brother's eyes widened. "It isn't proper for you to ride alone with an unmarried gentleman."

"Sean has an open curricle, so I can assure you nothing improper will happen."

Snickers came from all around them, this sort of exchange being exactly what nosy busybodies loved to overhear. Cainewood's jaw seemed to be clenched. Suspecting none of this was helping him earn the marquess's approval, Sean turned to Corinna. "I need to take Deirdre with me, *a rún,*" he told her apologetically. "The curricle seats only two."

"Your sister is welcome to ride with my husband and myself," Lady Stafford piped up at the same time Cainewood said, "*What* did you just call my sister?"

Deirdre smiled. "*A rún.* It means 'my love.'" She didn't seem to notice Cainewood's reaction as she turned to his middle sister.

"And I would be pleased to ride with you, Lady Stafford. Thank you for the offer."

"I think you should call me Juliana," Lady Stafford told her. "I've a feeling we'll be related soon."

The buzz around their little group was becoming deafening. Cainewood's next words came from between his teeth. "I think—"

"Oh, let them ride together, Griffin," Corinna's eldest sister interrupted, wheeling a squeaky perambulator back and forth. "My goodness, what do you think could happen in an open curricle? There's my carriage now." A large vehicle crept to a stop in the snarl of traffic. "Let's all go," she said, pushing the perambulator toward it.

Her husband followed. Lady Stafford took her own husband's arm and smiled at Deirdre. "Our carriage is this way, Lady Lincolnshire."

"Call me Deirdre," Deirdre said. "I won't be Lady Lincolnshire for long."

As the three of them walked off, a lovely young woman moved to stand squarely before Corinna's fuming brother. "It seems your sister may be getting married a lot sooner than you expected, hmm?" she purred.

"Good gracious," Cainewood said, blanching, and walked off, too.

A delighted smile on her face, the girl joined three others that looked like they might be her sisters and brother. "I want you to drop me off at Griffin's house," she said as they all departed.

Leaving Sean and Corinna alone.

Well, except for the dozens of buzzing busybodies.

"Who was that?" Sean asked.

"My cousin Rachael. I think Juliana is about to get even more smug. Where is your curricle?"

"In a mews about two streets from here." Still holding her hand, he drew her in the right direction. The crowd parted to let them through, but Sean felt at least a hundred eyes on his back.

"Am I dreaming?" Corinna asked, seemingly oblivious to all the curious gazes. "Just an hour ago, all was lost. Now suddenly your reputation is restored—no, more than that, it's golden—and we can get…"

Her voice trailed off, as though she were afraid to say what came next.

"Married?" Sean supplied.

"You never actually asked me." They turned a corner, and she threw herself into his arms. "Oh, Sean, I've never been so happy!"

He held her tight and risked a short kiss, since they'd escaped the prying eyes. She felt incredible in his arms and against his lips. But he couldn't bring himself to share in her happiness quite yet.

"Let's not count our chickens before they're hatched," he advised, remembering Cainewood's clenched jaw. "Lincolnshire's endorsement notwithstanding, your brother may not approve."

"Oh, don't worry about Griffin," she said gaily, rising to her toes for another quick kiss. He obliged her, of course. "I have a plan to persuade him."

"What do you mean?"

"Never mind." A bounce in her step, she turned and resumed walking. "We're all going to live happily ever after, just like in a Minerva Press novel."

"Not all of us," he pointed out. "Not Hamilton."

"No one will buy his paintings now, will they? He's going to *need* half the income from his uncle's trust."

"Very clever, that stipulation." They turned into the mews where his curricle was waiting. "Lincolnshire knew it would get him to free Deirdre."

"She looked so happy."

"Believe me, she is." Digging a coin from his pocket, he handed it to one groom as another helped Corinna climb up. Sean walked around to the driver's side and swung up beside her. "And I'm relieved to know she won't be living in sin," he added as he lifted the reins. "Or at least, not for long."

As the horses clip-clopped out of the mews, Corinna leaned against him, sighing contentedly. "What do you mean?"

"Deirdre won't be waiting for the divorce to come through before she moves in with Raleigh," he said with a sigh, turning onto the street. "That will take a long while, and she won't be patient. Impulsive, my sister is, not to mention a wee bit wild."

"I guess wildness runs in your family," Corinna said, grinning up at him. "Her brother posed nearly naked for an artist, you know."

FIFTY-EIGHT

A SHORT TIME later, Griffin found himself seated on a sofa in his drawing room, surrounded by members of his family and a couple of near strangers with Irish accents. And each and every one of them—except for the baby—wanted something.

His two brothers-in-law wanted to go home. *That* he could understand. If he weren't already home, he would want to go home now, too.

Alexandra wanted to know how Lincolnshire had come to learn everything his will had revealed. He couldn't blame her for that, as he'd be clamoring for the information himself if he didn't already have it.

Juliana wanted Corinna to marry Delaney. Corinna wanted to marry Delaney. Delaney's sister wanted Delaney to marry Corinna. And Delaney wanted to marry Corinna.

These four people were responsible for half of the new cracks in his teeth.

And then there was Rachael, sitting beside him on the sofa, enveloping him in her heady, floral scent. *She* wanted to marry *him*.

Which made her responsible for the rest of the cracks.

The beginnings of a headache pulsed in his temples. Alexandra wasn't seated. Holding little Harry, she was bouncing him unceasingly in a rather frantic, rhythmic fashion. While it worked to keep the baby from crying, Griffin's headache escalated just watching her.

"How on earth did Lord Lincolnshire learn everything?" she asked for the third time.

He decided to give her what she wanted first.

But before he could unclench his jaw to do so, Delaney answered. "I'm thinking Lincolnshire got the facts from your brother," the fellow told her. "A mere two days before he died." Sitting on a sofa across the drawing room, with Corinna beside him —*right* beside him—he looked to Griffin for confirmation. "That morning he summoned you…it wasn't to say goodbye, was it?"

"No, it wasn't," Griffin said. "He wanted information. I take it he asked you to find future employment for all of his staff?"

"He asked me to continue employing them all at Lincolnshire House, which I knew his real nephew wouldn't agree to. So I offered to find alternative employment for them instead."

"Well, you did too good a job of it, raising his suspicions. He subsequently requested that Mr. Lawless hire someone to investigate the various concerns where his servants would eventually work, to make certain they all existed and his people would be treated well. In the process, Lawless discovered all of the establishments were owned by a single man, a certain Mr. Sean Delaney." Griffin paused, rather impressed despite his hunch that this fellow might have kissed his little sister. "You own a *lot* of property, Delaney."

"Among other things. You needn't worry that your sister might ever want for anything."

Griffin snorted. "You'll keep her in dresses, I expect—if I agree to let you have her." When Corinna opened her mouth to protest, he forged ahead. "From there, Lawless made further inquiries and learned you were posing as Hamilton, and furthermore, that Hamilton was your brother-in-law. Feeling you were a good man"—this uttered with more than a little irony—"Lincolnshire summoned me to ask if I knew why you might have done such a thing."

"And you confirmed his suspicions?" Corinna asked.

"He was close enough to confirming them for himself. I told him Delaney agreed to the hoax for his sister's sake and attested that Hamilton was quite deserving of his less-than-stellar reputation. Lincolnshire seemed especially furious that his nephew had refused Mrs. Hamilton the divorce she wanted." He looked to Delaney's sister. "He was quite taken with you, if you didn't know."

"I loved him, too," she whispered, tears in her eyes.

"He considered your brother a saint, and he compared you to the angels. He wanted you happy. And he requested that I not reveal what he knew. He wanted to settle everything his own way. I expect his will was rewritten that very afternoon."

"Didn't you think we'd have wanted to know?" Corinna asked rather indignantly. "I was devastated, and Sean thought he was being set up to take a fall—"

"I agreed to keep the secret in order to make Lincolnshire happy. The exact reason you kept secrets, if you'll recall. I followed through after his death because I like to think I'm a man of my word. I felt Lincolnshire deserved to resolve the matter as he wished. And furthermore"—he glared daggers at her—"I had no knowledge the two of you were involved with each other, so I had no reason to worry for your happiness, Corinna. You denied any interest in him, and you told me you were upset over the loss of Lord Lincolnshire and because your painting isn't likely to be accepted for the Summer Exhibition, if you'll remember."

That tirade rendered his youngest sister speechless, a rare state for Corinna. Griffin found a measure of satisfaction in that.

He was going to allow her to marry Delaney, of course. He was thinking a late summer wedding at Cainewood Castle, after the season ended, would be perfect. While he wished he knew Delaney better, he liked what he'd learned of the fellow thus far. Lincolnshire had considered him worthy, and Griffin trusted the earl's judgment. Most important, Corinna was in love, and Griffin wanted to see her happy.

But he was sick and tired of being manipulated by all the women in his life.

Before he granted his permission, he planned to make everyone else squirm for a change. And he planned to enjoy it.

"Do you not *like* Sean?" Corinna finally asked.

"I would *like* to have his skill at investing," Griffin said dryly, leaving it at that for now. He shifted to look at Delaney. "Given Lincolnshire's reaction, I assumed he wasn't planning to punish you for lying to him. But I felt no responsibility, anyway. As far as I was concerned, you had made your bed."

Slowly Delaney nodded. "And now I expect I shall have to lie in it."

"No, you won't," Corinna disagreed heatedly. "Griffin will allow us to marry. I have a secret that will ensure it."

"Another secret?" Suddenly Griffin wasn't finding this so enjoyable. His headache was getting worse. "What sort of blasted secret?"

"Maybe he kissed her for half an hour," Rachael suggested sweetly.

Griffin nearly cracked another tooth.

"Open your eyes, Griffin," Juliana put in. "A blind man could see they belong together."

"I see they seem to be *glued* together," he said sharply.

Delaney immediately put space between himself and Corinna, and Corinna immediately scooted right back against him. Griffin found that amusing, which helped to calm him down a bit.

Delaney's pretty blond sister cleared her throat. "Lord Cainewood, you admired Lord Lincolnshire, didn't you? I'm thinking you should trust his judgment regarding my brother."

"I'm thinking this is none of your concern," he said, thinking she was the only one with an intelligent argument.

Unsurprisingly, Juliana wasn't ready to give up. "What do *you* think, James?"

Her husband looked at her as though doves had just flown out of her ears. "I think I'm staying out of this."

"Alexandra, Tristan?"

They both shook their heads, Alexandra doing so while still maniacally bouncing the baby.

Crossing her arms, Juliana looked back to Griffin. "You have to let them marry."

"I don't *have* to do anything."

"They can elope to Gretna Green," she pointed out with more than a little smugness.

"I won't do that," Delaney put in quickly. "I won't go behind her brother's back."

"I *knew* you'd say that," Corinna said. "That's why I'm prepared to use the secret."

Griffin swung back to her. "*What* secret?"

"Maybe he kissed her for *more* than half an hour," Rachael suggested.

Which made Griffin wonder if maybe things had gone beyond kissing. "Did he paw you, Corinna?"

She looked confused. "Did he what?"

An awful thought occurred to him. "You aren't in the family way, are you?"

"No, I'm not in the family way!" Her cheeks flushed red with anger or embarrassment. Perhaps both. "He didn't do anything that could get me in the family way. Sean's much too honorable to even consider such a thing. He's the son of a vicar, you know."

Griffin hadn't known, and he was rather pleased to hear it. "So, then, what's the secret? What *did* he do?"

She hesitated, her gaze darting about the room. She appeared to be holding her breath. Beside her, Delaney looked like he wished the floor would open up and swallow him. Alexandra stopped bouncing, and the baby began crying.

Griffin saw Corinna's breath rush out, saw her suck in another one—a single, shuddering, ragged breath—and then she opened her mouth—

"You know what? I don't want to hear it." Suddenly, he didn't. He was absolutely certain it was something that would make him furious, something that would make him demand the fellow marry his sister immediately.

In fact, he was going to do just that, just in case.

So much for a late summer wedding at Cainewood.

"You two will be married tomorrow."

Corinna finally left Delaney's side, rushing over to smother Griffin in a hug. "Oh, thank you, thank you, thank you for not making me use my secret. You won't be sorry."

"I'm sorry already," he muttered. "It's a miracle I have any teeth left in my mouth."

"They cannot marry tomorrow," Juliana said. Smugly. "They'll need a special license. And she'll need a dress."

"She has dozens of dresses. I know, because I paid for all of them." Griffin disentangled himself from his sister and set her away. "Very well, then, you have until Friday to get a license and pick a dress. Not a day later. And you and the vicar's son will not be alone together until then." The baby was still bawling, a racket loud enough to rattle his aching teeth. He had a raging headache. "Leave, all of you, please. Except for Corinna. Now."

Most of the family shuffled out. Mercifully, the baby's cries faded away with them, and as they left the house, the noise ceased altogether.

"I'm going to walk Sean and Deirdre to the door," Corinna said quietly. "I'm not leaving." The three of them walked into the foyer.

Rachael had stayed put, naturally. Now she moved closer, enveloping Griffin in her blasted floral scent again. Against his better judgment, he shifted to face her.

"I've reconsidered your offer," she said in her low, sultry voice.

"What do you mean?" he asked, fearing he knew what she meant.

"I said I wouldn't wait until your sister married. But as I can wait until Friday without becoming a shriveled old lady, I've changed my mind."

She moved closer, so close her mouth was a whisper from his.

And she licked her lips.

"Do you want to kiss me, Griffin?"

His head hurt. He felt beaten down. And he was being manipulated again, blast it.

But he very much wanted to kiss her.

He loved Rachael. She was clever and beautiful. Open and refreshing. Having managed an earldom for a number of years, she would make a fine partner, helping him manage the Cainewood holdings. He didn't want to lose her to some son of a gun with the gall to put his hand where it didn't belong.

The next fellow to put his hand where it didn't belong was going to be *him*.

Her lovely blue eyes bore into his, her lips curving into a tantalizing smile. Struggling for control, his heart and head pounding in unison, he moved closer. She met him halfway and brushed her lips over his, and he yanked her close, feeling his restraint snap, crushing her to him.

A bloodcurdling scream came from the foyer.

He jumped to his feet and rushed out to see who was being murdered.

No one was dead. But it was difficult to be thankful for that when he saw the way Corinna was wrapped around Delaney. No one should ever have to see his sister in such an embrace. She was literally hanging on the fellow, her arms around his neck, her legs around his waist.

She was sobbing, and she clutched a crumpled letter. Delaney's sister plucked it out of her hand and brought it to Griffin.

Somerset House, Monday 26 May

Lady Corinna Chase:

The Royal Academy's Summer Exhibition Committee is pleased to inform you that your painting has been accepted for our 1817 Exhibition. Please be advised that Varnishing Day will take place Friday 30 May in preparation for the Exhibition's opening on Monday 2 June.

Congratulations,
Benjamin West
President

"I cannot believe it," Corinna choked out through a sob.

"I'm not at all surprised," Griffin said.

She slid off Delaney, thank heavens, and dashed the tears from her face. "You're not?"

"You're very talented, Corinna." He was ecstatic for her. "Since Varnishing Day is Friday, we'll move the wedding to Saturday."

"And make it a double wedding," a sultry voice added behind him.

FIFTY-NINE

THE GREAT ROOM, which housed the Summer Exhibition, had been built at the very top of Somerset House so it could be illuminated by skylights. It was accessed by a wide, winding staircase that seemed endless. Corinna's knees trembled as she climbed up it on Friday afternoon, gripping her paint box like a life preserver.

"Are you getting tired?" Sean asked, taking her arm to steady her.

"A little," she said.

She was glad Griffin had relented and allowed Sean to accompany her. But unfortunately, he'd done so only after extracting a solemn promise from the "vicar's son" that he would take her here and straight back, and she knew Sean was so honorable he'd stick to that promise.

Which meant this would be another day without any kissing.

The four days since Griffin had agreed to their marriage seemed the longest four days of her life. Two special licenses had been procured, and the minister booked, and nothing much more had happened. The double wedding tomorrow was going to be a very quiet affair, even smaller than Lady Cavanaugh's.

Besides the two brides and grooms, only Corinna's family and Deirdre, Rachael's siblings, and the ABC sisters would be attending. Aunt Frances couldn't come, as she was still in confinement —new mothers stayed at home for the first month.

The wedding would take place in the afternoon in the Berkeley Square house's drawing room, and then they'd have a little dinner, and then everyone would go home.

Juliana was very disappointed. She'd wanted more of a fuss made about everything. But Corinna didn't care about the wedding, just like she didn't care that she didn't have a new dress to wear for it. The wedding was only something to get past.

"I'm a little tired *and* a little nervous," she admitted, still climbing. "What if my painting is hung up very high? Or down near the floor?"

"Why should it matter where it's hung? It's an honor just to be in the Exhibition, isn't it?"

"The room is designed with a line going around it, a strip of molding mounted eight feet above the floor. The pictures placed with the bottom edges of their frames along the line are considered the best. It's an extra honor to be hung not high or low, but right there in the middle. I'm afraid to look."

"Well, I don't see how not looking is going to change anything. But if you want, I'll look for you and let you know."

"You can't." On the landing, she stopped before the Great Room's open door to catch her breath. "You won't recognize my painting." That was another thing she was nervous about. "It's not Lord Lincolnshire's portrait."

"It's not?" He looked totally nonplussed. "Well, what is it, then?"

"My secret," she said and stepped in, hurrying to the center of the room.

Varnishing Day seemed to be chaos. Artists were everywhere, on chairs and ladders and their knees, blocking Corinna's view of all the pictures on the soaring walls. They hung frame-to-frame, fitted like puzzle pieces floor to ceiling. She turned in circles, frantically searching for her own.

"Sweet mercy!" Sean burst out.

"Where? Where is it?"

He took her by the shoulders and swung her around. "There. And begorrah, it's *quite* some secret."

She stared at it, feeling breathless, and not because she'd climbed a hundred stairs. "They liked it."

"They wouldn't have accepted it had they not liked it, *críona*."

"But it's on the line. In the place of honor. They *really* liked it."

"Hamilton loved it," he said dryly. "He described his favorite submission to me precisely. 'A rather outrageous depiction of a golden-haired young man, half-clothed and bathed in candlelight.' I had no idea the half-clothed young man was *me*."

"And neither did he, a person who's known you since childhood. No one will recognize you, Sean." Tearing her gaze from her picture, she turned to him. "I changed your coloring."

"But Deirdre will want to come see it, and your brother—"

"I didn't end up telling Griffin my secret," she reminded him, extremely thankful she hadn't needed to. "It won't occur to them it could be you. You're not cross with me, are you? No one here is recognizing you, either. And it's not because they haven't noticed the painting." Indeed, several artists not involved in their own work stood before it, discussing it, a sight that made her heart sing. "Why didn't you tell me Hamilton liked it so much?"

"Well, I had no idea he was speaking of your painting, did I?
"

He shook his head in apparent disbelief, but he didn't seem truly upset. Her hand went up to touch her claddagh necklace. She was so lucky to have him.

"Are you going to varnish it now, then?" he asked.

"In a minute." She wanted to let it all sink in for a while first. She shifted her paint box to her other hand, looking around. "Sean," she whispered, thrilled. "It's J.M.W. Turner. There, in the top hat and tails. I've heard he always dresses like that."

"His painting doesn't look finished."

The artist had hung an all but monochrome canvas. "You're color-blind. How can you tell?"

"It's a landscape, and the sky isn't even blue. How on earth did it get accepted?"

"Academicians are allowed to hang six paintings each without going through the selection process," Corinna explained in an undertone. "And Varnishing Day isn't just for varnishing; it's also for fixing little things. Turner is rather famous for this trick. While his fellow artists—"

"That's you," Sean interrupted.

"Holy Hannah, it is, isn't it?" She beamed. "While the rest of us struggle to fix some tiny mistake, he practically paints an entire picture."

"Thus proving his technical virtuosity?"

"And awing everyone else in the process." She watched the dull painting blaze to life as Turner swiftly transformed it with glorious chrome and brilliant vermilion and costly ultramarine. He stood so close to his canvas he appeared to paint with his eyes and nose as well as his hands. "He's legendary," she whispered. "They call him the painter of light. He first exhibited here at the age of fifteen."

"While you're an ancient seventeen?"

"I suppose I should feel lucky you're willing to marry such an old hag."

"We'd best wed quickly, *a rún*, before you get any older."

"Is tomorrow soon enough?"

"An hour from now wouldn't be soon enough."

She laughed, a joyous sound that felt like a cool breeze across

Sean's soul. To think, only four days ago, he'd believed he'd never hear that laugh again.

"I don't know how Turner does it," she said. "He's been known to produce two hundred and fifty pictures in a single year. It takes me at least two weeks to complete a painting."

"Not that one." Sean gestured to his image on the wall.

"That one *was* rather quick," she admitted, her cheeks flushing. "I guess I'll varnish it now."

She looked nervous as she walked toward it, paint box in hand. Sean followed, moving a step stool so that she could reach it.

"Is that yours?" someone asked as she climbed up, setting off a volley of comments.

"She's unknown!"

"A woman painted that?"

"She's a genius."

"I think it's shameful," a disgruntled man disagreed.

Through it all, Corinna held her head high, nerves notwithstanding. She made her own way in the world, just like Sean did. That was why he loved her.

Well, that and because she was the most captivating girl he'd ever met.

Only one more day until he made her his forever. Standing back, he smiled as she dipped her brush in varnish and began swiping it over his bare chest.

SIXTY

"**WELL**," **GRIFFIN** said. "That's it." Upstairs in the Berkeley Square town house, he shut the master bedroom door and leaned his hands against it. "Corinna is on her way to Hampstead, to a house I've never even seen."

"You'll see it soon," Rachael said behind him, where he knew she was slipping off her shoes.

He heard the soft give of the mattress as she sat on the bed across the room, and he imagined her rolling down her stockings. He remained facing away, listening to the sound of swishing silk.

"And I'm sure it's a fine house," she continued, her sultry voice settling around him like a blanket. "Deirdre told me it's enormous, and set in acres of gardens and woodland, and it was built by Robert Adams. She said her brother has more money than a pot of gold at the end of a rainbow."

"I swear, Rachael, that fellow could eat a pot of gold for breakfast and never notice it was missing. But it doesn't matter. He has Corinna now, and that's all that counts. Corinna wanted him, and I wanted her happy."

"You did the right thing, Griffin. She loves him, and he loves her. And I love you."

"I love you, too." He straightened and turned to look at her. She rose and took a few slow steps toward him, barefooted and gorgeous. Hopping on one foot and then the other, he pulled off his own boots and stockings, then shrugged out of his tailcoat and waistcoat, leaving it all littering the floor as he went.

He couldn't believe he'd wed Rachael. He couldn't believe anything that had happened this week, all the incredible events that had led to him marrying his last, youngest sister to someone he hardly knew and simultaneously getting married himself.

"You're wearing your mother's wedding dress," he said, walking toward her, remembering her pulling it out of the heavy oak trunk, and how he'd thought it looked lacy and beautiful. It fit her perfectly, as he'd known it would. Rachael was all willowy, graceful curves, and the sight of her in his bedroom, in the white dress, made his skin heat. It made his palms itch.

He couldn't believe she'd been his for half a day and he still hadn't touched her.

"You look lovely," he told her.

"You look better." She was standing before him now, so close their noses nearly touched. "I'm a Chase now," she said.

Her heady scent was overwhelming him, making him dizzy. "Is that why you wanted to marry me? So you could think of yourself as a Chase again?"

"No, that's just a bonus. I wanted to marry you because I love you."

He loved her, too. And she was his.

And he still hadn't touched her.

Her face was raised, her cerulean eyes fastened on his. They sparkled with mischief as she licked her lips. "Do you want to kiss me, Griffin?"

"I do," he said.

But first he wanted to put his hands where they belonged.

He did that, and then he used his hands to yank her against him, and then he kissed her. He was mad for her. He'd always been mad for her, it seemed, but now she was his.

Rachael kissed him back with abandon, wanting to belong to him, wanting him to belong to her. She'd thought she'd been in control of this relationship, but something about the way Griffin was holding her, like she was precious—but not fragile, not at all —seemed to flip a switch inside her, and suddenly she was heedless, senseless, frantic. She wasn't losing herself in him, not exactly. Maybe they were losing themselves in each other. It didn't signify, and she didn't care.

He'd always been the one for her. Realizing that now, she cursed herself for all the wasted time, all the months she'd spent denying her feelings, thinking of him as a cousin or a brother and concentrating on things that didn't really matter. Happy as she was to have discovered Mama's family, the person most important to her had been by her side all that time, and she was grateful beyond belief that she'd seen the truth before it was too late.

He broke the kiss and pulled back, his intense green gaze burning into hers. What she saw there made her heart squeeze. Lust, yes, but also devotion and affection and understanding. And most of all love.

She grinned and pulled his head back down to press her lips to his. Her heart singing, she held him tight and knew she would never let go.

～

*A*LTHOUGH SEAN'S house was just a few minutes' walk from Hampstead Heath and the High Street, Corinna found herself amazed when the curricle started up the long, serpentine drive. The property seemed in a different world, the setting idyllic, a picturesque, pastoral landscape. As they approached the classical villa, the sun was setting low on the horizon, its last rays glinting off glossy arched windows in the creamy white building.

"Oh," she breathed, "it's beautiful."

"It's glad I am it pleases you, *a rún*," Sean said in his melodic Irish lilt.

She nestled against him with a happy sigh. "We're almost there. You'll be able to kiss me."

His arm tightened around her shoulders. "I can kiss you now," he said, and gave her a peck on the cheek.

"Not the way I want."

"My straightforward Corinna." A low chuckle rumbled in his throat as he grabbed her hand and kissed the back. "Like that? Is that how you want me to kiss you?"

"Not quite," she said tartly.

He turned her hand over and kissed her palm. "Here, then?"

"Sean…"

He leaned sideways and took his eyes off the lane for half a second, just long enough to plant a kiss on her neck. "Closer?"

"You're getting closer." Her stomach did a little flip-flop. "I feel like I've been waiting forever."

He pulled the curricle to a halt. "Well, you won't have to wait much longer, *críona*."

He leapt down and came around to her side, but instead of handing her down, he scooped her into his arms.

"Put me down!" she said with a laugh.

"Oh, no," he said, striding toward the house. "They say the groom must carry the bride over the threshold to protect her from evil spirits."

He carried her so easily. Feeling cradled against his warm body, she linked her arms about his neck. "Do you believe in evil spirits, Sean?"

"I believe they're a good excuse to carry you." He dropped a kiss on her chin as the door opened, revealing a portly, gray-haired servant. "Good evening to you, Simpson," Sean said, stepping inside. "This is your new mistress, Lady Corinna Delaney."

Simpson kept an admirably straight face as he shut the door. "Welcome, my lady."

"I'm pleased to meet you." Corinna glanced around the entrance hall, a square room with a polished wooden floor and pale blue walls trimmed in white. "Put me down, Sean."

He didn't. "If the bedroom is ready, Simpson, I'll thank you to make yourself scarce and see that everyone else does as well."

"Sean!" Corinna shrieked, laughing at the expression on Simpson's face.

While the butler walked off in one direction, Sean carried Corinna in another. "You'll meet the rest of the staff tomorrow, *mo chroí.*"

She wondered what he meant by the bedroom being ready. "We're inside now, so you can put me down."

"I think not." Holding her close, he carried her through a dining room with blue walls and a crystal chandelier. "I'm finding I rather like carrying you."

In truth, she rather liked being carried. No one had carried her since she was a child, and the pure romance of it made her head swim. Sean swept her through a drawing room carpeted in blue with blue sofas. "I don't need a tour tonight," she said breathlessly. "Just your bedroom will do. I'm ready for a real kiss."

"*Our* bedroom, you mean," he said, his voice deep with meaning. He carried her past a library with white columns and plush ultramarine-blue velvet chairs, and on into a small, cobalt-blue lobby. "There's another wing and two more levels you can see tomorrow."

"I expect all of those rooms are blue, too?"

"Except for Deirdre's. I don't know what color it is. Maybe you can tell me."

"Not tonight," she said, thankful his sister had gone to Daniel Raleigh's house.

"I haven't any paintings," he said apologetically as he started up a grand staircase with a blue runner. "You can buy any paintings you want and hang them wherever you'd like."

She turned her face into his neck, inhaling his clean, soapy scent. "I don't care about paintings, Sean."

"And everything doesn't have to stay blue. You can have the rooms repainted any colors you'd like. You can have the furniture reupholstered or buy all new things."

"I don't care what color the rooms are." She was melting. Liquefying in his arms. "All I care about is you," she told him as they finally reached the master bedroom.

Set before a huge blue-toned tapestry, the bed was covered with a plush, sapphire blue counterpane and piled with lighter blue pillows. He walked to it, laying her upon it so gently, so reverently, that she could swear every bone in her body dissolved.

She gazed up at him as he stepped back. He looked better than a Greek god, but even better than that, he was the best person she'd ever known.

And she saw what he'd meant by *ready*. Candles flickered everywhere—on the windowsill, along the marble mantel, atop every piece of furniture—bathing the room in shadows and dancing light. Dozens of them. He must have set them about before leaving for the wedding and instructed a servant to light them when they arrived. Like a Minerva Press hero, she thought, her heart doing a slow roll in her chest.

"It's a wonderland," she breathed.

"Every bride should have a wonderland, *mo chroí.*"

Sean thought she was a wonder herself, a vision in a simple white dress, those brilliant blue eyes looking dreamy as he'd ever seen them. His necklace glinted silver against her skin, and he loved the way it seemed to mark her as his own. He couldn't believe dear Lincolnshire had fixed everything, had made it work out so he could have her—it seemed a miracle, and much more than he deserved. She was his, and he was hers, and nothing had ever been so right.

Watching her face, which glowed with candlelight and love, he slowly leaned down and finally kissed her the way she wanted.

For his part, he just wanted this night to be perfect.

And it was.

AUTHOR'S NOTE

∽

DEAR READER,

During the Regency, a female artist like Corinna might have had her picture accepted for the Summer Exhibition—but it's a sad truth that she probably never would have been elected to the Royal Academy of Arts. In 1768, the founding membership did include two women, Angelica Kauffmann and Mary Moser. However, ladies weren't admitted to the Royal Academy schools until 1861, and the next female Academician, Dame Laura Knight, wasn't elected until 1936.

Although we think of art from Corinna's era as classic, it was the contemporary art of its time, and the Royal Academy's Summer Exhibition is the largest contemporary art show in the world. Held every year since 1769, the Exhibition is and always has been the place to see a wide range of new work by both established and unknown living artists. Admission cost one shilling in the nineteenth century, and the exhibit has been extraordinarily popular all along. Attendance grew from 60,000 in 1780 to 390,000 by 1879. In 2006, the show drew over 150,000 visitors (including us!), and more than 1,200 works were included.

The Summer Exhibition Selection Committee members who attended Lady A's reception were the actual committee members in 1817, with the exception of Thomas Phillips. We removed him to make room for the fictional John Hamilton. We do apologize to Mr. Phillips, but we had to choose someone, and he was the man with the least biographical information to draw on.

It's been said that the modern novel was born in 1740, when Samuel Richardson wrote *Pamela or Virtue and Reward*. A tale of frustrated desires, it sparked controversy that created a thirst for more of the same. As a result, reading Gothic and romance fiction became a decades-long craze. Or maybe it still is a craze... as a romance reader, what do you think?

In about 1790, an Englishman named William Lane saw an opportunity and established Minerva Press. For a number of years, Lane dominated the novel publishing industry. Over half the popular books were printed by Minerva Press, and Lane reportedly made a fortune. According to the poet Samuel Rogers, Lane was often seen tooling around London in a splendid carriage, attended by footmen with cockades and gold-headed canes. All of the lines from books that Corinna recalls in her story are real quotes from Minerva Press novels that she could have purchased in 1817.

Most of the homes in our books are inspired by real places. We modeled Lincolnshire House on Devonshire House, which was designed by William Kent and served as the London residence of the Dukes of Devonshire for nearly two hundred years. Because we wanted Lord Lincolnshire to live in Berkeley Square, we turned this house around—in reality, the house fronted on Piccadilly Street and its gardens backed up to the square. Devonshire House is no longer standing, but before it was demolished in the 1920s, many of the interior furnishings were moved to Chatsworth, the duke's residence in the countryside. You can still see some of them there.

Sean's house was inspired by Kenwood House in Hampstead. Set in an idyllic landscape beside Hampstead Heath, the house was expanded by Robert Adam between 1764 and 1779. Although Sean didn't have any paintings, the real house is a veritable gallery. Edward Cecil Guinness, brewing magnate and first Earl of Iveagh, bought Kenwood House in 1925, and when he died in 1927, he bequeathed the estate and part of his art collection to Britain. The house is open daily all year round, and if you visit you will see important paintings by many great artists including Rembrandt, Vermeer, Constable, Turner, Reynolds, and Gainsborough. We like to imagine that, with Sean's vast fortune at her disposal, Corinna might have put together such a collection!

The Chases' town house at 44 Berkeley Square has been described as "the finest terrace house of London." It was designed in 1742 by William Kent for Lady Isabella Finch. Unfortunately, you cannot visit, because the building is currently being used as a private club, but if you go to Berkeley Square, you can see it from the outside. Look for the blue door.

Stafford House, Juliana's home in St. James's Place, is based on Spencer House, one of the great architectural landmarks of London. Built in the eighteenth century by John, 1st Earl Spencer (an ancestor of Diana, Princess of Wales), it was immediately recognized as a building of major importance. Should you ever find yourself in London, we highly recommend a visit. Spencer House is open to the public every Sunday except during January and August.

Noah is the Earl of Greystone, and in this book Rachael and Griffin pay a visit to his family's seat, Greystone Castle, in the countryside. Do you remember Noah saying, "I noticed that old portrait of the first earl over the fireplace"? The first earl was Colin Chase, and he and his bride Amethyst (commonly called Amy) have their own romance in *The Earl's Unsuitable Bride*, the first book in our *Sweet Chase Brides* series.

In fact, all the Chases in this series—Griffin's whole family and all their cousins except for Rachael—are descended from the Chase family generation whose stories are told in our 9-book *Sweet Chase Brides* series. Griffin inherited his looks from Jason, who stars in Book 2 of the series, and Juliana looks like Caithren, Jason's love. Claire has Amy's amethyst eyes and her talent for making jewelry.

When Rachael opens the box of jewels she inherited from her parents, she and Griffin see jewelry that Amy made, as well as jewelry that Amy herself inherited, made by her father, grandfather, and more ancestors going back. While Griffin's townhouse is newish (for its time!), the townhouse in Lincoln's Inn Fields, where Rachael and her family live, is old enough that all the Chase ancestors lived in it, too. If you read the *Sweet Chase Brides* series, you'll find many other fun tidbits that tie these two series and generations together.

I hope you enjoyed *Corinna!* Next up, meet more of the Chase family in *The Earl's Unsuitable Bride*. Please read on for an excerpt as well as more bonus material!

Always,

Lauren Royal

Read on for an excerpt from

The Earl's Unsuitable Bride

Book 1 of the
Sweet Chase Brides series
by Lauren & Devon Royal

Colin Chase, the Earl of Greystone, finds his carefully planned life turned upside down when the Great Fire of London lands a lowly jeweler's daughter in his arms.

London
April 22, 1661

THE DAY AMETHYST Goldsmith was born, her king was beheaded. Now, twelve years later, his son was returning to England, and Amy wanted to see every exciting second of his triumphant procession. Without taller people blocking her view.

Unfortunately, it seemed nearly everyone was taller than she.

She shouldered her way through the crowd, her parents and aunt murmuring apologies in her wake. "Here, there's room!" Finally reaching a few bare inches of rail, she clasped it with both hands and turned to flash them a victorious smile. "Come along, it's starting!"

Hugh and Edith Goldsmith joined her, shaking their heads at their daughter's tenacity. Hugh's sister, Amy's Aunt Elizabeth, squeezed in behind. Ignoring the grumbling of displaced spectators, Amy spread her feet wide to save more room at the front. "Robert, over here!"

Robert Stanley tugged on her long black plait as he wedged himself in beside her. She shot him a grin; he was fun. Although he'd arrived just last week to train as her father's apprentice, Amy had known since birth that she was to marry him—or at least since she was old enough to understand such things. So far they seemed to be compatible, although he'd been surprised to find she was far more skilled as a jeweler than he. Surprised and none too pleased, Amy suspected. But he would get over those feelings.

She might be a girl, but, as her father always said, her talent was a God-given gift. She'd never give up her craft. Robert would just have to get used to it.

With a sigh of pleasure, Amy shuffled her shoes on the scrubbed cobblestones. "Look, Mama! Everything is so clean and glorious." She breathed deep of the fresh air, blinking against the bright sun. "The rain has stopped...even the weather is welcoming the monarchy back to England! Have you ever seen so many people? All London must be here."

"These cannot all be Londoners." Her mother waved a hand, encompassing the crowds on the rooftops, the mobbed windows and overflowing balconies. "I think many have come in from the countryside."

A handful of tossed rose petals drifted down, landing on Amy's dark head like scented snowflakes. She shook them off, laughing. "Just look at all the tapestries and banners!"

"Just look at all that wasted wine," Robert muttered, with a nod toward the fragrant red river that ran through the open conduit in the street.

Amy opened her mouth to protest, then decided he must be fooling. "Marry come up, Robert! You must be pleased King Charles will be crowned tomorrow. Our lives have been so dreary until now. But now Cromwell is gone, and we have music and dancing!" She felt like dancing, like spreading her burgundy satin skirts and twirling in a circle, but the press of the crowd made such a maneuver impossible, so she settled for bobbing a little curtsy. "We've beautiful clothes, and the theater—"

"And drinking and cards and dice," Robert added.

But Amy wasn't listening. She'd turned back to ogle the mounted queue of nobility parading their way from the Tower to Whitehall Palace. Such jewels and feathers and lace! Fingering the looped ribbons adorning her new gown, she pressed harder against the rail, wishing she too could join the procession.

"Where did they possibly find so many ostrich feathers in all of England?" she wondered aloud, then burst into giggles.

Her aunt laughed and wrapped an affectionate arm around her shoulders. "Where do you find the energy, child? You must come to Paris. Uncle William and I could use your happy smiles."

Feeling a stab of sympathy, Amy hugged her around the waist. Aunt Elizabeth had lost her three children to smallpox last year.

"We need her artistry here," Amy's father protested, poking his sister good-naturedly. "Your shop will have to do without."

"Ah, Hugh, how selfish you are!" Aunt Elizabeth chided. "Hoarding my niece's talent for your own profit." She aimed a teasing smile at her brother. "No wonder we moved to France to escape the competition."

Amy grinned. Aunt Elizabeth and Uncle William had been forced to move their shop when business fell off during the Commonwealth years. But they'd flourished in Paris, becoming jewelers to the French court, and wouldn't think of returning now.

"I'm glad you came for the coronation, Aunty. It wouldn't be the same without you."

"I wouldn't have missed it," Aunt Elizabeth declared. "Old Noll drove me out of England, so my home is elsewhere now. But heaven knows no one here is happier than I."

"Listen!" Amy cried. A joyous roar rolled westward toward them, marking the slow passage of His Majesty in the middle of the procession. "Can you hear King Charles coming? There are his attendants!" The noise swelled as the king's footguards marched by, their plumes of red and white feathers contrasting with those of his brother, the Duke of York, whose guard was decked out in black and white.

All at once, the roar was deafening. Amy grasped her mother's hand. "It's him, Mama," she whispered. "King Charles II."

Glittering in the sunshine, the Horse of State caught and held her gaze. "Oh, look at the embroidered saddle, the pearls and rubies —look at our diamonds!"

Amy didn't care for horses—she was terrified of them, truth be told—so she paid no attention to the magnificent beast himself. But three hundred of her family's diamonds sparkled on the gold stirrups and bosses, among the twelve thousand lent for the occasion.

"Oh, Papa," she breathed, "I wish we could have designed that saddle."

Aunt Elizabeth's hand suddenly tightened on Amy's shoulder. "Charles is looking at me," she declared loudly.

Amy's father snorted. "Always the flirt, sister mine."

Amy's gaze flew from the dazzling horse to its rider. Smiling broadly beneath his thin mustache, the tall king waved to the crowd. His cloth-of-silver suit peeked from beneath ermine-lined crimson robes. Rubies and sapphires winked from gold shoe buckles and matching gold garters, festooned with great poufs of silver ribbon. Long, shining black curls draped over his chest, framing a weathered face; the result, Amy supposed, of having suffered through exile and the execution of his beloved father.

But his black eyes were quick and sparkling. Some women around Amy swooned, but she just stared, willing the king to look at her.

When he did, she flashed him a radiant smile. "No, Aunty, he's looking at *me*."

Before her family even stopped laughing, the king was gone, as suddenly as he had arrived. But the spectacle wasn't over. Behind him came a camel with brocaded panniers and an East Indian boy flinging pearls and spices into the crowd. And then more lords and ladies, more glittering costumes, more decorated stallions, more men-at-arms, all bedecked in gold and silver and the costliest of gems.

Yet none of it mattered to Amy, for there was a young nobleman riding her way.

He looked to be maybe sixteen, a bit older than Robert—but she thought he looked much more mature. It wasn't the richness of his clothing that caught Amy's eye, for in truth his garb was rather plain. His black velvet suit was trimmed with naught but gold braid; his wide-brimmed hat boasted only a single white plume. He wore no fancy crimped periwig; instead his own raven-black hair fell in gleaming waves past his chin.

Eyes the color of emeralds bore into Amy's as he set his horse in her direction. His glossy black gelding breathed close, but she felt no fear, for the young man held her safe with his piercing green gaze. It seemed as though he could see through her eyes right into her soul. Her cheeks flamed; never in her life had a boy looked at her like that.

He tipped his plumed hat. Flustered, she turned and glanced about, certain he must be saluting someone else. But everyone was laughing and talking or watching the procession; no one focused their attention his way. She looked back, and he grinned as he passed, a beautiful flash of white that made Amy melt inside.

Long after he rode out of sight around the bend, she stared to where he had disappeared.

"Amy?" Robert tugged on her hand.

She turned and gazed into his eyes: pale blue, not green. They didn't see into her soul, didn't make her feel anything.

Robert smiled, revealing teeth that overlapped a bit. She hadn't really noticed that before. "It's over," he said.

"Oh."

The sun set as they walked home to Cheapside, skirting merrymakers in the streets. Her father paused to unlock their door. Overhead, a wooden sign swung gently in the breeze. A nearby bonfire illuminated the image of a falcon and the gilt letters that proclaimed their shop GOLDSMITH & SONS, JEWELLERS.

There came a sudden brilliant flash and a stunned "Ooooh" from the crowd, as fireworks lit the sky. Amy dashed through the shop and up the stairs to their balcony.

Gazing toward the River Thames, she watched the great fiery streaks of light, heard the soaring rockets, smelled the sulfur in the air. It was the most spectacular display England had ever seen, and the sights and sounds filled her with a wondrous feeling.

If only life could be as exhilarating as a fireworks show.

When the last glittering tendril faded away, she listened to the fragments of song and rowdy laughter that filled the night air. Couples strolled by, arm in arm. Robert stepped onto the balcony and moved close.

His voice was quiet beside her. "This is a day I'll never forget."

"I'll never forget it, either," she said, thinking of the boy on the black steed, the young nobleman with the emerald eyes.

Robert reached out to tilt her face up. Was he going to kiss her? She'd never been kissed—what a day this was turning out to be! Her heart pounded as he bent his head and brushed his lips softly, chastely against hers.

Her heart stopped pounding.

It was her first kiss; she was supposed to feel fireworks.

But she felt nothing.

Five years later

"**ARE YOU TELLING** me *you* made this bracelet? A girl? This shop is Goldsmith and *Sons*, is it not?" Robert puckered his freckled face and made his voice high and wavering. "Where are the sons?"

From where she stood by the stone oven, Amy's laughter rang through the workshop. "Lady Smythe! A perfect imitation."

"Well done, Robert." Her father smiled as he brushed past them both and through the archway into the shop's showroom.

Robert's pale blue eyes twinkled, but he stayed in character, cupping a hand to his ear. "Imitation? Imitation, did you say? I was led to believe this was a *quality* jewelry shop, madame. I expect genuine—"

"Stop!" Amy fought to control her giggles. "You'll make me slip and scald myself."

Robert's gaze fell to Amy's hands. As he watched her pour a thin stream of molten gold into a plaster mold, his expression sobered. "I like Lady Smythe," he muttered. "At least she buys the things *I* make."

"Oh, Robert." She sighed. "Why should it matter who made something, as long as we're selling a piece?"

"I'm a good goldsmith."

"You're an excellent goldsmith," Amy agreed. Although she also thought he was a bit unimaginative, she kept that to herself. "What does that have to do with anything?"

"You're a girl."

She clenched her jaw and tapped the mold on her workbench, imagining the gold flowing to fill every crevice of her design. "I'm also a jeweler," she said under her breath.

"Never mind." He walked to his own workbench and plopped onto his stool, lifting the pewter tankard of ale that sat ever-present amongst his tools.

Ignoring him, Amy picked up a knife and a chunk of wax, intending to whittle a new design while the gold hardened. The windowless workroom seemed stifling today—hot, close, and dark. She dragged a lantern nearer, but the weak, yellowish glow did little to lift her mood.

Five years she'd lived and worked with Robert Stanley, her father's apprentice, and he still didn't understand her. She couldn't believe it. She was marrying him in two weeks, and she couldn't believe that, either.

Once it had seemed like a lifetime stretched ahead of her before she had to wed. But now she was seventeen, and Robert was twenty-one, and his apprenticeship had ended. Which meant it was time for them to marry.

She'd asked for more time, but her father had refused. According to the betrothal agreement that had been signed when she was born, Robert was now due a share of the shop—and Hugh Goldsmith wasn't about to share his family's hard-earned business with a man who wasn't his son-in-law. So he'd set a date, and that had been that.

No matter that Robert thought his wife should stay upstairs and mend his clothes; no matter that he resented it when Amy's designs sold faster and she received more custom orders than he did.

No matter that she didn't love him. Not the way a wife should love a husband. Not the way it was in the French novels she smuggled into her bedchamber. Not the way she had felt, five years ago at the coronation procession, when that young nobleman's emerald eyes had locked on hers.

Never mind that she'd been but a fanciful girl of twelve at the time—she'd felt something, and that feeling was something she'd never forgotten.

She would learn to love Robert, her father said. But it hadn't happened—not yet, anyway. Not even close.

Amy sighed and lifted the plait off her neck, fanning the hot skin beneath. She'd set out to talk to her father dozens of times, to beg him to reconsider. But her courage always failed her. Since the death of her mother in last year's Great Plague, it seemed she could take anything but her father's disapproval.

When the casting was set, Amy plunged it into the tub of water by Robert's workbench. She rubbed the mold's gritty plaster surface, feeling it dissolve away in her hands, watching Robert's knife send wax shavings flying as he sculpted a model.

She scowled at his curved back. "I believe I fancied you more as Lady Smythe."

Robert turned and stared at her for a moment, then hunched over suddenly. His face transformed, taking on a Lady Smythe look. "Are you certain, madame?" he asked in that high, wavering tone. "I hear tell you've had dancing lessons and speak fluent French. Such pretensions. I don't hold with women reckoning account books, you know. Not at all." His voice deepened into his own. "Or making jewelry, either."

Amy flinched. She pulled the casting from the water and carried it to her workbench to brush off the remaining bits of plaster.

He rose and came up behind her, tilting her head back with a hand beneath her chin. "Two more weeks, and a proper wife you'll be," he said and clamped his mouth on hers.

The faint scent of his breakfast had her squeezing her eyes shut and praying for the end to this torment.

"Part your lips, will you?" he said against her mouth.

She didn't. She wished he'd use one of those newfangled little silver toothbrushes Aunt Elizabeth had sent from Paris.

Finally he raised his head. "Two weeks," he repeated.

Her eyes snapped open and burned into his. "Papa will never allow you to keep me from making jewelry." Looking down, she brushed at the casting harder.

He shrugged. "Your papa won't be here forever." His hand moved to grip her waist.

Amy's gaze flickered toward the showroom in warning.

Sighing, he wrenched away and strode back to his workbench, back to his ale. "At least soon I'll be allowed to touch you whenever I please." Grinning, he lifted the tankard in a salute. "Two weeks."

Amy had once thought his grins shy and engaging…but of late they only made her uneasy.

The bell on the outside door tinkled, giving Amy a start. She stood and whipped off her apron. "I'll get it."

"Your father is out there," Robert reminded her. "He can handle it."

Paying him no mind, she straightened her gown and smoothed back a few damp strands that had escaped her plait. She put a shopgirl smile on her face before heading through the swinging doors into the cool, bright showroom.

"A locket," a girl at the far end of the L-shaped case was saying, smiling up at a tall gentleman with his back to Amy.

Deep red curls draped to the young lady's rather scandalously bare shoulders; her lavish golden brocade gown had a wide, scooped neckline Amy's father would never allow. Was she the gentleman's mistress?

The gentleman addressed Papa. "My sister would like a locket." He urged the girl—his sister, not his mistress—forward. "Go on, Kendra, see what you fancy."

Though the gentleman seemed determined to work with her father, Amy stepped closer, poised to turn the corner and help close the sale. Papa glanced at her, then smiled. "Have you a style in mind, or a price, Lord…?"

"Greystone." His back still to Amy, he waved an impatient hand. "Whatever she likes."

Papa cleared his throat. "Perhaps my daughter can help you decide. Amethyst, please show Lord Greystone the lockets."

She took a tray from the case and moved to set it before the gentleman's sister instead.

"They're all so pretty!" Lady Kendra exclaimed in delight. When she bent her head to look closer, her beautiful red curls shimmered to rival the glitter of jewels in the case.

Amy's hand went reflexively to her own head, as though she could rearrange her hated black hair into something more fashionable than its serviceable plait. Resisting the urge to sigh, she lifted an oval locket with tiny engraved flowers.

"See the gold ribbons forming the bale?" As her father had taught her, her voice was sweet and confident, reflecting her certainty of both the quality of the piece and her ability to sell it. She snapped open the locket and extended it, looking from Lady Kendra to Lord Greystone. "It's—"

Her voice failed her.

Her father nudged her, frowning. "Amy?"

"It-it's quite feminine," she stammered out, telling herself Lord Greystone couldn't be the young nobleman she remembered.

But then his emerald green eyes locked on hers—as they'd done five years earlier.

It *was* him.

The nobleman from the coronation procession, the one she'd been unable to forget. Only now he was all grown up. Her heart seemed to pause in her chest, and for a second she thought she would drown in those eyes; then she looked away, with an effort, and down to the locket she was holding.

Lady Kendra reached to take the locket from Amy. "Oh, look how pretty it is, Colin." She held it up to her bodice, turning to model it for her brother.

With seeming reluctance, Lord Greystone swung his gaze toward his sister. "I'm not sure I care for it."

"Notice the fine engraving, my lord," Papa rushed to put in. "Truly first quality."

Lord Greystone ignored him and looked back to Amy. When his eyes narrowed, Amy found herself studying him in return. Classic symmetrical features: a long, straight nose, sculpted planes, a slight dimple in his chin. His complexion appeared more golden than was the fashion.

Marry come up, he was beautiful.

When he finally spoke, his voice, smooth and deep, sent an

odd shiver down her spine. "Have you a locket with...amethysts?"

Amethysts...

She opened her mouth to answer, but the words refused to come out.

"I'm sorry, my lord, we don't," Papa said. "But emeralds would suit the lady—"

"Yes," Amy interrupted, finally finding her voice. "Yes, we do have amethysts! If you'll but wait one moment." She reached to grab the key ring off her father's belt, then turned and bolted for the workshop.

"What are you in such a rush for?" Robert asked as she jammed the key into the first padlock on their iron safe chest.

"Customers are waiting." Having removed the second padlock, she knelt on the floor and began working the twelve bolts in their complicated sequence.

Robert wandered over, wiping blunt hands on his apron, leaving streaks of abrasive gray slurry. "What customers?"

"A gentleman and his sister," she said as the last bolt slid into place, allowing her to access the final lock. She opened it with the largest key, then lifted the lid and rummaged inside.

Luckily, the locket she was after was there in the top tray. "Ah, here it is." Just seeing the piece, the shimmering gold, the sparkling gems, made her smile.

She rose and headed back to the showroom, Robert at her heels. He lounged against the archway and fixed Lord Greystone with a distrustful blue stare.

Well, she would just ignore him.

"I found it," she announced, handing the locket to Lord Greystone. She watched for his reaction even as she plunked the key ring into her father's outstretched palm.

Lord Greystone blinked at the piece in his hand. "Beautiful. It's truly beautiful."

Amy's heart swelled. "It does have amethysts, my lord, and diamonds, too."

"I can see that," he said, staring at the locket. "It's splendid."

"Splendid doesn't do it justice!" Lady Kendra's eyes had gone wide and round.

The piece had taken Amy weeks to make, so many hours she could still see it with her eyes closed. On top, a cutwork pattern of diamond-set leaves surrounded an amethyst flower. The lozenge-shaped locket dangled beneath, encrusted with amethysts and diamonds, its lid enameled with delicate violets. Swinging from the bottom, a large baroque pearl gleamed.

Lord Greystone finally looked to her father. "It's remarkable."

"*I* made it." Amy felt a flush blossom on her cheeks.

Lady Kendra's mouth dropped open in surprise. Lord Greystone's startled gaze swung to Amy, over to her father, who nodded proudly, then back to Amy. "I don't believe it. You're—"

"A girl?" She heard the challenge in her own voice.

His grin was a bit sheepish. "However did you learn to make something like this?"

Her father cleared his throat. "We hadn't much to do during the Commonwealth, my lord. I expect you were abroad?"

Lord Greystone nodded.

"Well, jewelry was much frowned upon, other than some mourning pieces. I had time aplenty to train Amy in the arts of goldsmithing." Amy's father placed a possessive hand on her shoulder. "She's a natural—even did the enameling herself."

"I must—I mean, *Kendra*—must have it."

Papa shook his head. "I'm afraid it's not for sale. It's Amy's own keepsake."

"Of course it's for sale, Papa." Amy regarded Lord Greystone with a speculative gaze. "But it's very expensive."

"I'd expect so. We'll take it."

Lady Kendra turned to him, a frown creasing the area between her light green eyes. "Are you sure, Colin?"

He looked down at his sister. "Don't you like it?"

"It's lovely, but…"

"I said I would buy whatever you chose for your birthday. I want you to have it." He fished a pouch of coins from his surcoat and handed it to Amy. "Here. Take whatever's fair. Include a chain; I want her to wear it now."

Shocked that he would leave the price up to her, Amy fumbled with the pouch. She drew out a few coins, then a few more. The materials had been costly, and the piece had taken a lot of her time—she didn't want to take advantage of Lord Greystone, but she wouldn't short herself, either.

"Papa?" Closing the pouch, Amy showed her father the gold she'd taken.

Papa nodded. "That's fine, Amy." He pocketed the coins and placed a gold chain on the counter.

As she returned the pouch to Lord Greystone, he handed her the locket. His fingers brushed her hand, and another brief, warm shiver rippled through her. She hoped no one noticed the way her breath caught.

Robert sullenly pulled a cloth from his apron pocket and moved from the archway to stand beside her. He polished the glass case as she threaded the chain through the bale on the locket, then held it up for Lady Kendra to see.

"Ooh," Lady Kendra breathed. "Will you put it on me?"

She turned, and Lord Greystone lifted her hair so Amy could fasten the clasp.

Lady Kendra faced Amy and touched the locket reverently. "Thank you so very much. I'll treasure it always."

"Thank *who*?" her brother prompted with a smile.

"Thank you, Colin," she said and turned to embrace him.

Amy bit her lip, feeling a twinge of envy. She envied the girl's shiny red curls and exquisite, fashionable gown, but most of all, she envied the way Lady Kendra was hugging Lord Greystone.

She glanced down at the counter, lest Robert catch sight of her telltale eyes.

Lord Greystone ushered his sister outside, then lingered in the doorway, looking strangely reluctant to leave.

"Can…" The long fingers of one hand drummed against his thigh, then stopped. "Can you make a signet ring?"

His question came low across the small shop, to Amy, not her father.

"A signet ring?" she said with a small smile. "Of course, it's a simple matter."

Beside her, Robert stopped polishing.

"Excellent." Lord Greystone paused, frowning a bit. "I'll send a messenger with a drawing of the crest," he said at last. "And my direction to deliver it when you're finished."

Amy nodded, feeling a quick stab of disappointment that she wouldn't be seeing him again. Robert's hand resumed its deliberate circular motion on top of the counter.

"I thank you," Lord Greystone said. Then he melted out the doorway and into the teeming streets of Cheapside.

The bell rang again when the door shut. Amy stared at the solid wood until her father cleared his throat.

"I cannot believe you sold your locket," he remarked. "I thought it was your favorite piece."

"It was," she answered dreamily. "But I can make another one."

Her stomach fluttered with happiness, just knowing Lord Greystone admired her craftsmanship and his sister would be wearing her locket. And soon, *he* would be wearing her ring.

"If you ask me, it was a clod-headed idea," Robert put in with a shake of his carrot-topped head. "You'll never find time to make another locket with all the custom orders you get."

Amy and her father shared a quizzical look.

"Besides, I didn't like him," Robert added. "I didn't like the way he looked at you."

Amy lowered her gaze and brushed past him into the work-shop. She'd liked the way Lord Greystone looked at her, very much.

Very much indeed.

COLIN ENTERED their carriage to find Kendra seated inside, her arms crossed. "What took you so long?"

He sat opposite her and looked out the window. The door of the jewelry shop had closed, so he couldn't see the girl with the amethyst-colored eyes and the long, thick, ribbon-entwined plait.

"I ordered a signet ring," he said.

"You *what*?"

Colin could have asked himself that question. But in all his twenty-one years he'd never met anyone like the girl who had made that exquisite locket. He'd wanted his sister to own it, and he'd wanted something she'd made for him, too. "I need a signet ring, for a seal."

Kendra shot him a look of patent disbelief. "You couldn't even afford this locket." She shook her bright head. "Something happened in that shop."

"Nothing happened," he said, although he knew very well something had. And he knew the girl—Amethyst—had felt it, too. An instantaneous pull of attraction. He smiled to himself. He was glad he'd met her, though nothing would ever come of it.

But he wasn't about to admit as much to his little sister.

Unfortunately, Kendra was observant as anything, a fact that could be deucedly inconvenient at times. "I just thought it was a beautiful piece of jewelry," he told her, "and I wanted you to have it."

"Od's fish, Colin, you're the one always lecturing us about saving funds…"

He turned off her voice in his head, instead remembering the little hitch in Amethyst's breath when he'd accidentally-on-purpose brushed her hand.

"…planning for the future…"

She was completely off limits, of course. A sheltered young woman of the merchant class, for certain she was nothing like the promiscuous ladies of the court.

"And then you ordered a ring. You never wear jewelry!"

Which would suit him just fine, in truth—he wasn't that sort of fellow anyhow. But well-suited though they might be, Colin Chase, Earl of Greystone, had no intention of marrying beneath himself.

"I cannot believe you bought this locket in the first place."

Besides, he was already betrothed to the perfect girl.

"I do love it, though."

As they passed Goldsmith & Sons, he glanced out the window. He would never go back there. He couldn't remember the last time he'd set foot in a jewelry shop, and…

No, he had no reason to ever return.

AVAILABLE NOW!
Learn more about *The Earl's Unsuitable Bride* at
www.DevonAndLaurenRoyal.com

ENTER FOR A CHANCE TO WIN
the sterling silver claddagh necklace that Sean gives Corinna
in this book!*

Visit the Contest page on Lauren & Devon's website
at www.LaurenandDevonRoyal.com
and answer a question to be
entered in the monthly drawing.

No purchase necessary. See complete rules on the site.

*Please note: Depending on when you enter, the prize may be another piece of jewelry
associated with one of Lauren & Devon's books. The authors reserve the right to discontinue
this promotion at any time.

ABOUT LAUREN & DEVON ROYAL

~

LAUREN ROYAL decided to become a writer in the third grade, after winning a "Why My Mother is the Greatest" essay contest. Now she's a *New York Times* and *USA Today* bestselling author of humorous historical romance novels. Lauren lives in Southern California with her family and their constantly shedding cat. She still thinks her mother is the greatest.

DEVON ROYAL is the daughter of romance novelist Lauren Royal. After attending film school, she wrote an award-winning TV comedy pilot and worked in digital video production before turning her focus to fiction writing. Devon lives in Southern California with her husband and son. She also thinks her mother is the greatest.

ACKNOWLEDGMENTS

~

OUR HEARTFELT THANKS:

To Deborah Alexander, MD, for helping us choose an appropriate illness for Lord Lincolnshire and spending much precious time describing all the pertinent details. (For anyone who may not know, dropsy is currently called edema and in Lord Lincolnshire's case was caused by heart failure.)

To Andrew Potter, research assistant at the Royal Academy Library, for the list of Academicians on the 1817 Selection Committee and historical information on the selection process.

To all the honorary Chase cousins in our Chase Family Readers Group, for their enthusiastic support.

And, once again, to our readers, because we do this for you.

Thank you, one and all!

CONTACT INFORMATION

～

Newsletter

littl.ink/News

Facebook Readers Group

facebook.com/groups/ChaseFamilyReaders

Website

www.DevonAndLaurenRoyal.com

Email

royall.ink/Email

www.ingramcontent.com/pod-product-compliance
Lightning Source LLC
Chambersburg PA
CBHW020524110726
47899CB00004B/1242